A Darker Shade of Blue

A
Darker
Shade
of
Blue

STORIES

John Harvey

PEGASUS CRIME
NEW YORK

A DARKER SHADE OF BLUE

Pegasus Crime is an Imprint of
Pegasus Books LLC
80 Broad Street, 5th Floor
New York, NY 10004

ISBN: 978-1-60598-284-7

10 9 8 7 6 5 4 3 2 1

Printed in the United States of America
Distributed by W. W. Norton & Company, Inc.

CONTENTS

For
James Crumley (1939–2008)
and
Townes Van Zandt (1944–1997)

A proportion of the author's royalties from the sale of this book will be donated to The Place2Be, specifically for the work it is doing to help foster the emotional development of children in Nottingham Primary Schools. For more information visit the website at www.theplace2be.org.uk

INTRODUCTION

'Crime seldom pays,' wrote James Crumley, 'love seldom works. Thankfully stories, like fishing, occasionally work. In ways inexplicable.' I don't know about the fishing; but about stories, as he was about a number of things, Jim had it right. 'Inexplicable.'

I remember reading one of the earlier Charlie Resnick stories at a short story seminar somewhere in the States and being confronted by a puzzled writing student afterwards: I loved your story, she said, but it did all the things we've been taught not to do.

Well, yes.

If I lined up a bunch of my favourite writers of short fiction and tried to use their work to make a template for the perfect story, it just wouldn't happen. How to match Hemingway with Katherine Mansfield; Alice Munro or Lorrie Moore with the Socrates Fortlow stories of Walter Mosley or the evocations of mining life in D. H. Lawrence; the southern Ireland of John McGahern with the Wyoming of Annie Proulx – for that matter, the Raymond Carver stories before they were heavily edited by his mentor, Gordon Lish, or after?

I think, in a way, short stories are like poems. Not in some airy-fairy, self-indulgent, fancy word and obscure metaphor kind of way (of course, no really good poems are like that, either) but like poetry in that they depend on the right, if often surprising, choice of word or phrase, upon exactness and the creation of atmosphere, upon the ability to make relatively few words carry more meaning than the page count suggests. Inference rather than explication.

I know I get a great deal of pleasure from writing them, something that wasn't always the case. They used to terrify me. Admirable, I thought, but out of reach. It wasn't until I'd been writing for almost twenty years – fiction, television, radio – that I allowed myself to be cajouled into doing my first ever story. A piece about Charlie Resnick, as it happened, Resnick and jazz – 'Now's the Time'; it ends with him making a visit to Ronnie Scott's. Now, there's (almost) nothing I like better. If I could make a comparable living out of writing short stories as opposed to the longer stuff, that's what I'd do. Someone gets in touch and wonders if you'd like to contribute to this or that collection, an email comes from Piacenza, or St Louis, Mo. . . . and you know one of the best things about it? Allowing for time later to polish and refine, it can be done and dusted inside a couple of weeks. Compare that to setting out on a new novel, all those months stretching into the distance with rarely an end in sight. That's what I find terrifying now.

In this collection, which brings together all of the short fiction I've written since the William Heinemann edition of *Now's the Time* in 1999, there are four stories featuring

Introduction

Charlie Resnick, seven featuring my north London-based private detective, Jack Kiley, and one – 'Trouble in Mind' – in which they both appear, though Kiley is perhaps the major player.

The Resnick stories I've often used to give a little more space to some of the characters and relationships that received somewhat short shrift in the novels – Eileen Cooke, who turns up in both 'Billie's Blues' and 'The Sun, the Moon, and the Stars' is a case in point. They also served as a way of letting dedicated readers know what Resnick himself was up to in the wilderness years between *Last Rites* and *Cold in Hand*.

Jack Kiley, before turning private eye a copper in the Met and, briefly, a professional footballer, has never set foot in a novel, nor do I think he ever will. As I see him, he's best suited to the short form – quick, generally small investigations, in and out. As a writer and a bit of a crime fiction *aficionado* (well, I was), Kiley gives me the chance to hark back to Hammett and Chandler, Ross Macdonald and the rest, letting him loose, angry and incorruptible, in the mean streets of Kentish Town. When Kiley's in his office and a woman's footsteps are heard approaching his door, you know things are going to get worse before they get better. These are the stories I think Jim Crumley would have liked best.

Short stories can also be invaluable for the opportunity they provide for trying out characters and situations you are unsure of – 'walking them round the block', as I believe Elmore Leonard once described it. 'I wrote "Karen Makes Out",' Leonard said, 'to see if I'd like Karen Sisco enough to develop a novel around her as a federal marshal.' Clearly, he did, and *Out of Sight* was the result; first the novel, and then the movie.

Frank Elder first saw the light of day in 'Due North'

and went on to be the main protagonist in three novels, *Flesh and Blood*, *Ash and Bone* and *Darkness and Light*, while police officers Will Grayson and Helen Walker, who make a belated appearance in 'Snow, Snow, Snow', on the trail of a prolific hit man who has so far eluded capture, handled most, but not all, of the detection in *Gone to Ground* and *Far Cry*.

Tom Whitemore, the leading character in 'Sack O' Woe', one of the most recent stories included here, had a walk-on part in the third Elder novel, *Darkness and Light*, and I remembered him as someone I wanted to return to. Now that he's been around his particularly difficult block a little more, who's to say he won't appear again?

'Drummer Unknown', which, as was pointed out to me, is the only piece I've written in the first person, was a relatively early attempt to write about the world of London's Soho between the late 50s and the mid-60s – a world of jazz clubs, street corner vice and petty crime (some not so petty) and a particularly British kind of bohemia that I skirted round and began tentatively to explore in my late teens and early twenties. The two stories towards the end of the book, 'Just Friends' and 'Minor Key', take this further, both revolving, as they do, around a central group of characters who might, one day, be dealt with at fuller length in the novel set in and around Soho I've been threatening to write for so long neither my editor nor my agent believe I'll ever actually do so. The stories are there, though – they're among my favourites in the collection – and the characters are starting to take shape, so you never know.

It's true to say that all of these stories exist because someone asked me to write them. Seba Pezzani, for instance, one of my Italian translators (and organiser of the rather wonderful blues and fiction festival, *Dal Mississippi al Po*) wanted something for a series in the Italian newspaper, *Il*

Introduction

Giornale, hence 'Ghosts'. My publisher in Finland, Otava, requested a Resnick piece to distribute at the Helsinki Book Fair, thus 'Well, You Needn't'.

Certain editors and compilers of short story collections have been assiduous and kind – Maxim Jakubowski, Otto Penzler, Robert J. Randisi come immediately to mind. Without them, this book would be a meagre thing, indeed. Ross Bradshaw, at Nottingham's Five Leaves, has been a consistent supporter, as have Ed Gorman and Martin Greenberg in the States. But perhaps the final thank you – on behalf of so many writers of crime stories as well as myself – should go to the estimable Janet Hutchings, editor of *Ellery Queen Mystery Magazine*, who has published many of my stories through the years, filtering out most of the extreme profanities but leaving the heart intact.

SACK O' WOE

The street was dark and narrow, a smear of frost along the roofs of the occasional parked car. Two of a possible six overhead lights had been smashed several weeks before. Recycling bins – blue, green and grey – shared the pavement with abandoned supermarket trolleys and the detritus from a score of fast-food take-aways. Number thirty-four was towards the terrace end, the short street emptying onto a scrub of wasteland ridged with stiffened mud, puddles of brackish water covered by a thin film of ice.

January.

Tom Whitemore knocked with his gloved fist on the door of thirty-four. Paint that was flaking away, a bell that had long since ceased to work.

He was wearing blue jeans, T-shirt and sweater, scuffed leather jacket, the first clothes he had grabbed when the call had come through less than half an hour before.

January twenty-seventh, three seventeen a.m.

Taking one step back, he raised his right leg and kicked

1

against the door close by the lock; a second kick, wood splintered and the door sprang back.

Inside it was your basic two-up, two-down house, a kitchen extension leading into the small yard at the back, bathroom above that. A strip of worn carpet in the narrow hallway, bare boards on the stairs. Bare wires that hung down, no bulb attached, from the ceiling overhead. He had been here before.

'Darren? Darren, you there?'

No answer when he called the name. A smell that could be from a backed-up foul water pipe or a blocked drain.

The front room was empty, odd curtains at the window, a TV set in one corner, two chairs and a sagging two-seater settee. Dust. A bundle of clothes. In the back room there were two more chairs, one with a broken back, and a small table; a pile of old newspapers, the remnants of an unfinished oven-ready meal, a child's shoe.

'Darren?'

The first stair creaked a little beneath his weight.

In the front bedroom a double mattress rested directly on the floor; several blankets, a quilt without a cover, no sheets. Half the drawers in the corner chest had been pulled open and left, miscellaneous items of clothing hanging down.

Before opening the door to the rear bedroom, Whitemore held his breath.

A pair of bunk beds leaned against one wall, a pumped-up Lilo mattress close by. Two tea chests, one spilling over with children's clothes, the other with toys. A plastic bowl in which cereal had hardened and congealed. A baby's bottle, rancid with yellowing milk. A used nappy, half-in half-out of a pink plastic sack. A tube of sweets. A paper hat. Red and yellow building bricks. Soft toys. A plastic car. A teddy bear with a waistcoat and a bright bow tie, still new enough to have been a recent Christmas gift.

And blood. Blood in fine tapering lines across the floor, faint splashes on the wall.

Tom Whitemore pressed one hand to his forehead and closed his eyes.

*

He had been a member of the Public Protection Team for almost four years: responsible, together with other police officers, probation officers and representatives of other agencies – social services, community psychiatric care – for the supervision of violent and high-risk-of-harm sex offenders who had been released back into the community. Their task, through maintaining a close watch, pooling information, getting offenders, where applicable, on to accredited programmes, assisting them in finding jobs, was to do anything and everything possible to prevent reoffending. It was often thankless, frequently frustrating – What was that Springsteen song? Two steps up and three steps back? – but unlike a lot of police work, it had focus, clear aims, methods, ambitions. It was possible – sometimes – to see positive results. Potentially dangerous men – they were mostly men – were neutralised, kept in check. If nothing else, there was that.

And yet his wife hated it. Hated it for the people it brought him into contact with, day after day – rapists, child abusers – the scum of the earth in her eyes, the lowest of the low. She hated it for the way it forced him to confront over and over what these people had done, what people were capable of, as if she feared the enormities of their crimes might somehow be contaminating him. Creeping into his dreams. Coming back with him into their home, like smoke caught in his hair or clinging to the fibres of his clothes. Contaminating them all.

'How much longer, Tom?' she would ask. 'How much longer are you going to do this hateful bloody job?'

'Not long,' he would say. 'Not so much longer now.'

Get out before you burn out, that was the word on the force. Transfer to general duties, traffic, fraud. Yet he could never bring himself to leave, to make the move, and each morning he would set off back into that world and each evening when he returned, no matter how late, he would go and stand in the twins' bedroom and watch them sleeping, his and Marianne's twin boys, safe and sound.

That summer they had gone to Filey as usual, two weeks of holiday, the same dubious weather, the same small hotel, the perfect curve of beach. The twins had run and splashed and fooled around on half-sized body boards on the edges of the waves; they had eaten chips and ice creams and, tired of playing with the big coloured ball that bounced forever down towards the sea, Tom had helped them build sandcastles with an elaborate array of turrets and tunnels, while Marianne alternately read her book or dozed.

It was perfect: even the weather was forgiving, no more than a scattering of showers, a few darkening clouds, the wind from the south.

On the last evening, the twins upstairs asleep, they had sat on the small terrace overlooking the promenade and the black strip of sea. 'When we get back, Tom,' Marianne had said, 'you've got to ask for a transfer. They'll understand. No one can do a job like that for ever, not even you.'

She reached for his hand and as he turned towards her, she brought her face to his. 'Tom?' Her breath on his face was warm and slightly sweet and he felt a lurch of love run through him like a wave.

'All right,' he said.

'You promise?'

4

'I promise.'

But by the end of that summer, things had changed. There had been the bombings in London for one thing, suicide bombers on the Tube; an innocent young Brazilian shot and killed after a bungled surveillance operation; suspected terrorists arrested in suburbs of Birmingham and Leeds. It was everywhere. Security alerts at the local airport; rumours that spread from voice to voice, from mobile phone to mobile phone. Don't go into the city centre this Saturday. Keep well away. Stay clear. Now it was commonplace to see, fully armed in the middle of the day, a pair of uniformed police officers strolling down past Pizza Hut and the Debenhams department store, Heckler & Koch sub-machine guns held low across their chests, Walther P990 pistols holstered at their hips, shoppers no longer bothering to stop and stare.

As the Home Office and security services continued to warn of the possibility of a new terrorist attack, the pressures on police time increased. A report from the chief inspector of constabulary noted that in some police areas surveillance packages intended to supervise high-risk offenders were now rarely implemented due to a lack of resources. 'Whether it is counter-terrorism or a sex offender,' explained his deputy, 'there are only a certain number of specialist officers to go round.'

'You remember what you promised,' Marianne reminded him. By now it was late September, the nights drawing in.

'I can't,' Tom said, slowly shaking his head. 'I can't leave now.'

She looked at him, her face like flint. 'I can, Tom. We can. Remember that.'

It hung over them after that, the threat, fracturing what had held them together for so long.

Of necessity, Tom worked longer hours; when he did

get home, tired, head buzzing, it was to find her turned away from him in the bed and flinching at his touch. At breakfast, when he put his arms around her at the sink, she shrugged him angrily away.

'Marianne, for God's sake . . .'

'What?'

'We can't go on like this.'

'No?'

'No.'

'Then do something about it.'

'Jesus!'

'What?'

'I've already told you. A hundred times. Not now.'

She pushed past him and out into the hall, slamming the door at her back. 'Fuck!' Tom shouted and slammed his fist against the wall. 'Fuck, fuck, fuck!' One of the twins screamed as if he'd been struck; the other knocked his cereal to the floor and started to cry.

*

The team meeting was almost over when Bridget Arthur, one of the probation officers, mid-fifties, experienced, raised her hand. 'Darren Pitcher, I think we might have a problem.'

Tom Whitemore sighed. 'What now?'

'One of my clients, Emma Laurie, suspended sentence for dealing crack cocaine, lives up in Forest Fields. Not the brightest cherry in the bunch. She's taken up with Pitcher. Seems he's thinking of moving in.'

'That's a problem?'

'She's got three kids, all under six. Two of them boys.'

Whitemore shook his head. He knew Darren Pitcher's history well enough. An only child, brought up by his

6

mother, who had given birth to him when she was just sixteen, Pitcher had only met his father twice: on the first occasion, magnanimous from drink, the older man had squeezed his buttocks and slipped two five-pound notes into his trouser pocket; on the second, sober, he had blacked the boy's eye and told him to fuck off out of his sight.

A loner at school, marked out by learning difficulties, readily bullied, from the age of sixteen Pitcher had drifted through a succession of low-paid jobs – cleaning, stacking supermarket shelves, hospital portering, washing cars – and several short-term relationships with women who enjoyed even less self-esteem than himself.

When he was twenty-five he was sentenced to five years' imprisonment for molesting half a dozen boys between the ages of four and seven. While in prison, in addition to numerous incidents of self-harming, he had made one attempt at suicide.

Released, he had spent the first six months in a hostel and had reported to both his probation officer and a community psychiatric nurse each week. Since which time, supervision had necessarily slackened off.

'Ben?' Whitemore said, turning towards the psychiatric nurse at the end of the table. 'He was one of yours.'

Ben Leonard pushed a hand up through his cropped blonde hair. 'A family, ready-made, might be what he needs.'

'The girl,' Bridget Arthur said, 'she's not strong. It's a wonder she's hung on to those kids as long as she has.'

'There's a father somewhere?'

'Several.'

'Contact?'

'Not really.'

For a moment, Tom Whitemore closed his eyes. 'The boys, they're how old?'

'Five and three. There's a little girl, eighteen months.'

'And do we think, should Pitcher move in, they could be at risk?'

'I think we have to,' Bridget Arthur said.

'Ben?'

Leonard took his time. 'We've made real progress with Darren, I think. He's aware that his previous behaviour was wrong. Regrets what he's done. The last thing he wants to do is offend again. But, yes, for the sake of the kids, I'd have to say there was a risk. A small one, but a risk.'

'Okay,' Whitemore said. 'I'll go and see him. Report back. Bridget, you'll stay in touch with the girl?'

'Of course.'

'Good. Let's not lose sight of this in the midst of everything else.'

They sat on the Portland Leisure Centre steps, a wan sun showing weakly through the wreaths of cloud. Whitemore had bought two cups of pale tea from the machines inside and they sat there on the cold, worn stone, scarcely talking as yet. Darren Pitcher was smoking a cigarette, a roll-up he had made with less than steady hands. What was it, Whitemore thought, his gran had always said? Don't sit on owt cold or you'll get piles, sure as eggs is eggs.

'Got yourself a new girlfriend, I hear,' Whitemore said.

Pitcher flinched then glanced at him from under lowered lids. He had a lean face, a sickly pallor, a few reddish spots around the mouth and chin; strangely long eyelashes that curled luxuriantly over his weak grey eyes.

'Emma? That her name?'

'She's all right.'

'Of course.'

Two young black men in shiny sportswear bounced past them, all muscle, on their way to the gym.

'It serious?' Whitemore asked.

'Dunno.'

'What I heard, it's pretty serious. The pair of you. Heard you were thinking of moving in.'

Pitcher mumbled something and drew on his cigarette.

'Sorry?' Whitemore said. 'I didn't quite hear . . .'

'I said it's none of your business . . .'

'Isn't it?'

'My life, yeah? Not yours.'

Whitemore swallowed a mouthful more of the lukewarm tea and turned the plastic cup upside down, shaking the last drops onto the stone. 'This Emma,' he said, 'she's got kids. Young kids.'

'So?'

'Young boys.'

'That don't . . . You can't . . . That was a long time ago.'

'I know, Darren. I know. But it happened, nonetheless. And it makes this our concern.' For a moment, his hand rested on Pitcher's arm. 'You understand?'

Pitcher's hand went to his mouth and he bit down on his knuckle hard.

*

Gregory Boulevard ran along one side of the Forest Recreation Ground, the nearest houses, once substantial family homes, now mostly subdivided into flats and falling, many of them, into disrepair. Beyond these, the streets grew narrower and coiled back upon themselves, the houses smaller with front doors that opened directly out on to the street. Corner shops with bars across the windows, shutters on the doors.

Emma Laurie sat on a lopsided settee in the front room; small-featured, a straggle of hair falling down across her face, her voice rarely rose above a whisper as she spoke. A wraith of a thing, Whitemore thought. Outside, a good wind would blow her away.

The three children huddled in the corner, watching cartoons, the sound turned low. Jason, Rory and Jade. The youngest had a runny nose, the older of the boys coughed intermittently, open-mouthed, but they were all, as yet, bright-eyed.

'He's good with them,' Emma was saying, 'Darren. Plays with them all the time. Takes them, you know, down to t'Forest. They love him, they really do. Can't wait for him to move in wi' us. Go on about it all the time. Jason especially.'

'And you?' Bridget Arthur said. 'How do you feel? About Darren moving in?'

'Be easier, won't it? Rent and that. What I get, family credit an' the rest, s'a struggle, right? But if Darren's here, I can get a job, afternoons, Asda. Get out a bit, 'stead of bein' all cooped up. Darren'll look after the kids. He don't mind.'

They walked down through the maze of streets to where Arthur had parked her car, the Park and Ride on the edge of the Forest.

'What do you think?' Whitemore said.

'Ben could be right. Darren, could be the making of him.'

'But if it puts those lads at risk?'

'I know, I know. But what can we do? He's been out a good while now, no sign of him reoffending.'

'I still don't like it,' Whitemore said.

Arthur smiled wryly. 'Other people's lives. We'll keep our fingers crossed. Keep as close an eye as we can.'

Sometimes, Whitemore thought, it was as if they were

trying to hold the world together with good intentions and a ball of twine.

'Give you a lift back into town?' Arthur said when they reached her car. It was not yet late afternoon and the light was already beginning to fade.

Whitemore shook his head. 'It's okay. I'll catch the tram.'

Back at the office, he checked his emails, made several calls, wrote up a brief report of the visit to Emma Laurie. He wondered if he should go and see Darren Pitcher again, but decided there was little to be gained. When he finally got back home, a little after six, Marianne was buckling the twins into their seats in the back of the car.

'What's going on?'

She was flushed, a scarf at her neck. 'My parents, I thought we'd go over and see them. Just for a couple of days. They haven't seen the boys in ages.'

'They were over just the other weekend.'

'That was a month ago. More. It is ages to them.'

One of the boys was marching his dinosaur along the top of the seat in front; the other was fiddling with his straps.

'You were just going to go?' Whitemore said. 'You weren't even going to wait till I got back?'

'You're not usually this early.'

'So wait.'

'It's a two-hour drive.'

'I know how far it is.'

'Tom, don't. Please.'

'Don't what?'

'Make this more difficult than it is.'

He read it in her eyes. Walking to the back of the car, he snapped open the boot. It was crammed with luggage, coats, shoes, toys.

'You're not just going for a couple of days, are you? This is not a couple of fucking days.'

'Tom, please . . .' She raised a hand towards him, but he knocked it away.

'You're leaving, that's what you're doing . . .'

'No, I'm not.'

'You're not?'

'It's just for a little while . . . A break. I need a break. So I can think.'

'You need to fucking think right enough!'

Whitemore snatched open the rear door and leaned inside, seeking to unsnap the nearest boy's belt and failing in his haste. The boys themselves looked frightened and close to tears.

'Tom, don't do that! Leave it. Leave them alone.'

She pulled at his shoulder and he thrust her away, so that she almost lost her footing and stumbled back. Roused by the shouting, one of the neighbours was standing halfway along his front garden path, openly staring.

'Tom, please,' Marianne said. 'Be reasonable.'

He turned so fast, she thought he was going to strike her and cowered back.

'Reasonable? Like this? You call this fucking reasonable?'

The neighbour had come as far as the pavement edge. 'Excuse me, but is everything all right?'

'All right?' Whitemore shouted. 'Yeah. Marvellous. Fucking wonderful. Now fuck off indoors and mind your own fucking business.'

Both the twins were crying now: not crying, screaming.

The car door slammed as Marianne slid behind the wheel. Whitemore shouted her name and brought down his fist hard on the roof of the car as it pulled away, red tail lights blurring in the half-dark.

He stood there for several moments more, staring off

into the middle distance, seeing nothing. Back in the house, he went from room to room, assessing how much she had taken, how long she might be considering staying away. Her parents lived on the coast, between Chapel St Leonards and Sutton-on-Sea, a bungalow but with room enough for Marianne and the twins. Next year they would be at school, next year would be different, but now . . .

He looked in the fridge, but there was nothing there he fancied. A couple of cold sausages wrapped in foil. Maybe he'd make himself a sandwich later on. He snapped open a can of lager, but the taste was stale in his mouth and he poured the remainder down the sink. There was a bottle of whisky in the cupboard, only recently opened, but he knew better than to start down that route too soon.

In the living room, he switched on the TV, flicked through the channels, switched off again; he made a cup of tea and glanced at that day's paper, one of Marianne's magazines. Every fifteen minutes, he looked at his watch. When he thought he'd given them time enough, he phoned.

Marianne's father came on the line. Soft-spoken, understanding, calm. 'I'm sorry, Tom. She doesn't want to speak to you right now. Perhaps tomorrow, tomorrow evening. She'll call you. . . . The twins? They're sleeping, fast off. Put them to bed as soon as they arrived. . . . I'll be sure to give them your love. Yes, of course. Of course. . . . Goodnight, Tom. Goodnight.'

Around nine, Whitemore called a taxi and went across the city to the Five Ways pub in Sherwood. In the back room Jake McMahon and a bunch of the usual reprobates were charging through Cannonball Adderley's 'Jeannine'. A Duke Pearson tune, but because Whitemore had first heard it on Adderley's *Them Dirty Blues* – Cannonball on alto alongside his trumpeter brother, Nat – it was forever associated with the saxophonist in his mind.

Whitemore's father had given him the recording as a sixteenth birthday present, when Tom's mind had been more full of T'Pau and the Pet Shop Boys, Whitney Houston and Madonna. But eventually he had given it a listen, late in his room, and something had stuck.

One of the best nights he remembered spending with his father before the older man took himself off to a retirement chalet in Devon had been spent here, drinking John Smith's bitter and listening to the band play another Adderley special, 'Sack O' Woe'.

Jake McMahon came over to him in the break and shook his hand. 'Not seen you in a while.'

Whitemore forced a smile. 'You know how it is, this and that.'

McMahon nodded. 'Your dad, he okay?'

'Keeping pretty well.'

'You'll give him my best.'

'Of course.'

Whitemore stayed for most of the second set then called for a cab from the phone alongside the bar.

*

Darren Pitcher moved in with Emma Laurie and her three children. October became November, became December. Most Sundays Whitemore drove out to his in-laws' bungalow on the coast, where the twins threw themselves at him with delight and he played rough and tumble with them on the beach if the cold allowed, and if not, tussled with them on the living-room settee. Marianne's parents stepped around him warily, keeping their thoughts to themselves. If he tried to get Marianne off on her own, she resisted, made excuses. Conversation between them was difficult.

'When will we see you again?' she asked one evening as he was leaving.

'When are you coming home?' he asked. Christmas was less than three weeks away.

'Tom, I don't know.'

'But you are coming? Coming back?'

She turned her face aside. 'Don't rush me, all right?'

It was just two days later that Bridget Arthur phoned Whitemore in his office, the first call of the day. Emma Laurie was waiting for them, agitated, at her front door. She had come back from work to find Pitcher with Jason, the elder of her two sons, on his lap; Jason had been sitting on a towel, naked, and Pitcher had been rubbing Vaseline between his legs.

Whitemore and Arthur exchanged glances.

'Did he have a reason?' Arthur asked.

'He said Jason was sore, said he'd been complaining about being sore . . .'

'And you don't believe him?'

'If he was sore,' Emma said, 'it was 'cause of what Darren was doing. You know that as well as me.'

'Where is Darren now?' Whitemore said.

'I don't know. I don't care. I told him to clear out and not come back.'

Whitemore found Pitcher later that morning, sitting cross-legged on the damp pavement, his back against the hoardings surrounding the Old Market Square. Rain was falling in fine slanted lines, but Pitcher either hadn't noticed or didn't care.

'Darren,' Whitemore said, 'come on, let's get out of this wet.'

15

Pitcher glanced up at him and shook his head.

Coat collar up, Whitemore hunkered down beside him. 'You want to tell me what happened?'

'Nothing happened.'

'Emma says—'

'I don't give a fuck what Emma says.'

'I do,' Whitemore said. 'I have to. But I want to know what you say, too.'

Pitcher was silent for several minutes, passers-by stepping over his legs or grudgingly going round.

'He'd been whingeing away,' Pitcher said, 'Jason. How the pants he was wearing was too tight. Scratching. His hand down his trousers, scratching, and I kept telling him to stop. He'd hurt himself. Make it worse. Then, when he went to the toilet, right, I told him to show me, you know, show me where it was hurting, point to it, like. And there was a bit of red there, I could see, so I said would he like me to put something on it, to make it better and he said yes and so . . .'

He stopped abruptly, tears in his eyes and shoulders shaking.

Whitemore waited.

'I didn't do anything,' Pitcher said finally. 'Honest. I never touched him. Not like . . . you know, like before.'

'But you could have?' Whitemore said.

Head down, Pitcher nodded.

'Darren?'

'Yes, yeah. I suppose . . . Yeah.'

Still neither of them moved and the rain continued to fall.

*

On Christmas morning Whitemore rose early, scraped the ice from the windows of the second-hand Saab he'd bought not so many weeks before, loaded up the back seat with presents, and set out for the coast. When he arrived the light was only just beginning to spread, in bands of pink and yellow, across the sky. Wanting his arrival to be a surprise, he parked some houses away.

The curtains were partly drawn and he could see the lights of the Christmas tree clearly, red, blue and green, and, as he moved across the frosted grass, he could see the twins, up already, still wearing their pyjamas, tearing into the contents of their stockings, shouting excitedly as they pulled at the shiny paper and cast it aside.

When he thought they might see him, he stepped quickly away and returned to the car, loading the presents into his arms. Back at the bungalow he placed them on the front step, up against the door, and walked away.

If he had waited, knocked on the window, rung the bell, gone inside and stayed, seen their happiness at close hand, he knew it would have been almost impossible to leave.

Emma Laurie appeared at the police station in early January, the youngest child in a buggy, the others half-hidden behind her legs. After days of endless pestering, she had allowed Pitcher back into the house, just for an hour, and then he had refused to leave. When she'd finally persuaded him to go, he had threatened to kill himself if she didn't have him back; said that he would snatch the children and take them with him; kill them all.

'It was wrong o'me, weren't it? Letting him back in. I never should've done it. I know that, I know.'

'It's okay,' Whitemore said. 'And I wouldn't pay too much attention to what Darren said. He was angry. Upset. Times like that, people say a lot of things they don't necessarily mean.'

'But if you'd seen his face . . . He meant it, he really did.'

Whitemore gave her his card. 'Look, my mobile number's there. If he comes round again, threatening you, anything like that, you call me, right? Straight away. Meantime, I'll go and have a word with him. Okay?'

Emma smiled uncertainly, nodded thanks and ushered the children away.

After spending time in various hostels and a spell sleeping rough, Pitcher, with the help of the local housing association, had found a place to rent in Sneinton. A one-room flat with a sink and small cooker in one corner and a shared bathroom and toilet on the floor below. Whitemore sat on the single chair and Pitcher sat on the sagging bed.

'I know why you're here,' Pitcher said. 'It's about Emma. What I said.'

'You frightened her.'

'I know. I lost me temper, that's all.' He shook his head. 'Being there, her an' the kids, a family, you know? An' then her chuckin' me out. You wouldn't understand. Why would you? But I felt like shit. A piece of shit. An' I meant it. What I said. Not the kids, not harmin' them. I wouldn't do that. But topping myself . . .' He looked at Whitemore despairingly. 'It's what I'll do. I swear it. I will.'

'Don't talk like that,' Whitemore said.

'Why the hell not?'

Whitemore leaned towards him and lowered his voice. 'It's hard, I know. And I do understand. Really, I do. But you have to keep going. Move on. Look – here – you've got this place, right? A flat of your own. It's a start. A new start. Look at it like that.'

He went across to Pitcher and rested a hand on his shoulder, not knowing how convincing his half-truths and platitudes had been.

'Ben Leonard, you talked to him before. I'll see if

I can't get him to see you again. It might help sort a few things out. Okay? But in the meantime, whatever you do, you're to keep away from Emma. Right, Darren? Emma and the children.' Whitemore tightened his grip on Pitcher's shoulder before stepping clear. 'Keep right away.'

It was a little over a week later the call came through, waking Whitemore from his sleep. The voice was brisk, professional, a triage nurse at the Queen's Medical Centre, accident and emergency. 'We've a young woman here, Emma Laurie, she's quite badly injured. Some kind of altercation with a partner? She insisted that I contact you, I hope that's all right. Apparently she's worried about the children. Three of them?'

'Are they there with her?'

'No. At home, apparently.'

'On their own?'

'I don't know. I don't think so. Maybe a neighbour? I'm afraid she's not making a lot of sense.'

Whitemore dropped the phone and finished pulling on his clothes.

*

The house was silent: the blood slightly tacky to the touch. One more room to go. The bathroom door was bolted from the inside and Whitemore shouldered it free. Darren Pitcher was sitting on the toilet seat, head slumped forward, one arm trailing over the bath, the other dangling towards the floor. Long, vertical cuts ran down the insides of both arms, almost from elbow to wrist, slicing through the horizontal scars from where he had harmed himself before. Blood had pooled along the bottom of the bath and around his

19

feet. A Stanley knife rested on the bath's edge alongside an oval of pale green soap.

Whitemore crouched down. There was a pulse, still beating faintly, at the side of Pitcher's neck.

'Darren? Can you hear me?'

With an effort, Pitcher raised his head. 'See, I did it. I said I would.' A ghost of a smile lingered in his eyes.

'The children,' Whitemore said. 'Where are they?'

Pitcher's voice was a sour whisper in his face. 'The shed. Out back. I didn't want them to see this.'

As Pitcher's head slumped forward, Whitemore dialled the emergency number on his mobile phone.

Downstairs he switched on the kitchen light; there was a box of matches lying next to the stove. Unbolting the back door, he stepped outside. The shed was no more than five feet high, roughly fashioned from odd planks of wood, the roof covered with a rime of frost. The handle was cold to the touch.

'Don't be frightened,' he said, loud enough for them to hear inside. 'I'm just going to open the door.'

When it swung back, he ducked inside and struck a match. The three children were clinging to one another in the furthest corner, staring wide-eyed into the light.

Darren Pitcher had lost consciousness by the time the paramedics arrived and despite their efforts and those of the doctors at A & E, he was pronounced dead a little after six that morning. Sutured and bandaged, Emma Laurie was kept in overnight and then released. Her children had been scooped up by the social services emergency duty team and would spend a short time in care.

Tom Whitemore drove to the embankment and stood on the pedestrian bridge across the river, staring down at the dark, glassed-over surface of the water, the pale shapes of sleeping swans, heads tucked beneath their wings. Overhead, the sky was clear and pitted with stars.

When finally he arrived home, it was near dawn.

The heating in the house had just come on.

Upstairs, in the twins' room, it felt cold nonetheless. Each bed was carefully made up, blankets folded neatly back. Just in case. He stood there for a long time, letting the light slowly unfold round him. The start of another day.

SNOW, SNOW, SNOW

Snow drifted, soft, against his face.

Earlier, the wind had whipped each succeeding fall into a virtual blizzard, slicing into him as he stood, barely sheltered, on the edge of the fen.

Now it was this: the snow of fairy tales and dreams.

A pair of swans floated, uncaring, along the shuffled surface of the water, at home in the gathering white.

Malkin checked his watch and continued to stand.

Fifteen minutes later, Fraser's SUV appeared on the raised strip of road, headlights pale through the mist of falling snow.

Malkin waited until, indicator blinking, the vehicle slowed into the left-hand turn that would take it along a narrow, barely made-up lane to where the new house was in the process of construction, further along the fen.

The main structure was already in place: varying shades of yellow brick at each end and to the rear, the front partly clad in as yet untreated wood. The frames for the large windows that would dominate the upper floor had recently

22

been set. No glass as yet. Ladders leaned against scaffolding, secured with rope. A bucket half-filled and frozen fast. Tarpaulins that flapped in each catch of wind.

Fastidious, Fraser changed soft leather shoes for green wellingtons and pulled on his sheepskin coat. Lifting back the mesh gates that guarded the site, he moved inside, and, after a few moments, disappeared into the building's shell.

Snow continued to fall.

Malkin stood no more than forty metres away, all but invisible against the washed-out sky, the shrouded earth.

Cautious, Fraser climbed the ladder to the upper floor and stared out. He'd expected the architect to be already at the site, not limping in late with some excuse about the weather. A bit of snow. February. What else did he expect?

Treading with care across the boards, Fraser eased aside a length of tarpaulin and stepped inside what would be the main room, running almost the entire length of the floor. Views right out across open land, unimpeded as far as the horizon. But not today. He failed to hear Malkin's foot on the ladder's bottom rung.

Angry, Fraser pushed back his cuff and double-checked his watch. Damned architect!

Hearing Malkin's footsteps now, he turned. 'What sort of time d'you call this?'

Malkin stepped through the space of the open doorway and out of the snow.

'Who the hell . . . ?' Fraser began, words fading from his lips.

Malkin smiled.

'Remember Sharon Peters?' he said.

For an instant, Fraser saw a tousle-haired girl of eight, playing catch ball up against the wall as she waited for her bus; her face, at the last moment, widening in a scream.

'You do remember,' Malkin said, 'don't you?'

23

The pistol was already in his hand.

'Don't you?'

Ashen, Fraser stumbled back, began to plead.

For jobs like this Malkin favoured a 9mm Glock 17. Light, plastic, readily disposable. Two shots were usually enough.

Or sometimes one.

At the sound, a solitary crow rose, shaking snowflakes from its wings, and began to circle round.

Blood was beginning to leak, already, from the back of Fraser's head, staining the untreated wood a dull reddish-brown. Snow swirled into Malkin's face as he descended the ladder, and with a quick shake of his head he blinked it away.

*

The train was no more than a third full and he had a table to himself, plenty of room to spread the paper and read. Every once in a while, he looked out at the passing fields, speckled as they were with snow. Hedgerows and rooftops gleamed white in the fresh spring sun.

He read again the account, all too familiar, of a prison suicide: a nineteen-year-old who had hanged himself in his cell. According to his family, the youth had been systematically beaten and bullied during the weeks leading up to his death, and prison staff had turned a blind eye.

'My son,' the mother was reported as saying, 'made complaint after complaint to the governor and the prison officer in charge of his wing, and they did nothing. Nothing. And now they're as guilty of his death as if they'd knotted the sheet themselves and kicked away the chair.'

Poetic, Malkin thought. A good turn of phrase. He tore the page from the newspaper, folded it neatly once and once again and slipped it into his wallet. One for a rainy day.

When the train pulled into the station, he left the remainder of the newspaper on the seat, pulled on his coat, and walked the length of the platform to the exit, taking his time.

The first thing he saw, stepping into the broad concourse, was a police officer in helmet and body armour, sub-machine gun held at an angle across his chest, and he was glad that he'd disposed of the Glock before boarding the train. Not that any of this was for him.

Two other officers, similarly armed, stood just outside the station entrance, at the head of the pavement steps. Anti-terrorism, Malkin thought, it had to be. A suspect being brought in that day for trial. Some poor bastard Muslim who'd made the mistake of visiting Afghanistan, or maybe just sent money to the wrong cause. Most likely now he'd be slammed up for a couple of years in Belmarsh or some other top-security hole, then released without charge.

But that wasn't why Malkin was here.

He crossed close to a Transit holding as many as ten officers in reserve and descended the cobbled slip road leading to the canal. A short distance along, the high glass and polished stone of the new courthouse was guarded by yet more police.

All it needed, Malkin thought, was a helicopter circling overhead.

He showed his ID and explained his reasons for entry. The case he was interested in was due to conclude today.

A little over two years before, Alan Silver had been woken in the night by the sound of intruders; he had armed himself with the licensed shotgun that he kept close by the bed, gone to the head of the stairs and emptied both barrels into the two youths he surprised below. One took superficial wounds to the arm and neck and was able to turn and run; the other was thrown backwards on to the tiles of the broad hallway, bleeding out, a hole torn in his chest.

Silver phoned emergency services, ambulance and police, but by the time the paramedics arrived, less than ten minutes later, it was too late. Wayne Michaels, seventeen, was pronounced dead on arrival at the hospital.

Alan Silver – a sometime song-and-dance man and minor celebrity – was both hero and villain. The more righteous of the media spoke of unnecessary force and questioned the rights of any civilians to own firearms at all, while others championed him as a hero. Right-of-centre politicians strutted in reflected glory, crowing about the right of every Englishman to protect house and home, his proverbial castle.

When Silver, described in court as a popular entertainer, pleaded guilty to manslaughter and was sentenced to three years' imprisonment, there was uproar. *'Is this all a young man's life is worth?'* demanded the *Independent*. *'Jailed for doing what was right!'* denounced the *Mail*.

Outside the court that day, Wayne Michaels' father, Earl, sweaty, clinging to his dignity in an ill-fitting suit, was asked how he felt about the verdict. 'My son is dead,' he said. 'Now let justice take its course.'

More recently, Silver's lawyers had earned the right to appeal; the sentence, they said, was punitive and over-severe. Punitive, Malkin remembered thinking: isn't that supposed to be the point?

Riding on the back of a popular hysteria about the rising rate of crime they had helped to create, the tabloid press rejoiced in seeing their circulations soar, inviting their readers to text or email in support of the campaign Free Silver Now!

'If this government,' proclaimed a Tory peer in the Lords, 'and this Home Secretary, have not totally lost touch with the people they are supposed to represent, they should act immediately and ensure that the sentence in this case be made to better reflect the nation's mood.'

Malkin settled into the back of the public gallery in time for the verdict: after due deliberation, and having reconsidered both his previously untarnished reputation and his unstinting work for charity, the judge reduced Alan Silver's sentence to eighteen months. Taking into account the time he had spent on remand awaiting trial, this meant Silver had little more than two months to serve.

Channel Five were rumoured to have offered him a six-figure contract to host a weekly chat show; a long-forgotten recording of 'Mama Liked the Roses', a sentimental country ballad initially made popular by Elvis Presley, had been reissued and was currently number seven in the charts.

As he was led out to the waiting Securicor van, Alan Silver, grey hair trimmed short and wearing his sixty-three years well, was, none too surprisingly, smiling.

Malkin found Michaels' father staring into the water of the canal, smoking a cigarette.

'You still think justice should be allowed to take its course?' Malkin said.

'Do I fuck!'

*

Earlier that morning, Will Grayson and his four-year-old son, Jake, had been building a snowman at the back of the house: black stones for the eyes, a carrot for a nose, one of Will's old caps, the one he'd worn when he was on the police bowling team, snug on the snowman's head.

Inside, Will could see his wife, Lorraine, through the

kitchen window, moving back and forth behind the glass. Pancakes, he wouldn't have minded betting. Lorraine liked to make pancakes for breakfast those mornings he didn't have to go in to work; Lorraine well into her eighth month and on maternity leave, the size of her such that their second kid must be almost ready to pop. Baby might come early, the midwife had said.

As Will crouched down and added a few finishing touches to their snowman, Jake sneaked round behind him and caught him with a snowball from close range. Will barely heard the phone through the boy's shrieks of laughter; didn't react until he saw Lorraine waving through the window, her knuckles banging on the pane.

Will touched her belly gently with the palm of his hand as he passed. Good luck.

'Hello?' he said, picking up the phone. 'This is Grayson.'

The change in his face told Lorraine all she needed to know and quickly she set to making a flask of coffee; a morning like this, more snow forecast, he would need something to keep out the cold.

Will laced up his boots, pulled on a fleece, took a weather-proof coat from the cupboard beneath the stairs; the first pancake was ready and he ate it with a smudge of maple syrup, licking his fingers before lifting his son into the air and swinging him round, kissing him, then setting him down.

Lorraine leaned forward and hugged him at the door. 'Be careful when you're driving home. In case it freezes over.'

'Don't worry.' He kissed her eyes and mouth. 'And call me if anything, you know, happens.'

She laughed. 'Go get the bad guys, okay?'

When the car failed to start first time, Will cursed, fearing the worst, but then the engine caught and turned and he was on his way, snaking tyre tracks through a film of fallen snow.

Some thirty minutes and two wrong turnings later, he pulled over into a farm gateway and unfolded the map. Out there in the middle of the fens, a day like this, everything looked the damned same.

It was another ten minutes before he finally arrived, wheels cracking the ice, and slid to a halt behind Helen Walker's blue VW, last in line behind the three police vehicles parked alongside the fen. There was an ambulance further back, closer to the road.

Helen Walker: how had she got there before him?

'Afternoon, Will,' she called sarcastically, leaning over the scaffolding on the upper level of the unfinished house. 'Good of you to join us.'

Will shot her a finger and began making his way up the ladder.

He and Helen had worked together the best part of three years now, Will, as detective inspector, enjoying the higher rank, but, most of the time, that wasn't how it worked. It was more as if they were partners, sometimes one would lead, sometimes the other.

'How's Lorraine?' Helen's first question when he stepped off on to the boards.

'She's fine.'

'The baby?'

'Kicking for England.'

She laughed at the grin on his face.

'What have we got?' Will asked.

Helen stepped aside.

The dead man lay on his back, one arm flung out, the other close to his side, legs splayed. Eyes opened wide. A dark hole at the centre of his forehead. The blood that had pooled out from the exit wound seemed to have frozen fast.

29

'Someone found him like this?'

'Kids. Playing around.'

Will crouched low then stood up straight. 'We know who he is?'

'Arthur Fraser.'

'How do we know that?'

'Wallet. Inside pocket.'

'Not robbery then?'

'Not robbery.'

'Any idea what he was doing here?'

'Checking on his new house, apparently. The architect's name's on the board below. I gave him a call. He was with a client the other side of Cambridge.' Helen took a quick look at her watch. 'Should be here, another thirty minutes or so.'

Will turned back towards the body. 'He come from round here? Fraser?'

'Not really. Address the other side of Coventry.'

'What's he doing having a house built here?'

'I asked the architect that. Making a new start, apparently.'

'Not any more.'

*

Malkin and Earl Michaels sat at one of a cluster of wooden tables out front of a canal-side pub. None of the other tables was occupied. The snow had held off but there was a wind, driving in from the north-west, though neither man seemed bothered by the cold. Both were drinking blended Scotch, doubles; Malkin nursing his second, Michaels on his third or fourth.

'How much,' Michaels asked, 'always assuming I wanted to go ahead, how much is this going to cost?'

When Malkin told him, he had to ask a second time.

'That friggin' much?'

'That much.'

'Then you can forget it.'

'Okay.' Downing the rest of his drink in one, Malkin got to his feet.

'No. Hey, hey. Wait a minute. Wait up.'

'Look,' Malkin said, 'no way I want to push you where you don't want to go.'

'Come on, it's not that. You know it's not that. Nobody wants that . . . Nobody wants it more than me. That bastard. I'd like to get hold of that fucking shotgun of his and let him have it myself.'

'And end up inside doing fifteen to life.'

'I know, I know.' Michaels shook his head. He was a heavy man and the weight sat ill upon him, his body lumpen, his face jowly and red.

Malkin sat back down.

'That sort of money,' Michaels said. 'I'd be lucky to earn that in a year. A good year at that.'

Malkin shrugged. 'You want a job well done . . .'

'Listen.' Leaning in, Michaels took hold of Malkin's sleeve. 'I could go down some pub in the Meadows, ask around. Time it takes to have a good shit, there'd be someone willing to do it for a couple of hundred quid.'

'Yes,' Malkin said. 'And ten days after that the police would have him banged up inside and he'd give you up first chance he got. Listen to him, you'd been the one talked him into it, forced him more or less, did everything except pull the trigger.'

Michaels knew he was right.

'You want another?' he said, eyeing his empty glass.

Malkin shook his head. 'Let's get this sorted first.'

'The money,' Michaels said, 'I don't see how . . .'

'Borrow it,' Malkin said. 'Building society. The bank. Tell them you want to extend. I don't know. Add on a conservatory. Put in a loft.'

'You make it sound easy.'

'It is if you want it to be.'

For several minutes neither man spoke. Whoever had been the centre of all the police attention at the court had been taken in under close guard and now, indeed, there was a helicopter making slow small circles above their heads.

'That bastard Silver,' Michaels said. 'He's going to make a fucking fortune out of this.'

'Yes.'

'Smelling of fucking roses won't be in it.'

'That's true.'

'All right, all right. But listen, I'm going to need a few days. The cash, you know?'

Malkin laid a hand on his arm. 'That's okay. Within reason, take all the time you need. Silver's not going anywhere quite yet. Meantime, I'll ask around, make a few plans.'

'We've got a deal, then?'

The skin around Malkin's grey eyes creased into a smile. 'We've got a deal.'

*

What was it they said about converts? They were always the strictest adherents to the faith? Since he'd turned away from a thirty-a-day habit two years ago, Will had been that way about smoking. Just about the only thing he found hard to take about Helen was the way her breath smelled when she'd come in from outside, sneaking a cigarette break at the rear of the building. Not so long back he'd given her a tube of extra-strong mints and she'd handed them back, saying they were bad for her teeth.

It was the day after Fraser's body had been found.

Careful examination of the scene had found little in the way of forensic evidence; no stray hairs or fingerprints, no snatches of fabric snagged by chance on ladder or doorway. A series of footprints, fading in the slow-melting snow, had been traced across two broad fields; at the furthest point, close in against the hedge, there were tyre tracks, faint but clear. A Ford Mondeo with similar patterned tyres, stolen in Peterborough the day previously, was discovered in the car park at Ely station. Whoever had killed Fraser could have had another car waiting or have caught a train. South to Cambridge and London; east towards Norwich, west to Nottingham and beyond.

It was an open book.

'Fraser,' Will said. 'I've been doing some checking. Fifty-two years old. Company director. Divorced five years ago. Two kids, both grown up. Firm he was running went under. Picked himself up since then, financially at least, but it seems to have been pretty bad at the time.'

'That was when the wife left him?'

'How d'you know she was the one who left?'

Helen touched her fingertips to her temple. 'Female intuition.'

'Bollocks!'

'Excuse me, is that a technical term?'

'Definitely. And you're right, she walked away. What with that and the business thing, Fraser seems to have fallen apart for a while, started drinking heavily. Two charges of driving with undue care, another for driving when over the limit. Just under three years ago he lost control behind the wheel, went up on to the kerb and hit this eight-year-old. A girl.'

Pain jolted across Helen's face. 'She was . . .'

Will nodded. 'She was killed. Not outright. Hung on in hospital for five days more.'

'What happened to Fraser?'

'Fined six thousand pounds, banned from driving for eighteen months . . .'

'Eighteen months?'

'Uh-huh.'

'And that was it?'

'Two years inside.'

'Of which he served half.'

Will nodded. 'Two-thirds of that in an open prison with passes most weekends.'

'That's justice?'

Will shook his head. 'Not so's you'd notice.'

Helen drew breath. 'What time's the post-mortem?'

'An hour from now?'

She nodded. 'My car or yours?'

*

Malkin showed the appropriate credit card and booked a room at the Holiday Inn under an assumed name. It was a city he knew, though not well, and it was doubtful that anyone there knew him. Average height, average build, he was blessed with one of those faces that were instantly forgettable, save possibly for the eyes.

At the central library he read through the coverage of Silver's appeal and then the reporting of the original shooting and trial. Aside from Silver's own faded celebrity, much was made of the delinquent lifestyle of Wayne Michaels and his companion that evening,

34

Jermaine Royal. Both young men had been in trouble with the police since their early teens; both had been excluded, at various times, from school. An accident, one compassionate reporter said of Wayne Michaels, just waiting to happen.

Malkin found a cut-and-paste biography on the shelves. *The Fall and Fall of Alan Silver*. He took it to one of the tables on the upper floor to read; just himself and a bunch of students beavering away at their laptops, listening to their iPods through headphones.

Silver's mother had been a chorus girl, his father a third-rate comedian in music hall and a pantomime dame; Alan himself first appeared on stage at the age of six, learning to be his father's stooge. A photograph showed him in a sailor suit, holding a silver whistle. By the age of seventeen he was doing a summer season at Scarborough, complete with straw hat and cane, Yorkshire's answer to Fred Astaire. There were spots on popular radio shows, *Variety Bandbox* and *Educating Archie*; even some early television, *Café Continental* with Hélène Cordet.

Three marriages, but none of them stuck; no children, apparently. A veiled suggestion that he might be gay. In the eighties, he had something of a comeback in the theatre, playing a failed music hall performer in a revival of *The Entertainer*, the part originally played by Laurence Olivier. Asked how he did it, Silver replied, 'I just close my eyes and think of my old man.'

Soon after this he was featured on *This is Your Life* and had some brief success with 'Mama Liked the Roses'. Somehow he kept working into his sixties, mostly doing pantomime, trotting out his father's old routines at the likes of Mansfield and Hunstanton.

Oh, no, it isn't!
Oh, yes, it is!

35

He bought an old farmhouse between Newark and Nottingham. Retired, more or less.

Malkin phoned Michaels that evening, wanting to make sure he was still on board; asked a few questions about Wayne's friends. Something Wayne's pal, Jermaine, had claimed at the trial, that they'd been out to Silver's place before and he'd told them come back any time. Did Michaels think there was any truth in that?

Michaels had no bloody idea.

'Besides,' Michaels said, 'what difference if there was?'

None, Malkin told him. None at all.

'Too bloody right,' Michaels said. 'Dead is fucking dead.'

*

The phone rang and before Will could reach it, Helen had snatched it up. Coat buttoned up against the cold, she had just come in from outside.

'Lorraine,' she said, passing the phone swiftly across.

Will's throat went dry and his stomach performed a double somersault, but all his wife wanted was to remind him to pick up an extra pint of milk on his way home if possible. Will assured her he'd do what he could.

'No news?' Helen asked, once he'd set down the phone.

'No news.'

'Well, I've got something.'

'You're not pregnant, too?'

'Chance would be a fine thing.'

Will stood back and looked her over. 'You want to get pregnant?'

'You're offering?'

He grinned. It was a good grin, took maybe ten years off his age and he knew it. 'Not today.'

'Damn!' Helen smiled back. She liked flirting with him;

36

it was something they did. Somehow it helped them along; kept them, Helen sometimes thought, from ever getting close to the real thing.

'You want to tell me your news?' Will said.

'You know that expanse of water the other side of Ely? Close to the railway line?'

'I think so.'

'These kids were out there the day Fraser was killed. Late morning. They'd taken a makeshift toboggan, thinking the water might have frozen over, but it hadn't. Just a little at the edges maybe, but that's all. Not worth taking any risks; near the centre it's pretty deep.'

Will nodded, waiting, perched on the edge of a desk. She'd get to it in her own time.

'While they were there, the Nottingham train went through. They didn't know it was that, but I've checked. One of the boys swears he saw someone throwing an object from the window between the carriages. Just for a moment, he thought it looked like a gun.'

'How old? This kid, how old is he?'

'Nine? Ten?'

'You think he's any way reliable?'

'According to his mother, he's not the kind to make things up.'

'Why's he only come forward now?'

'Mentioned it to his mum at the time. She didn't think anything of it till she saw something about the investigation on the local news.'

'You know what the boss is going to say. Divers don't come cheap.'

'Not even if they're our divers?'

'Not even then.'

'Think you can persuade him?'

'What else have we got?'

37

'So far? Diddly-squat.'
'Why don't I tell him that?'

*

Instant Tanning read the sign in the window. *Manicure, Pedicure* in similar lettering below. *Top Notch Beauty Salon* above the door. Lisa was sitting on the step outside, pink tunic, sandals, tights, smoking a cigarette.

Malkin crossed towards her and as he came close she glanced up and then away.

'Busy?' Malkin said.

She looked at him through an arc of smoke. 'Takin' the piss, right?'

By appearance she was a mixture of African-Caribbean and Chinese, but her accent was East Midlands through and through, Notts rather than Derby.

'Lisa?'

'Yeah?'

Malkin squatted low on his haunches, face close to hers. 'You used to know Wayne Michaels.'

'So what if I did?'

'I'm sorry. About what happened.'

'Yeah, well. Been and gone now, i'n't it?'

'You've moved on.'

'Something like that.'

'Good.'

Something about his voice made her feel ill at ease. 'Look, this place.' She looked up at the sign. 'It's what it says it is, you know. Not one of them massage parlours, if that's what you're thinking.'

'Not at all. It's just, if you've got the time, I thought we could talk a bit about Wayne? Maybe his mate, Jermaine? You were friendly with both of them, weren't you?'

38

Lisa narrowed her eyes. 'You're not the police, are you?'

'Perish the thought.'

'Not some reporter?'

Malkin shook his head. 'I used to know Wayne's father a little, that's what it is.'

'Him told you 'bout me, I s'pose, were it?'

'That's right.'

Lisa lit a new cigarette from the butt of the last. 'Got a good twenty minutes till my next, why not?'

*

There was a pair of divers, borrowed for the occasion from the Lincolnshire force, and they struck lucky within the first hour. Will grateful he could assure his boss there'd be no need for overtime. The weapon was a Glock 17, its bulky stock immediately recognisable. Any serial numbers had, of course, been removed. If they begged and pleaded with the technicians, another twenty-four hours should tell them if it was the gun responsible for Arthur Fraser's death.

Will and Helen were both parked up at the side of the road, a lay-by off the A10, the Ely to Cambridge road. They were sitting in Will's car, a faint mist beginning to steam up the insides of the windows.

'You thinking what I'm thinking?' Will said.

'Most probably.' A hint of a smile on Helen's face.

'This shooting. Nothing to suggest any kind of fight or quarrel. Nothing personal. Every sign of careful planning: preparation. A single shot to the head with a weapon that's almost certainly clean. A professional job. It has to be.'

'Someone hired to make a hit on Fraser?'

'It looks that way.'

'Then you have to ask why.'

'And there's only one answer,' Will said. 'Sharon Peters.'

Helen nodded. 'The family, the parents, we should go and talk to them?'

'Let's wait,' Will said. 'Till tomorrow. Make sure the ballistics match up.'

'Okay.'

It was warm inside the car. Their arms close but not touching. An articulated lorry went past close enough to rock them in its slipstream. Still neither one of them made a move to go.

Finally, it was Helen who looked at her watch. 'Shouldn't you be getting back?'

'If anything had happened, Lorraine would have called on my mobile.'

'Even so.'

He left her leaning against the roof of her VW, smoking a cigarette.

When Will arrived home, Lorraine was wandering from room to room, Cowboy Junkies on the stereo, singing quietly along. 'A Common Disaster' playing over and over, the track programmed to repeat. To Will, it wasn't a good omen.

'Lol?'

'Huh?'

'Can we change this?'

'Change?'

'The music. Can we . . . ?'

'I like it.'

Okay, Will thought, go with the flow.

A good few years back, when he and Lorraine had first started going together, she would fetch her little stash from where she kept it upstairs in the bedroom – her dowry, as she called it – and roll them both a joint. Now that he no longer smoked cigarettes and, Will supposed, with this latest promotion, if she ever suggested it, he passed.

Lorraine, he was sure, still partook from time to time, the sweet smell lingering in the corners of the house and in her hair. Maybe, looking at her slight, slow sway, she was stoned right now.

How would that be for the baby, he wondered, if it were so?

Would it make him a cool kid or slightly crazy?

There were some cans of beer in the fridge and he took one and went into the living room and switched on the TV. Lorraine had been vague about dinner, but he thought she was entitled, hormones all over the place like they were. Later he'd phone for a curry or, better still, a Chinese. It was ages since they'd eaten Chinese.

They were in bed before ten thirty, Lorraine set to read a chapter or so of whatever book she had on the go, Will rolling away from her and on to his side, arm raised to shield his eyes from the light.

He must have fallen asleep straight away, because the next thing he knew it was pitch dark and the bed beside him was empty. Lorraine was sitting on the toilet with her nightgown pulled high across her thighs.

'You all right?' Anxiety breaking in his voice.

'Yes. Yes, just woke with this pain.' She indicated low in her abdomen.

'But you're okay? I mean, nothing's happened?'

'Nothing's happened.'

When he bent to kiss her forehead it was damp and seared with sweat. 'Why don't you let me get you something? A drink of water? Tea? How about some peppermint tea?'

'Yes. Peppermint tea. That would be nice.'

He kissed her chastely on the lips and went downstairs.

Back in bed, he found it near impossible to get back to sleep, dozed fitfully and got up finally at five.

Jake was fast off, thumb in his mouth, surrounded by his favourite toys.

Will made coffee and toast and sat at the kitchen table staring out, willing it to get light. At six thirty he gave in and dialled Helen's number. She answered on the second ring.

'Not asleep then?'

'Hardly.'

'Yesterday,' Will said, 'you think I was being over-cautious?'

'In the car?'

'What I said in the car, yes. About waiting to see if we had a match.'

'You don't think there's any doubt?'

'Has to be some. But, shit, not really, no.'

'You want to go over there now? Sharon Peters' parents?'

'What do you reckon? A couple of hours' drive? More?'

'Coventry? This time of the morning maybe less.'

'I'll meet you by the Travelodge on the A14. This side of the turn-off for Hemingford Grey.'

'It's a deal.' Will could hear the excitement rising in her voice.

The traffic moving into and out of the city was heavy and it was close to nine before they arrived at the house, a twenties semi-detached in a quiet street with trees, leaf-less still, at frequent intervals. Cars parked either side.

There was a van immediately outside the house with decorating paraphernalia in the rear, partly covered by a paint-splodged sheet. The man who came to the door was wearing off-white dungarees, speckled red, blue and green.

'Mr Peters?'

He looked Will and Helen up and down, as if slowly making up his mind. Then he stepped back and held the door wide. 'You'd best come in. Don't want everyone knowing our business up and down the street.'

One wall of the room into which he led them was a virtual shrine to Sharon when she'd been alive, photographs almost floor to ceiling.

'The wife's out,' Peters said. 'Dropping off our other girl at school. Usually goes and does a bit of shopping after that.'

Our other girl, Will was thinking. Of course, to them she's still alive.

'You know why we're here?' Helen asked.

'Something to do with that bastard getting shot, I imagine.'

'You know about it, then?'

'Not at first, no. One of neighbours come round and told us. Saw it, like, on TV.'

'And you didn't know anything about it till then?'

'Course not, what d'you think?'

'To be frank, Mr Peters,' Will said, 'we think someone paid to have Fraser killed.'

'You reckon?' Peters laughed. 'Well, I'll tell you what, if they'd come round here asking for a few quid toward it, I'd have shelled out double-quick. What he did to our Sharon, shooting's too good for him.' Looking at Will, he narrowed his eyes. 'Quick was it?'

'I think so, yes.'

'More's the sodding pity.'

They talked to him for three-quarters of an hour, pushing and prodding, back and forth over the same ground, but if he had anything to give away, it never showed.

Just as they were on the point of leaving, a key turned

in the front door and Mrs Peters stepped through into the hall, shopping bags in both hands. One look at her husband, another at Will and Helen and the bags dropped to the floor. 'Oh Christ, they know, don't they? They bloody know.'

Will contacted the local police station and arranged for an interview room to be placed at their disposal. Donald and Lydia Peters were questioned separately and together, always with a lawyer present. After her initial outburst, Lydia would say nothing; Donald, brazening it out, would not say a great deal more. Without an admission, without tangible evidence – letters, emails, recordings of phone calls – their involvement in Fraser's murder would be difficult to prove. All they had was the wife's slip of the tongue. *They know, don't they?* In a court of law, it could have meant anything.

Their one chance was a court order to examine the Peterses' bank records, turn their finances inside out. If they had, indeed, paid to have Fraser killed, the money would have had to have come from somewhere. Unless they'd been especially careful. Unless it had come from other sources. Family. Friends.

Will knew full well that if he went to the Crown Prosecution Service with what they had now, they'd laugh in his face.

*

It had taken a little time for Malkin to gain Lisa's confidence enough for her to take him to see Jermaine. Jermaine having served his time for attempted burglary and been released into the care of his probation officer, one of the conditions that he move away from where he'd been living,

44

steer clear of his former friends. Where Lisa took Malkin
was no more than ten miles away, Sutton-in-Ashfield,
Jermaine's gran's.

Jermaine and Malkin sat in the small front room, the
parlour his gran had called it, Lisa and the old lady in the
other room, watching TV.

Jermaine was fidgeting constantly, never still.

'What you said in court,' Malkin asked, 'about having
been to Silver's place before, was that true?'

'Course it was true. No one fuckin' believed it, though,
did they?'

'You'd both been there? You and Wayne?'

'Yeah. What's this all about, anyway? What's it matter
now?'

'Why were you there, Jermaine?'

'What d'you mean, why?'

'I mean Alan Silver's a has-been in his sixties and you're
what? Seventeen. I wouldn't have thought you'd got a lot
to talk about, a lot of common ground.'

Jermaine's head swung from side to side. 'He was all
right, you know, not stuck up, not tight. Plenty to drink,
yeah? Southern Comfort, that's what he liked.'

'And money? He gave you money?'

Now Jermaine was staring at the floor, not wanting to
look Malkin in the eye.

'He gave you money?' Malkin said again.

'He gave Wayne money.' Jermaine's voice was little more
than a whisper.

'Why did he give Wayne money, Jermaine? Why did he
give—'

'For sucking his cock,' Jermaine suddenly shouted. 'Why
d'you think?'

Just for an instant, Malkin closed his eyes. 'And that's
why you went back?' he said.

'No. We went back to rip him off, didn't we? Fucking queer!'

Malkin leaned, almost imperceptibly, forward. 'Silver's house,' he said. 'If I gave you some paper, paper and a pencil, d'you think you could draw me some kind of plan of the inside?'

*

'Look,' Will called across the office. 'Take a look at this.'

Helen pushed aside what she was doing and made her way to where Will was sitting at the computer.

'There, you see. This has been nagging at me and there it is. Two years ago. Lincoln. This man Royston Davies. Nightclub bouncer. Found dead in the back of a taxi. Single bullet through the head. 9mm.'

'All right,' Helen said. 'I see the connection.'

'Just wait. There's more.' Will scrolled down the page. 'See. That was February. The August before there was a fracas outside the club where Davies was working. Nineteen-year-old youth was struck with something hard enough to put him into hospital. Bottle, baseball bat. Went into a coma and never came out of it.' Will closed the file. 'I rang someone I know at Lincoln this morning. Seems Davies was brought in for questioning, quite a few witnesses pointing the finger, but they never got enough to make a case.'

'Wait, wait. Wait a minute.' Helen held both hands in front of her, palms out, as if to ward off the idea. 'What you're suggesting, unless I've got this wrong, what you're saying, there's someone out there, some professional assassin, some hitman, specialising in taking out people who've killed and got away with it. Is that it?'

'That's it exactly.'

'You're crazy.'

'Why? Look at it, look at the evidence.'

'Will, there is no evidence. Not of what you're saying.'

'What is it then?'

'Coincidence.'

'And if I could show otherwise?'

'How?'

'If these weren't the only two instances, would you believe me then?'

'You telling me there are more?'

'I don't know yet. But I can find out.'

Helen laughed and pushed a hand back through her hair. 'Tell you what, Will, when you do, let me know.'

He watched her walk, still laughing, back across the room.

*

Alan Silver's house was pitched between Colston Bassett and Harby, on the western edge of the Vale of Belvoir. Nice country. Hunting country, when the time was right.

Malkin had driven past it several times, learning the lie of the land. Earlier that evening, the light fading, he had parked close by the canal and made his way across the fields. Now he was there again, close to midnight, tracing a path back between the trees.

Cold, he thought, pausing at a field end to glance up at the sky. Cold enough for snow.

*

At just about the time Malkin had made his first visit to Alan Silver's house, Lorraine had been sitting with her feet up on the settee, watching television, one of those chat shows Will abhorred. *Richard & Judy? Richard & Jane?*

He was in the other room, leafing through the paper, when she called him.

'Look. That man who shot the boy trying to burgle him. The one there was all the fuss about, remember?'

Will remembered.

'He's on now.'

As Will came into the room a black-and-white image of a young Alan Silver was on the screen. White suit, straw hat and cane.

'My God!' said Silver in mock surprise. 'Was that me? I'd never have known.'

'But that was how you started?' said Richard. 'A bit of a song-and-dance man.'

'Absolutely.'

'You don't suppose,' said Jane or Judy, 'you could still do a few steps for us now?'

Sprightly for a man of his years, Silver sprang to his feet and did a little tap dance there and then. Jane or Judy marvelled and the studio audience broke into spontaneous applause.

'Not bad for sixty-odd,' Lorraine said.

Will said something non-committal and walked back out of the room.

Alan Silver plumped up his pillows and reached for the glass of water he kept beside the bed. He was tired; his legs ached. The show had gone well, though, he thought. Sparkled, that's what he'd done. Sparkled. Still smiling, he switched out the bedside light. It wouldn't take him long to get to sleep tonight.

A short while later he was wide awake.

Something had woken him but what?

A dream? A noise on the stairs?

Imagination, surely?

But no, there it was again.

Silver felt his skin turn cold.

It couldn't be happening twice.

Carefully, he eased back the heavy covers and rolling on to his stomach, reached beneath the bed.

It wasn't there. The bloody thing wasn't there.

The bedroom door swung open and Silver, turning clumsily, jabbed on the light.

'Looking for something?' Malkin said, levelling the shotgun towards the centre of the bed.

PROMISE

The way it would usually be: Kiley would be in the pub enjoying a quiet drink when someone would walk over to him or intercept him on his way to the bar. 'Excuse me, but aren't you that bloke . . .' And then it would start and Kiley would nod and grin and hear it all again, some blurred version of it anyway, before signing whatever scrap of paper was within reach and shaking hands. 'Always wondered what happened to you.'

Jack Kiley at forty. A tall man with a barely discernible limp as he carried his pint of Worthington back to his corner table. The face fuller now, the hair as thick, though touched with grey; the eyes a safer shade of blue. His body softer, but not soft, some fifteen pounds heavier than when he came from nowhere to score that hat-trick in extra time. The FA Cup quarter final, 1989.

'Hey, aren't you . . . ?'

Kiley had been a police officer at the time, a detective in the Met, CID. Seven years in. He'd never stopped playing

50

soccer since he was a kid. Turned out for the force, of course he did. And as an amateur, without contract, for a string of semi-pro clubs, Kidderminster Harriers, Canvey Island, Gravesend. When Stevenage Borough in the Conference came in for him, needing cover for an injured striker, an understanding detective superintendent cleared Kiley's rota for most Saturdays in the season, only for him to spend the best part of each game on the bench, waiting to be thrown on in the dying stages – 'Go get 'em, Jack. Show 'em what you can do.' – Kiley clogging through the churned-up mud in search of an equalising goal.

Each year the Cup threw up its giant killer, a team from the lower reaches riding their luck and ground advantage to harry and chase the top pros with their fancy boots and trophy wives, each earning more in a month than Kiley's team would graft in a brace of years. And in '89 it was Stevenage, a home draw against the Villa promising them a place in the last four. One all at the end of the ninety and five minutes into extra time, Kiley, frustrated and cold inside his tracksuit, got the call. 'Go get 'em, Jack.'

With his first touch he played the ball straight into the path of the opposing centre half, the second slid beneath his boot and skidded out of touch; his third, a rising shot struck full off the meat of the right boot on the run, swerved high and wide past the goalie's outstretched hand and Kiley's side were in the lead, nineteen minutes to go.

Five minutes later Villa drew level, and then, from the midst of a nine-man goal-mouth melee, Kiley toe-poked the ball blindly over the line.

Kiley's marker, who'd already been trying to kick six shades of shit out of him, clattered against him as they headed back towards the centre circle. 'Don't think that makes you fucking clever. 'Cause you're not, you're fuckin' shite!' And as the ball arced away towards the left wing, unobserved, he elbowed Kiley in the kidneys and left him face down in the dirt.

Which is why Kiley was unmarked, moments later, when the ball came ballooning towards him out of the Villa defence, Kiley thirty yards from goal, open space in front of him and he met it on the half-volley, sweet like driving a passing shot down the line on Centre Court, or pulling a six head-high to the boundary at Lord's, that rare and perfect combination of technique and relaxation, and he knew, even before the roar of the crowd or the sight of his own players cartwheeling in pleasure, that he had scored.

At the final whistle, with the home crowd chanting his name, his marker sought him out, and with a toothless grin, threw an arm around his shoulder. 'No hard feelings, eh?' And when Kiley looked back at him, 'Swap shirts, then? What d'you say?'

Kiley nodded and waited till the player had lifted his arms above his head. And punched him once, a short right to the ribs that dropped the man, breathless, to his knees.

The referee red-carded him for that, which meant Kiley was ineligible for the semi-final, which they lost seven–one to Liverpool, a necessary corrective to their uppity behaviour. In professional soccer, each giant-killer – so valuable for filling column inches and the turnstiles both – is only allowed so many sacrificial giants.

For Kiley, though, fame lingered on, his hat-trick the stuff of innumerable sports-show repeats, and it was no surprise when someone offered him the chance to turn professional a few months short of his twenty-ninth birthday. The manager of Charlton Athletic had something of a reputation for making silk purses from sow's ears, turning grit into gold. And Kiley knew it was the only chance he would get. With too few second thoughts, he resigned from the Met.

Most of his first season was spent in the reserves or on the bench: in all he made just three first team starts, scoring once. The following summer he trained hard, determined; played in all three pre-season friendlies, looking sharp; in the first league game he hit a volley from twenty-five yards that slammed against the bar, and narrowly missed with a diving header inside the box. The second game, away, he was stretching for a ball that was never really his when the tackle came in, two-footed, late, and broke his leg. Some legs, young legs, mend. After two operations, rest, light training, lots of physio, Kiley called it a day. The club were more generous than many, the insurance settlement better than he might have hoped. For months he did little or nothing, left books half-read, watched afternoon movies, moped. Considered a civilian job with the Met. Then a former colleague from the force offered him work with the security firm he was running. 'No uniform, Jack. No bullshit. Just wear a suit, look large and smile.' For the best part of three years, he was a paid bodyguard to B-list celebrities, obscure overseas royals, sports personalities and their hangers-on.

At Wimbledon, Kiley found himself sharing overpriced strawberries and champagne with Adrian Costain, a sports agent he'd brushed up against a few times in his soccer days, and when Costain rang him a week later with the offer of some private work, he thought, why not?

So here he was, ten years down the line from his twenty-five minutes of fame, a private investigator with an office, a computer, pager, fax and phone; a small but growing clientele, a backlog of successfully resolved, mostly sports-associated cases.

Jack Kiley, whatever happened to him?
Well, now you know.

*

Kiley was alone in his office, August third. Two rooms
above a bookshop in Belsize Park. A bathroom he shared
with the financial consultant whose office was on the upper
floor.

'So what d'you think?' Kate had asked him the first
time they'd looked round. 'Perfect, no?' Kate having been
tipped off by her friend, Lauren, who managed the shop
below.

'Perfect, maybe. But rents in this part of London . . .
There's no way I could afford it.'

'Jack!'

'It's all I can do to keep up with the payments on the flat.'

'Then let it go.'

'What?'

'The flat, let it go.'

Kiley had stared around. 'And live here?'

'No, fool. Move in with me.'

So now Kiley's name was there in neat lettering, upper
and lower case, on the glass of the outer door. The office
chair behind the glass-topped desk was angled round,
suggesting his secretary had just popped out and would be
back. As she might, were she to exist. In her stead, there
was Irena, a young Romanian who waited on tables across
the street, and two mornings a week did Kiley's filing for
him, a little basic word processing, talked to him of the
squares and avenues of Bucharest, excursions to the Black
Sea, of storks that nested by the sides of country roads.

In Kiley's inner sanctum were a smaller desk, oak-faced,
an easy chair, a couch on which he sometimes napped, a

54

radio, a TV whose screen he could span with one outstretched hand. There was a plant, jasmine, tiny white flowers amongst a plethora of glossed green leaves; a barely troubled bottle of single malt; a framed print Kate had presented him with when he moved in: two broad bands of cream resting across a field of mottled grey, the lines between hand-drawn and slightly wavering.

'It'll grow on you,' she'd said.

He was still waiting.

The phone chirruped and he lifted it to his ear.

'Busy, Jack?' Costain's voice was two-thirds marketing, one-third market stall.

'That depends.'

'Victoria Clarke.'

'What about her?'

'Get yourself down to Queen's. Forty-five minutes to an hour from now, she should be towelling down.'

Kiley was enough of a Londoner to know car owning for a mug's game. Within three minutes, he'd picked up a cab travelling south down Haverstock Hill and they'd set off on the zigzag course that would shuttle them west, Kiley wondering how many billboards of Victoria Clarke they would pass on the way.

That damp June and July she had been a minor sensation at the Wimbledon Championships, the first British woman to reach the semi-finals since Boadicea, or so it seemed, and ranked currently twenty-three in the world. And she had sprung from nowhere, or somewhere near the Essex end of the Central line at best; a council flat she had shared growing up with her sister, stepdad and mum. And like the Williams sisters, Serena and Venus, in the States, she had learned to play on public courts, enjoying none of the privilege that usually attended the luckless Amandas and Betinas of the English tennis world. Nor did

55

it end there. Her face, which freckled slightly in the sun, was beautiful in a Kate Moss kind of a way, her legs slender and long; the quality of the sports photographer's long lens and of television video ensured that not one salted bead of sweat that languished on her neck then slowly disappeared into the décolletage of the thin cotton tops she liked to wear was spared from public view.

Before the tournament was over, Costain had the contracts signed, the company's ad campaign agreed. Less than a fortnight later, the first of the advertisements appeared: Clarke crouching on the baseline, racket in hand, lips slightly parted, waiting to receive. In another she is watching the high toss of the ball, back arched, about to serve, white cotton top stretched tight across her breasts. For these and others, the strapline is the same: 'A Little Honest Sweat!' Just that and a discreet Union Jack, the deodorant pictured lower right, close by the product's name.

Unreconstructed feminists protested and sprayed slogans late at night; students tore them down as trophies for their rooms; Kate devoted her column in the *Independent* to the insistent eroticising of the everyday. One giant billboard near an intersection on the A1 north was removed after advice from the Department of Transport.

In the *Observer Sport Monthly*'s annual list of '*Britain's Top 20 Sportswomen*', Victoria Clarke was number seven with a bullet, the only tennis player to appear at all.

'Forgot your racket,' the cabbie joked, glancing at Kiley, empty-handed, waiting outside Queen's Club for his change and his receipt.

Kiley half-grinned and shook his head. 'Different game.'

Costain was in the bar: tousled hair, rimless glasses, Paul Smith suit and large gin. He bought Kiley a small Scotch and water and they moved to a pair of low leather chairs

56

by the far wall. Good living, Kiley noticed, had brought Costain the beginnings of a belly the loose cut of his suit just failed to disguise.

'So how is it really?' Costain asked with a smile.

'You know.'

'Still with Kate?'

Kiley nodded.

'How long's that now?' And then, quickly, 'I know, I know, who's counting?'

In a week's time it would be two years since they'd started seeing one another; nine months, almost to the day, since he'd moved into Kate's house in Highbury Fields. Kate, Kiley knew, had gone out with Costain a few times some few years back; kissing him, she said, was like being force-fed marinated eel.

'Victoria Clarke,' Kiley said, 'what's the problem? There is a problem, I suppose.'

Costain drank a little more gin. 'She's being blackmailed.'

'Don't tell me she was a Page Three Girl for the *Sun*.'

For an answer, Costain took an envelope from the inside pocket of his suit coat and passed it across. Inside, a black-and-white copy of a photograph had been pasted to a single sheet of paper: a young woman in a park, holding a small girl, a toddler, high above her head; in the background, another woman, beside an empty buggy, looks on. The first woman, and the girl, are smiling, more than smiling, laughing; the second woman is not. The quality of the copy was such, it took a keen eye to identify the former as Victoria Clarke. Even then, there was room for doubt.

'Is this all there is?' Kiley asked.

'It arrived this morning, first post. A phone call some forty minutes later, man's voice, disguised.' He nodded towards the paper in Kiley's hand. 'I imagine the original's a lot clearer, wouldn't you?'

57

'And the child?'

'Hers. Victoria's.'

Kiley looked at the picture again; the relationship between the two women was there, but it wasn't yet defined. 'Whoever sent this, what do they want?'

'A quarter of a million.'

'For what?'

'The negative, all originals, copies. We've got two days before they sell it to the highest bidder. The tabloids'd go ape shit.'

Kiley tasted his Scotch. 'Why now?' he asked.

'We're in the middle of renegotiating Victoria's advertising contract. Very hush-hush. Big, big money involved. If nothing slips out of sync, everything should be finalised by the end of the week.'

'Then, hush-hush or not, somebody knows.'

'What?' Costain said, mouth twisting in a wry grin. 'You don't believe in blind luck?' And, because Victoria Clarke was now walking through the bar towards them, he rose to his feet and smiled a reassuring smile.

She was tall, taller even than Kiley, who knew the stats, had thought, and wore a dark blue warm-up suit, name monogrammed neatly along the sleeve with something close to style. Sports bag slung over one shoulder, hair still damp from the shower and tied back, the only signs of distress were in the hollows of her eyes, the suggestion of a tremor when she shook Kiley's hand.

'You want something?' Costain asked. 'Mineral water? Juice?'

She shook her head. Standing there devoid of make-up, she almost looked what she was: nineteen.

The envelope lay on the table between two unfinished drinks. 'I don't want to talk about this here,' Victoria said.

'I thought just—' Costain began.

'Not here.' The voice wasn't petulant, but firm.

Costain shrugged and, with a glance at Kiley, downed his gin and led the way towards the door.

Costain owned a flat in a mansion block close to the Thames – in fact, he owned several between there and the Cromwell Road – and for the past several months it had been Victoria's home. Near enough to Queen's for her to hit every day.

'You'll have to excuse the mess,' she said.

Kiley moved an armful of discarded clothing and a paperback copy of Navratilova's life story. The room resembled a cross between a Conran window and the left luggage department at Euston station.

Victoria left them to each other's company and re-emerged some minutes later in a pale cotton top and faded jeans, hair brushed out and a little make-up around the eyes.

Sitting in an easy chair opposite Kiley, she tucked as much of her long legs beneath her as she could. 'Can you help?' She had a way of looking directly at you when she spoke.

'It depends.'

'On what?'

Kiley shook his head. 'Timing. Luck. You. The truth.'

Only for an instant did she lower her eyes, fingers of one hand sliding between those of the other then out again. 'Adrian,' she said over her shoulder. 'Get me some water, would you? There's some in the fridge in . . .' But Costain had already gone to do her bidding.

'I had Alicia – Alicia, that's her name – when I was fifteen. Fifteen years and ten months. The year before I'd been runner-up in the National Under-Sixteens at Hove. I was on the fringes of the county team. I thought if I can

59

get through to the last eight of the Junior Championships this next Wimbledon, I'm on my way. And then there was this lump that wouldn't go away.'

She paused to judge the effect of what she'd just said.

Costain placed a tumbler of still mineral water in her hand and then retreated back across the room.

'Why didn't you have an abortion?' Kiley asked.

She looked back at him evenly. 'I'd already made one bad mistake.'

'So you asked your sister – that is your sister, isn't it? In the photo?' Victoria bobbed her head. 'You asked your sister to look after her . . . No, more than that. To say Alicia was hers; bring her up as her own.'

'Yes.' In the wide, high-ceilinged room, Victoria's voice was suddenly very small.

'And she didn't mind?'

A shadow passed across Victoria's eyes. 'You have to understand. Cathy, that's my sister, I mean, she's wonderful, she's lovely with Alicia, really, but she just isn't . . . Well, we're different, chalk and cheese, she isn't like me at all, she doesn't . . .' Victoria drank from her glass and went back to balancing it on her knee. 'All she's ever wanted was to settle down, have kids, a place of her own. She didn't want to . . .' Victoria sighed. '. . . *do* anything. She and Trevor, they'd been going steady since she was fifteen; they were saving up to get married anyway. Mum chipped in, help them get started. Trevor, he was bringing in good money by then, Ford's at Dagenham. Of course, now I can pay towards whatever Alicia needs, I do.'

'A good percentage of her disposable income,' Costain interrupted. 'First-class holiday in Florida last year for the three of them, four weeks.'

'Cathy and Trevor,' Kiley said, 'they haven't had children of their own?'

60

Victoria lifted her gaze from Kiley's face towards the window, where a fly was buzzing haphazardly against the glass. 'She can't. I mean, I suppose she could try IVF. But, no, she can't have children of her own.'

Kiley let the moment settle. 'And Alicia?'

Victoria's lower lip slid over the upper and the water glass tipped from hand and knee onto the floor. 'She thinks I'm her auntie, of course. What else?'

Adrian reached out for her as she ran but she swerved around him and slammed the bedroom door.

'What do you think?' he said.

'I think,' said Kiley, 'I need a drink.'

Victoria had been seeing Paul Broughton ever since her fifteenth birthday. Broughton, twenty-three years old, a butcher boy in Leytonstone by day, by night the drummer in a band which might have been the Verve if the Verve hadn't already existed. A nice East London line on post-Industrial grime and angst. With heavily amplified guitars. After a gig at Walthamstow Assembly Rooms, he and Victoria got careless – either that, or Broughton's timing was off.

'For fuck's sake!' he said when Victoria told him. 'What d'you think you're gonna do? Get rid of it, of course.'

She didn't waste words on him again. She talked to her mum and her mum, who had some experience in these things, told her not to worry, they'd find a way. Which of them first had the idea about asking Cathy, they could never be sure. Nor how Cathy persuaded Trevor. But there was big sister, half nine to half five in the greetings-card shop and hating every minute. Victoria wore looser clothes, avoided public showers; her sister padded herself out, chucked in her job, practised walking with splayed legs and pain in the lower back. They chose the name together from a book. After the birth – like shelling peas, the midwife said – Victoria held the baby, kissed her close, and handed her across, a smear of blood and mucus on her cheek. Still, sometimes when she woke, she felt a baby's breath pass warm across her face.

As a Wimbledon junior, she reached the semi-finals before dropping a set, strode out to take the final, as she thought, by right, and went down two and love to the LTA's new white hope in thirty minutes flat. Costain, who had been monitoring Victoria's progress, waited till the hurt had eased and offered her a contract, sole representation, which her mother, of course, had to sign on her behalf. Costain's play: retreat, lie low, for now leave domestic competition alone; he financed winters in Australia, the United States. Wait till they've forgotten who you are then hit them smack between the eyes.

So far it had worked.

'I assume you don't want to pay?' Kiley said to Costain. Victoria was still in the bedroom, door locked.

'Quarter of a million? No, thanks!'

'But you'd pay something?'

Costain shrugged and pursed his lips; of course he would.

'Sooner or later, you know it'll come out.'

'Of course. I just want to be able to manage it, that's all. And now . . . the timing . . . you can imagine what this company's going to be saying about their precious image. If they don't walk away completely, and I think they might, they'll strip what they're offering back down to what we're getting now. Or worse.'

'You couldn't live with that?'

'I don't want to live with that.'

'All right, all right. When are they getting in touch again?'

'Five this evening.'

Kiley looked at his watch. One hour fifteen to go. 'Try and stall them, buy another twenty-four hours.'

'They'll never wear it.'

'Tell them if they want payment in full, they don't have any choice.'

'And if they still say no?'

Kiley rose to his feet. 'In the event the shit does hit the fan, I assume you've damage limitation planned.'

'What do you think?'

'I think you should make sure your plan's in place.'

*

'So what did you think of her?' Kate asked. 'Ms Teen Sensation.'

'I liked her.'

'Really?'

'Yes, really.'

They were lying, half-undressed, across the bed, Kate picking her way through an article by Naomi Klein, seeking something with which to disagree in print. Kiley had been reading one of the Chandlers Kate had bought him for his birthday – give you some idea of how a private eye's supposed to think – and liking it well enough. Although it was still a book. Before that, they had been making love.

'You fancied her, that's what you mean?'

'No. I liked her.'

'You didn't fancy her?'

'Kate . . .'

'What?' But she was laughing and Kiley grinned back and shook his head and she shifted so that one of her legs rested high across his and he began to stroke her shoulder and her back.

'You got your extra twenty-four hours,' Kate said.

'Apparently.'

'Is that going to be enough?'

'If it's someone close, someone obvious, then, yes. But if it's somebody outside the loop, there's no real chance.'

'And he knows that, Costain?'

Kiley nodded. 'I'm sure he does.'

'In which case, why not involve the police?'

'Because the minute he does, someone inside the force will sell him out to the media before tomorrow's first edition. You should know that better than me.'

'Jack,' she said, smiling, 'you'll do what you can.' And rolled from her side on to her back.

*

Victoria's mum, Lesley, was a dead ringer for Christine McVie. The singer from Fleetwood Mac. Remember? Not the skinny young one with the Minnie Mouse voice, but the other one, older, more mature. Dyed blonde hair and lived-in face and a voice that spoke of sex and forty cigarettes a day; the kind of woman you might fancy rotten if you were fifteen, which was what Kiley had been at the time, and you spotted her or someone like her behind the counter in the local chemist or driving past in one of those white vans delivering auto parts, nicotine at her finger ends and oil on her overalls. *Rumours*. Kiley alone upstairs in his room, listening to the record again and again. Rolling from side to side on the bed, trying to keep his hands to himself.

'Won't you come in?' Lesley Clarke said. She was wearing a leisure suit in pale mauve, gold slippers with a small heel. Dark red fingernails. She didn't have a cigarette in her hand, but had stubbed it out, Kiley thought, when the doorbell rang; the smell of it warm and acrid on

her as he squeezed past into the small lobby and she closed the double-glazed Tudor-style external door and ushered him into the living room with its white leather-look chairs and neat little nest of tables and framed photographs of her granddaughter, Alicia, on the walls.

'I made coffee.'

'Great.'

Kiley sat and held out his cup while Lesley poured. Photographs he had expected, but of a triumphant Victoria holding trophies aloft. And there were photos of her, of course, a few, perched around the TV and along the redundant mantelpiece; Cathy, too, Cathy and Trevor on their wedding day. But little Alicia was everywhere and Lesley, following Kiley's gaze, smiled a smile of satisfaction. 'Lovely, isn't she. A sweetheart. A real sweetheart. Bright, too. Like a button.'

Either way, Kiley thought, Victoria or Cathy, Lesley had got what she wanted. Her first grandchild.

'Vicky bought me this house, did you know that? It's not a palace, of course, but it suits me fine. Cosy, I suppose that's what it is. And there's plenty of room for Alicia when she comes to stay.' She smiled and leaned back against white vinyl. 'I always did have a hankering after Buckhurst Hill.' Unable to resist any longer, she reached for her Benson & Hedges, king size. 'Coffee okay?'

'Lovely.' The small lies, the little social ones, Kiley had found came with surprising ease.

They talked about Victoria then, Victoria and her sister, whatever jealousies had grown up between them, festered maybe, been smoothed away. Trevor, was he resentful, did he ever treat Alicia as if she weren't really his? But Trevor was the perfect dad and as far as money was concerned since his move to Luton, to Vauxhall, some deal they done with the German owners, the unions that is, and Trev had got himself off the shop floor – well, it wasn't a

they were actually throwing it around, but, no, cash was something they weren't short of, Lesley was sure of that.

'What about Victoria's father?' Kiley asked.

Lesley threw back her head and laughed. 'The bastard, as he's affectionately known.'

'Is he still around? Is there any chance he might be involved?'

Lesley shook her head. 'The bastard, bless him, would've had difficulties getting the right stamp on to the envelope, never mind the rest. Fifteen years, the last time I laid eyes on him; working on the oil rigs he'd been, up around Aberdeen. Took a blow to the head from some piece of equipment in a storm and had to be stretchered off. Knocked the last bit of sense out of him. The drink had seen to the rest long since.' She drew hard on her cigarette. 'If he's still alive, which I doubt, it's in some hostel somewhere.' And shivered. 'I just hope the poor bastard isn't sleeping rough.'

*

Paul Broughton was working for a record company in Camden, offices near the canal, more or less opposite the Engineer. Olive V-neck top and chocolate flat-front mole-skin chinos, close-shaven head and stubbled chin, two silver rings in one ear, a stud, emerald green, at the centre of his bottom lip. A & R, developing new talent, that was his thing. Little bands that gigged at the Dublin Castle or the Boston Dome, the Rocket on the Holloway Road. He was listening to a demo tape on headphones when Kiley walked towards him across a few hundred feet of open plan; Broughton's desk awash with take-away mugs from Caffè Nero, unopened padded envelopes and hopeful flyers.

Kiley waited till Broughton had dispensed with the head-phones, then introduced himself and held out his hand.

66

'Look,' Broughton said, ignoring the hand, 'I told you on the phone—'

'Tell me again.'

'I ain't seen Vicky in fuckin' years.'

'How many years?'

'I dunno. Four, five?'

'Not since she told you she was carrying your child.'

'Yeah, I s'pose.'

'But you've been in touch.'

'Who says?'

'Once you started seeing her picture in the paper, those ads out on the street. Read about all that money she was bringing in. And for what? It wouldn't have been difficult to get her number, you used your mobile, gave her a call.'

Broughton glared back at him, defiant. 'Bollocks!' And then, 'So what if I did?'

'What did she tell you, Paul? The same as before? Get lost.'

'Look, I ain't got time for this.'

'Was that when you thought you'd put the bite on her, a little blackmail? Get something back for treating you like shit?'

Broughton clenched his fists. 'Fuck off! Fuck off out of here before I have you thrown out. I wouldn't take money from that stuck-up tart if it was dripping out of her arse. I don't need it, right?'

'And you don't care she had your child against your will, kept her out of your sight?'

Broughton laughed, a sneer ugly across his face. 'You don't get it, do you. She was just some cunt I fucked. End of fuckin' story.'

'She was barely fifteen years old,' Kiley said.

'I know,' Broughton said, and winked.

Kiley was almost halfway towards the door before he

turned around. Broughton was sitting on the edge of his desk, headphones back in place, watching him go. Kiley hit him twice in the face with his fist, hauled him back up on to his knees and hit him once more. Then left. Perhaps it shouldn't have made him feel a whole lot better, but it did.

*

They'd bought a nice house on the edge of Dunstable, with views across the Chiltern Hills. They'd done well. Alicia was in the back garden, on a swing. The apple trees were rich in fruit, the roses well into bloom. Cathy stood by the French windows, gazing out. Her expression when Kiley had arrived on the doorstep had told him pretty much all he needed to know.

Trevor was in the garage, tinkering. Tools clipped with precision to the walls, tools that shone with pride of owner-ship and use. Kiley didn't rush him, let him take his time. Watched as Trevor tightened this, loosened that.

'It's the job, isn't it?' Kiley eventually said.

Trevor straightened, surprised.

'You sold up, left friends, invested in this place. Not just for Cathy and yourself. For her, Alicia. A better place to grow up, country, almost. A big mortgage, but as long as the money's coming in . . .'

'They promised us,' Trevor said, not looking at Kiley now, staring through the open door towards the trees. 'The Germans, when we agreed the deal. Jobs for life, that's what they said. Jobs for sodding life. Now they're closing down the plant, shifting production to Portugal or Spain. No longer economic, that's us.' When he did turn, there were tears in his eyes. 'They bent us over and fucked us up the arse and all this bastard government did was stand by with the Vaseline.'

Kiley put a hand on his shoulder and Trevor shrugged

it off and they stood there for a while, not speaking, then went inside and sat around the kitchen table drinking tea. Alicia sat in Cathy's lap, playing with her mother's hair. Her mother: that's what she was, what she had become.

'You could have asked,' Kiley said. 'Asked Victoria outright, explained.'

'We've tried before,' Cathy said bitterly. 'It's hateful, like pulling teeth.'

Trevor reached across and gave her lower arm a squeeze. 'Vicky's not the problem,' he said, 'not really. It's him, the money man.'

'Costain?'

Trevor nodded.

'Leave him to me,' Kiley said. 'I'll make sure he understands.'

'Mum,' Alicia said. 'Let's read a book.'

Trevor walked Kiley down the path towards his hired car, stood with one hand resting on the roof. The sun was just beginning to fade in the sky. 'I'd go round to their house,' he said. 'Evenings, you know, when I was seeing Cathy, and she'd be there. Victoria. I doubt she was much more than fourteen then.' He sighed and kicked at the ground with his shoe. 'She could've put a ring through my nose and had me crawling after her, all fours around the room.' Slowly, he drew air down into his lungs. 'You're right, it's nice out here. Quiet.'

The two men shook hands.

'Thanks,' Trevor said. 'I mean it. Thanks a lot.'

*

Kiley didn't see Victoria Clarke until the following year, the French Open. He and Kate had travelled Eurostar to Paris for the weekend, stayed in their favourite hotel near the Jardin du Luxembourg. Kate had a French author to

69

interview, a visit to the Musée d'Art Moderne planned;
Kiley thought lunch at the brasserie across from Gare du
Nord, then a little tennis.

Costain, buoyant after marshalling Victoria's advertising
contract safely through, had struck a favourable deal with
Cathy and Trevor: five per cent of Victoria's gross income
to be paid into a trust fund for Alicia, an annual payment
of ten thousand pounds towards her everyday needs, this
sum to be reviewed; as long as Trevor remained unem-
ployed, the shortfall on the mortgage would be picked up.
In exchange, a secrecy agreement was sworn and signed,
valid until Alicia reached eighteen.

On court at Roland Garros, rain threatened, the sky a
leaden grey. After taking the first set six–two, Victoria was
struggling against a hefty left-hander from Belarus.
Concentration gone, suddenly she was double-faulting on
her serve, over-hitting her two-fisted backhand, muttering
to herself along the baseline. Five all and then the set had
gone, unravelled, Victoria slump-shouldered and staring at
the ground. The first four games of the final set went with
serve and Kiley could feel the muscles across his shoulders knot as he willed Victoria to break clear of whatever
was clouding her mind, shake free. It wasn't until she was
four–three down that it happened, a skidding return of
serve whipped low across the net and some instinct causing
her to follow it in, her volley unplayable, an inch inside
the line. After that, a baseline smash that tore her opponent's racket from her hand, a topspin lob judged to perfec-
tion; finally, two aces, the first swinging away unplayably,
the second hard down the centre line, and she was running
to the net, racket raised to acknowledge the applause, a
quick smile and touch of hands. On her way back to her
chair, she glanced up to where Kiley was sitting in the
stands, but if she saw him she gave no sign.

When he arrived back at the hotel, Kate was already there, damp from the shower, leaning back against the pillows with a book. The shutters out on to the balcony were partway open.

'So?' Kate said as Kiley shrugged off his coat. 'How was it?'

'A struggle.'

'Poor lamb.'

'No call to be bitchy.'

Kate poked out her tongue.

Stretched out on the bed beside her, Kiley bent his head. 'Are you reading that in French?'

'Why else d'you think I'm moving my lips?'

The skin inside her arm was taut and sweet.

TRUTH

Before Jack Kiley had moved, courtesy of Kate, to the comparatively rarefied splendours of Highbury Fields, home had been a second-floor flat in the dodgy hinterland between the Archway and the arse end of Tufnell Park. Upper Holloway, according to the *London A–Z*. A bristle of indistinguishable streets that clung to the rabid backbone of the Holloway Road: four lanes of traffic which achieved pollution levels three times above those recommended as safe by the EC.

Undaunted, Kiley would, from time to time, stroll some half a mile along the pavements of this great highway, past the innumerable Greek Cypriot and Kurdish convenience stores and the fading splendour of the five-screen Odeon, to drink at the Royal Arms. And why not? One of the few pubs not to have been tricked out with shamrocks and fake antiquities, it boasted reasonable beers, comfortable chairs and more than adequate sight lines should Kiley fancy watching the Monday night match on wide-screen TV.

It was here that young Nicky Cavanagh, nineteen and

72

learning a trade at U-Fit Instant Exhausts and Tyres, got
into an argument with one of the Nealy brothers, one of
five. What the argument was about, its starting point and
raison d'être, was still in dispute. Some comment passed
about last Sunday's game at Highbury, a jostled arm, a
look that passed between Cavanagh and the girl, under-
dressed and underaged, by Nealy's side. Less uncertain
were the details of what followed. After a certain amount
of mouthing off, a shove here and a push there, the pair
of them, Nealy and Cavanagh, stood facing one another
with raised fists, an empty bottle of Miller Lite reversed
in Cavanagh's spare hand. Nealy, cursing, turned on his
heels and left the bar, hauling his companion with him.
Less than thirty minutes later, he returned. Three of the
brothers were with him, the fourth enjoying time in Feltham
Young Offenders Institution at the government's expense.
His place was taken by a bevy of friends and hangers-on,
another four or five. Pick handles, baseball bats. They
trapped Cavanagh by the far wall and dragged him out on
to the street. By the time the first police sirens could be
heard, Cavanagh, bloodied and beaten, lay curled into a
broken ball beside the kerb.

Now, some months later, Nicky Cavanagh was in a
wheelchair, his only drinking done at home or in the sketch
of park which edged the main road near Kiley's old flat,
and Kiley himself had found another pub. Despite state-
ments taken from several witnesses at the time, none of
Cavanagh's attackers had so far been charged.

The Lord Nelson was a corner pub, for Kiley a longer
walk though none the worse for that; refurbishment had
brought in stripped pine tables and Thai cuisine, wide-
screen satellite TV, but left the cellar pretty much intact –
John Smith's and Marston's Pedigree. The occasional

Saturday night karaoke he tolerated, quiz nights he avoided like the plague: which non-league footballer, coming on in extra time, scored a hat-trick in the quarter finals of the FA Cup? Embarrassing when they misremembered his name – Keeley, Kelsey, Riley – worse when he was recognised and some good-hearted fellow, full of booze and bonhomie, insisted on introducing him to the room.

But he had been more than a soccer player and there were those who knew that as well.

'Jack Kiley, isn't it? You were in the Met.'

The face Kiley found himself looking into was fleshy, dark-eyed, receding hair cut fashionably short, a small scar pale across his cheek. 'Dave Marshall.'

Kiley nodded and shook the proffered hand; rough fingers, calloused palms.

'Mind?' Marshall gestured towards an empty chair.

'Help yourself.'

Marshall set down his glass, angled out the chair and sat. Late thirties, Kiley thought, a few years younger than himself. Marshall wearing a waist-length leather jacket, unzipped, check shirt and jeans.

'I was in the job myself,' Marshall said. 'South, mostly. Tooting, Balham. Too many rules and regs. Shifts. Better now I'm me own boss. Damp-proofing, plastering. Bit of heavy rain and you're quids in. But you know all about that, working for yourself, I mean. Not that it ever really appealed, not to me, like. Going private.' He shook his head. 'Missing persons, mispers, lot of those, I reckon. Them an' wives frightened their old man's goin' over the side.'

Kiley shifted his weight, waiting for Marshall to get to it.

'Here,' Marshall said, taking a folded sheet from his inside pocket and smoothing it out. 'Take a look at this.'

It was a poster, A3 size, composed by someone on a dodgy home computer and run off at Prontaprint or somewhere similar. The photograph of Marshall was just recognisable, the print jammed too close together but the message clear enough.

DAVID MARSHALL
Six months ago David Marshall walked out on his
family, leaving a gorgeous little baby girl behind.
Since then he has refused to pay a penny towards
the upkeep of his child. If you're approached by this
man to do building work of any kind, look the other
way. Don't put money into his pockets so he can
spend it on whores and ignore his responsibilities.
DO NOT TRUST THIS MAN.

'Where was this?' Kiley asked.

'On some hoarding up by the Nag's Head. And there's more of 'em. All over. Here. The Archway. Finsbury fucking Park.' The anger in Marshall's face was plain, the line of his scar white as an exclamation mark. 'What am I s'posed to do? Go round and tear every one of 'em down?'

'What do you want me to do?' Kiley said.

'Go see her. Talk to her. Here.' He pushed a slip of paper towards Kiley's hand. 'Tell her it's not fuckin' on.'

'Wouldn't it be better if you did that yourself?'

Marshall laughed, a grating sound that finished low in his throat.

Kiley glanced at the poster again. 'Is it true?'

'What?'

'What it says.'

'What do you think?'

'Did you leave her?'

'Course I left her. There weren't no livin' with her.'

'And child support? Maintenance?'

75

'Let whichever bloke she's screwing pay fuckin' maintenance.' Marshall laughed again, harsh and short. 'And
she's got the mouth to accuse me of goin' with whores.
Ask her what she was doing when I met her, ask her that.
She's the biggest whore of the fuckin' lot.'

'I still think if you could go and talk to her . . .'

Marshall leaned sharply forward, slopping his beer.
'She's trying to make me look a cunt. And she's got to be
stopped.'

'I'm sorry,' Kiley said, a slow shake of the head. 'I don't
think I want to get involved.'

'Right.' Marshall's chair cannoned backwards as he got
to his feet. The poster he screwed up and tossed to the
floor. 'You ain't got the stomach for it, believe me, there's
plenty who have.'

Kiley watched him go, barging people aside on his way
to the door. The piece of paper Marshall had given him
was lined, the writing small and surprisingly neat. Jennie
Calder, an address in N8. He refolded it and tucked it out
of sight.

*

He had met Kate at a film festival, the premiere of a new
Iranian movie, the organisers anticipating demonstrations
and worse. The security firm for whom Kiley had then been
working were hired to forestall trouble at the screening and
the reception afterwards. Late that night, demonstrations
over, only a handful of people lingering in the bar, Kiley
had wandered past the few discarded placards and leaned
on the Embankment railing, staring out across the Thames.
Leaving Charing Cross station, a train clattered across
Hungerford Bridge; shrouded in tarpaulin, a barge ghosted
bulkily past, heading downriver towards the estuary. In their

wake, it was quiet enough to hear the water, lapping against stone. When he turned, there was Kate, her face illuminated as she paused to light a cigarette. Dark hair, medium height, he had noticed her at the reception, asking questions, making notes. At one point she had been sitting with the young Iranian director, a woman, Kate's small tape recorder on the table between them.

'What did you think of the film?' Kiley asked, wanting to say something.

'Very Iranian,' Kate said and laughed.

'I doubt if it'll come to the Holloway Odeon, then.'

'Probably not.'

She came and stood alongside him at the Embankment edge.

'I should get fed up with it,' Kate said after some moments. 'This view – God knows I've seen it enough – but I don't.' She was wearing a loose-fitting suit, the jacket long, a leather bag slung from one shoulder. When she pitched her cigarette, half-smoked, towards the water, it sparkled through the near dark.

'There's another showing,' she said, looking at Kiley full on. 'The film, tomorrow afternoon. If you're interested, that is.'

'You're going again?'

'I shouldn't think so.' She was smiling with her eyes, the merest widening of the mouth.

The opening images aside, a cluster of would-be teachers, blackboards strapped awkwardly to their backs as they struggle along a mountain road in a vain search for pupils, it turned out to be the longest eighty-five minutes Kiley could recall. Kate's piece in the *Independent on Sunday*, complete with photographs of Samira Makhmalbaf and suitable stills, he thought far more interesting than the film itself.

Plucking up a certain amount of courage, he phoned to tell her so.

Well, it had been a beginning.

*

'I'm still not clear,' Kate said, 'why you turned it down.'

They were sitting in Kate's high bed, a bottle of red wine, three-parts empty, resting on the floor. Through the partly opened blinds, there was a view out across Highbury Fields. It was coming up to a quarter past ten and Kiley didn't yet know if he'd be invited to stay the night. He'd tried leaving his toothbrush once and she'd called down the stairs after him, 'I think you've forgotten something.'

'I didn't fancy it,' Kiley said.

'You didn't fancy the job or you didn't like the look of him?'

'Both.'

'Because if you're only going to take jobs from decent, upstanding citizens with good credit references and all their vowels in the right place . . .'

'It's not that.'

'What then?'

'It's what he wanted me to do.'

'Go round and talk to her, persuade her to ease off, reach some kind of accommodation.'

'That wasn't what he wanted. He wanted me to warn her, frighten her.'

'And now you're not going to do it?'

Kiley looked at her. Pins out of her hair, it fell across her shoulders, down almost to the middle of her back. 'What d'you mean?'

'Now you've turned him down, what will happen?'

'He'll get somebody else.'

'With fewer scruples.'

Kiley shrugged.

'Maybe it would've been better for her,' Kate said, 'if you'd said yes.' The way she was looking at him suggested that pretty soon he'd be climbing back into his clothes and setting out on the long walk home.

*

Some housing department official lacking a sense of irony had named the roads after areas of New Orleans. Anything further from the Crescent City would have been hard to find. Kiley walked past a triangle of flattened mud masquerading as a lawn and headed for the first of several concrete walkways. '*Do Not Let Your Dogs Foul the Estate*', read one sign. '*No Ball Games*', read another. A group of teenagers lounged around the first stairwell, listening to hard-core hip-hop at deafening volume and occasionally spitting at the ground. They gave no sign of moving aside to let Kiley pass, but then, at the last moment, they did. Laughter trailed him up towards the fifth floor.

Two of the glass panels in the front door had been broken and replaced by hardboard. Kiley rang the bell and waited.

'Who is it?'

He could see a shape, outlined through the remaining glass.

'Jennie Calder?'

'Who's this?' The voice was muffled yet audible.

'Kiley. Jack Kiley.'

'Who?'

He took a card from his wallet and pushed it through the letter-box. The shape came closer.

'Who sent you? Did he send you?'

'You mean Marshall?'

'Who else?'

'Not exactly.'

She unbolted the door but kept it on the chain. Through a four-inch gap Kiley could see reddish hair, unfashionably curly, grey-green eyes, a full mouth. She tapped Kiley's card with the tip of a fingernail.

'Private investigator? What is this, some kind of joke?'

Kiley grinned. 'I'm beginning to wonder.'

Out of sight, a child started crying.

'You here to do his dirty work for him?'

'No.'

As the crying grew in intensity, the woman looked hard at Kiley, making up her mind. Then, abruptly, she pushed the door to, unfastened the chain and opened it wide enough for him to step inside.

'Wait there,' she said, leaving him in a square hallway the size of a telephone booth. When she reappeared, it was with a tow-haired child astride her hip. Eighteen months? Two years? Kiley wasn't sure.

'This is Alice.'

'Hello, Alice.'

Alice hid her face against her mother's arm.

'Why don't we go through,' Jennie said, 'and sit down?'

There were pieces of Lego and wooden bricks here and there across the floor, a small menagerie of lions and bears; on one of the chairs, a doll, fully dressed, sat staring blankly out. Toys apart, the room was neat, tidy: three-piece suite, TV, stereo, dining table pushed into a corner near the window.

Without putting her daughter down, Jennie made tea and brought it through, with biscuits and sugar, on a tray.

Only when she sat opposite him, Alice clambering from one side of her chair to the other, did Kiley see the tiredness in her face, the strain behind her eyes. Jennie wearing blue jeans and a soft blue top, no-name trainers without socks; late twenties, Kiley thought, though she could have passed for older.

'So?' she said.

Kiley held his mug of tea in both hands. 'These posters . . .'

'Got to him, have they?' A smile now.

'You could say.'

'And you were meant to warn me off?'

'Something like that. Only I'm not.'

'You said.'

The tea was strong. Kiley spooned in sugar and stirred it round.

'Biscuit,' Alice said, the word just this side of recognition. Jennie reached down and broke a digestive in half. 'So what are you doing here?' she asked.

'If it's not me it'll likely be somebody else. I thought you should know.'

'I didn't think he was going to be leading the applause.'

'Isn't there somewhere you could go?' Kiley asked. 'Until it blows over.'

'No.'

'Friends, a relative?'

'No.' The child's piece of biscuit broke and pieces crumbled across her mother's top. Automatically, Jennie brushed them away and reached for the other half. 'Besides, who says it's going to blow over? The day he puts his hand in his pocket, faces up to his responsibilities, that's when it'll blow over. Not before.'

*

For the time being, Kiley was working out of his flat: he had a fax, an answerphone, directories, numbers on a

Rolodex. What he didn't have, the faithful secretary secretly lusting for him in the outer office, the bottle of Scotch in the desk drawer alongside the .38. When he'd jacked in his job with the security firm – no hard feelings, Jack, keep in touch – he'd contacted those officers he still knew inside the Met and let them know what he was doing. Adrian Costain, a sports agent he knew, had thrown a couple of things his way, but since then nothing. A local firm of solicitors likewise.

Recently, he'd spent a lot of time watching movies in the afternoons, starting paperbacks he never finished, staring at the same four walls. He would have sat diligently doing his accounts if there were any accounts to do. Instead he took out ads in the local press and waited for the phone to ring.

When he got back from Jennie Calder's flat, two red zeros stared back at him from the answerphone. The people in the flat upstairs were playing 'Green Green Grass of Home' again. He had a bacon sandwich at the nearest greasy spoon and skimmed the paper twice. Each time he reached the sports page, Charlton Athletic had lost away.

Still it kept nagging at him. A brisk walk through the back doubles and he was back at the estate, keeping watch on Jennie Calder's place from below.

He didn't have too long to wait. There were two of them, approaching from the opposite direction and moving fast. The one at the front, bulkily built, shoulders hunched, wool hat tight on his head; the other, younger, taller, tagging along behind.

By the time Kiley arrived, the front door was half off its hinges, furniture overturned, the front of the television kicked in. Alice was clinging tight to her mother and screaming, Jennie shouting over the noise and close to tears.

'Company,' the youth said.

On his way over, Kiley had picked up a piece of two-by-four from a building site, solid wood.

'What the fuck do you want?' the big man said.

Just time for Kiley to think he recognised him before swinging the length of wood hard against the side of his head. Twice, and the man was down on his knees.

The lanky kid standing there, not knowing what to do.

'Get him out of here,' Kiley said. 'And don't come back.'

Blood ran between the man's fingers; one eye was swelling fast and all but closed. The pair of them stumbled to the door, mouthing threats, Kiley watching them go.

Alice was whimpering now, tears wet against her mother's neck.

'Thanks,' Jennie said. She was shaking.

Bending forward, Kiley righted one of the chairs.

'You think they'll be back?'

'Not yet.'

Kiley went into the kitchen and filled the kettle, set it on the gas, made tea; he tracked down an emergency locksmith and told him to fit extra bolts top and bottom, metal reinforcements behind both hinges and locks.

'Who's going to pay for all that?' Jennie asked.

'I will,' Kiley said.

Jennie started to say something else but thought better of it. She put Alice down in her cot and almost immediately the child was asleep. When she came back into the room, Kiley was clearing the last of the debris from the floor.

'Why?' Jennie asked, arms folded across her chest. 'Why're you doing all this?'

'Job satisfaction?'

'Nobody hired you.'

'Ah.' He set one of his cards down on a corner of the settee. 'Here. In case you lost the first one. Ring me if there's a need.' Leaving, he leaned the splintered piece of two-by-four against the wall by the front door. 'Just in case. And don't let anybody in unless you're certain who they are, okay? Not anybody.'

He found Dave Marshall later that evening, at a table in the Royal Arms. Two others with him. The big man was still wearing his wool hat, only now there was a good inch of bandage visible beneath it, plaster sticking to his cheek. One eye was bruised and two-thirds closed. Their companion – loose suit, dark shirt, blue patterned tie – Kiley didn't recognise.

He crossed the floor towards them.

'What the fuck . . . ?' the big man started, half out of his seat.

The one in the suit reached out and caught hold of his arm, gave a slow shake of the head. Grudgingly, the big man sat back down.

'You've got some balls,' Marshall said.

'I told you to go and talk to her,' Kiley replied. 'Sort things out. Not this.'

Marshall nodded. 'You said you didn't want to get involved, an' all. Remember that?'

'Talk to her,' Kiley said again.

'What is this?' Marshall scoffed. 'Marriage guidance? Social fuckin' services?'

Kiley shrugged and took a step away.

'You,' the big man said, lurching back to his feet. 'Your life ain't worth livin'.'

Which was when Kiley knew who he was, the place, the occasion reminding him, the family resemblance now clear.

'Nealy, isn't it?' Kiley said.

'Eh?'

'Nealy.'

'What's it to you?'

'What're you fixing to do? Get those boys of yours? Wade in mob-handed like you did with Nicky Cavanagh?'

Nealy moved close enough for Kiley to smell the sourness on his breath. 'I'll fuckin' have you,' he said.

'Bob,' loose suit said quietly from the table. 'Let it go.'

Reluctantly, Nealy lowered his hands to his sides.

Kiley took a last look at each of them, turned and left.

*

The phone went at a quarter to seven, Kiley not quite awake, wondering if he should turn over again or push back the covers and face another day.

Jennie's voice was angry, frightened. 'It's the police. They're arresting me. They . . .'

Abruptly, the line went dead.

Kiley ran the bathroom tap, splashed water on his face, cleaned his teeth and dressed.

They'd taken her to the police station on Hornsey Road, the officer on the desk fending off enquiries like Atherton on the fourth day of the Test. A Jennie Calder had been taken into custody and was currently being interviewed, that was all he would confirm. 'What are the charges?' Kiley demanded. The officer's eyes switched focus. 'Next,' he called into the small crowd at Kiley's back.

Margaret Hamblin's offices were in Kentish Town. Hamblin, Laker and Clarke. When Kiley had been building up his overtime in CID, Margaret had been a lowly solicitor's clerk, forever in this police station or that, picking up cases

85

nobody else wanted, learning on the hoof. Now, even if Kiley had still been in the force, overtime was pretty much a thing of the past and Margaret was a senior partner with a taste for good wines and stylish clothes. This morning she was wearing a cord drawstring jacket and chevron skirt from Ghost. She listened to Kiley intently then reached for the phone. Ten minutes later, a car was taking them back to Hornsey Road, Margaret sensibly lyrical about her recent holiday in northern Spain.

This time Kiley got past the enquiry desk but not a great deal further. He was kicking his heels outside the custody suite, trying not to notice the smell of disinfectant, when two officers, one in uniform, one plain clothes, pushed their way through the double doors. Neither looked to be in the best of humour. The CID man had changed his shirt from the previous night in the Royal Arms, but the suit and tie were the same. If he recognised Kiley, he gave no sign.

An hour later, no more, they were sitting, the four of them – Kiley, Margaret Hamblin, Jennie and Alice – in Margaret's office. An assistant had brought in coffee, Danish and bottled water. Jennie's face was strained and pale without make-up; Alice, released from the tender mercies of a broody WPC, clung to her mother's neck, whimpering softly.

Margaret sipped at her espresso and set it aside. 'Jennie's charged with keeping a brothel.'

'She's what?' Kiley exclaimed.

Jennie looked away.

'I persuaded them to release her on police bail, but it seems they're considering instituting care proceedings . . .'

'They can't!' Jennie pressed her face down against her daughter's head and held her tight.

86

'On what grounds?' Kiley asked.

Margaret leaned back in her chair. 'That Alice is exposed to moral danger where she is.'

'Surely that's a nonsense?'

'Not if the brothel charge can be made to stick.'

'How can it?' Kiley asked.

Margaret looked across at Jennie and Kiley did the same. It was a while before she spoke, her voice shaky and quiet.

'This friend of mine, Della – we were at school together – she's been seeing this bloke, married of course. Della, she's living with her mum, got two kids of her own. Car parks and hotels aside, they didn't have anywhere to go. So I've been letting them use my place, afternoons. Just, maybe, once or twice a week.'

'And you and Alice,' Margaret asked, 'while they were in the bedroom, whatever, you'd both be in the flat?'

Jennie shook her head. 'Not as a rule. I'd take Alice up the park, swings and slides. You know, a walk.'

'And if it rained?'

Jennie hung her head; all too clearly, she could see where this was going. 'If it was really bad, yes, we stayed in.'

Margaret looked across at Kiley, one eyebrow raised.

'This was an affair, right?' Kiley said. 'Two people having an affair. There's no suggestion of any money changing hands.'

'Is that true, Jennie?' Margaret asked.

Jennie paused. 'Sometimes he'd give me a fiver on the way out. A tenner. So I could get something for Alice. Just as a way of saying thanks.'

'And your friend, Della? Did he give her money, too?'

'I don't know. He might have. Sometimes. I don't know.'

'They're friends,' Kiley said. 'They're never going to testify.'

'It depends what kinds of pressure are put on them,' Margaret said. 'And besides, payment's not the crucial thing, not according to the law. A brothel is a house, room or other place, used for the purposes of illicit sexual inter-course and/or acts of lewdness.'

'It's still not enough, is it?' Kiley said. 'Even if they make up stuff about men traipsing up and down the stairs at all hours, it's not enough.'

Tears began to fall, unbidden, down Jennie's face.

'What?' Kiley asked.

'Six, seven years ago, I was done for soliciting. King's Cross.'

'It went to court?' Margaret asked.

'Yes.'

'And you were fined?'

'Yes.'

'How many times?' Margaret asked. 'Was it just the once?'

Jennie shook her head.

Kiley reached for his coffee and set it back down.

'Is there anything else?' Margaret asked.

An ambulance went shrilly by outside.

'Della and I, we used to work at a massage parlour. Over Stroud Green. Where I met him, wasn't it? Marshall.' She laughed a short, disparaging laugh. 'Girl like you, you shouldn't be working in a place like this – I think he'd heard it somewhere, some trashy film on TV.'

'While you were there,' Margaret asked, 'the massage parlour, was it raided by the police?'

'You're kidding, right? Only regular as clockwork.'

'And were you ever charged with any offence?'

'No, no. Took our names, that was it. Too concerned with getting their freebies, half of 'em, to do much else.'

*

Margaret called up a car to take Jennie and Alice home and she and Kiley carried on their conversation over lunch at Pane Vino.

'What do you think?' Kiley asked. 'Is any of this really going to stand up?'

'The brothel charge, no. I can't see it getting past first post. But the other, getting the little girl taken into care, if they were to really push it, get social services on board, I'm not so sure.'

Kiley forked up a little more chicken and spinach risotto. 'Let's take a step backwards, remind ourselves what's at the root of this.'

'Okay.'

'Dave Marshall is angry. He doesn't like having his name plastered over half the billboards in North London.'

'Who would?' Margaret reached across for the bottle of wine.

'That aside, there's going to be all manner of stuff between himself and Jennie, unresolved. I think he's just striking out in any way he can.'

'To what end?'

'To see her hurt; have her climb down, leave him alone.'

'You don't think it's a way of getting eventual custody of the child?'

Kiley shook his head. 'I think that's the last thing on his mind.'

Margaret drank some wine. 'So what do we do? Prepare a defence for Jennie in the remote possibility things get to court? File a report with the Child Support Agency, suggesting they re-examine Marshall's financial position?'

'The arresting officer,' Kiley said, 'that was him leaving the custody suite just before you this morning? Around forty, suit, bright blue tie?'

'DS Sandon, yes, why?'

'I saw him having a drink with Marshall last night; Marshall and the guy who trashed Jennie's flat.'

'No law against that.'

'But more than a coincidence.'

'Probably. But unless you had your Polaroid camera in your back pocket . . .'

'I might be able to do better than that.'

'How so?'

'Marshall isn't the only one with friends inside the Met.' Seeing his expression, Margaret smiled.

*

At two thirty the following afternoon, they were both sitting in the fifth-floor office of Paul Bridge, Deputy Assistant Commissioner (CID). Margaret, feeling that Ghost might be deemed frivolous, had opted for a Donna Karan suit; Kiley had ironed his shirt.

Bridge was pretty much the same age as the pair of them, fast-tracking his way up the ladder, Deputy Commissioner well within his sights. He was clean-shaven, quietly spoken, two degrees and a nice family home out at Cheshunt, a golf handicap of three. He listened attentively while Margaret outlined the relationship between Sandon and Marshall, beginning when they were stationed together in Balham, DC and DS respectively. Drinking pals. Close friends. Still close now, some few years on, Sandon apparently at Marshall's beck and call.

'I'm not altogether clear,' Bridge said, when he'd finished listening, 'if misconduct is where we're heading here.'

'Given the evidence—' Margaret began.

'Entirely circumstantial.'

'Given the evidence, it's a distinct possibility.'

'Depending,' said Kiley.

90

Bridge readjusted his glasses.

'Sandon's not just been harassing Peter's ex-partner, he was also the officer in charge of investigating the assault on Nicky Cavanagh.'

Almost imperceptibly, Bridge nodded.

'Which was carried out, as almost everyone in Holloway knows, by four of Bob Nealy's sons. And yet, questioning a few of the Nealys and their mates aside, nothing's happened. No one's been arrested, no one charged. And Nicky Cavanagh's still in a wheelchair.'

Bridge sighed lightly and leaned back into his chair.

'Marshall, Sandon, Nealy,' Kiley said. 'It's a nice fit.'

'One wonders,' Margaret said, anxious not to let the Assistant Commissioner off the hook, 'how a case like this, a serious assault of this nature, could have been allowed to lie dormant for so long.'

Bridge glanced past his visitors towards the window, a smear of cloud dirtying up the sky. 'The lad Cavanagh,' he said, 'he should've been black. Asian or black. There'd have been pressure groups, demonstrations, more official inquiries than you could shake a stick at. Top brass, myself included, bending over backwards to show the investigation was fair and above board. But this poor sod, who gives a shit? Who cares? A few bunches of flowers in the street and a headline or two in the local press.'

Bridge removed his glasses and set them squarely on his desk.

'I can make sure the investigation's reopened, another officer in charge. As to the other business, the woman, I should think it will all fade away pretty fast.'

'And Sandon?' Kiley asked.

'If you make moves to get the Police Complaints Authority involved,' Bridge said, 'that's your decision, of course. On the other hand, were Sandon to receive an informal warning, be transferred to another station, you might, after due consideration of all the circumstances, think that sufficient.'

He stood and, smiling, held out his hand: the meeting was over.

*

Whenever Kiley bought wine, which wasn't often, he automatically drew the line at anything over five pounds. Kate had no such scruples. So the bottle they were finishing, late that Friday evening, had been well worth drinking. Even Kiley could tell the difference.

'I had a call today,' he said. 'Margaret Hamblin. She managed to sit Marshall and Jennie Calder down long enough to hammer out an agreement. He makes monthly payments for Alice, direct debit, Jennie signed an undertaking to stop harassing him in public.'

'You think he'll stick to it?'

'As long as he has to.'

'You did what you could,' Kate said.

Kiley nodded.

There was perhaps half a glass left in the bottle and Kate shared it between them. 'If you stayed over,' she said, 'we could have breakfast out. Go to that gallery off Canonbury Square.'

Kiley shot her a look, but held his tongue.

*

Almost a year after his first encounter with Dave Marshall, Kiley was in a taxi heading down Crouch End Hill. Mid-morning, but still the traffic was slow, little more than a crawl. Outside the massage parlour near the corner of

92

Crescent Road, two women were standing close together, waiting for the key holder to arrive so they could go in and start work. Despite the fact that she'd changed her hair, had it cut almost brutally short, he recognised Jennie immediately, a cigarette in her hand, talking to someone who might have been Della. But it was probably Della's turn to look after the kids.

'Hang on a minute,' Kiley called to the driver, thinking he'd jump out, say hello, how's it all going, walk the rest of the way to his meeting near the clock tower. But then, when the driver, questioning, turned his head, Kiley sat back again in his seat. 'No, it's okay, never mind.'

When he looked back, a little further down the hill, the women had gone inside.

BILLIE'S BLUES

Angels, that was what he thought. The way she lay on her back, arms spread wide, as if making angels in the snow. The front of her coat tugged aside, feet bare, the centre of her dress stained dark, fingers curled. A few listless flakes settled momentarily on her face and hair. Porcelain skin. In those temperatures she could have been dead for hours or days. The pathologist would know.

Straightening, Resnick glanced at his watch. Three forty-five. Little over half an hour since the call had come through. Soon there would be arc lights, a generator, yellow tape, officers in coveralls searching the ground on hands and knees. As Anil Khan, crouching, shot off the first of many Polaroids, Resnick stepped aside. The broad expanse of the Forest rose behind them, broken by a ragged line of trees. The city's orange glow.

'The woman as called it in,' Millington said, at his shoulder. 'You'll likely want a word.'

She was standing some thirty metres off, where the scrub of grass and the gravel of the parking area merged.

94

'A wonder she stayed around,' Resnick said.

Millington nodded and lit a cigarette.

She was tall, taller than average, dark hair that at closer range was reddish-brown, brown leather boots which stopped below the knee, a sheepskin coat she pulled across herself protectively as Resnick came near. A full mouth from which most of the lipstick had been worn away, eyes like seawater, bluey-green. The fingers holding her coat close were raw with cold.

Still Resnick did not recognise her until she had fumbled in her pockets for a pack of cigarettes, a lighter, the flame small yet sudden, flaring before her eyes.

'Eileen? Terry's Eileen?'

She looked at him then. 'Not any more.'

It had been two years, almost to the day, since the last time he had seen her, trapped out in widow's weeds. Since then, the seepage that had followed Terry Cooke's funeral had submerged her from Resnick's sight. Cooke, a medium-range chancer who had punched his weight but rarely more – aggravated burglary, the occasional lorry hijack, once a payroll robbery of almost splendid audacity – and who had ended his own life with a bullet through the brain, administered while Eileen lay in bed alongside him.

'You found her.' Resnick's head nodded back in the direction of the corpse.

As a question, it didn't require answer.

'How come?'

'She was there, wasn't she? Lyin' there. I almost fell over her.'

'I mean, three in the morning, how come you were here? On the Forest?'

'How d'you think?'

Resnick looked at her, waiting.

95

She gouged the heel of her boot into the frozen ground.
'Business. What else?'

'Christ, Eileen.'

'I was here doin' business.'

'I didn't know.'

'Why should you?' For the space of seconds, she looked
back at him accusingly.

Resnick had talked to her several times in the weeks
before Terry Cooke had died, Eileen seeking a way out of
the relationship but too scared to make the move. And
Resnick listening sympathetically, hoping she would give
him an angle, a way of breaking through Cooke's camouflage and alibis. Give him up, Eileen. Give us something
we can use. Once he's inside, he'll not be able to reach
you, do you any harm. In the end, Resnick had thought,
the only harm Cooke had done had been to himself. Now,
looking at Eileen, he was less sure.

'I'm sorry,' Resnick said.

'Why the hell should you be sorry?'

He shrugged, heavy shouldered. If he knew why, he
couldn't explain. Behind, the sound of transport pulling
off the road, reinforcements arriving.

'When you first knew me, Terry too, I was stripping,
right? This i'n't so very different.' They both knew that
wasn't so. 'Besides, get to my age, those kind of jobs,
prime ones, they can get few and far between.'

She was what, Resnick thought, twenty-six, twenty-
seven? Shy of thirty, to be sure. 'You'd best tell me what
happened,' he said.

Eileen lit a fresh cigarette from the butt of the last. 'This
punter, he said he weren't going to use a condom, couldn't
understand why an extra twenty didn't see it right. Chucked
me out and drove off. I was walking up on to Forest Road,
thought I might pick up a cab, go back into town. Which

96

was when I saw her. Ducked through that first lot of bushes and there she was.'

'You could have carried on walking,' Resnick said. 'Skirted round.' At his back, he could hear Millington's voice, organising the troops.

'Not once I'd seen her.'

'So you called it in.'

'Had my mobile. Didn't take but a minute.'

'You could have left her then.'

'No, I couldn't.' Her eyes fastened on his, challenging.

The pathologist was driving slowly across the pitted surface towards them, mindful of the paintwork on his new Volvo.

'I'll get someone to take you to the station,' Resnick said. 'Get a statement. No sense you freezing out here any more than you have to.'

Already he was turning away.

*

The dead woman was scarcely that: a girl, mid-teens. Below medium height and underweight; scars, some possibly self-inflicted, to her legs and arms; bruising across the buttocks and around the neck. The thin cotton of her dress was stuck to her chest with blood. Scratches to exposed parts of the body suggested that she could have been attacked elsewhere then dragged to the spot where she was found and dumped. No bag nor purse nor any other article she might have been carrying had been discovered so far. Preliminary examination suggested she had been dead not less than twenty-four hours, possibly more. Further tests on her body and clothing were being carried out.

Officers would be out on the streets around Hyson Green and the Forest with hastily reproduced photographs, talking to prostitutes plying their trade, stopping cars, knocking on doors. Others would be checking missing persons on the computer, contacting social services, those responsible for the care and custody of juveniles. If no one had come forward with an identification by the end of the day, public relations would release a picture to the press for the morning editions, push for the maximum publicity on local radio and TV.

In his office, Resnick eased a now lukewarm mug of coffee aside and reached again for the transcript of Lynn Kellogg's interview with Eileen. As a document in a murder investigation it was unlikely to set the pulses racing; Eileen's responses rarely rose above the monosyllabic, while Lynn's questioning, for once, was little more than routine.

In the CID room, Lynn Kellogg's head was just visible over the top of her VDU. Resnick waited until she had saved what was on the screen and dropped the transcript down on her desk.

'You didn't get on, you and Eileen.'

'Were we supposed to?'

'You didn't like her.'

'What was to like?'

A suggestion of a smile showed on Resnick's face. 'She dialled 999. Hung around. Agreed to make a statement.'

'Which was next to useless.'

'Agreed.'

Lynn touched her index finger to the keyboard and the image on the screen disappeared. 'I'm sorry, sir, but what exactly's your point?'

'I'm just wondering if we've missed something, that's all.'

'You want me to talk to her again?'

'Perhaps not.'

Lynn's eyes narrowed perceptibly. 'I see.'

'I mean, if she sensed you didn't like her . . .'

'Whereas she might open up to you.'

'It's possible.'

With a slow shake of the head, Lynn flipped back through the pages of her notebook for the address and copied it onto a fresh sheet, which Resnick glanced at quickly before folding it down into the breast pocket of his suit.

'She's a tart, sir. A whore.'

If, on his way to the door, Resnick heard her, he gave no sign.

*

It was a two-up, two-down off the Hucknall Road, opening into the living room directly off the street: one of those old staples of inner-city living that are gradually being bulldozed from sight, some would say good riddance, to be replaced by mazes of neat little semis with miniature gardens and brightly painted doors.

Eileen answered the bell in jeans and a baggy sweat-shirt, hair tied back, no trace of make-up on her face.

'Lost?' she asked caustically.

'I hope not.'

She stood back and motioned him inside. The room was neat and comfortably furnished, a framed photograph of herself and Terry on the tiled mantelpiece, some sunny day in both their pasts. Set into the old fireplace, a gas fire was going full blast; the television playing soundlessly, racing from somewhere, Newmarket or Uttoxeter, hard going under leaden skies.

'Nice,' Resnick said, looking round.

'But not what you'd've expected.'

'How d'you mean?'

'Terry, leaving me half of everything. You'd have reck-oned something posh, Burton Joyce at least.'

'Maybe.'

'Yes, well, half of everything proved to be half of nothing much. Terry, bless him, all over. And by the time that family of his had come scrounging round, to say nothing of all his mates, Frankie Farmer and the rest, oh, Terry owed me this, Terry promised me that, I was lucky to get away with what I did.'

'You could always have said no, turned them down.'

'You think so?' Eileen reached for her cigarettes, bent low and lit one from the fire. 'Farmer and his like, no's not a word they like to hear.'

'They threatened you?'

Tilting back her head, she released a slow spiral of smoke towards the ceiling. 'They didn't have to.'

Nodding, Resnick began to unbutton his overcoat.

'You're stopping then?' Almost despite herself, a smile along the curve of her mouth.

'Long enough for a coffee, maybe.'

'It's instant.'

'Tea then.' Resnick grinned. 'If that's all right.'

With a short sigh, Eileen held out her hand. 'Here. Give me your coat.'

She brought it through from the kitchen on a tray, the tea in mugs, sugar in a blue-and-white Tate & Lyle bag, three digestive biscuits, one of them chocolate-faced.

'You did want milk?'

'Milk's fine.'

Eileen sat opposite him in the second of matching chairs, stirred two sugars into her tea, leaned back and lit another cigarette.

'The last thousand I had left—' she began.

'You don't have to tell me,' Resnick said.

'What was I doing, out on the Forest, your question.'

'You still don't have—'

'Maybe I do.'

Resnick sat back and listened.

'The last thousand from what Terry left me – after I'd bought this place, I mean – this pal of mine – least, I'd reckoned her for a pal – she persuaded me to come in with her on this sauna she was opening, Mapperley Top. Money was for the deposit, first three months' rent, tarting the place up – you know, a lick of paint and a few posters – buying towels and the like.' She rested her cigarette on the edge of the tray and swallowed a mouthful of tea. 'Vice Squad raided us five times in the first fortnight. Whether it was one of the girls refusing a freebie or something more – backhanders, you know the kind of thing – I never knew. Either way, a month after we opened we were closed and I was left sorting out the bills.'

'I'm sorry.'

'So you keep saying.'

'Maybe it's true.'

'And maybe it's you.'

'How d'you mean?'

She gave a little snort of derision. 'It's what you do. Your way of getting what you want. Kind word here, little smile there. All so bloody understanding. It's all bollocks, Charlie. You told me to call you that, remember? When you were buttering me up before, trying to use me to get Terry locked away.'

Resnick held his tea in both hands, fingers laced around the mug, saying nothing.

'Well, I didn't. Wouldn't. Never would. But Terry didn't know that, did he? Saw you and me together and thought the worst. If you'd been screwing me, it wouldn't've been so bad, he could have coped with that, I reckon, come to terms. But no, he thought I was grassing him up. And that was what he couldn't live with. The thought that I was betraying him. So he topped himself.'

Both of them knew it hadn't been that simple.

Tears had appeared at the corners of Eileen's eyes and with the back of her hand she brushed them away. 'I reckon there was a lot of unsolved business written off that day, eh, Charlie? Anything that Terry might've had his hand in and a lot more besides. A lot of your blokes lining up to pat your back and buy you a drink and help you spit on Terry's grave.'

Resnick waited until the worst of the anger had faded from her eyes. 'I deserve that. Some of it.'

'Yes, you bastard, you do.'

'And I am—'

'Don't.' She stretched a hand towards his face, fingers spread. 'Just don't bother with sorry. Just tell me what you're doing here, sitting there in my front room, taking all that shit from me.'

Resnick set his mug down on the tray. 'The girl,' he said, 'the one whose body you found. I think there's something about her you're still keeping back.'

'Christ!' Up on her feet, she paced the room. 'I should've left her, shouldn't I? Poor stupid cow. Minded my own bloody business.'

Resnick followed her with his eyes. 'Stupid, Eileen. What way was she stupid?'

'She was a kid, a girl, I doubt she was old enough to have left school.'

'You did know her then?'

'No.'

'A kid, you said . . .'

'I saw her lyin' there, didn't I.'

'And that was all?'

Eileen stood at the window, her breath warming circles on the glass. A heavy bass echoed faintly through the side wall, the same rhythm over and again. Traffic stuttered in and out of the city along the Hucknall Road.

'I saw her a few nights back,' Eileen said. 'Corner of Addison Street. Skirt up to her arse and four-inch heels. She must've been freezing.' Her back was still to Resnick, her voice clear in the small room. 'This van had been up and down, two, maybe three times. Blue van, small. Post office van, that sort of size. Just the one bloke inside. He'd given me the once-over, going past real slow, the girl too. Finally he stops alongside her and leans out. I thought she was going to get in, but she didn't. To and fro about it for ages they was before he drives off and she goes back to her stand. Fifteen, twenty minutes later he's back, straight to her this time, no messing, and this time get in is what she does.'

Eileen turned to face him, hands behind her pressed against the wall.

'A few nights back,' Resnick said. 'Is that three or four?'

'Three.'

'Monday, then?'

'I suppose.'

'The driver, you knew him?'

'No.' The hesitation was slight, slight enough that Resnick, going over the conversation later, couldn't be certain it was his imagination.

'You're sure?'

'Course.'

'And the van?'

She shook her head.

'The driver, though. You'd recognise him again?'

'I don't know. I might.'

Resnick set the mug down on the tray, tea barely touched. 'Thanks, Eileen. Thanks for your time.'

She waited until he was at the door. 'When the van came back the second time, I can't be sure, but I think there were two of them, two blokes, the second one leaning forward from the back. Like I say, I can't be sure.'

The temperature seemed to have dropped another five degrees when Resnick stepped out from the comparative warmth of the house on to the street and clouds hung low overhead, laden with snow.

*

The pathologist was a short, solid man with stubby fingers that seemed unsuited to his daily tasks. Despite the cold, they stood at one corner of the parking area to the building's rear, Resnick and himself, allowing the pathologist to smoke.

'Weather, eh, Charlie.'

Resnick grunted in reply.

'All right for you, up off the Woodborough Road; where I am, down by the Trent, bloody river freezes over, soon as the bugger thaws you're up to your ankles in floodwater and bailing out downstairs like the place has sprung a leak.'

'The girl,' Resnick nudged.

The pathologist grinned. 'Hamlet, Charlie. Act one, scene two.'

'Come again?'

'Had you down as a bit of a scholar. On the quiet at least. "Seems, madam? Nay, it is. I know not seems." That poor kid, stretched out in the snow, clothes stuck to her with blood, jumped to the same conclusions, you and me, I'll wager. Cut. Stabbed. Sliced.' He sucked noisily on the end of his cigar. 'Not a bit of it. Not her blood. Different

104

type altogether. No, she was strangled, Charlie. Throttled. Bare hands. Likely passed out within minutes, that's one mercy. Bruising in plenty elsewhere, mind you, some consistent with being struck by a fist and some not. Something hard and narrow. Old-fashioned poker, something similar. And semen, Charlie, generous traces of, inside and out.'

For a moment, without his willing it, Resnick's eyes shut fast.

'Marks round her wrists,' the pathologist continued, 'as if at some point she'd been tied up. Tight enough to break the skin.'

'Rope or metal?'

'Metal.'

'Like handcuffs?'

'Very like.'

Unbidden, instinctive, the scene was beginning to play out in Resnick's mind.

'One person's or more?' he asked. 'The semen.'

'I'll get back to you.'

Resnick nodded. 'Anything else?'

'Fragments of material beneath her fingernails. Possibly skin. It's being analysed now.'

'How close can you pin down the time of death?'

'Likely not as close as you'd like.'

'Try me.'

'Twenty-four hours, give or take.'

'So if she was killed elsewhere and then dumped . . .'

'Which everything else suggests.'

'She'd likely been on the Forest since the early hours of yesterday morning, Wednesday.'

'Where she was found, not unfeasible.' The pathologist stubbed out the last smoulderings of the cigar on the sole of his shoe. 'Noon tomorrow, Charlie, I'll have more for you then.'

105

Resnick cupped both hands together and lifted them to his face, breathing out warm air.

Back upstairs in the CID room, Lynn Kellogg was talking to a Mrs Marston from a village just north of Melton Mowbray, arranging for her and her husband to be picked up and driven into the city, there to assist in the identification of the body of a fifteen-year-old girl who corresponded to the description of their missing daughter.

*

Her name was Clara. She'd run away twice before without getting further than Leicester services on the M1. The usual things: clothes, boys, forever missing the last bus home, the silver stud she'd had put through her nose, the ring she wanted through her navel. Fifteen years and three months. Pills. Sex. Her father ran a smallholding, found it hard; four mornings a week her mum worked in a newsagent in Melton, cycling the seven or so miles so she could open up first thing. Weekends they helped out at the local nature reserve, her mum made scones, coffee and walnut cake, the best.

'For Christ's sake,' Resnick had said, 'if it is her, don't tell them any more than they need to know.'

Ashen faced, Ted Marston held his wife by the shoulders as she beat her fists against his chest, her screams of denial tearing the sterile air.

The morning papers were full of it. Schoolgirl sex. Prostitution. Murder. An ordinary family grieves. Photographs of Clara in her school uniform vied for space with close-ups of her parents, stolen with a telephoto lens. The police are seeking to trace the driver of a blue van, seen in the vicinity of Addison Street and Forest Road East.

The pathologist beat his deadline by close on an hour. DNA samples taken from the girl's body confirmed that the semen came from two different men, one of whom was the source of the blood that had soaked her dress. Scrapings of skin found beneath her fingernails were from the second man. Filaments of a muddy green synthetic material, also taken from under her nails, seemed to have come from cheap, generic carpeting.

Two men, one young girl. A room without windows, a locked door. Do they take it in turns, one watching through a peephole while the other performs? A video camera? Polaroids? When she screams, as Resnick assumes she must, why are those screams not heard? And the hand-cuffs – is she cuffed to a bed or somehow to the floor?

Anil Khan took Eileen to Central Station and watched while she went through book after book of mugshots, barely glancing at each page. Resnick was there on the spread of pavement when she left.

'Don't go out tonight, Eileen. Stay close to home.'

He turned and watched as she continued on down Shakespeare Street towards the taxi rank on Mansfield Road.

*

Back in his own kitchen, the cats winding between his legs, anxious to be fed, Resnick poured himself a generous shot of Scotch and drank it down, two swallows then a third. Blood on the walls. Was there blood on the walls? He forked tinned food into four bowls, poured water and milk. Officers had contacted accident and emergency at Queen's and the other hospitals, the only serious stab wounds seemingly the result of drunk and disorderly or domestics, but these were all being checked. He rinsed his hands beneath the tap before assembling a sandwich on slices of dark rye, grinding coffee. Skin beneath the girl's fingernails. Fighting back. Had she somehow got hold of a knife, seized it when, for whatever reason, the cuffs were undone? Or had there been a falling-out between the two men? Jealousy? Fear?

The front room struck cold, the radiators likely in need of bleeding; switching on the light, Resnick pulled across the curtains, thankful for their weight. Why strangle her? Take her life. A fit of anger, irrational, unplanned? A response to being attacked? Somehow, had things gone too far, got out of hand? He crossed to the stereo where a CD still lay in place: Billie Holiday on Commodore. 'I'll Be Seeing You'. 'Strange Fruit'.

Less than forty minutes later, sandwich and coffee long finished, Billie's voice still ringing in his head, he prised the smallest cat from his lap, switched off the amplifier, lifted down his topcoat from the pegs in the hall, and went out to where the elderly Saab was parked alongside the house. Slowly, doubtless looking like a punter himself, he drove around the Forest, doubling back through a succession of interlocking streets until he was sure Eileen was not there. When, later, he passed her house, lights were burning upstairs and down.

His sleep was patchy and by five he was fully awake, listening to the breathing of the two cats entwined near the foot of his bed, the faint fall of snow against the pane.

They would have known, wouldn't they, that Eileen had seen the girl getting into their van.

*

Next morning, the snow on the streets was just a memory. Sunshine leaked, pale and weak, through clouds smeared

108

purplish-grey. At the obligatory press conference, Resnick made a brief statement, responded to questions without ever really answering, showed a right and proper concern for the Marstons in their bereavement. 'Good job,' said the public relations officer approvingly as they left the platform. Resnick scowled.

The job was being done in the CID office, the incident room, men and women accessing computer files, cross-checking messages, transcripts of interviews. So easy to let things slip, fail to make the right connection, wrongly prioritise. In addition to the sex offenders' register, they would check through the Vice Squad's list of men stopped and cautioned trawling the red light district in their cars. Married men. Businessmen. Men who were inadequate, law-abiding, lonely, unhinged. Men with a record of violence. Men who cuddled up to their wives each night in the matrimonial bed, never forgot an anniversary, a birthday, kissed the children and wished them happiness, sweet dreams.

Neither of the DNA samples taken from Clara Marston's body found a positive match. Follow-up calls relating to reported stab wounds yielded nothing.

Time passed.

Four days after the inquiry had begun, the burned-out skeleton of a blue Ford Escort van was found at the end of a narrow track near Moorgreen Reservoir, some dozen miles north-west of the city centre.

Late on that same Sunday evening, as Resnick was letting himself back into the house after a couple of hours at the Polish Club, accordions and reminiscence, bison grass vodka, the phone rang in the hall. The sergeant out at Carlton wasted few words: name's Eileen, sir, hell of a state, asking for you.

Within minutes, driving with particular care, Resnick

was heading south on Porchester Road, cutting through towards Carlton Hill.

*

She was pale, shaken, huddled inside a man's raincoat, the collar upturned. There were grazes to her face and hands and knees, a swelling high on her right temple; below her left cheekbone, a bruise slowly emerging like soft fruit. A borrowed sweater, several sizes too large, covered the silver snap-front uplift bra and matching G-string: she had got a job stripping after all. Her feet were bare. She had climbed out of the bathroom window of a house off Westdale Lane, jumped from the roof of the kitchen extension to the ground and fallen heavily, run through the side gate on to the road, throwing herself, more or less, in front of the first car which came along. The duty sergeant had calmed her down as best he could, taken a brief statement, provided tea and cigarettes.

Eileen saw Resnick with relief and tugged at his sleeve, her words tumbling over one another, breathlessly. 'It was him. I swear it. At the house.'

'Which house? Eileen, slow down.'

'Someone called, set up this private session, his brother's birthday. Half a dozen of them there, all blokes. Just as I was getting into it, he showed himself, back of the room. I don't know if he meant to, not then. Anyhow, I just panicked. Panicked and ran. Shut myself in the bathroom and locked the door behind me.'

'And it was him, the driver from the van? You're certain?'

'Not the driver,' Eileen said. 'The other man.'

'This address,' Resnick said, turning towards the sergeant, 'off Westdale Lane, you've checked it out?'

'No, sir. Not as yet.'

110

'Why in God's name not?'

'Way I saw it, sir, seeing as she'd asked for you, I thought to wait, just, you know, in case—'

'Get some people out there now. I doubt you'll find anyone still inside, but if you do, I want them brought in so fast their feet don't touch the ground. And get the place sealed. I'll want it gone over tomorrow with a fine-tooth comb. Knock up the neighbours, find out who lives there, anything else you can. Whatever you get, I want it passed through to me direct. Understood?'

'Yes, sir.'

'Then snap to it.'

Resnick turned towards Eileen. 'Whoever made this booking, did he leave a name?'

'Phil.'

'That was it?'

'Yes.' Instead of looking at him now, she was staring at the floor. 'There's something else,' she said, her voice so quiet he could only just make out the words.

'Go on.'

'Not here,' she said, glancing round. 'Not here.'

Taking her arm, Resnick led Eileen outside to where the Saab was parked at the kerb. 'I'll take you home. We can talk there.'

'No.' Fear in her eyes. 'He knows, doesn't he? He knows where I live.'

'Okay,' Resnick said, holding open the car door. 'Get in.'

Less than ten minutes later they were standing in the broad hallway of Resnick's house, a small commotion of cats scurrying this way and that.

'Charlie . . .'

'Yes?' It still took him by surprise, the way she used his name.

'Before anything else, can I have a bath?'

'Of course. Follow the stairs round and it's on the left. I'll leave you a towel outside the door.'

'Thanks.'

'And that trick with the bathroom window,' he called after her. 'I wouldn't recommend it twice in the same evening.'

Taking his time, he grilled bacon, sliced bread, broke eggs into a bowl; when he heard her moving around in the bathroom, the water running away, he forked butter into a small pan and turned the gas up high, adding shavings of Parmesan to the eggs before they set.

Eileen appeared in the kitchen doorway wearing an old dressing gown he scarcely ever bothered with, a towel twisted around her head.

'I thought you should eat,' Resnick said.

'I doubt if I can.'

But, sitting across from him at the kitchen table, she wolfed it down, folding a piece of the bread in half and wiping the last of the egg from her plate.

Uncertain, Pepper and Miles miaowed from a distance.

'Don't you feed them, Charlie?'

'Sometimes.'

Eileen pushed away her plate. 'You know what I need after that?'

'A cup of coffee?'

'A cigarette.'

She stood in the rear doorway, looking out across the garden, a few stunted trees in silhouette and, beyond the wall, the land falling away into darkness.

Resnick rinsed dishes at the sink.

When she came back inside and closed the door behind her, her skin shone from the cold. 'He's one of yours,' she said.

Resnick felt the breath stop inside his body.

'Vice, at least I suppose that's what he is. The sauna, that's where I saw him, just the once. With one of the girls. Knocked her around. Split her lip. It wasn't till tonight I was sure.'

'You scarcely saw him in the van. You said so yourself.'

'Charlie, I'm sure.'

'So the description you gave before . . .'

'It was accurate, far as it went.'

'And now?'

'He's got – I don't know what you'd call it – a lazy eye, the left. It sort of droops. Just a little. Maybe you'd never notice at first, but then, when you do . . . The way he looks at you.'

Resnick nodded. 'The driver, did you see him there tonight as well?'

Eileen shook her head. 'I don't know. No. I don't think so. I mean, he could've been, but no, I'm sorry, I couldn't say.'

'It's okay.' Now that the shock had faded, Resnick caught himself wondering why the allegation was less of a surprise than it was.

'You don't know him?' Eileen asked. 'Know who he is?'

Resnick shook his head. 'It won't take long to find out.'

In the front room he sat in his usual chair and Eileen rested her back against one corner of the settee, legs pulled up beneath her, glass of Scotch balancing on the arm.

'You'll go after him?'

'Oh, yes.'

'On my word?'

'Yes.'

She picked up her drink. 'You'll need more than that, Charlie. In court. The word of a whore.'

113

'Yes. Agreed.'

The heating had clicked off and the room was slowly getting colder. He wondered why it didn't seem stranger, her sitting there. Refilling both their glasses, he switched on the stereo and, after a passage of piano, there was Billie's voice, half-broken, singing of pain and grieving, the pain of living, the loving kiss of a man's hard hand.

'Sounds like,' Eileen said, 'she knows what she's talking about.'

Less than ten minutes later, she was stretching her arms and yawning. 'I think I'll just curl up on here, if that's the same to you.'

'No need. There's a spare room upstairs. Two.'

'I'll be okay.'

'Suit yourself. And if any of the cats jump up on you, push them off.'

Eileen shook her head. 'I might like the company.'

It was a little after two when she climbed in with him, the dressing gown discarded somewhere between the door and the bed. Startled awake, Resnick thrashed out with his arm and only succeeded in sending the youngest cat skittering across the floor.

'Budge up, Charlie.'

'Christ, Eileen!'

Her limbs were strong and smooth and cold.

'Eileen, you can't—'

'Shush.'

She lay with one leg angled over his knee, an arm across his midriff holding him close, her head to his chest. Within minutes the rhythm of her breathing changed and she was asleep, her breath faint and regular on his skin.

How long, Resnick wondered, since he had lain with a woman like this, in this bed? When his fingers touched

114

the place between her shoulder and her neck, she stirred slightly, murmuring a name that wasn't his.

It was a little while later before the cat felt bold enough to resume its place on the bed.

'Is there anywhere you can go?' Resnick asked. 'Till all this blows over.'

'You mean, apart from here.'

'Apart from here.'

They were in the kitchen, drinking coffee, eating toast.

'Look, if it's last night . . .'

'No, it's not.'

'I mean, it's not as if—'

'It's what you said yourself, at the moment everything's hanging on your word. It just needs someone to make the wrong connection between you and me . . .'

'Okay, you don't have to spell it out. I understand.'

The radio was still playing, muffled, in the bathroom. Politics: the same evasions, the same lies. As yet the outside temperature had scarcely risen above freezing, the sky several shades of grey.

'I've got a friend,' Eileen said, 'in Sheffield. I can go there.' She glanced down at what she was now wearing, one of his shirts. A morning-after cliché. 'Only I shall need some clothes.'

'I'll drive you round to your place after breakfast, wait while you pack.'

'Thanks.'

Resnick drank the last of his coffee, pushed himself to his feet. 'You'll let me have a number, in case I need to get in touch?'

'Yes. Yes, of course.'

She took one more mouthful of toast and left the rest.

*

They were gathered together in Resnick's office, the clamour of the everyday going on behind its closed door: Graham Millington, Anil Khan and Sharon Garnett. Sharon had been a member of the Vice Squad before being re-assigned to Resnick's team and had maintained her contacts.

'Burford,' Sharon said once Resnick had relayed the description. 'Jack Burford, it's got to be.'

Millington whistled, a malicious glint in his eye. 'Jack Burford – honest as the day is long.'

It wasn't so far from the shortest day of the year.

'How well do you know him?' Resnick asked.

'Well enough,' Sharon said. 'We'd have a drink together once in a while.' She laughed. 'Never too comfortable in my company, Jack. A woman who speaks her mind and black to boot, more than he could comfortably handle. No, a bunch of the lads, prize fights, lock-ins and lap dancers, that was more Jack's mark. Gambling, too. In and out of Ladbroke's most afternoons.'

'These lads, anyone closer to him than the rest?'

She gave it a few moments' thought. 'Jimmy Lyons, if anyone.'

'Left the force, didn't he?' Millington said. 'About a year back. Early retirement or some such.'

'There was an inquiry,' Sharon said. 'Allegations of taking money to turn a blind eye. Massage parlours, the usual thing. Didn't get anywhere.'

'And they worked together?' Resnick asked. 'Burford and Lyons?'

Sharon nodded. 'Quite a bit.'

'Lyons,' Resnick said. 'Anyone know where he is now?'

Nobody did.

'Okay. Sharon, chase up one or two of your contacts at

Vice, those you think you can trust. See what the word is on Burford. Anil, see if you can track down Lyons. He might still be in the city somewhere, in which case he and Burford could still be in touch.'

Millington was already at the door. 'I'd best get myself out to Carlton, see how they're getting on. You'll not want them dragging their feet on this.'

By four it was pretty much coming into place. The carpet fibres found beneath Clara Marston's fingernails matched the floor covering throughout the upstairs of the house off Westdale Lane. And traces of blood, both on the carpet and in the bathroom, were identical with that on the girl's clothing.

The house had been let a little over two years back to a Mr and Mrs Sadler, Philip and Dawn. None of the neighbours could recall seeing Dawn Sadler for a good six months and assumed the couple had split up; since then Philip Sadler had been sharing the place with his brother, John. John Sadler was known to the police: a suspended sentence for grievous bodily harm eight years before and, more recently, a charge of rape which had been dropped by the CPS at the last moment because some of the evidence was considered unsafe. Unusually, the rape charge had been brought by a prostitute, who claimed Sadler had threatened her with a knife and sodomised her against her will. What made it especially interesting – the arresting officers had been Burford and Lyons.

Lyons was still in the city, Khan confirmed, working with a security firm which provided bouncers for nightclubs and pubs; rumour was that he and Burford were still close. And Lyons had not been seen at work since the night Clara Marston had been killed.

Resnick crossed to the deli on Canning Circus, picked up a large filter coffee and continued into the cemetery on the far side. Burford and Lyons or Burford and Sadler, cruising the Forest in the van, looking for a likely girl. Finally, they get her back to the house and somewhere in the midst of it all things start to go awry.

He sat on a bench and levered the lid from his cup; the coffee was strong and still warm. It had to be Burford and Lyons who had sex with the girl; Sadler's DNA was likely still on file and no match had registered. So what happened? Back on his feet again, Resnick started to walk downhill. Burford and Lyons are well into it when Sadler takes it into his head to join in. It's Sadler who introduces the knife. But whose blood? Jimmy Lyons' blood. He's telling Sadler to keep out of it and Sadler won't listen; they argue, fight, and Lyons gets stabbed, stumbles over the girl. Grabs her as he falls.

Then if she doesn't do the stabbing, why does she have to die?

She's hysterical and someone – Burford? – starts slapping her, shaking her, using too much force. Or simply this: she's seen too much.

Resnick sits again, seeing it in his mind. Is it now that she struggles and in desperation fights back? Whose skin then was with those carpet fibres, caught beneath her nails? He sat a little longer, finishing his coffee, thinking; then walked, more briskly, back towards the station. There were calls to make, arrangements to be put in place.

*

Burford spotted Sharon Garnett the second she walked into the bar, dark hair piled high, the same lift of the head,

118

self-assured. It was when he saw Resnick behind her that he understood.

'Hello, Jack,' Sharon said as she crossed behind him. 'Long time.'

Some part of Burford told him to cut and run, but no, there would be officers stationed outside he was certain, front and back, nothing to do now but play it through.

'Evening, Charlie. Long way off your turf. Come to see how the other half live?'

'Something like that.'

'Get you a drink?'

'No, thanks.'

'Sharon?'

Sharon shook her head.

'Suit yourself.' Burford lifted the shot glass from the counter and downed what remained in one.

Without any attempt to disguise what he was doing, Resnick picked up the glass with a clean handkerchief and deposited it in a plastic evidence bag, zipping the top across.

'Let's do this decent, Charlie,' Burford said, taking a step away. 'No cuffs, nothing like that. I'll just walk with you out to the car.'

'Suit yourself,' Resnick said.

'Decent,' said Sharon. 'That word in your vocabulary, Jack?'

Millington was outside in the car park, Anil Khan.

'You know I'm not saying a word without a solicitor,' Burford said. 'You know that.'

'Shut up,' Resnick said, 'and get in the car.'

When Lynn Kellogg hammered on the door of Jimmy Lyons' flat near the edge of the Lace Market, Lyons elbowed her aside and took off down the stairs smack into

119

the arms of Kevin Naylor. Blood had already started to seep through the bandages across his chest.

John Sadler had skipped town and his brother, Philip, claimed no knowledge of where he might be. 'How about Mrs Sadler?' Millington asked. 'Been a while, I under-stand, since anyone's clapped eyes on her.' Philip Sadler turned decidedly pale.

Under questioning, both Burford and Lyons agreed to picking up Clara Marston and taking her back to the house for sex. They claimed they had left her alone in the upstairs room, which was where Sadler, drunk, had threatened her with a knife and then attacked her. By the time they'd realised what was going on and ran back upstairs, he had his hands round her throat and she was dead. It was when Lyons tried to pull him off that Sadler had stabbed him with the knife.

Burford claimed he then used his own car to take Lyons back to his flat and tended his wound. Sadler, he assumed, carried the dead girl out to the van and left her on the Forest, disposing of the van afterwards.

Without Sadler's side of things, it would be a difficult story to break down and Sadler wasn't going to be easy to find.

*

About a week later, media interest in the case beginning to fade, Resnick left the Polish Club early, a light rain falling as he walked back across town. Indoors, he made himself a sandwich and poured the last of the Scotch into a glass. Billie's voice was jaunty and in your face, even in defeat. Since the time she had sat across from him in

120

his chair, slipped into his bed, he had never quite managed to shake Eileen from his mind. When he crossed the room and dialled again the number she had given him, the operator's message was the same: number unobtainable. The music at an end, the sound of his own breathing seemed to fill the room.

THE SUN, THE MOON AND THE STARS

Eileen had done everything she could to change his mind. Michael, she'd said, anywhere else, okay? Anywhere but there. Michael Sherwood not his real name, not even close. But in the end she'd caved in, just as he'd known she would. Thirty-three by not so many months and going nowhere; thirty-three, though she was still only owning up to twenty-nine.

When he'd met her she'd been a receptionist in a car showroom south of Sheffield, something she'd blagged her way into and held down for the best part of a year; fine until the head of sales had somehow got a whiff of her past employment, some potential customer who'd seen her stripping somewhere most likely, and tried wedging his podgy fingers up inside her skirt one evening late. Eileen had kneed him in the balls, then hit him with a solid glass ashtray high across the face, close to taking out an eye. She hadn't bothered waiting for her cards.

She'd been managing a sauna, close to the city centre, when Michael had found her. In at seven, check the towels, make sure the plastic had been wiped down, bottles of massage oil topped up, the come washed from the walls; once the girls arrived, first shift, ready to catch the early punters on their way to work, she'd examine their hands, ensure they'd trimmed their nails; uniforms they took home and washed, brought back next day clean as new or she'd want the reason why.

'Come on,' Michael had said, 'fifty minutes down the motorway. It's not as if I'm asking you to fucking emigrate.' Emigration might have been easier. She had memories of Nottingham and none of them good. But then, looking round at the tatty travel posters and old centrefolds from *Playboy* on the walls, he'd added, 'What? Worried a move might be bad for your career?'

It hadn't taken her long to pack her bags, turn over the keys.

Fifty minutes on the motorway.

A house like a barn, a palace, real paintings on the walls.

When he came home earlier than usual one afternoon and found her sitting in the kitchen, polishing the silver while she watched TV, he snatched the cloth from her hands. 'There's people paid for that, not you.'

'It's something to do.'

His nostrils flared. 'You want something to do, go down the gym. Go shopping. Read a fucking book.'

'Why?' she asked him later that night, turning towards him in their bed.

'Why what?'

'Why am I here?'

He didn't look at her. 'Because I'm tired of living on my own.'

He was sitting propped up against pillows, bare-chested, thumbing through the pages of a climbing magazine. Eileen couldn't imagine why: anything more than two flights of stairs and he took the lift.

The light from the lamp on his bedside table shone a filter of washed-out blue across the patterned quilt and the curtains stirred in the breeze from the opened window. One thing he insisted on, one of many, sleeping with at least one of the windows open.

'That's not enough,' Eileen said.

'What?'

'Enough of a reason for me being here. You being tired of living alone.'

After a long moment, he put down his magazine. 'It's not the reason, you know that.'

'Do I?' She leaned back as he turned towards her, his fingers touching her arm.

'I'm sorry about earlier,' he said. 'Snapping at you like that. It was stupid. Unnecessary.'

'It doesn't matter.'

'Yes, it does.'

His face was close to hers, too close for her to focus; there was a faint smell of brandy on his breath.

After they'd made love he lay on his side, watching her, watching her breathe.

'Don't,' she said.

'Don't what?'

'Don't stare. I hate it when you stare.' It reminded her of Terry, her ex, the way his eyes had followed her whenever he thought she wasn't looking; right up until the night he'd slipped the gun out from beneath the pillow and, just when she'd been certain he was going to take her life, had shot himself in the head.

'What else am I supposed to do?' Michael said.

'Go to sleep? Take a shower?' Her face relaxed into a smile. 'Read a fucking book?'

Michael grinned and reached across and kissed her. 'You want to know how much I love you?'

'Yeah, yeah.' Mocking.

After a little searching, he found a ballpoint in the bedside-table drawer. Reaching for the magazine, he flicked through it till he came to a picture of the Matterhorn, outlined against the sky.

'Here,' he said, and quickly drew a hasty, childlike approximation of the sun, moon and stars around the summit. 'That's how much.'

Smiling, Eileen closed her eyes.

Resnick had spent the nub end of the evening in a pub off the A632 between Bolsover and Arkwright Town. Peter Waites and himself. From the outside it looked as if the place had been closed down months before and the interior was not a lot different. Resnick paced himself, supping halves, aware of having to drive back down, while Waites worked his way assiduously from pint to pint, much as he had when he'd been in his pomp and working at the coalface, twenty years before.

Whenever it came to Waites' round, Resnick was careful to keep his wallet and his tongue well zipped, the man's pride buckled enough. He had lost his job in the wake of the miners' strike and not worked steady since.

'Not yet forty when they tossed me on the fuckin' scrapheap, Charlie. Me and a lot of others like me. Nigh on a thousand when that pit were closed and them panty-waist civil bloody servants chucking their hands up in the air on account they've found sixty new jobs. Bloody disgrace.'

He snapped the filter from the end of his cigarette before lighting up.

'Lungs buggered enough already, Charlie. This'll not make ha'porth of difference, no matter what anyone says. Besides, long as I live long enough to see the last of that

125

bloody woman and dance on her bloody grave, I don't give
a sod.'

That bloody woman: Margaret Hilda Thatcher.

In that company especially, no need to speak her name.

When they stepped outside the air bit cold. Over the
carefully sculpted slag heap, now slick with grass, the
moon hung bright and full. Of the twenty terraced houses
in Peter Waites' street, fourteen were now boarded up.

'You'll not come in, Charlie?'

'Some other time.'

'Aye.' The two men shook hands.

'Look after yourself, Peter.'

'You, too.'

Resnick had first met the ex-miner when his son had
joined the Notts force as a young PC and been stationed
for a while at Canning Circus, under Resnick's wing. Now
the boy was in Australia, married with kids, something in
IT, and Resnick and Waites still kept in touch, the occasional pint, an odd Saturday at Bramhall Lane or down in
Nottingham at the County ground, a friendship based on
mutual respect and a sense of regret for days gone past.

Eileen would never be sure what woke her. The flap of
the curtain as the window opened wider; the soft tread
on the carpeted floor. Either way, when she opened her
eyes there they were, two shrouded shapes beyond the foot
of the bed. Beside her, Michael was already awake, pushing
up on one elbow, hand reaching out towards the light.

'Leave it,' said a voice.

Already the shapes beginning to flesh out, take on detail.

'We don't need the fucking light,' the shorter one said.
A voice Eileen didn't recognise: one she would never
forget.

Michael switched on the light and they shot him, the

tall one first and then the other, the impact hurling Michael back against the headboard, skewing him round until his face finished somehow pressed up against the wall.

Moving closer, the shorter of the two wrenched the wire from the socket and the room went dark. Too late to prevent Eileen from seeing what she had seen: the taller man bare-headed, more than bare, shaven, bald, a child's mask, Mickey Mouse, covering the centre of his face; his companion had a woollen hat pulled low, a red scarf wrapped high around his neck and jaw.

Some of Michael's blood ran, slow and warm, between Eileen's arm and her breast. The rest was pooling between his legs, spreading dark across the sheets. The sound she hadn't recognised was her own choked sobbing, caught like a hair-ball in her throat. She knew they would kill her or rape her or both.

'You want it?' the shorter one said, gesturing towards the bed.

The tall one made a sound like someone about to throw up and the shorter one laughed.

Eileen closed her eyes and when she opened them again they had gone.

Welcoming the rare chance of an early night, Lynn had been in bed for a good hour by the time Resnick returned home. Through several layers of sleep she registered the Saab slowing into the drive outside, the front door closing firmly in its frame, feet slow but heavy on the stairs; sounds from the bathroom and then his weight on the mattress as he lowered himself down. More than two years now and she still sometimes felt it strange, this man beside her in her bed. His bed, to be more precise.

'God, Charlie,' she said, shifting her legs. 'Your feet are like blocks of ice. And you stink of beer.'

His mumbled apology seemed to merge with his first snore.

His feet might be cold, but the rest of him seemed to radiate warmth. Lynn moved close against him and within not so many minutes she was asleep again herself.

Short of four, the phone woke them both.

'Yours or mine?' Resnick said, pushing back the covers.

'Mine.'

She was already on her feet, starting to pull on clothes.

'Shooting,' she said, when she'd put the phone back down. 'Tattershall Drive.'

'You want me to come?'

Lynn shook her head. 'No need. Go back to sleep.'

When they'd started living together, Lynn had transferred from Resnick's squad into Major Crime; less messy that way. Her coat, a hooded black anorak, windproof and waterproof, was on a hook in the hall. Despite the hour, it was surprisingly light outside, not so far off a full moon.

The body had not yet been moved. Scene of Crime were taking photographs, measuring, assiduously taking samples from the floor. The pathologist was still on his way. It didn't need an expert, Lynn thought, to see how he'd died.

Anil Khan stood beside her in the doorway. He had been the first officer from the Major Crime Unit to arrive.

'Two of them, so she says.' His voice was light, barely accented.

'She?'

'Wife, mistress, whatever. She's downstairs.'

Lynn nodded. When she had been promoted, three months before, detective sergeant to detective inspector, Khan had slipped easily into her shoes.

'Any idea how they got in?'

'Bedroom window, by the look of things. Out through the front door.'

Lynn glanced across the room. 'Flew in then, like Peter Pan?'

Khan smiled. 'Ladder marks on the sill.'

Eileen was sitting in a leather armchair, quilt round her shoulders, no trace of colour in her face. Someone had made her a cup of tea and it sat on a lacquered table, untouched. The room itself was large and unlived in, heavy dark furniture, dark paintings in ornamental frames; wherever they'd spent their time, Lynn thought, it wasn't here.

She lifted a high-backed wooden chair and carried it across the room. Through the partly open door she saw Khan escorting the pathologist towards the stairs. She set the chair down at an angle, close to Eileen, and introduced herself, name and rank. Eileen continued to stare into space, barely registering that she was there.

'Can you tell me what happened?' Lynn said.

No reply.

'I need you to tell me what happened,' Lynn said. For a moment, she touched Eileen's hand.

'I already did. I told the Paki.'

'Tell me. In your own time.'

Eileen looked at her then. 'They killed him. What more d'you want to know?'

'Everything,' Lynn said. 'Everything.'

His name was Michael Sherwood: Mikhail Sharminov. He had come to England from Russia fifteen years before. Born in Tbilisi, Georgia to Russo-Armenian parents, as a young man he had quickly decided a life devoted to the production of citrus fruits and tung oil was not for him. He went, as a student, to Moscow, and by the time he was thirty he had a thriving business importing bootlegged rock music through East Germany into Russia, everything from the Beatles to Janis Joplin. Soon, there were video tapes, bootlegged also: *Apocalypse Now*, *The Godfather*, *E.T.* By the standards of the Russian black economy, Mikhail was on his way to being rich.

But then, by 1989 the Berlin Wall was crumbling and, in its wake, the Union of Soviet Socialist Republics was falling apart. Georgia, where his ageing parents still lived, was on the verge of civil war. Free trade loomed.

Go or stay?

Mikhail became Michael.

In Britain he used his capital to build up a chain of provincial video stores, most of whose profits came from pirated DVDs; some of his previous contacts in East Berlin were now in Taiwan, in Tirana, in Hong Kong. Truly, a global economy.

Michael Sherwood, fifty-eight years old. The owner outright of property to the value of two million five, together with the leases of more than a dozen stores; three bank accounts, one offshore; a small collection of paintings, including a small Kandinsky worth an estimated eight hundred and fifty thousand pounds; three cars, a Lexus and two BMWs; four .38 bullets, fired from close range, two high in the chest, one to the temple, one that had torn through his throat.

Most of this information Lynn Kellogg amassed over the following days and weeks, piecing together local evidence with what could be gleaned from national records and HM Customs and Excise. And long before that, before the end of that first attenuated conversation, she realised she had seen Eileen before.

'Charlie,' she said, phoning him at home. 'I think you'd better get over here after all.'

*

130

The first time Resnick had set eyes on Eileen, she'd been sitting in a basement wine bar, smoking a cigarette and drinking Bacardi and Coke, her hair redder then and falling loose around her shoulders. The harshness of her make-up, in that attenuated light, had been softened; her silver-grey top, like pale filigree, shimmered a little with each breath she took. She knew he was staring at her and thought little of it: it was what people did. Men, mostly. It was what, until she had taken up with Terry Cooke, had paid her way in the world.

The sandwich Resnick had ordered arrived and when he bit into it mayonnaise smeared across the palm of his hand; through the bar stereo Parker was stripping the sentiment from 'Don't Blame Me' – New York City, 1947, the closing bars of Miles' muted trumpet aside, it's Bird's alto all the way, acrid and languorous, and when it's over there's nothing left to do or say.

'You bastard!' Eileen had yelled later. 'You fucking bastard! Making out you're so fucking sympathetic and understanding and all the while you're screwing me just as much as those bastards who think for fifty quid they can bend me over some car park wall and fuck me up the arse.'

A nice turn of phrase, Eileen, and Resnick, while he might have resisted the graphic nature of her metaphor, would have had to admit she was right. He had wanted to apply pressure to Terry Cooke and his burgeoning empire of low-grade robbers and villains, and in Eileen, in what he had misread as her weakness, he thought he had seen the means.

'Leave him,' he'd said. 'Give us something we can make stick. Circumstances like this, you've got to look out for yourself. No one would blame you for that.'

In the end it had been Terry who had weakened and

whether it had been his fear of getting caught and being locked away that had made him pull the trigger, or his fear of losing Eileen, Resnick would never know. After the funeral, amidst the fallout and recriminations, she had slipped from sight and it was some little time before he saw her again, close to desperate and frightened, so frightened that he had offered her safe haven in that same big sprawling house where he now lived with Lynn, and there, in the long sparse hours between sleeping and waking, she had slid into his bed and fallen fast asleep, one of her legs across his and her head so light against his chest it could almost have been a dream.

Though his history of relationships was neither extensive nor particularly successful, and though he prized honesty above most other things, he knew enough never to have mentioned this incident to Lynn, innocent as he would vainly have tried to make it seem.

He stood now in the doorway, a bulky man with a shapeless suit and sagging eyes, and waited until, aware of his presence, she turned her head.

'Hello, Eileen.'

The sight of him brought tears to her eyes. 'Christ, Charlie. First Terry and now this. Getting to be too much of a fucking habit, if you ask me.'

She held out a hand and he took it, and then she pressed her head against the rough weave of his coat, the too-soft flesh beneath, and cried. After several moments, Resnick rested his other hand against her shoulder, close to the nape of her neck, and that's how they were some minutes later when Lynn looked into the room through the open door, then looked away.

'What did she have to say for herself?' Lynn asked. They were high on the Ropewalk, the light breaking through the sky, bits and pieces of the city waking south and west below them.

'No more, I dare say, than she told you,' Resnick said.

'Don't tell me all that compassion went for nothing.'

Resnick bridled. 'She'd just seen her bloke shot dead alongside her, what was I supposed to do?'

Lynn gave a small shake of the head. 'It's okay, Charlie. Just teasing.'

'I'm glad to hear it.'

'Though I do wonder if you had to look as if you were enjoying it quite as much.'

At the end of the street they stopped. Canning Circus police station, where Resnick was based, was only a few minutes away.

'What do you think?' Lynn asked. 'A paid hit?'

'I doubt it was a couple of local tearaways out to make a name for themselves. Whoever this was, they'll be well up the motorway by now. Up or down.'

'Someone he'd crossed.'

'Likely.'

'Business, then.'

'Whatever that is.'

Lynn breathed in deeply, drawing the air down into her lungs. 'I'd best get started.'

'Okay.'

'See you tonight.'

'Yes.'

She stood for a moment, watching him walk away. Her imagination, or was he slower than he used to be? Turning, she retraced her steps to where she'd parked her car.

Much of the next few days Lynn spent accessing and exchanging information on the computer and speaking on the telephone, building up, as systematically as she could, a picture of Mikhail Sharminov's activities, while forensic staff analysed the evidence provided by Scene of Crime.

At the start of the following week, Lynn, armed with a bulging briefcase and a new Next suit, went to a meeting at the headquarters of the Specialist Crime Directorate in London; also present were officers from the National Criminal Intelligence Service and the National Crime Squad, as well as personnel from HM Customs and Excise, and observers from the Interpol team that was carrying out a long-term investigation into the Russian Mafia.

By the time the meeting came to a halt, some six hours and several coffee breaks later, Lynn's head was throbbing with unfamiliar names and all-too-familiar motivations. Sharminov, it seemed, had been seen as an outsider within the Soviet diaspora; as far as possible he had held himself apart, relying instead on his contacts in the Far East. But with the increased capability for downloading not only CDs but now DVDs via the Internet, the logistics of his chosen field were changing, markets were shifting and becoming more specialised. There was a burgeoning trade in hard-core pornography which certain of Sharminov's former compatriots were keen to further through the networks he'd established. For a price. It wasn't clear whether he had resisted on moral grounds or because the price wasn't right.

Eileen was questioned at length about Sharminov's business partners and shown numerous photographs, the faces in which, for the most part, she failed to recognise. One man, middle-aged, with dark close-cropped hair and eyes too close together, had been to the house on several occasions, hurried conversations behind closed doors; another, silver-haired and leonine, she remembered seeing once, albeit briefly, in the rear seat of a limousine. There were others, a few, of whom she was less certain.

134

'Did he seem worried lately?' they asked her. 'Concerned about business?'

'No,' she said. 'Not especially.'

Perhaps he should have been. The silver-haired man was Alexei Popov, whose organisation encompassed drugs and pornography and human trafficking in a network that stretched from the Bosporus and the Adriatic to the English Channel, and had particularly strong links with the Turkish and Italian Mafia. Tony Christanidi was his go-between and sometime enforcer, the kind of middle-management executive who never left home without first checking that his two-shot .22 Derringer was snug alongside his mobile phone.

The line back through Christanidi to Popov was suspected of being behind three recent fatal shootings, one in Manchester, one in Marseilles, the other in Tirana.

'Would they carry out these shootings themselves?' Lynn had asked.

'Not usually. Sometimes they'll make a deal with the Turks or the Sicilians. You do one for me, I'll do one for you. Other times, they'll simply contract it out. Usually overseas. Someone flies in, picks up the weapons locally, junks them straight after, twelve hours later they're back on the plane.'

'So they wouldn't necessarily be English?'

'Not at all.'

'The two men who shot Sharminov, the only witness we have swears they were English.'

'This is the girlfriend?'

'Eileen. Yes.'

'I don't understand.'

'What?'

'Why they didn't kill her too.'

'You don't think she could have been involved?'

'In setting him up? I suppose it's possible.'

They questioned Eileen again, pushed her hard until her confidence was in shreds and her voice was gone.

'I don't think she knows anything,' the National Crime Squad officer said after almost four hours of interrogation. 'She was just lucky, that's all.'

She wasn't the only one. Good luck and bad. In the early hours of the morning, almost two weeks and two days after Mikhail Sharminov was murdered, there was a shooting in the city. At around two in the morning, there was an altercation at the roundabout linking Canal Street with London Road, a Range Rover cutting across a BMW and causing the driver to brake hard. After a lot of gesturing and angry shouting, the Range Rover drove off at speed, the other vehicle following. At the lights midway along Queen's Drive, where it runs beside the Trent, the BMW came alongside and the man in the passenger seat leaned out and shot the driver of the Range Rover five times.

The driver was currently in critical condition in hospital, hanging on.

Forensics suggested that the shots had been fired from one of the same weapons that had been used to kill Mikhail Sharminov, a snub-nosed .38 Smith & Wesson.

'It could mean whoever shot Sharminov was recruited locally after all,' Lynn said. 'Didn't see any need to leave town.'

They were in the kitchen of the house in Mapperley, Saturday afternoon: Lynn ironing, a glass of white wine close at hand; Resnick putting together a salad with half an ear cocked towards the radio, the soccer commentary on Five Live.

'Well, he has now,' Resnick said, wondering why the bottle of walnut oil was always right at the back of the

136

cupboard when you needed it. Neither the driver nor passenger of the BMW had so far been traced.

'You think it's possible?' Lynn said.

Resnick shook a few drops of the oil over rocket and romaine and reached for the pepper. 'I think you're on safer ground following the gun.' He broke off a piece of lettuce to taste, scowled, and began ferreting for the Tabasco.

'Don't make it too hot, Charlie. You always do.'

'Assume they've flown in. Birmingham, Leeds-Bradford, East Midlands. There's a meeting with whoever's supplying the weapons, prearranged. After the job, either they're dumped or, more likely, handed back.'

'Recycled.'

'I could still tell you which pub to go to if you wanted a converted replica. A hundred in tens handed over in the gents. But this is a different league.'

'Bernard Vitori,' Lynn said. 'He's the best bet. Eddie Chambers, possibly. One or two others. We'll start with Vitori first thing.'

'Sunday morning?' Resnick said. 'He won't like that.'

'Disturbing his day of rest?'

'Takes his mother to church. Strelley Road Baptists. Regular as clockwork.' Resnick ran a finger round the inside of the salad bowl. 'Here. Taste this. Tell me what you think.'

They followed Vitori and his mum to church, thirty officers, some armed, keeping the building tightly surrounded, mingling inside. The preacher was delighted by the increase in his congregation. Sixty or so minutes of energetic testifying later, Vitori reluctantly unlocked the boot of his car. Snug inside were a 9mm Glock 17 and a Chinese-made A15 semi-automatic rifle. Vitori had been taking them to a potential customer after the service. Faced with the possibility of eight to ten inside, he cut a deal. Contact with the Russians had been by mobile phone, using numbers which were now untraceable, names which were clearly fake. Vitori had met two men in the Little Chef on the A60, north of Arnold. Leased them two clean revolvers for twenty-four hours, seven hundred the pair. Three days later, he'd sold one of the guns to a known drug dealer for five hundred more.

No matter how many times officers from Interpol and NICS showed him photographs of potential hit men, Vitori claimed to recognise none. He was not only happy to name the dealer, furnishing an address into the bargain, he gave them a likely identity for the driver of the car. Remanded in custody, special pleading would get him a five-year sentence at most, of which he'd serve less than three.

'Bloody Russians, Charlie,' Peter Waites said, sitting opposite Resnick in their usual pub. 'When I was a kid we were always waiting for them to blow us up. Now they're over here like fucking royalty.'

Sensing a rant coming, Resnick nodded non-committally and supped his beer.

'That bloke owns Chelsea football club. Abramovich? He's not the only one, you know. This Boris, for instance – what's his name? – Berezovsky. One of the richest people in the fucking country. More money than the fucking Queen.'

Resnick sensed it was not the time to remind Waites that as a dedicated republican, he thought Buckingham Palace should be turned into council housing and Her Majesty forced to live out her remaining years on her old age pension.

'You know how many Russians there are in this country, Charlie? According to the last census?'

138

Resnick shook his head. Waites had been spending too much time in Bolsover library, trawling the Internet for free. 'I give up, Peter,' he said. 'Tell me.'

'Forty thousand, near as damn it. And they're not humping bricks for a few quid an hour on building sites or picking cockles in Morecambe fucking Bay. Living in bloody luxury, that's what they're doing.' Leaning forward, Waites jabbed a finger urgently towards Resnick's face. 'Every third property in London sold to a foreign citizen last year went to a bloody Russian. Every fifteenth property sold for over half a million the same.' He shook his head. 'This country, Charlie. Last ten, twenty years, it's turned upside fucking down.' He wiped his mouth with the back of his hand.

'Another?' Resnick said, pointing to Waites' empty glass.

'Go on. Why not?'

For a good few minutes neither man spoke. Noise and smoke spiralled around them. Laughter but not too much of that. The empty trill of slot machines from the far side of the bar.

'This soccer thing, Charlie,' Waites said eventually. 'Yanks buying into Manchester United and now there's this President of Thailand or whatever, wants forty per cent of Liverpool so's he can flog Steven Gerrard shirts and Michael Owen boots all over South-East Asia. It's not football any more, Charlie, it's all fucking business. Global fuckin' economy.' He drank deep and drained his glass. 'It's the global fucking economy as has thrown me and hundreds like me on to the fucking scrapheap, that's what it's done.' Waites sighed and shook his head. 'Sorry, Charlie. You ought never to have let me get started.'

'Stopping you'd take me and seven others.'

'Happen so.'

At the door Waites stopped to light a cigarette. 'You

know what really grates with me, Charlie? It used to be a working-class game, football. Now they've took that from us as well.'

'Some places,' Resnick said, 'it still is.'

'Come on, Charlie. What's happening, you don't think it's right no more'n me.'

'Maybe not. Though I wouldn't mind some oil billion-aire from Belarus taking a fancy to Notts County for a spell. Buy 'em a halfway decent striker, someone with a bit of nous for midfield.'

Waites laughed. 'Now who's whistling in the dark?'

For several months Customs and Excise and others did their best to unravel Sharminov's financial affairs; his stock was seized, his shops closed down. A further six months down the line, Alexei Popov would buy them through a twice-removed subsidiary and begin trading in DVDs for what was euphemistically called the adult market. He also bought a flat in Knightsbridge for a cool five million, close to the one owned by Roman Abramovich, though there was no indication the two men knew one another. Abramovich's Chelsea continued to prosper; no oil-fed angel came to Notts County's rescue as they struggled against relegation.

Lynn began to wonder if a sideways move into the National Crime Squad might help to refocus her career.

Resnick saw Eileen one more time. Although most of the money belonging to the man she knew as Michael Sherwood had been confiscated, she had inherited enough for new clothes and an expensive makeover, new suitcases which were waiting in the taxi parked outside.

'I thought I'd travel, Charlie. See the world. Switzerland, maybe. Fly round some mountains.' Her smile was near to perfect. 'You know the only place I've been abroad?

140

If you don't count the Isle of Man. Alicante. Apart from the heat, it wasn't like being abroad at all. Even the announcements in the supermarket were in English.'

'Enjoy it,' Resnick said. 'Have a good time.'

Eileen laughed. 'Come with me, why don't you? Chuck it all in. About time you retired.'

'Thanks a lot.'

For a moment her face went serious. 'You think we could ever have got together, Charlie?'

'In another life, maybe.'

'Which life is that?'

Resnick smiled. 'The one where I'm ten years younger and half a stone lighter; not already living with somebody else.'

'And not a policeman?'

'Maybe that too.'

Craning upwards, she kissed him quickly on the lips. 'You're a good man, Charlie, and don't let anyone tell you otherwise.'

Long after she had gone, he could feel the pressure of her mouth on his and smell the scent of her skin beneath the new perfume.

§ § §

For K. C. Constantine, with gratitude and admiration, in particular for his marvellous novel, Blood Mud, *from which the salad finger episode was stolen.*

DUE NORTH

Elder hated this: the after-midnight call, the neighbours penned back behind hastily unravelled tape, the video camera's almost silent whirr; the way, as if reproachful, the uniformed officers failed to meet his eye; and this especially, the bilious taste that fouled his mouth as he stared down at the bed, the way the hands of both children rested near the cover's edge, as if at peace, their fingers loosely curled.

*

He had been back close on two years, long enough to view the move north with some regret. Not that north was really what it was. A hundred and twenty miles from London, one hour forty minutes, theoretically, by train. Another country nonetheless.

For weeks he and Joanne had argued it back and forth, reasons for, reasons against, two columns fixed to the refrigerator door. Cut and Dried, the salon where Joanne worked as a stylist, was opening branches in Derby and

142

Nottingham and she could manage either one she chose. Derby was out of the question.

On a visit, Katherine trailing behind them, they had walked along the pedestrianised city centre street: high-end fashion, caffè latte, bacon cobs; Waterstone's, Ted Baker, Café Rouge.

'You see,' Joanne said, 'we could be in London. Chiswick High Road.'

Elder shook his head. It was the bacon cobs that gave it away.

The empty shop unit was just off to one side, secluded and select. '*Post no Bills*' plastered across the glass frontage, '*Sold Subject to Contract*' above the door. Joanne would be able to hire the staff, set the tone, everything down to choosing the shade of paint on the walls.

'You know I want this, don't you?' Her hands in his pockets as she pulled him back against the glass.

'I know.'

'So?'

He closed his eyes and, slow at first, she kissed him on the mouth.

'God!' Katherine exclaimed, whacking her father in the back.

'What?'

'Making a bloody exhibition of yourselves, that's what.'

'You watch your tongue, young lady,' Joanne said, stepping clear.

'Sooner that than watching yours.'

Katherine Elder: eleven going on twenty-four.

'What say we go and have a coffee?' Elder said. 'Then we can have a think.'

Even a casual glance in the estate agent's window made it clear that for the price of their two-bedroom first-floor flat off Chiswick Lane, they could buy a house in a decent area, something substantial with a garden front and back.

For Katherine, moving up to secondary, a new start in a new school, the perfect time. And Elder . . . ?

He had joined the police as a twenty-year-old in Huddersfield, walked the beat in Leeds; out of uniform, he'd been stationed in Lincolnshire: Lincoln itself, Boston, Skegness. Then, married, the big move to London, this too at Joanne's behest. Frank Elder a detective sergeant in the Met. Detective inspector when he was forty-five. Moving out he'd keep his rank at least, maybe push up. There were faces he still knew, a name or two. Calls he could make. A week after Joanne took charge of the keys to the new salon, Elder had eased himself behind his desk at the head-quarters of the Nottinghamshire Major Crime Unit: a telephone, a PC with a splintered screen, a part-eaten Pork Farms pie mildewing away in one of the drawers.

Now, two years on, the screen had been replaced, the keyboard jammed and lacked the letters R and S; photographs of Joanne and Katherine stood beside his in-tray in small frames. The team he'd been working with on a wages hijack north of Peterborough had just brought in a result and shots of Scotch were being passed around in polystyrene cups.

Elder drank his down, a single swallow, and dialled home. 'Jo, I'm going to be a bit late.'

A pause in which he visualised her face, a tightening around the mouth, the corners of her eyes. 'Of course.'

'What do you mean?'

'It's the end of the week, the lads are raring to go, of course you'll be late.'

'Look, if you'd rather—'

'Frank, I'm winding you up. Go and have a drink. Relax. I'll see you in an hour or so, okay?'

'You're sure?'

'Frank.'

'All right. All right. I'm going.'

When he arrived home, two hours later, not so much more, Katherine was closeted in her room, listening to music, and Joanne was nowhere to be seen.

Barely pausing to knock, he pushed open his daughter's door.

'Dad!'

'What?'

'You're supposed to knock.'

'I did.'

'I didn't hear you.'

Reaching past her, he angled the volume control of the portable stereo down a notch, a half-smile deflecting the complaint that failed to come.

'Where's Mum?'

'Out.'

'Where?'

'Out.'

Cross-legged on the bed, fair hair splashed across her eyes, Katherine flipped closed the book in which she had been writing with a practised sigh.

'You want something to eat?' Elder asked.

A quick shake of the head. 'I already ate.'

He found a slice of pizza in the fridge and set it in the microwave to reheat, opened a can of Heineken, switched on the TV. When Joanne arrived back, close to midnight, he was asleep in the armchair, unfinished pizza on the floor close by. Stooping, she kissed him lightly and he woke.

'You see,' Joanne said, 'it works.'

'What does?'

'You turned into a frog.'

Elder smiled and she kissed him again; he didn't ask her where she'd been.

Neither was quite in bed when the mobile suddenly rang.

'Mine or yours?'

145

Joanne angled her head. 'Yours.'

Elder was still listening, asking questions, as he started reaching for his clothes.

*

Fourteen miles north of the city, Mansfield was a small industrial town with an unemployment rate above average, a reputation for casual violence and a soccer team just keeping its head above water in Division Three of the Nationwide. Elder lowered the car window a crack, broke into a fresh pack of extra-strong mints and tried not to think about what he would find.

He missed the turning first and had to double back, a cul-de-sac built into a new estate, just shy of the road to Edwinstowe and Ollerton. An ambulance snug between two police cars, lights in the windows of all the houses, the periodic yammering of radios. At number seventeen all of the curtains were drawn closed. A child's scooter lay discarded on the lawn. Elder pulled on the protective coveralls he kept ready in the boot, nodded to the young officer in uniform on guard outside and showed his ID just in case. On the stairs, one of the Scene of Crime team, whey-faced, stepped aside to let him pass. The smell of blood and something else, like ripe pomegranate on the air.

The children were in the smallest bedroom, two boys, six and four, pyjamed arms outstretched; the pillow with which they had been smothered lay bunched on the floor. Elder noticed bruising near the base of the older boy's throat, twin purpling marks the size of thumbs; he wondered who had closed their eyes.

'We were right to call you in?'

For a big man, Saxon moved lightly; only a slight nasal heaviness to his breathing had alerted Elder to his presence in the room.

146

'I thought, you know, better now than later.'

Elder nodded. Gerry Saxon was a sergeant based in the town, Mansfield born and bred. The two of them had crossed paths before, swapped yarns and the occasional pint; stood once at the Town ground, side by side, as sleet swept near horizontally goalwards, grim in the face of a nil-nil draw with Chesterfield. Elder thought Saxon thorough, bigoted, not as slow-witted as he would have you believe.

'Where's the mother?' Elder asked.

Lorna Atkin was jammed between the dressing table and the wall, as if she had been trying to burrow away from the pain. One slash of a blade had sliced deep across her back, opening her from shoulder to hip. Her night-dress, once white, was matted here and there to her body with stiffening blood. Her throat had been cut.

'The police surgeon . . . ?'

'Downstairs,' Saxon said. 'Few preliminaries, nothing more. Didn't like to move her till your say-so.'

Elder nodded again. So much anger: so much hate. He looked from the bed to the door, at the collision of bottles and jars across the dressing-table top, the trajectory of blood along the walls. As if she had made a dash for it and been dragged back, attacked. Trying to protect her children or herself?

'The weapon?'

'Kitchen knife. Least that's what I reckon. Downstairs in the sink.'

'Washed clean?'

'Not so's you'd notice.'

There were footsteps on the landing outside and then Maureen Prior's face in the doorway, eyes widening as she took in the scene; one slow intake of breath and she stepped into the room.

'Gerry, you know DS Prior. Maureen, Gerry Saxon.'

147

'Good to see you again, Gerry.' She scarcely took her eyes from the body. The corpse.

'Maureen, check with Scene of Crime. Make sure they've documented everything we might need. Let's tie that up before we let the surgeon get to work. You'll liaise with Gerry here about interviewing the neighbours, house to house.'

'Right.'

'You'll want to see the garage next,' Saxon said.

There were two entrances, one from the utility room alongside the kitchen, the other from the drive. Despite the latter being open, the residue of carbon monoxide had yet to fully clear. Paul Atkin slumped forward over the driver's wheel, one eye fast against the windscreen's curve, his skin sacking grey.

Elder walked twice slowly around the car and went out to where Saxon stood in the rear garden, smoking a cigarette.

'Any sign of a note?'

Saxon shook his head.

'A note would have been nice. Neat at least.'

'Only tell you what you know already.'

'What's that then, Gerry?'

'Bastard topped his family, then himself. Obvious.'

'But why?'

Saxon laughed. 'That's what you clever bastards are going to find out.' He lit a fresh cigarette from the butt of the last and as he did Elder noticed Saxon's hands had a decided shake. Probably the night air was colder than he'd thought.

*

There was no note that came to hand, but something else instead. Traced with Atkin's finger on the inside of the misting glass and captured there by Scene of Crime, the first

148

wavering letters of a name – '*C O N N*' and then what might have been an '*I*' trailing weakly down towards the window's edge.

Mid-afternoon the following day, Elder was driving with Maureen Prior out towards the small industrial estate where Atkin had worked, head of sales for Pleasure Blinds. Prefabricated units that had still to lose their shine, neat beds of flowering shrubs, no sign of smoke in sight. Sherwood Business Park.

If someone married's going over the side, chances are it's with someone from where they work. One of Frank Elder's rules of thumb, rarely disproved.

Some few years back, close to ten it would be now, his wife Joanne had an affair with her boss. Six months it had gone on, no more, before Elder had found out. The reasons not so very difficult to see. They had just arrived in London, uprooted themselves, and Joanne was high on the speed of it, the noise, the buzz. Since having Katherine, she and Elder had made love less and less; she felt unattractive, oddly sexless, over the hill at thirty-three. And then there had been Martyn Miles, all flash and if not Armani, Hugo Boss; drinks in the penthouse bar of this hotel or that, meals at Bertorelli's or Quo Vadis.

Elder had his fifteen minutes of crazy, smashed a few things around the house, confronted Miles outside the mews apartment where he lived and restrained himself from punching his smug and sneering face more than just the once.

Together, he and Joanne had talked it through, worked it out; she had carried on at the salon. 'I need to see him every day and know I don't want him any more. Not turn my back and never know for sure.'

Elder had told Maureen all of this one day: one night, actually; a long drive down the motorway from Fife, the road surface slick with rain, headlights flicking by. She had listened and said very little, a couple of comments only. Maureen with a core of moral judgement clear and unyielding as the Taliban. Neither of them had ever referred to it again.

Elder slowed the car and turned through the gates of the estate; Pleasure Blinds was the fourth building on the right.

'Constance Seymour' read the sign on the door. *'Personnel'*.

As soon as she saw them, her face crumpled inwards like a paper bag. Spectacles slipped, lopsided, down on to the desk. Maureen fished a Kleenex from her bag; Elder fetched water from the cooler in a cone-shaped cup. Connie blew her nose, dabbed at her eyes. She was somewhere in her thirties, Elder thought, what might once have been called homely, plain. Sloped shoulders, buttoned blouse, court shoes. Elder could imagine her with her mother, in town Saturdays shopping arm in arm, the two of them increasingly alike.

The eyes that looked at him now were tinged with violet, palest blue. She would have listened to Atkin like that, intense and sympathetic, pained. Whose hand would have reached out first, who would first have comforted whom?

Maureen came to the end of her expressions of condolence, regret.

'You were having an affair with him,' she said. 'Paul Atkin. A relationship.'

Connie sniffed and said yes.

'And this relationship, how long . . .'

'A year. More. Thirteen months.'

'It was serious, then?'

'Oh, yes.' Her expression slightly puzzled, somewhat hurt. What else could it have been?

'Mr Atkin, was there . . . was there any suggestion that he might leave his wife?'

150

'Oh, no. No. The children, you see. He loved the children more than anything.'

Maureen glanced across, remembering the faces, the pillow, the bed. Killed with kindness: the proverb eddied up in Elder's mind.

'Have you any idea why he might want to harm them?' Elder asked.

'No,' she gasped, moments ahead of the wash of tears. 'Unless . . . unless . . .'

*

Joanne was in the living room, feet tucked beneath her, watching TV. Katherine was staying overnight at a friend's. On screen, a bevy of smartly dressed and foul-mouthed young things were dissecting the sex lives of their friends. A laughter track gave hints which Joanne, for the most part, ignored.

'Any good?' Elder asked.

'Crap.'

'I'm just going out for a stroll.'

'Okay.'

'Shan't be long.'

Glancing towards the door, Joanne smiled and puckered her lips into the shape of a kiss.

Arms swinging lightly by his sides, Elder cut through a swathe of tree-lined residential streets on to the main road; for a moment he was distracted by the lights of the pub, orange and warm, but instead walked on, away from the city centre and then left to where the houses were smaller than his own and huddled together, the first part of a circular walk that would take him, an hour or so later, back home.

Behind the curtains of most front rooms, TV sets flickered and glowed; muffled voices rose and fell; the low rumble of a sampled bass line reverberated from the windows of a passing Ford. Haphazardly, dogs barked. A child cried. On the corner, a group of black youths wearing ripped-off Tommy Hilfiger eyed him with suspicion and disdain.

Elder pictured Gerry Saxon leaning up against a darkened tree, his hands trembling a little as he smoked a cigarette. Almost a year now since he had given up himself, Elder fumbled in his pocket for another mint.

He knew the pattern of incidents similar to that at the Atkins house: the man – almost always it was the man – who could find no other way to cope; debt or unrequited love or some religious mania, voices that whispered, unrelenting, inside his head. Unable or unwilling to leave his family behind, feeling it his duty to protect them from whatever loomed, he took their lives and then his own. What differed here was the intensity of the attack upon the wife, that single fierce and slashing blow, delivered after death. Anger at himself for what he had done? At her, for giving cause?

A cat, tortoiseshell, ran two-thirds of the way across the road, froze, then scuttled back.

'She was seeing someone, wasn't she?' Connie Seymour had said, voice parched with her own grief. 'Lorna. His wife, Lorna. Paul was terrified she was going to leave him, take his kids.'

No matter how many times he and Maureen had asked, Connie had failed to give them a name. 'He wouldn't tell me. Just wouldn't tell. Oh, he knew all right, Paul knew. But he wouldn't say. As if he was, you know, as if he was ashamed.'

Maureen had got Willie Bell sifting through the house-to-house reports already; tomorrow Matt Dowland and Salim Shukla would start knocking on doors again. For Karen Holbrook the task of contacting Lorna Atkin's family and friends. Elder would go back to the house and take Maureen with him.

Why? That's what you clever bastards are going to find out.

Joanne was in the bathroom when he got back, smoothing cream into her skin. When he touched her arm, she jumped.

'Your hands, they're like ice.'

'I'm sorry.'

The moment passed.

In bed, eyes closed, Elder listened to the fall of footsteps on the opposite side of the street, the window shifting uncertainly inside its frame. Joanne read for ten minutes before switching out the light.

*

They found a diary, letters, nothing of real use. In a box file shelved between two albums of photographs, Maureen turned up a mishmash of guarantees and customer instructions, invoices and bills.

'Mobile phones,' she called into the next room. 'We've had those checked.'

'Yes,' Elder said, walking through. 'He had some kind of BT cell phone leased by his work, she was with – who was it? – One to One.'

'Right.' Maureen held up a piece of paper. 'Well, it looks as if she might have had a second phone, separate account.'

'Think you can charm some details out of them, recent calls especially?'

'No. But I can impress on them the serious nature of the situation.'

*

'You sure you want to do this alone?' Maureen said.

They were parked in a lay-by on the road north from

153

the city, arable land to their left shading into a small copse of trees. Lapwings rose sharply in the middle distance, black and white like an Escher print.

'Yes. I think so.'

'You don't want . . . ?'

'No,' Elder said. 'I'll be fine.'

Maureen nodded and got back into her car and he stood there, watching her drive away, rehearsing his first words inside his head.

It was a square brick-built house in a street full of square brick-built houses, the front of this one covered in white pebbledash that had long since taken on several shades of grey. Once council, Elder assumed, now privately owned. A Vauxhall Astra parked outside. Roses in need of pruning. Patchy grass. Close against the kitchen window, a damson tree that looked as if it rarely yielded fruit.

He rattled the knocker and for good measure rang the bell.

No hesitation in the opening of the door, no delay.

'Hello, Gerry,' Elder said. 'Late shift?'

'You know,' Saxon said. 'You'd've checked.' And when Elder made no further remark, added, 'You'd best come in.'

It was tea or instant coffee and Elder didn't really want either, but he said tea would be fine, one sugar, and sat, mug cradled in both hands, in the middle of the cluttered living room while Saxon smoked and avoided looking him squarely in the eye.

'She phoned you, Gerry. Four days ago. The day before she was murdered. Phoned you when you were on duty. Twice.'

'She was upset, wasn't she? In a real state. Frightened.'

'Frightened?'

'He'd found out about us, seen us. The week before.'

Saxon shook his head. 'It was stupid, so fucking half-arsed stupid. All the times we . . . all the times we saw one another, we never took no chances. She'd come here, afternoons, or else we'd meet up miles away, Sheffield or Grantham, and then this one bloody Saturday she said let's go into Nottingham, look round the shops. He was supposed to be off taking the kids to Clumber Park and there we are coming out of the Broad Marsh Centre on to Lister Gate and they're smack in front of us, him with the little kid on his shoulders and the other one holding his hand.'

Saxon swallowed down some tea and lit another cigarette.

'Course, we tried to pass it off, but you could see he wasn't having any. Ordered her to go home with them there and then and of course when they did there was all merry hell to pay. Ended up with him asking her if she intended leaving him and her saying yes, first chance she got.' Saxon paused. 'You'll take the kids, he said, over my dead body.'

'She didn't leave?'

'No.'

'Nor try to?'

Saxon shook his head. 'He seemed to calm down after the first couple of days. Lorna, she thought he might be going to get over it. Thought, you know, if we lay low for a spell, things'd get back to normal, we could start up again.'

'But that's not what happened?' Elder said.

'What happened was, this idea of her taking the kids, he couldn't get it out of his head. Stupid, really. I mean, I could've told him, a right non-starter.' Saxon looked around. 'You imagine what it'd be like, two lads in here. Someone else's kids. Place is mess enough as it is. Anyway . . .' Leaning forward now, elbows on his knees. '. . . you know what it's like, the kind of life we lead. The hours and all the rest of it. How many couples you know, one or both of them in the force, children, how many d'you know make it work?'

Elder's tea was lukewarm, tannin thick in his mouth. 'The last time she phoned you, you said she was frightened. Had he threatened her or what?'

'No. I don't think so. Not in as many words. It was more him coming out with all this guff. Next time we're in the car I'll drive us all into the back of a lorry. Stuff like that.'

'And you didn't think to do anything?'

'Such as what?'

'Going round, trying to get him to talk, listen to reason; suggesting she take the boys away for a few days, grandparents, somewhere like that?'

'No,' Saxon said. 'I kept well out of it. Thought it best.'

'And now?'

'What do you mean, and now?'

'You still think it was for the best?'

The mug cracked across in Saxon's hand and tea spilled with blood towards the floor.

'Who the fuck?' he said, on his feet now, both men on their feet, Saxon on his feet and backing Elder towards the door. 'Who the fuck you think you are, coming in here like you're some judge and fucking jury, some tinpot fucking god. Think you're fucking perfect? That what you think, you pompous sack of shit? I mean, what the fuck are you here for anyway? You here to question me? Arrest me? What? There was some fucking crime here? I committed some fucking crime?'

He had Elder backed up against the wall, close alongside the door, the sweat off his skin so rank that Elder almost gagged.

'Crime, Gerry?' Elder said. 'How much d'you want?

Three murders, four deaths. Two boys, four and six. Not that you'll be losing much sleep over them. I mean, they were just a nuisance, an irrelevance. Someone to mess up this shit heap of a home.'

'Fuck you!' Saxon punched the wall, close by Elder's head.

'And Lorna, well, you probably think that's a shame, but let's face it, you'll soon find someone else's wife to fuck.'

'You bastard!' Saxon hissed. 'You miserable, sanctimonious bastard!'

But his hands fell back down to his sides and slowly he backed away and gazed down at the floor and when he did that, without hurrying, Elder let himself out of the house and walked towards his car.

*

He and Joanne were sitting at either end of the settee, Elder with a glass of Jameson in his hand, the bottle nearby on the floor; Joanne was drinking the white Rioja they had started with dinner. The remains of their take-away Chinese was on the table next door. Katherine had long since retreated to her room.

'What will happen?' Joanne asked. It was a while since either of them had spoken.

'To Saxon?'

'Um.'

'A bollocking from on high. Some kind of official reprimand. He might lose his stripes and get pushed into going round schools sweet-talking kids into being honest citizens.' Elder shook his head. 'Maybe nothing at all. I don't know. Except that it was all a bloody mess.'

He sighed and tipped a little more whiskey into his glass

and Joanne sipped at her wine. It was late but neither of them wanted to make the first move towards bed.

'Christ, Jo! Those people. Sometimes I wonder if everyone out there isn't doing it in secret. Fucking one another silly.'

He was looking at Joanne as he spoke and there was a moment, a second, in which he knew what she was going to say before she spoke.

'I've been seeing him again. Martyn. I'm sorry, Frank, I—'

'Seeing him?'

'Yes, I—'

'Sleeping with him?'

'Yes. Frank, I'm sorry, I—'

'How long?'

'Frank—'

'How long have you been seeing him?'

'Frank, please . . .'

Elder's whiskey spilled across the back of his hand, the tops of his thighs. 'How fucking long?'

'Oh, Frank . . . Frank . . .' Joanne in tears now, her breath uneven, her face wiped clear of colour. 'We never really stopped.'

Instead of hitting her, he hurled his glass against the wall.

'Tell me,' Elder said.

Joanne foraged for a tissue and dragged it across her face. 'He's . . . he's got a place . . . up here, in the Park. At first it was just, you know, the odd time, if we'd been working late, something special. I mean, Martyn, he wasn't usually here, he was down in London, but when . . . Oh, Frank, I wanted to tell you, I even thought you knew, I thought you must . . .'

She held out a hand and when Elder made no move to take it, let it fall.

'Frank . . .'

He moved quickly, up from the settee, and she flinched and turned her face away. She heard, not saw him leave the room, the house, the home.

It wasn't difficult to find out where Martyn Miles lived when he was in the city, a top-floor flat in a seventies apartment block off Tattershall Drive. Not difficult to slip the lock, even though stepping across the threshold set off the alarm. 'It's okay,' he explained to an anxious neighbour, 'I'll handle it. Police.' And showed his ID.

He had been half-hoping Miles would be there but he was not. Instead, he searched the place for signs of what? Joanne's presence? Tokens of love? In the built-in wardrobe, he recognised some of her clothes: a dove-grey suit, a blouse, a pair of high-heeled shoes; in the bathroom, a bottle of her perfume, a diaphragm.

Going back into the bedroom, he tore the covers from the bed, ripped at the sheets until they were little more than winding cloths, heaved the mattress to the floor and, yanking free the wooden slats on which it had rested, broke them, each and every one, against the wall, across his knee.

Back in the centre of the city, he booked into a hotel, paid over the odds for a bottle of Jameson and finally fell asleep, fully clothed, with the contents two-thirds gone. At work next day, he barked at anyone who as much as glanced in his direction. Maureen left a bottle of aspirin on his desk and steered well clear. When he got home that evening, Joanne had packed and gone. *Frank – I think we both need some time and space.* He tore the note into smaller and smaller pieces till they filtered through his hands.

Katherine was in her room and she turned off the stereo when he came in.

Holding her, kissing her hair the way he didn't think he'd done for years, his body shook.

'I love you, Kate,' he said.

Lifting her head she looked at him with a sad little smile. 'I know, but that doesn't matter, does it?'

'What do you mean? Of course it does.'

'No. It's Mum. You should have loved her more.'

*

Two weeks later, Joanne back home with Katherine, and Elder in a rented room, he knocked on the door of the Detective Superintendent's office, walked in and set his warrant card down on the desk, his letter of resignation alongside.

'Take your time, Frank,' the Superintendent said. 'Think it over.'

'I have,' Elder said.

SMILE

Soho, Manchester, Birmingham – why was it that Chinatown and the gay quarter were in such close proximity? Cantonese restaurants, pubs and bars, Ocean Travel, the Chang Ving Garden, City Tattooing, Clone Zone, the Amsterdam Experience Adults Only Shop and Cinema. Kiley turned down an alley alongside a shopfront hung liberally with wind-dried chickens and within moments he was lost amidst an uneven criss-cross of streets which seemed to lead nowhere except back into themselves. When he had stepped off the London train less than thirty minutes earlier and set off on the short walk down from New Street station, it had all seemed so simple. Instead of the dog-eared copy of *Farewell, My Lovely* he'd brought to read on the journey, a *Birmingham A–Z* would've been more useful.

Finding his way back onto Hurst Street, Kiley ducked into the first bar he found. He ordered a bottle of Kronenbourg 1664 and a glass from an Australian with cropped red hair and carried his drink over to a seat near

161

the window, where, taking his time over his beer, he could think again about what he was doing and watch the couples strolling by outside, holding hands.

When he went back to the bar, the barman greeted him as though they were old friends. 'Ready for another? Kronenbourg, right?'

Kiley shook his head. 'You know a place called Kicks?'

'Kicks? No, I don't think so. What kind of a place is it?'

'It's a club.'

'No, sorry.' The barman shook his head and two gold rings danced in the lobe of his left ear. 'Wait up, though, I'll ask.'

'Thanks.'

Inside a few minutes, he was back. 'You're in luck. Tina says it's off the underpass near the library. Paradise Circus. Some name, huh? Just take a right out of here and follow your nose.'

'Okay,' Kiley said. 'Thanks again.'

'Drop back later. I'll keep one cold for you.'

Kiley nodded and turned away, the limp in his right leg barely noticeable as he crossed towards the door.

The steps led down below several lanes of fast-moving traffic, the subway itself tiled and surprisingly clean, the muted stink of urine cut through with disinfectant and the smoky-sweet drift of petrol fumes. Discarded newspapers and fast-food wrapping clotted here and there in corners, but not so much.

He followed round the slow curve of the arcade, a faint, accented clip from his heels. Several small restaurants were open and as yet, largely empty; shopfronts were barred and shuttered across. Forty, fifty yards more and there it was facing him, the name in green neon over the top of a bright pink door. More fuchsia than mere pink. The door itself was closed, windows either side discreet with frosted glass. Posters gave some idea of what to expect inside, a smiling mostly naked woman spilling out of her leopard-skin bra, Mel B twinned with Lara Croft. Alongside the licensing details above the door was a sign: *'PLEASE NOTE THIS IS A GENTLE-MENS ONLY CLUB.'*

Kiley was surprised there wasn't a doorman outside, muscles threatening the seams of his rented suit. No bell to ring, he pushed at the centre of the door and it swung slowly back, inviting him into a pool of tinted violet light. A sharp-faced blonde greeted him from inside a kiosk to his right and treated him to a smile that would have had no trouble cutting glass.

'Good evening, sir. Are you a member?' And when Kiley shook his head, 'Membership fee is fifty pounds. That includes your first night's admission. We take Visa,' she added helpfully. 'American Express.'

Heavy velvet curtains shielded the interior of the club itself. The sounds of music, muffled, seventies disco but with a different beat.

'Suppose I just want to pay for tonight?'

'I'm afraid that's not possible.'

'Look, the thing is . . .' Kiley moving closer, trying on the charm. As well try to charm an anaconda. '. . . there's a girl, I think she works here. Adina.'

'We have no Adina.'

'I just wanted to check, you know. As long as she's working then—'

'We have no Adina.'

'I knew her, in London.'

But now she was looking past his shoulder, maybe she'd pressed some warning buzzer, Kiley didn't know, but when he turned there was his doorman, two of them in fact, the Lennox Lewis twins.

'Is there a problem here?'

'No, no problem.'

''Cause if there's a problem we can talk about it outside.' One spoke, the other didn't, his voice a soft mix of Caribbean and Brummie.

'He was asking about one of the girls,' said the blonde.

They moved towards him; Kiley stood his ground. 'Sir, please, why don't we just step outside?' Polite. Threateningly polite.

'Look,' Kiley said. 'Suppose I pay the membership fee and—?'

'I'm sorry, sir, I'm afraid membership's closed. Now if we can step outside.'

Kiley shrugged. The two men exchanged glances; the silent one pulled the door open and the talker escorted Kiley through.

Wind rattled an empty food tray along one side of the underpass. The man was taller than Kiley by three or four inches, heavier by some forty pounds.

'You not from round here.'

Kiley shook his head.

'In town for business?'

'Something like that.'

The man held out his hand. 'No hard feelings, huh? Why not try somewhere else?' His grip was swift and strong.

'Look,' Kiley said, stepping back. 'I wonder if you'd take a look at this?'

He had scarcely reached inside the lapel of his coat when a fist caught him low, beneath the heart. Before he could touch the ground with his knees, two hands seized him and swung him round. The brickwork alongside the club door closed on him fast. As he buckled and started to slide, another blow struck him in the kidneys and finally a punch to the side of the head. A pool of darkness opened at his feet and he dived into it – as Chandler might have said.

*

Kiley worked out of two rooms above a bookshop in Belsize Park, a chancy business with a good address. A little over a year now since Kate had rescued him from the lower depths of Upper Holloway and invited him, lock, stock and baggage, to her flat in Highbury Fields, thus enabling him, most weeks, to pay the quite exorbitant office rent.

'You do realise,' he'd said, the first or second evening after supper in her three-storey late-Victorian house, 'keeping that place going's not going to leave me much to contribute here.'

'Contribute?'

'You know, towards the electricity, gas, the council tax.'

'We'll think of something,' Kate had laughed, and poured the last of the white burgundy into her glass.

In the outer office were a filing cabinet, a computer with printer attached, a Rolodex, a telephone with answering machine and fax. Two mornings a week, Irena, the young Romanian who worked across the street at Café Pasta, did his secretarial work, updated his accounts. In Bucharest, she had been a high-school teacher with a good degree; here she fetched and carried through six long shifts, linguine con capesante, penne con salsiccia – black pepper, sir? Parmesan? – bottles of house red.

It had been earlier that month that Irena had mentioned her friend, Adina, for the first time.

'She wants to meet you.' Irena blushed. 'She thinks you are my lover.'

'I'm flattered.'

Irena was slender as a boy, slim-hipped and small-breasted, with deep brown eyes just a fraction too large and a mouth that was generous and wide. Her hair was cut short, close-cropped, severe enough in strong light for her scalp to show through.

'I tell her,' Irena said, 'of course, it is not true.'

'Of course.'

'You are making fun of me.'

'No, not at all. Well, yes, maybe a little.'

Irena returned his smile. 'This afternoon, when I finish my shift. She comes then.'

'Okay.'

What, Kiley wondered, was the Romanian for chalk and cheese? Adina was taller than Irena and more voluptuously built, raven hair falling past her shoulders to her middle back, lips a rich purply-red, eyeshadow a striking blue. She wore a slinky top, one size too small, tight jeans, high heels.

'Irena has told me much about you.'

'I'll bet.'

Irena blushed again.

It was warm enough for them to be sitting at one of the pavement tables outside the café where Irena worked.

'So,' Kiley said, 'you and Irena, you're from the same part of Romania?'

Adina tossed her head. 'No, not really. I am from Constanza. It is on the Black Sea coast. Irena came for one year to teach in our school.'

'She taught you? Irena?'

'Yes.' Adina laughed. 'She is much older than me. Did you not know?'

'Not so much,' Irena protested.

For a moment, Adina touched Kiley's arm with her own. 'I am only nineteen, what do you think?'

Kiley thought he would change the subject. He signalled to one of Irena's colleagues and ordered coffee for himself, mineral water for Irena, for Adina Coke with ice and lemon.

'So what are you doing in London?' Kiley asked, once Adina had offered them both a cigarette and lit her own.

'I am dancer.'

'A dancer?'

'Yes. Perhaps you do not believe?'

Kiley believed her, though he doubted it was Ballet Rambert. 'Where do you dance?'

'Club Maroc. It is on Finchley Road.'

'I have seen her,' Irena said. 'Pole dance. It is remarkable.'

'I'll bet.'

'I study for three weeks,' Adina said seriously.

'Pole dancing?'

'Of course. Table dancing also. I have diploma.'

Irena leaned forward, glass in both hands. 'Adina thinks I should take lessons, go and work with her.'

'Instead of this, of course. With me you can earn two hundred, two hundred fifty pounds one night. Here you are slave.'

'At least,' Irena said, 'I keep on my clothes.'

Adina poked out her tongue.

*

Kiley saw her again two weeks later, unannounced in his outer office, her hair tied back in a pony tail and her make-up smeared. 'Adina, what is it?'

She looked at him helplessly, suddenly awash with tears.

167

'Come through here; come and sit down.' Helping her first to the couch, he hurried to the bathroom he shared with the financial consultant upstairs.

'Here. Drink this.'

She sipped from the glass of water, then set it aside. Dabbed at her eyes.

'All right, now tell me; tell me what's wrong.'

It was enough to set her off again, and Kiley pressed several clean tissues into her hands, sat back in the chair opposite and waited for her to become calm.

After several moments, she blew her nose and reached inside her bag for a cigarette; while she fumbled with her lighter, Kiley fetched the saucer that served as an ashtray and placed it near her feet. An ambulance siren, sudden and shrill, broke through the steady churn of traffic passing outside.

'Coming to this country,' she began falteringly, 'it was not easy for me. I pay, I have to pay much money. A lot of money.'

'How much?'

'Five thousand pounds.'

'You had that much?'

'No, of course not. I pay it back now. That is why . . . why I work as I do. I pay, each week, as much as I can. And last night . . . last night the man who arrange for me to come here, he tell me I must give him more. Five thousand more. The same again. Or he will report me and I will be sent home.' Ash spilled from the end of her cigarette and she brushed it across her jeans. 'Since Ceauşescu, there has been much change in my country. My parents say, yes, this is better, we can do, say what we like. Travel if we want. But what I see, there is no work. No money. Not for me. For Irena, maybe, she has qualifications, degree. She can work there if she wish. But me . . . you think I

168

can dance in Bucharest, earn money, wear nice clothes, you think this?'

Kiley didn't know what he thought. He got to his feet and didn't know where to go. The light through the window was muted and pale, the sky a mottled grey.

'What if you refuse to pay?'

Adina laughed: there was no pleasure in the sound.

'One of the other girls did this. He cut her face. Oh, not himself. He told someone. Someone else.' Lightly, she touched one hand against her cheek. 'Either that or he will have me sent back home.' She stubbed out her cigarette. 'You know what will happen to me if I go back home? Where I will be? Standing beside the road from Bucharest to Sofia, waiting for some lorry driver to pull over and fuck me in his cab for the price of a meal and a pack of cigarettes.'

The room was suddenly airless and Kiley opened the window a crack and the sound of voices rolled in; early afternoon and people, some of them, were heading back to work after lunch. Others would be waiting for the first performance at the cinema up the street, going into the bookshop downstairs to browse and buy.

'This man, the one who says you owe him money, does he have a name?'

'Aldo. Aldo Fusco.'

'You want me to talk to him?'

'Oh, yes. Yes, please, if you will.'

'When are you meant to see him again?'

'I don't know. For certain, I mean. Sometimes he comes to the club, sometimes he sends message for me to meet him. Usually it is Soho, Berwick Street.' She placed the emphasis on the first syllable, sounded the middle letter. 'He has office above shop that sells jewellery.'

'You meet him there, his office?'

Adina shook her head. 'Coffee bar across the street.'

'If he contacts you, phone me,' Kiley said, giving her one of his cards. 'Let me know. Meantime, I'll do what I can.'

'Thank you. Thank you.' She caught his arm and kissed him hard, leaving what remained of her lipstick like a purple bruise beside his mouth.

There was little he could do but wait. Walking in and confronting Fusco direct, always assuming he could find him, would likely cause more trouble than it was worth. For Adina as well as for himself. So Kiley waited for the phone to ring, attended to other things. One morning, after meeting Kate for coffee in Maison Bertaux, he strolled up through Soho and located the shop in Berwick Street, costume jewellery in the window, the door leading to the upper floors firmly closed, several bells with no name attached. In a café a little way up the street, half a dozen men, leather-jacketed, dark-haired, sat around a table playing cards. When one of them chanced to look up and see Kiley through the glass, he held his stare till Kiley turned and walked away.

Two more days, three, then four. Irena came across from Café Pasta, concern clouding her eyes. 'I went to the club looking for Adina and they told me she didn't work there any more. That is all they would tell me. Her flat, the place she shared with two of the other girls, most of her clothes have gone too.'

'The girls, did they have any idea where she went?'

'No. All they knew, that man came to the club, the one she owed money to. The next thing she was packing her things into a bag, there was a car waiting downstairs.'

Irena sighed and closed her eyes and Kiley placed one hand on her shoulder and she lowered her head until it rested on his chest. 'It'll be okay,' he said quietly. 'Don't worry.' When he kissed the top of her head, he was amazed at the softness of her hair.

'Aldo fucking Fusco. Claims he's Italian. Sicilian even. It's all so much horse shit. His real name's Sali, Sali Mejdani. He's Albanian. From Tirana.'

Kiley had called his friend, Margaret, a solicitor who dealt with a lot of cases involving refugees, applications for asylum – 'Was there anybody in Immigration who might talk to him, off the record?' Which was why he and Barker were walking between Westminster Bridge and Vauxhall, tour boats slowly passing both ways along the river. Two fortyish men in topcoats, talking over old times.

'This girl,' Barker said. 'Adina? You think she'd give evidence? In court?'

Kiley shook his head.

Barker broke his stride to light another cigarette. 'They never do. Even if they say they will, when it comes down to it, they won't. Too frightened about what might happen. Getting deported back to whatever shithole it is they come from. So these people go on squeezing money out of them. The lucky ones, like your Adina, they work the clubs. For others, it's massage parlours, brothels. Twelve, fourteen hours a day; hundred, hundred and fifty cocks a week.'

'You haven't got enough,' Kiley said, 'without her, to have him arrested?'

'Sure. Every once in a while we do.' Barker released a plume of smoke out on to the air. 'He can afford a better solicitor, better barrister. We can never hold him. So we keep a watch, as much as we can, wait for him to slip up. A container ship stuffed full of asphyxiated bodies we can trace back to him direct. That would do the trick.'

'And he knows?'

'Fusco? That we're watching him? Oh, yes. And he loves it, makes him feel big. Important. A made guy.'

'If I want to talk to him, you've no quarrel?'

Barker shook his head. 'I'll come along. Ride shotgun. Margaret might not forgive me if I let you get hurt.'

They were playing blackjack, five of them. Fusco had just bought another card on eighteen and gone over the top. 'Fuck!' he said.

'Nice,' Barker said from the doorway, 'that you know your name.'

Three of the men round the table started to rise, but Fusco waved them back down. A couple by the wall drank their last mouthfuls of cappuccino and headed for the door. Barker and Kiley stood aside to let them past.

'Hey,' Fusco said, looking at Barker. 'You never give up.'

'You know a girl called Adina?' Kiley said. 'The Club Maroc.'

Fusco eased back into his chair, tilting it on to its rear legs. 'Sure, what of it?'

'She says she owes you money.'

'Not any more.'

Kiley moved closer. Behind him, someone came breezily through the café door, caught the eye of the woman behind the counter and stepped back out. 'You mean she paid you? What?'

Amusement played in Fusco's eyes. 'No, she didn't pay me. I sold her, that's what.'

'Sold her? What d'you mean, sold her? Where the fuck d'you think you are?'

The man nearest to Kiley was half out of his chair and Kiley levered him back down, hand tight against his neck.

Across the room Barker was thinking a little more back-up might've been nice.

'You are right,' Fusco said, 'she owe me money. Did not want to pay. I sell the debt.'

'You sold the debt?'

'Hey,' Fusco laughed. 'You hear pretty good.'

Kiley went for him then, fists raised, and there were two men quick to block his path, holding his arms till he shook them off.

'Jack,' Barker said, clear but not loud. 'Let's not.'

Slowly, Fusco lowered his chair back on to all four legs. He was still grinning his broad grin and Kiley wanted to tear it from his face.

'Jack,' Barker said again.

Kiley eased back.

'I tell you this because of your friend,' Fusco said, indicating Barker with a nod of the head. 'The one who took over the debt, he is called O'Hagan. He has a club in Birmingham. Kicks. You best hope she is working there. If not, get someone to drive you up and down the Hagley Road.' Scooping up the cards, he proceeded to shuffle and deal.

'The Hagley Road,' Barker said when they were back on the street. 'It's—'

'I know what it is.'

They set off south towards the Tube. 'You'll go? Brum?'

Kiley nodded. 'Yes.'

'Tread carefully.'

'You know this O'Hagan?'

'Not personally. But I could give you the name of someone who might.'

On the corner of Old Compton Street, Barker stopped and wrote a name inside the top of a cigarette pack, tore it off and pushed it into Kiley's hand. 'West Midlands Crime Squad. You can use my name.'

'Thanks.'

At the station they went their separate ways.

*

The last thing Kiley wanted, the last thing he wanted there and then, following the altercation outside Kicks, was several hours spent in A & E. Hailing a cab, he got the driver to take him to the nearest late-night chemist where he stocked up on plasters, bandages and antiseptic cream. When he asked for suggestions for a hotel, the cabbie took him to his sister-in-law's B & B on the Pershore Road, near Pebble Mill. Clean sheets, a pot of tea and a glass of Scotch, full breakfast in the morning and change from fifty pounds.

'You look like warmed-over shit,' Mackay said next day, drinking an early lunch in the anonymity of an All Bar One. Mackay, detective sergeant in the West Midlands Crime Squad, Birmingham by way of Aberdeen. Suit from Top Man, shirt and tie from Next.

Kiley thought they could skip the small talk and asked about O'Hagan instead.

Mackay laughed. A cheery sound. 'Casinos, that's his thing. Any kind of gambling. That club you got yourself thrown out of, as much for show as anything. Entertaining. When one of our lot had his retirement bash six months back, that's where it was. O'Hagan's treat. Sign of respect.' He laughed again. 'Not an official donor to the Police Benevolent Fund, you understand, but here and there he does his bit.'

'Widows and orphans.'

'That type of thing.'

174

'How about nineteen-year-olds from Romania?'

'He has his share.' Mackay drained his whisky glass and pushed it across a foot or so of polished pine. Kiley sought a refill at the bar, another coffee for himself.

'You're not drinking?' Mackay asked, eyebrow raised.

'How does he treat his girls?' Kiley asked.

'O'Hagan? Well enough, I'd suppose. So long as they stay in line.'

'And if not?'

Mackay tasted his Scotch, lit a cigarette. 'A wee bit of trouble with his enforcers once or twice. But that was gambling, debts not paid. The local lads sorted it as I recall.'

'These enforcers – a couple of big guys, black, look as if they could box.'

Mackay laughed again. 'Cyril and Claude. Brothers. Twins. And, aye, box is right. But they're straight enough, not the kind of enforcers I meant at all. Those bastards are still in the open-razor stage. Cyril and Claude, much more smooth.' He chuckled into his glass. 'Which one was it, I wonder, rearranged your face?'

'The talkative one.'

'That'd be Claude. He works out in a gym not far from here. You know, he's really not so bad a guy.' Finishing his drink, Mackay got to his feet. 'If you bump into him again, make sure you give him my best.'

Kiley watched Claude spar three rounds with a big-boned Yugoslav, work out on the heavy bag, waited while he towelled down. They sat on a bench off to one side of the main room, high on the scent of sweat and wintergreen, the small thunder of feet and fists about their ears.

'Sorry about last night,' Claude offered.

Kiley shook his head.

'Like, when I saw you reach inside your coat, I thought
. . . See, not so long back, me and Cyril we're escorting this
high-roller out of the club and he's offerin' money, all sorts,
to let him stay. We get him outside an' I think he's reachin'
for his wallet an' suddenly he's wavin' this gun . . .' Claude
grinned, almost sheepishly. 'I wasn't goin' to make that
mistake again.'

Kiley nodded to show he understood.

'This girl you looking for . . .'

'Adina.'

'Adina, yes, she there. Nice lookin', too. You and
she . . . ?'

'No.'

'Just lookin' out for her, somethin' like that.'

'Something like that.'

'Mr O'Hagan, he heard you was there, askin' for her.'
Claude frowned. 'I don't know. I think he had words with
her. Somethin' about stickin' by the rules. He don't like
no boyfriends, no one like that comin' round.'

'She's okay?'

'I reckon so.'

'I'd like to see her. Just, you know, to make sure. Make
sure she's all right. She has a friend in London, works for
me. Worried about her. I promised I'd check. If I could.'

Claude tapped his fists together lightly as he thought.
'Come by the club later, you can do that? But not so late,
you know? Around nine. Mr O'Hagan, no way he's there
then. Cyril or I, we meet you out front, take you in another
door. What d'you say?'

Kiley said thank you very much.

The dressing room was low-ceilinged and small, a brightly
lit mirror the length of one wall, make-up littered along
the shelf below. Clothes hung here and there from wire

hangers, were draped over the backs of chairs. The other girls were working, the sound of Gloria Gaynor distinct enough through the closed door. Adina sat on a folding chair, cardigan across her shoulders, spangles on her micro-skirt and skimpy top. Her carefully applied foundation and blusher didn't hide the bruise discolouring her cheek.

Gently, Kiley turned her face towards the light. Fear stalked her eyes.

'I slip,' she said hastily. 'Climbing down from the stage.'

'Nothing to do with O'Hagan, then,' Kiley said.

She flinched at the sound of his name.

Kiley leaned towards her, held her hand. 'Adina, look, I think if you came with me now, walked out of here, with me, it would be all right.'

'No, no, I—'

'Come back down to London, maybe you could stay with Irena for a bit. She might even be able to wangle you a job. Or some kind of course, college. Then you could apply for a visa. A student visa.'

'No, it is not possible.' She pulled herself free from his hand and turned aside. 'I must . . . I must stay here. Pay what I owe.'

'But you don't—'

'Yes. Yes, I do. You don't understand.'

'Adina, listen, please . . .'

Slowly, she turned back to face him. 'I can earn much money here, I think. In a year maybe, debt will be no more. What I have to do: remember rules, be respectful. Remember what I learn for my diploma. Which moves. And my hands, always look after my hands. This is impor-tant. A manicure. When you dance at table, be good listener. Smile. Always smile. Make eye contact with the guests. Look them in the eye. Look at the bridge of the nose, right between the eyes. And smile.'

Tears were tracing slowly down her cheeks and around the edges of her chin, running down her neck, falling onto bare thighs.

'Please,' she said. 'Please, you must go now. Please.'

'I Will Survive' had long finished, to be replaced by something Kiley failed to recognise.

He took one of his cards from his wallet and set it down.

'Call,' he said. 'Either Irena or myself. Call.'

Adina smiled and reached for some tissues to wipe her face. Another fifteen minutes and she was due on stage. The Basic Spin. The Lick and Flick. The Nipple Squeeze. The Bump and Grind. And smile. Always smile.

*

In the following months, Adina phoned Irena twice; both calls were fragmentary and short, she seemed to have been speaking on someone else's mobile phone. Sure, everything was okay, fine. Lots of love. Then, when Kiley arrived one morning at his office, there was a message from Claude on his answerphone. Adina had quit the club, something to do with complaints from a customer, Claude wasn't sure; he had no idea where she'd gone.

Nothing for another three months, then a card to Irena, posted in Bucharest.

Dear Irena, I hope you remember me. As you can see, I am back in our country now, but hope soon to return to UK. Pray for me. Love, Adina.
PS A kiss for Jack.

It is cold and trade on the autoroute north towards Budapest is slow. Adina pulls her fake fur jacket tighter across her chest and lights another cigarette. The seam of her denim shorts sticks uncomfortably into the crack of her behind, but at least her boots cover her legs above the knee. Her forearms and thighs are shadowed with the marks of bruises, old and new. An articulated lorry, hauling aggregate towards Oradea, slows out of the road's curve and approaches the makeshift lay-by where she has stationed herself. The driver, bearded, tattoos on his arms, leans down from his cab to give her the once-over, and Adina steps towards him. Smile, she tells herself, smile.

CHANCE

The second or third time Kiley went out with Kate Keenan, it had been to the theatre, an opening at the Royal Court. Her idea. A journalist with a column in the *Independent* and a wide brief, she was on most people's B list at least.

The play was set in a Brick Lane squat, two shiftless young men and a meant-to-be fifteen-year-old girl: razors, belt buckles, crack cocaine. Simulated sex and pain. One of the men seemed to be under the illusion, much of the time, that he was a dog. At the interval, they elbowed their way to the bar through louche suits and little black dresses with tasteful cleavage, New Labour voters to the core. 'Challenging,' said a voice on Kiley's left. 'A bit full on,' said another. 'But relevant. Absolutely relevant.'

'So what do you think?' Kate asked.

'I think I'll meet you outside later.'

'What do you mean?'

She knew what he meant.

They took the Tube, barely talking, to Highbury and

180

Islington, a stone's throw from where Kate lived. Across the road, she turned towards him, a hand upon his arm.

'I don't think this is going to work out, do you?'

Kiley shrugged and thought probably not.

Between Highbury Corner and the Archway, almost the entire length of the Holloway Road, there were only three fights in progress, one between two women in slit skirts and halter tops, who clawed and swore at each other, rolling on the broad pavement outside the Rocket while a crowd bayed them on. Propped inside a telephone box close by the railway bridge, a man stared out frozen-eyed, a hypodermic needle sticking out of the scabbed flesh of his bare leg. Who needs theatre, Kiley asked himself?

*

His evenings free, Kiley was at liberty to take his usual seat in the Lord Nelson, a couple of pints of Marston's Pedigree before closing, then a slow stroll home through the back-doubles to his second-floor flat in a shabby terraced house amongst other shabby houses, too far from a decent primary school for the upwardly mobile middle-class professionals to have appropriated in any numbers.

Days, he sat and waited for the telephone to ring, the fax machine to chatter into life; the floor was dotted with books he'd started to read and would never finish, pages from yesterday's paper were spread out haphazardly across the table. Afternoons, if he wasn't watching a film at the local Odeon, he'd follow the racing on TV – Kempton, Doncaster, Haydock Park. '*Investigations*', read the ad in the local press, '*Private and Confidential. All kinds of security work undertaken. Ex-Metropolitan Police.*' Kiley was never certain whether that last put off as many potential clients as it impressed.

Seven years in the Met, two seasons in professional soccer and then freelance: Kiley's CV so far.

The last paid work he'd done had been for Adrian Costain, a sports agent and PR consultant Kiley knew from one of his earlier lives. Kiley's task: babysitting an irascible yet charming American movie actor in London on a brief promotional visit. After several years of mayhem and marriages to Meg or Jennifer or Julia, he was rebuilding his career as a serious performer with a yearning to play Chekhov or Shakespeare.

'For Christ's sake,' Costain had said, 'keep him away from the cocaine and out of the tabloids.'

It was fine until the last evening, a celebrity binge at a members-only watering hole in Soho. What exactly went down in the small men's toilet between the second and third floors was difficult to ascertain, but the resulting black eye and bloodied lip were front-page juice to every picture editor between Wapping and Faringdon. Today the UK, tomorrow the world.

Costain was incandescent.

'What did you expect me to do?' Kiley asked. 'Go in there and hold his dick?'

'If necessary, yes.'

'You're not paying me enough, Adrian.'

He thought it would be a while before Costain put work his way again.

He put through a call to Margaret Hamblin, a solicitor in Kentish Town for whom he sometimes did a little investigating, either straining his eyes at the local land registry or long hours hunkered down behind the wheel of his car, waiting for evidence of some small near-lethal indiscretion.

But Margaret was in court and her secretary dismissed him with a cold promise to tell her he'd called. The connection was broken almost before the words were out of her mouth. Kiley pulled on his coat and went out on to the street; for early December it was almost mild, the sky opaque and indecipherable. There was a route he took when he wanted to put some distance beneath his feet: north up Highgate Hill, past the spot where Dick Whittington was supposed to have turned again, and through Waterlow Park, down alongside the cemetery and into the Heath, striking out past the ponds to Kenwood House, a loop then that took him round the side of Parliament Hill and down towards the tennis courts, the streets that would eventually bring him home.

Tommy Duggan was waiting for him, sitting on the low wall outside the house, checking off winners in the *Racing Post*.

'How are you, Tommy?'

'Pretty fine.'

Duggan, deceptively slight and sandy-haired, had been one of the best midfielders Kiley had ever encountered in his footballing days, Kiley on his way up through the semi-pro ranks when Duggan was slipping down. During Kiley's brace of years with Charlton Athletic, Duggan had come and gone within the space of two months. Bought in and sold on.

'Still like a flutter,' Kiley said, eyeing the paper at Duggan's side.

'Academic interest only nowadays,' Duggan smiled. 'Isn't that what they say?'

The addictions of some soccer players are well documented, the addiction and the cure. Paul Merson. Tony Adams. Stories of others running wild claim their moment in the news then fade. But any manager worth his salt will know the peccadilloes of those he might sign: drugs, drink, gambling, having at least one of his teammates watch as he snorts a line of cocaine from between the buttocks of a four-hundred-pounds-an-hour whore. You look at your need, your place in the table, assess the talent, weigh up the risk.

When Tommy Duggan came to Charlton he was several

thousand in debt to three different bookmakers and spent more time with his cell phone than he did on the training ground. Rumour had it, his share of his signing-on fee was lost on the back of a spavined three-year-old almost before the ink had dried on the page.

Duggan went and Kiley stayed: but not for long.

'Come on inside,' Kiley said.

Duggan shrugged off his leather coat and chose the one easy chair.

'Tea?'

'Thanks, two sugars, aye.'

What the hell, Kiley was wondering, does Tommy Duggan want with me?

'You're not playing any more, Tom?' Kiley asked, coming back into the room.

'What do you think?'

Watching Sky Sport in the pub, Kiley had sometimes glimpsed Duggan's face, jostling for space amongst the other pundits ranged across the screen.

'I had a season with Margate,' Duggan said. 'After I come back this last time from the States. Bastard'd shove me on for the last twenty minutes – "Get amongst 'em, Tommy, work the magic. Turn it round."' Duggan laughed. 'Every time the ball ran near, there'd be some donkey anxious to kick the fuck out of me. All I could do to stay on my feet, never mind turn bloody round.'

He drank some tea.

'Nearest I get to a game nowadays is coaching a bunch of kids over Whittington Park. Couple of evenings a week. That's what I come round to see you about. Thought you might like to lend a hand. Close an' all.'

'Coaching?'

'Why not? More than a dozen of them now. More than I can handle.'

'How old?'

'Thirteen, fourteen. Best of them play in this local league. Six-a-side. What d'you think? 'Less your evenings are all spoken for, of course.'

Kiley shook his head. 'Can't remember the last time I kicked a ball.'

'It'll come back to you,' Duggan said. 'Like falling off a bike.'

Kiley wasn't sure if that was what he meant or not.

*

There were eleven of them the first evening Kiley went along, all shapes and sizes. Two sets of dreadlocks and one turban. One of the black kids, round-faced, slightly pudgy in her Arsenal strip, was a girl. Esther.

'I ain't no mascot, you know,' she said, after Duggan had introduced them. 'I can run rings round this lot.'

'My dad says he saw you play once,' said a lad whose mum had ironed his David Beckham shirt straight from the wash. 'He says you were crap.'

'Your dad'd know crap right enough, wouldn't he, Dean,' Duggan said. 'Living with you.'

The rest laughed and Dean said, 'Fuck off,' but he was careful to say it under his breath.

'Okay, let's get started,' Tommy Duggan said. 'Let's get warmed up.'

After a few stretching exercises and a couple of circuits of the pitch, Duggan split them up into twos and threes practising basic ball skills, himself and Kiley moving between them, watching, offering advice.

No more than twenty minutes or so of that and their faces were bright with sweat under the floodlights.

'Now,' Duggan said, 'let's do a little work on corners,

attacking, defending, staying alert. Jack, why don't you send a few over, give us the benefit of that sweet right foot.'

Kiley was sweating like the rest, feeling his forty years. Either his tracksuit had shrunk or he'd put on more weight than he'd thought. The first corner was struck too hard and sailed over everyone's heads, but after that he settled into something of a rhythm and was almost disappointed when Duggan called everyone together and divided them into teams.

Like most youngsters they had a tendency to get drawn out of position and follow the ball, but some of the passing was thoughtful and neat and only luck and some zealous defending prevented a hatful of goals. Dean, in his Beckham shirt, hand forever aloft demanding the ball, was clearly the most gifted but also the most likely to kick out in temper, complain loudly if he thought he'd been fouled.

When he slid a pass through for Esther to run on to and score with a resounding drive, the best he could muster was, 'Jammy cow!'

Game over, kids beginning to drift away, Duggan offered to buy Kiley a pint. There was a pub on the edge of the park that Kiley had not been into before.

'So what did you think?' Duggan asked. They were at a table near the open door.

'About what?'

'This evening, you enjoy it or what?'

'Yeah, it was okay. They're nice enough kids.'

'Most of them.'

Kiley nodded. The muscles in the backs of his legs were already beginning to ache.

'You'll come again then?'

'Why not? Not as if my social calendar's exactly full.'

'No girlfriend?'

'Not just at present.'

'But there was one?'

186

'For a while, maybe.'

'What happened?'

Kiley shrugged and supped his beer. 'You?' he said.

Duggan lit a cigarette. 'The only women I meet are out for a good time and all they can get. Either that or else they've got three kids back home with the babysitter and they're looking for someone to play dad.'

'And you don't fancy that?'

'Would you?'

Kiley wasn't certain; there were days – not so many of them – when he thought he might. 'No,' he said.

Without waiting to be asked, Duggan fetched two more pints. 'Where d'you meet her anyway?' he said. 'This ex of yours.'

'I was working,' Kiley said. 'Security. Down on the South Bank. She'd just come out from this Iranian movie.'

'She's Iranian?'

'No. The film was Iranian. She's English. Kate. Kate Keenan.'

'Sounds Irish.'

'Maybe. A generation or so back maybe.'

'You're cut up about it,' Duggan said.

'Not really.'

'No, of course not,' Duggan said, grinning. 'You can tell.'

*

Kate's column in the *Indy* questioned the morality of making art out of underclass deprivation and serving it up as a spectacle for audiences affluent enough to afford dinner and the theatre and then a taxi home to their three-quarters-of-a-million-plus houses in fashionable Islington and Notting Hill.

Under Duggan's watchful eye and with Kiley's help, the six-a-side team won their next two games, Dean being sent off in the second for kicking out at an opponent in retaliation and then swearing at the referee.

Margaret Hamblin offered Kiley three days' work checking up on a client who had been charged with benefit fraud over a period in excess of two years.

'Come round my gaff, why don't you?' Tommy Duggan said one night after training. 'See how the other half lives.' And winked.

Drained by two lots of child support, which he paid intermittently but whenever he could, Duggan had sold his detached house in Totteridge and bought a thirties semi in East Finchley, half of which he rented out to an accountant struggling with his MBA.

In the main room there were framed photographs of Duggan's glory days on the walls and soiled grey carpet on the floor. Clothes lay across the backs of chairs, waiting to be washed or ironed. On a table near the window were a well-thumbed form book, the racing pages, several cheap ballpoints, a telephone.

'Academic?' said Kiley, questioningly.

Duggan grinned. 'Man's got to have a hobby.'

He took Kiley to a Hungarian restaurant on the high street where they had cherry soup and goulash spiced with smoked paprika. A bottle of wine.

'Good, uh?' Duggan said, pushing away his plate.

'Great,' Kiley said. 'What's the pitch?'

Duggan smiled with his eyes. 'Just a small favour.'

*

The casino was on a narrow street between Soho and Shaftesbury Avenue, passing trade not one of its concerns. Instead of a bouncer with overfed muscles, Kiley was greeted at the door by a silvered blonde in a tailored two-piece.

'I'm here to see Mr Stephen.'

'Certainly, sir. If you'll come this way.' Her slight accent was Scandinavian.

Mr Stephen's name wasn't really Stephen. Not originally, at least. He had come to England from Malta in the late fifties when the East End gangsters were starting to lose their grip on gambling and prostitution up West; had stood his ground and received the razor scars to prove it, though these had since been surgically removed. Now gambling was legal and he was a respectable businessman. Let the Albanians and the Turks fight the Yardies over heroin and crack cocaine, he had earned his share portfolio, his place in the sun.

The blonde handed Kiley over to a brunette who led him to a small lift at the far side of the main gaming room. There was no background music, no voice raised above the faint whirring of roulette wheels, the hushed sounds of money being made and lost.

Kiley was glad he'd decided to wear his suit, not just his suit but his suit and tie.

'Have you visited our casino before?' the brunette asked him.

'I'm afraid not, no.'

One of her eyes was brown and the other a greyish green.

When he stepped out of the lift there was an X-ray machine, the kind you walk through in airports; Kiley handed the brunette his keys and small change and she gave them back to him at the other side.

'Mr Kiley for Mr Stephen,' she said to the man at the end of the short corridor.

The man barely nodded; doors were opened and closed. Stephen's inner sanctum was lined with books on two sides, mostly leather bound; screens along one wall afforded high-angle views of the casino's interior. Stephen himself sat behind a desk, compact, his face the colour of walnut, bald head shining as if he had been recently buffed.

A few days before, Kiley had spoken to one of his contacts at Scotland Yard, a sergeant when he and Kiley had served together, now a detective superintendent.

'The casino's a front,' the superintendent told him. 'Prestige. He doesn't lose money on it exactly, but with all those overheads, that area, he'd make more selling the site. It's the betting shops that fetch in the money, one hundred and twenty nationwide. That and the fact he keeps a tight ship.'

'Can you get me in to see him?' Kiley had asked.

'Probably. But nothing more. We've no leverage, Jack, I'm sorry.'

Now Kiley waited for Stephen to acknowledge him, which he did with a small gesture of a manicured hand, no suggestion that Kiley should take a seat.

'Tommy Duggan,' Kiley said. 'He owes you money. Not a lot in your terms, maybe, but . . .' Kiley stopped and waited then went on. 'He says he's been threatened. Not that you'd know about that directly, not your concern, but I imagine if you wanted you could get it stopped.'

Stephen looked at him through eyes that had seen more than Kiley, far more, and survived.

'Do you follow soccer at all, Mr Stephen?' Kiley asked. No response.

'With some players it's speed, with others it's power, sheer force. Then there are those who can put their foot on the ball, look up and in that second see the perfect pass and have the skill to make it, inch perfect, thirty, forty yards crossfield.'

Something moved behind the older man's eyes. 'Liam Brady,' he said. 'Rodney Marsh.'

'Right,' said Kiley. 'Hoddle. Le Tissier. Tommy, too. On his day Tommy was that good.'

Stephen held Kiley's gaze for a moment longer, then slipped his wristwatch free and placed it on the desk between them. 'Your Tommy Duggan, he owes close to one hundred thousand pounds. Each time the hands of that watch move round, he owes more.' He picked up the watch and weighed it in the palm of his hand. 'You tell him if he makes payments, regular, if the debt does not increase, I will be patient. Bide my time. But if he loses more . . .'

'I'll tell him,' Kiley said.

Stephen set the watch back on his wrist. 'Do you gamble, Mr Kiley?'

Kiley shook his head.

'In gambling, there is only one winner. In the end.'

'Thanks for your time,' Kiley said.

Almost imperceptibly Stephen nodded and his eyes returned their focus to the screens on the wall.

'Good evening, sir,' said the brunette in the lift; 'Good evening, sir,' said the blonde. 'Be sure to come again.'

'Jack, you're a prince,' Duggan said, when Kiley recounted the conversation.

Kiley wasn't certain what, if anything, he'd achieved.

'Room for manoeuvre, that's what you've got me. Pressure off. Time to recoup, study the field.' He smiled. 'Don't worry, Jack. Nothing rash.'

There was a message from Kate on his answerphone. 'Perhaps I was a little hasty. How about a drink, Wednesday evening?'

Wednesday was soccer training. Kiley called back and made it Thursday. The wine bar at Highbury Corner was only a short walk from Kate's house; from there it was only two flights of stairs to her bed.

'Something on your mind, Jack?'

There was and then there wasn't. Only later, his head resting in the cleft between Kate's bare calf and thigh, did it come back to him.

'He'll carry on gambling, won't he?' Kate said, when she had finished listening.

'Probably.'

'It's an illness, Jack, a disease. If he won't get proper help, professional help, there's nothing you can do.'

He turned over and she stroked his back and when he closed his eyes he was almost immediately asleep. In a short while she would wake him and send him home, but for now she was comfortable, replete. Maybe, she was thinking, it was time for another piece on gambling in her column.

*

Duggan had returned from his second spell in the States with a fondness for Old Crow over ice and country music, bluegrass and pedal steel and tales of love gone wrong. Nothing flash, no rhinestones, the real thing.

Back in England he toned down his new-found love of bourbon but still listened to the music whenever he could. In a music store off Upper Street, less than a week ago, he'd picked up a CD by Townes Van Zandt, *A Far Cry from Dead*.

> *Sometimes I don't know where this dirty road is*
> *   taking me*
> *Sometimes I can't even see the reason why*
> *I guess I'll keep on gamblin', lots of booze and*
> *   lots of ramblin'*
> *It's easier than just a-waitin' round to die*

Chance
===

Playing it was like pushing your tongue against an abscessed tooth.

He had seen Van Zandt in London in '97, one of the last gigs he ever played. Standing sweating in the Borderline, a crowded little basement club off Charing Cross Road, he had watched as Van Zandt, pale and thin and shaking, had begun song after song only to stop, mid-verse, forgetting the words, hearing another tune. His fingers failed to grip the neck of the guitar, he could scarcely balance on the stool. Embarrassed, upset, voices in the crowd began to call out, telling him to take a break, rest, telling him it was okay, but still he stumbled on. Dying before their eyes.

Two days before buying the CD, Duggan had placed the first instalment of his payback money on a four-horse accumulator and, on the small betting-shop screen, watched the favourite come through on the inside in the final race and leave his horse stranded short of the line.

Flicking the remote, he played the song again.

The money from the recording, some of it at least, would go to Van Zandt's widow and their kids. Duggan hadn't seen either his daughter or his two sons in years; he didn't even know where one of the boys was.

There were some cans of lager in the fridge, the tail end of a bottle of Scotch; when he'd finished those he put on his coat and followed the familiar path to the Bald-Faced Stag.

Ten minutes short of closing, a motorbike pulled up outside the pub. Without removing his helmet, the pillion rider jumped off and went inside. Duggan was standing at the bar, drink in hand, staring up aimlessly at the TV. The pillion rider pulled an automatic pistol from inside his

193

leather jacket, shot Duggan twice in the head at close range, and left.

Duggan was dead before he hit the floor.

*

Several evenings later, Kiley called the kids around him behind one of the goals. In the yellowing light, their breath floated grey and clear. He talked to them about Tommy Duggan, about the times he had seen him play; he told them how much Duggan wanted them to do well. One or two had tears in their eyes, others scuffed their feet in the ground and looked away.

'Who cares?' Dean said when Kiley had finished. 'He was never any bloody good anyway.'

Without deliberation, without meaning to, Kiley hit him: an open-handed slap across the face which jolted the boy's head back and round.

'You bastard! You fuckin' bastard!'

There were tears on his face now and the marks left by Kiley's hand stood out livid on his cheek.

'I'm sorry,' Kiley said. Some part of him felt numb, shocked by what he'd done.

'Fuck you!' the boy said and turned on his heel for home.

Dean lived in one of the flats that bordered Wedmore Street, close by the park. The man who answered the door was wearing jeans and a fraying Motorhead T-shirt and didn't look too happy to be pulled away from whatever was playing, over-loud, on the TV.

'I'm Jack Kiley,' Kiley said.

'You hit my boy.'

'Yes.'

'You've got some balls, showing up round here.'
'I wanted to explain, apologise.'
'He says you just laced into him, no reason.'
'There was a reason.'
'Dean,' the man called back over his shoulder, 'turn that fuckin' thing down.' And then, 'All right then, let's hear it.'
Kiley told him.
The man sighed and shook his head. 'That mouth of his, I'm always telling him it's going to get him into trouble.'
'I should never have lost my temper. I shouldn't have hit him.'
'My responsibility, right?' Dean's father said. 'Down to me.'
Kiley said nothing.
'What you did, maybe knock a bit of sense into him.'
'Maybe,' Kiley said, unconvinced.
'There's nothing else?'
'No.' Kiley took a step away.
'Tommy Duggan, what happened to him. It was wrong.'
'Yes.'
'Now that he's, you know, you think you might take over the team, the coaching?'
'For a bit, maybe,' Kiley said. 'It was Tommy's thing really, not mine.'
'Yeah. Yeah, that's right, I suppose.'
The door closed and Kiley took the stairs two at a time.

*

When he phoned Kate, she began by putting him off, a piece to finish, an early start, but then, hearing something in his voice, she changed her mind.
'Come round.'

The first glass of wine she poured, Kiley finished almost before she had started hers.

'If you just wanted to get drunk you could have done that on your own.'

'That's not what I wanted.'

He leaned against her and she held him, her breath warm on the back of his neck.

'I'm sorry about your friend,' she said.

'It's a waste.'

'It always is.'

After a while, Kiley said, 'I keep thinking there was something more I could've done.'

'It was his life. His choice. You did what you could.'

It was quiet. Often at Kate's there would be music playing but not this evening. From the hiss of tyres on the road outside it had started to rain. At the next coaching session, Kiley thought, he would apologise to Dean again in front of everyone, see if he couldn't get the lad to acknowledge what he'd said was wrong: start off on a new footing, give themselves a chance.

WELL, YOU NEEDN'T

November the third, '94, and it was Resnick's birthday. He just wasn't saying which one. Two days more and he would have been celebrating alongside scores of others, fireworks and bonfires, the burns unit at Queen's Medical on full alert and the Fire Service stretched to near breaking. As it was, he treated himself to a rare cooked breakfast, eggs and ham and some leftover potatoes fried to the point of crispness, two mugs of coffee instead of the usual one. The cats hovered around his feet, hoping for titbits of rind.

Outside, it was as cold as Margaret Thatcher's heart.

Ten years since she had broken the miners; broken them with the help, if not of Resnick himself then men like him. Her Majesty's Constabulary. Even now, Resnick shrivelled at the thought.

He had a pal, Peter Waites, who had stood shoulder to shoulder on the picket line until he was clubbed to the ground. Still lived in the same two-up, two-down Coal Board house in Arkwright Town. Ten years on the dole.

When his son, Jack, had joined the force as a young PC, Peter Waites had buckled with the shame.

'It's not coppers as is the enemy,' Jack had said. 'They're just takin' orders, same as everyone else.'

Waites had stared away, remembering the clash and clatter of horses' hoofs on cobbled streets, the flare of pain as the truncheon struck his shoulder blade, chipping bone.

Now his lad was attached to CID and stationed at Canning Circus under Resnick's command.

'Congratulations in order, I hear,' Millington said, greeting Resnick at the top of the stairs. 'Another year closer to retirement.' A smile hovered furtively beneath the edges of his moustache. 'Be drinks all round tonight, I dare say. Bit of a celebration.'

Resnick grunted and carried on past: inside his office he firmly closed the door. When it opened again, some forty minutes later, it was Jack Waites, notebook in hand.

'Come in, lad,' Resnick said. 'Take a seat.'

Waites preferred to stand.

'How's your dad?

'Bitter. Bloody-minded. Same as bloody ever.' The young man had held his gaze.

'What can I do for you?' Resnick asked.

'That break-in at the Green Man. Looks like it was Shotter right enough. Prints all over window frame in back.'

Resnick sighed. Three nights before, someone had broken into the rear of a pub off the Alfreton Road and made off with a small haul of spirits and cigarettes, the petty cash from the till.

Like Jack Waites' father, Barrie Shotter's life had been shattered by the Miners' Strike: in common with many in the Nottinghamshire pits, he had ignored the strike call

198

and continued to report for work. The windows of his house were smashed. 'SCAB' in foot-high paint on his walls and scratched into his front door. Wife and kiddies jostled in the streets. One morning a group of flying pickets overturned his car; stones were thrown and a sliver of glass spooned out his right eye like the yolk of a boiled egg, neat and entire.

For months he sat in a darkened room and drank: drank away the rent money and the furniture and what little bit they'd saved. When his wife borrowed the bus fare and took the kids back to her mum's in Derby, he tried to hang himself but failed. Took to thieving instead. He was already on probation following his last offence: prison this time, without fail.

Waites was eager to pick him up, make an arrest.

'Later,' Resnick said wearily. 'Later. He's not going anywhere.'

That morning Resnick had a meeting scheduled with the Assistant Chief Constable, himself and a dozen other officers of similar rank – strategy, long-term goals, deference and long words. On the way back he dropped into a record shop on one of the arcades between Upper Parliament Street and Angel Row. Mostly CDs now, of course, but still some racks of vinyl, second-hand. A double album with a slightly dog-eared cover caught his eye: *Thelonious Monk Live at the Jazz Workshop*. The titles were mostly tunes he recognised. 'Round Midnight'. 'Misterioso'. 'Blue Monk'. Recorded in San Francisco over two nights in 1964. November third and fourth. Resnick smiled and reached for his wallet: what better gift?

Barrie Shotter lived in the Meadows, a terraced house not so far from the recreation ground. Jack Waites and two other officers had presented the warrant at the door, Resnick

199

hanging back. Now while they searched the upstairs, cock-a-hoop over finding bottles of vodka and Scotch, Bensons king size by the score, Resnick sat across from Shotter in the small kitchen, neither man speaking, the kettle boiling away behind them, ignored.

There were pictures of Shotter's children, three boys and a girl, all under ten, thumbtacked to the cupboard by the stove. Spotted now and splashed with grease.

Resnick made tea while his men made an inventory.

Shotter mumbled thanks, stirred in two spoons of sugar and then a third.

'You're a daft bugger, Barrie,' Resnick said.

'Tell me something I don't know,' Shotter said.

They took him away and double-locked the door.

There was a wedge of bread pudding waiting on his desk with a candle sticking out of it, Millington's idea of a joke. He stood the troops a couple of rounds in the pub across the street, put fifty pounds behind the bar and left them to it.

At home he fed the cats then made himself a sandwich, toasted cheese. A shot of whisky in a water glass. His birthday present to himself was on the stereo. A jinking upturned phrase from Monk's piano, the same repeated twice, three times, before the advent of bass and drums and then the saxophone. 'Well You Needn't', November third.

Resnick leaned back in the chair to listen and when the smallest of the cats jumped up on to his lap he let it stay.

HOME

Resnick was unable to sleep. All those years of living alone, just the weight of the cats, one and occasionally more, pressing lightly down on the covers by his feet or in the V behind his legs, and now, with Lynn away for just forty-eight hours, he was lost without her by his side. The warmth of her body next to his, the small collisions as they turned from their respective dreams into a splay of legs, her arm sliding across his chest. 'Lay still, Charlie. Another five minutes, okay?' Musk of her early-morning breath.

He pushed away the sheet and swivelled round, then rose to his feet. Through an inch of open window, he could hear the slight swish of cars along the Woodborough Road. Not so many minutes short of two a.m.

Downstairs, Dizzy, the oldest of the four cats, a warrior no longer, raised his head from the fruit bowl he had long since appropriated as a bed, cocked a chewed and half-torn ear and regarded Resnick with a yellow eye.

Padding past, Resnick set the kettle to boil and slid a

tin of coffee beans from the fridge. A flier announcing Lynn's course was pinned to the cork board on the wall – *'Unzipping the Agenda: A Guide to Creative Management and Open Thinking'*. Lynn and forty or so other officers from the East Midlands and East Anglia at a conference centre and hotel beside the A1 outside Stevenage. Promotion material. High fliers. When she had joined the Serious Crime Unit a little more than two years ago, it has been as a sergeant; an inspector now and barely thirty, unless somehow she blotted her copybook, the only way was up. Whereas for Resnick, who had turned down promotion and the chance to move on to a bigger stage, little more than a pension awaited once his years were in.

While the coffee dripped slowly through its filter, Resnick opened the back door into the garden and, as he did so, another of the cats slithered past his ankles. Beyond the allotments, the lights of the city burned dully through a haze of rain and mist. Down there, on the streets of St Ann's and the Meadows, armed officers patrolled with Walther P990s holstered at their hips. Drugs, of course, the cause of most of it, the cause and the core: all the way from after-dinner cocaine served at trendy middle-class dinner parties alongside squares of Green and Black's dark organic chocolate, to twenty-five-pound wraps of brown changing hands in the stairwells of dilapidated blocks of flats.

Bolting the door, he carried his coffee through into the living room, switched on the light and slid a CD into the stereo. *Art Pepper Meets the Rhythm Section*, Los Angeles, nineteenth January 1957. Pepper only months out of jail on drugs offences, his second term and still only thirty-two. And worse to come.

Resnick had seen him play in Leicester on the British leg

of his European tour; Pepper older, wiser, allegedly straightened out, soon to be dead three years shy of sixty, a small miracle that he survived that long. That evening, in the function room of a nondescript pub, his playing had been melodic, and inventive, the tone piping and lean, its intensity controlled. Man earning a living, doing what he can.

Back in '57, in front of Miles Davis' rhythm section, he had glittered, half-afraid, inspired, alto saxophone dancing over the chords of half-remembered tunes. 'Star Eyes', 'Imagination', 'Jazz Me Blues'. The track that Resnick would play again and again: 'You'd Be So Nice To Come Home To'.

For a moment Pepper's namesake cat appeared in the doorway, sniffed the air and turned away, presenting his fine tail.

Just time for Resnick, eyes closed, to conjure up a picture of Lynn, restlessly sleeping in a strange bed, before the phone began to ring.

It was the sergeant on duty, his voice stretched by tiredness: '. . . ten, fifteen minutes ago, sir. I thought you'd want to know.'

That stretch of the Ilkeston Road was a mixture of small shops and residential housing, old factories put to new use, student accommodation. Police cars were parked, half on the kerb, either side of a black Ford Mondeo that, seemingly, had swerved wildly and collided, broadside-on, into a concrete post, amidst a welter of torn metal and splintered glass. Onlookers, some with overcoats pulled over their night clothes and carpet slippers on their feet, stood back behind hastily strung-out police tape, craning their necks. An ambulance and fire engine stood opposite, paramedics and fire officers mingling with uniformed police at the perimeter of the scene. Lights flashing, a second ambulance was pulling away as Resnick arrived.

Driving slowly past, he stopped outside a shop, long boarded-up, '*High Class Butcher*' in faded lettering on the brickwork above.

Anil Khan, once a DC in Resnick's squad and now a sergeant with Serious Crime, came briskly down to meet him and walked him back.

'One dead at the scene, sir, young female; one on his way to hospital, the driver. Female passenger, front near side, her leg's trapped against the door where it buckled in. Have to be cut out most likely. Oxyacetylene.'

Resnick could see the body now, stretched out against the lee of the wall beneath a dark grey blanket that was darker at the head.

'Impact?' Resnick said. 'Thrown forward against the windscreen?'

Khan shook his head. 'Shot.'

It stopped Resnick in his tracks.

'Another car, as best we can tell. Three shots, maybe four. One of them hit her in the neck. Must have nicked an artery. She was dead before we got her out.'

Illuminated by the street light above, Resnick could see the blood, sticky and bright, clinging to the upholstery like a second skin. Bending towards the body, he lifted back the blanket edge and looked down into the empty startled eyes of a girl of no more than sixteen.

Fifteen years and seven months. Shana Ann Faye. She had lived with her mother, two younger sisters and an older brother in Radford. A bright and popular student, a lovely girl. She had been to an eighteenth birthday party with her brother, Jahmall, and his girlfriend, Marlee. Jahmall driving.

They had been on their way home when the incident occurred, less than half a mile from where Shana and

Jahmall lived. A blue BMW drew up alongside them at the lights before the turn into Ilkeston Road, revving its engine as if intent on racing. Anticipating the green, Jahmall, responding to the challenge, accelerated downhill, the BMW in close pursuit; between the first set of lights and the old Radford Mill building, the BMW drew alongside, someone lowered the rear window, pushed a handgun through and fired four times. One shot ricocheted off the roof, another embedded itself in the rear of the front seat; one entered the fleshy part of Jahmall's shoulder, causing him to swerve; the fourth and fatal shot struck Shana low in the side of the neck and exited close to her windpipe.

An impulse shooting, is that what this was? Or a case of mistaken identity?

In the October of the previous year a gunman had opened fire from a passing car, seemingly at random, into a group of young people on their way home from Goose Fair, and a fourteen-year-old girl had died. There were stories of gun gangs and blood feuds in the media, of areas of the inner city running out of control, turf wars over drugs. Flowers and sermons, blame and recriminations and in the heart of the city a minute's silence, many people wearing the dead girl's favourite colours; thousands lined the streets for the funeral, heads bowed in respect.

Now this.

Understaffed as they were, low on morale and resources, policing the city, Resnick knew, was becoming harder and harder. In the past eighteen months, violent crime had risen to double the national average; shootings had increased fourfold. In Radford, Jamaican Yardies controlled the trade in heroin and crack cocaine, while on the Bestwood estate, to the north, the mainly white criminal fraternity was forging an uneasy alliance with the Yardies, all the while fighting amongst themselves; at either side of the city centre, multiracial gangs from St Ann's and the Meadows, Asian and Afro-Caribbean, fought out a constant battle for trade and respect.

So was Shana simply another victim in the wrong place at the wrong time? Or something more? The search for the car was on: best chance it would be found on waste land, torched; ballistics were analysing the bullets from the scene; Jahmall Faye and his family were being checked through records; friends would be questioned, neighbours. The public-relations department had prepared a statement for the media, another for the Assistant Chief Constable. Resnick sat in the CID office in Canning Circus station with Anil Khan and Detective Inspector Maureen Prior from Serious Crime. His patch, their concern. Their case more than his.

Outsides, the sky had lightened a little, but still their reflections as they sat were sharp against the window's plate glass.

Maureen Prior was in her early forties, no nonsense, matter-of-fact, wearing loose-fitting grey trousers, a zip-up jacket, hair tied back. 'So what do we think? We think they were targeted or what?'

'The girl?'

'No, not the girl.'

'The brother, then?'

'That's what I'm thinking.' The computer printout was in her hand. 'He was put under a supervision order a little over two years back, offering to supply a class A drug.'

'That's when he'd be what?' Khan asked 'Fifteen?'

'Sixteen. Just.'

'Anything since?'

'Not according to this.'

'You think he could still be involved?' Resnick said.

'I think it's possible, don't you?'

'And this was what? Some kind of payback?'

'Payback, warning, who knows? Maybe he was trying to step up into a different league, change his supplier, hold back his share of the cut, anything.'

'We've checked with the Drug Squad that he's a player?' Resnick asked.

Maureen Prior looked over at Khan, who shook his head. 'Haven't been able to raise anyone so far.'

The detective inspector looked at her watch. 'Try again. Keep trying.'

Freeing his mobile from his pocket, Khan walked towards the far side of the room.

'How soon can we talk to Jahmall, I wonder?' Resnick said.

'He's most likely still in surgery. Mid-morning, I'd say. The earliest.'

'You want me to do that?'

'No, it's okay. I've asked them to call me from Queen's the minute he's out of recovery. There's an officer standing by.' She moved from the desk where she'd been sitting, stretching out her arms and breathing in stale air. 'Maybe you could talk to the family?' She smiled. 'They're on your patch, Charlie, after all.'

There were bunches of flowers already tied to the post into which the car had crashed, some anonymous, some bearing hastily written words of sympathy. More flowers rested up against the low wall outside the house.

The victim support officer met Resnick at the door.

'How they holding up?' he asked.

'Good as can be expected, sir.'

Resnick nodded and followed the officer into a narrow hall.

'They're in back.'

Clarice Faye sat on a green high-backed settee, her youngest daughter cuddled up against her, face pressed to her mother's chest. The middle daughter, Jade, twelve or thirteen, sat close but not touching, head turned away. Clarice was slender, light-skinned, lighter than her daughters, shadows scored deep beneath her eyes. Resnick was reminded of a woman at sea, stubbornly holding on against the pitch and swell of the tide.

The room itself was neat and small, knick-knacks and framed photographs of the children, uniform smiles; a crucifix, metal on a wooden base, hung above the fireplace. The curtains, a heavy stripe, were still pulled partway across.

Resnick introduced himself and expressed his sympathy; accepted the chair that was offered, narrow with wooden arms, almost too narrow for his size.

'Jahmall – have you heard from the hospital?'

'I saw my son this morning. He was sleeping. They told me to come home and get some rest.' She shook her head and squeezed her daughter's hand tight. 'As if I could.'

'He'll be all right?'

'He will live.'

The youngest child began to cry.

'He is a good boy, Jahmall. Not wild. Not like some. Not any more. Why would anyone . . . ?' She stopped to sniff away a tear. 'He is going to join the army, you know that? Has been for an interview already, filled in the forms.' She pulled a tissue, screwed and damp, from her sleeve. 'A man now, you know? He makes me proud.'

Resnick's eyes ran round the photographs in the room. 'Shana's father,' he ventured, 'is he . . . ?'

'He doesn't live with us any more.'

'But he's been told?'

'You think he cares?'

The older girl sprang to her feet and half-ran across the room.

'Jade, come back here.'

The door slammed hard against the frame.

Resnick leaned forward, drew his breath. 'Jahmall and Shana, last night, you know where they'd been?'

'The Meadows. A friend of Jahmall's, his eighteenth.'

'Did they often go around together like that, Jahmall and Shana?'

'Sometimes, yes.'

'They were close then?'

'Of course.' An insult if it were otherwise, a slight.

'And his girlfriend, she didn't mind?'

'Marlee, no. She and Shana, they were like mates. Pals.'

'Mum,' the younger girl said, raising her head. 'Shana didn't like her. Marlee. She didn't.'

'That's not so.'

'It is. She told me. She said she smelled.'

'Nonsense, child.' Clarice smiled indulgently and shook her head.

'How about Shana?' Resnick asked. 'Did she have any boyfriends? Anyone special?'

The hesitation was perhaps a second too long. 'No. She was a serious girl. Serious about her studies. She didn't have time for that sort of thing. Besides, she was too young.'

'She was sixteen.'

'Too young for anything serious, that's what I mean.'

'But parties, like yesterday, that was okay?'

'Young people together, having fun. Besides, she had her brother to look after her . . .' Tears rushed to her face and she brushed them aside.

The phone rang and the victim support officer answered it in the hall. 'It's Jahmall,' he said from the doorway. 'They'll be taking him back up to the ward any time.'

'Quickly,' Clarice said to her daughter, bustling her off the settee. 'Coat and shoes.'

Resnick followed them out into the hall. Door open, Jade was sitting on one of the beds in the room she and Shana had obviously shared. Aware that Resnick was looking at her, she swung her head sharply towards him, staring hard until he moved away.

Outside, clouds slid past in shades of grey; on the opposite side of the narrow street, a couple slowed as they walked by. Resnick waited while the family climbed into the support officer's car and drove away. . . . *a good boy, Jahmall. Not wild. . . . Not any more.* The crucifix. The mother's words. Amazing, he thought, how we believe what we want to believe, all evidence aside.

On the Ilkeston Road, he stopped and crossed the street. There were more flowers now, and photographs of Shana, covered in plastic against the coming rain. A large teddy bear with black ribbon in a bow around its neck. A dozen red roses wrapped in cellophane, the kind on sale in garage forecourts. Resnick stooped and looked at the card. *For Shana. Our love will live for ever. Michael.* Kisses, drawn in red biro in the shape of a heart, surrounded the words.

Resnick was putting the last touches of a salad together when he heard Lynn's key in the lock. A sauce of spicy sausage and tomato was simmering on the stove; a pan of gently bubbling water ready to receive the pasta.

'Hope you're good and hungry.'

'You know . . .' Her head appearing round the door. '. . . I'm not sure if I am.'

But she managed a good helping nonetheless, wiping the spare sauce from her plate with bread, washing it down with wine.

'So – how was it?' Resnick asked between mouthfuls.

'All right, I suppose.'

'Not brilliant then.'

No, some of it was okay. Useful even.'

'Such as?'

'Oh, ways of avoiding tunnel vision. Stuff like that.'

Resnick poured more wine.

'I just wish,' Lynn said, 'they wouldn't get you to play these stupid games.'

'Games?'

'You know, if you were a vegetable, what vegetable would you be? If you were a car, what car?'

Resnick laughed. 'And what were you?'

'Vegetable or car?'

'Either.'

'A first-crop potato, fresh out of the ground.'

'A bit mundane.'

'Come on, Charlie, born and brought up in Norfolk, what do you expect?'

'A turnip?'

She waited till he was looking at his plate, then clipped him round the head.

Later, in bed, when he pressed against her back and she turned inside his arms, her face close to his, she said, 'Better watch out, Charlie, I didn't tell you what kind of car.'

'Something moderately stylish, compact, not too fast?'

'A Maserati Coupé 4.2 in Azuro Blue with full cream leather upholstery.'

He was still laughing when she stopped his mouth with hers.

The bullet that had struck Jahmall's shoulder was a 9mm, most likely from a plastic Glock. Patched up, replenished with blood, Jahmall was sore, sullen, and little else. Aside from lucky. His girlfriend, Marlee, had twenty-seven stitches in a gash in her leg, several butterfly stitches to one side of her head and face and bruises galore. The BMW was found on open ground near railway tracks on the far side of Sneinton, burned out. No prints, no ejected shell cases, nothing of use. It took the best part of a week, but thirty-seven of the fifty or so people who had been at the party in the Meadows were traced, tracked down and questioned. For officers, rare and welcome overtime.

The Drug Squad had no recent information to suggest that Jahmall was, again, dealing drugs, but there were several people at the party well known to them indeed. Troy James and Jason Fontaine in particular. Both had long been suspected of playing an active part in the trade in crack cocaine: suspected, arrested, interrogated, charged. James had served eighteen months of a three-year sentence before being released; Fontaine had been charged with possession of three kilos of amphetamine with intent to supply, but due to alleged contamination of evidence, the case against him had been dismissed. More recently, the pair of them had been suspected of breaking into a chemist's shop in Wilford and stealing several cases of cold remedies in order to manufacture crystal meth.

James and Fontaine were questioned in the street, questioned in their homes; brought into the police station and questioned again. Jahmall spent as much as fourteen hours, broken over a number of sessions, talking to Maureen Prior and Anil Khan.

Did he know Troy James and Jason Fontaine?

No.

He didn't know them?

No, not really.

Not really?

Not, you know, to talk to.

But they were at the party.
If you say so.
Well, they were there. James and Fontaine.
Okay, so they were there. So what?
You and Fontaine, you had a conversation.
What conversation?
There are witnesses, claim to have seen you and Fontaine in conversation.
A few words, maybe. I don't remember.
A few words concerning . . . ?
Nothing important. Nothing.
How about an argument . . . a bit of pushing and shoving?
At the party?
At the party.
No.
Think. Think again. Take your time. It's easy to get confused.
Oh, that. Yeah. It was nothing, right? Someone's drink got spilled, knocked over. Happens all the time.
That's what it was about? The argument?
Yeah.
A few punches thrown?
Maybe.
By you?
Not by me.
By Fontaine?
Fontaine?
Yes. You and Fontaine, squaring up to one another.
No. No way.
'There's something there, Charlie,' Maureen Prior said. 'Something between Jahmall and Jason Fontaine.'
They were sitting in the Polish Diner on Derby Road, blueberry pancakes and coffee, Resnick's treat.

213

'Something personal?'

'To do with drugs, has to be. Best guess, Fontaine and James were using Jahmall further down the chain and some way he held out on them, cut the stuff again with glucose, whatever. Either that, or he was trying to branch out on his own, their patch. Radford kid poaching in the Meadows, we all know how that goes down.'

'You'll keep on at him?'

'The girlfriend, too. She's pretty shaken up still. What happened to Shana. Keeps thinking it could have been her, I shouldn't wonder. Flaky as anything. One of them'll break sooner or later.'

'You seem certain.'

Maureen paused, fork halfway to her mouth. 'It's all we've got, Charlie.'

Resnick nodded and reached for the maple syrup: maybe just a little touch more.

The flowers were wilting, starting to fade. One or two of the brighter bunches had been stolen. Rain had seeped down into plastic and cellophane, rendering the writing for the most part illegible.

Clarice Faye came to the door in a dark housecoat, belted tight across; there were shadows still around her eyes.

'I'm sorry to disturb you,' Resnick said.

A slight shake of the head: no move to invite him in.

'When we were talking before, you said Shana didn't have any boyfriends, nobody special?'

'That's right.'

'Not Troy James?'

'I don't know that name?'

'How about Jason? Jason Fontaine?'

The truth was there on her face, a small nerve twitching at the corner of her eye.

214

'She did go out with Jason Fontaine?'

'She saw him once or twice. The end of last year. He came round here in his car, calling for her. I told him, he wasn't suitable, not for her. Not for Shana. He didn't bother her again.'

'And Shana . . . ?'

'Shana understood.' Clarice stepped back and began to close the door. 'If you'll excuse me now?'

'How about Michael?' Resnick said.

'I don't know no Michael.'

And the door closed quietly in his face.

He waited until Jade was on her way home from school, white shirt hanging out, coat open, skirt rolled high over dark tights, clumpy shoes. Her and three friends, loud across the pavement, one of them smoking a cigarette.

None of the others as much as noticed Resnick, gave him any heed.

'I won't keep you a minute,' Resnick said as Jade stopped, the others walking on, pace slowed, heads turned.

'Yeah, right.'

'You and Shana, you shared a room.'

'So.'

'Secrets.'

'What secrets?'

'Jason Fontaine, was she seeing him any more?'

Jade tilted back her head, looked him in the eye. 'He was just a flash bastard, weren't he? Didn't care nothin' for her.'

'And Michael?'

'What about him?'

'You tell me.'

'He loved her, didn't he?'

Michael Draper was upstairs in his room: computer, stereo, books and folders from the course he was taking at City

College, photographs of Shana on the wall, Shana and himself somewhere that might have been the Arboretum, on a bench in front of some trees, an old wall, Michael's skin alongside hers so white it seemed to bleed into the photo's edge.

'She was going to tell them, her mum and that, after her birthday. We were going to get engaged.'

'I'm sorry.'

The boy's eyes empty and raw from tears.

Maureen Prior was out of the office, her mobile switched off. Khan wasn't sure where she was.

'Ask her to call me when she gets a chance,' Resnick said. 'She can get me at home.'

At home he made sure the chicken pieces had finished defrosting in the fridge, chopped parsley, squashed garlic cloves flat, opened a bottle of wine, saw to the cats, flicked through the pages of the *Post*, Shana's murder now page four. Art Pepper again, turned up loud. Lynn was late, no later than usual, rushed, smiling, weary, a brush of lips against his cheek.

'I need a shower, Charlie, before anything else.'

'I'll get this started.' Knifing butter into the pan.

It cost Jahmall a hundred and fifteen, talked down from one twenty-five. A Brocock ME38 Magnum air pistol converted to fire live ammunition, .22 shells. Standing there at the edge of the car park, shadowed, he smiled: an eye for an eye. Fontaine's motor, his new one, another Beamer, was no more than thirty metres away, close to the light. He rubbed his hands and moved his feet against the cold, the rain that rattled against the hood of his parka, misted his eyes. Another fifteen minutes, no more, he'd be back out again, Fontaine, on with his rounds.

Less than fifteen, it was closer to ten.

Fontaine appeared at the side door of the pub, calling out to someone inside before raising a hand and turning away.

Jahmall tensed, smelling his own stink, his own fear; waited until Fontaine had reached towards the handle of the car door, back turned.

'Wait,' Jahmall said, stepping out of the dark.

Seeing him, seeing the pistol, Fontaine smiled. 'Jahmall, my man.'

'Bastard,' Jahmall said, moving closer. 'You killed my sister.'

'That slag!' Fontaine laughed. 'Down on her knees in front of any white meat she could find.'

Hands suddenly sticky, slick with sweat despite the cold, Jahmall raised the gun and fired. The first shot missed, the second shattered the side window of the car, the third took Fontaine in the face splintering his jaw. Standing over him, Jahmall fired twice more into his body as it slumped towards the ground, then ran.

After watching the news headlines, they decided on an early night. Lynn washed the dishes left over from dinner, while Resnick stacked away. He was locking the door when the phone went and Lynn picked it up. Ten twenty-three.

'Charlie,' she said, holding out the receiver. 'It's for you.'

DRUMMER UNKNOWN

There's a photograph taken on stage at Club Eleven, early 1950 or perhaps late '49, the bare bulbs above the stage picking out the musicians' faces like a still from a movie. Ronnie Scott on tenor sax, sharp in white shirt and knotted tie; Dennis Rose, skinny, suited, a hurt sardonic look in his eyes; to the left of the picture, Spike Robinson, on shore leave from the US Navy, a kid of nineteen or twenty, plays a tarnished silver alto. Behind them, Tommy Pollard's white shirt shines out from the piano and Lennie Bush, staring into space, stands with his double bass. At the extreme right, the drummer has turned his head just as the photo has been taken, one half of his polka-dot bow tie in focus but the face lost in a blur of movement. The caption underneath reads *drummer unknown*.

That's me: drummer unknown.

Or was, back then.

In ten years a lot of things have changed. In the wake of a well-publicised drug raid, Club Eleven closed down;

218

the only charges were for possession of cannabis, but already there were heroin, cocaine.

Ronnie Scott opened his own club in a basement in Chinatown, Spike Robinson sailed back across the ocean to a life as an engineer, and Dennis Rose sank deeper into the sidelines, an almost voluntary recluse. Then, of course, there was rock 'n' roll. Bill Haley's 'Rock Around the Clock' at number one for Christmas 1955 and the following year Tony Crombie, whose drum stool I'd been keeping warm that evening at Club Eleven, had kick-started the British bandwagon with his Rockets: grown men who certainly knew better, cavorting on stage in blazers while shouting about how they were going to teach you to rock, to the accompaniment of a honking sax. Well, it paid the rent.

And me?

I forget now, did I mention heroin?

I'm not usually one to cast blame, but after the influx of Americans during the last years of the war, hard drugs were always part of the scene. Especially once trips to New York to see the greats on 52nd Street had confirmed their widespread use.

Rumour had it that Bird and Diz and Monk changed the language of jazz the way they did – the complex chords, the flattened fifths, the extreme speeds – to make it impossible for the average white musician to play. If that was true, well, after an apprenticeship in strict tempo palais bands and pick-up groups that tinkered with Dixieland, where I was concerned they came close to succeeding. And it was true, the drugs – some drugs – helped: helped you to keep awake, alert. Helped you to play an array of shifting counter rhythms, left hand and both feet working independently, while the right hand drove the pulse along the top cymbal for all it was worth. Except that in my case, after a while, it wasn't the drumming that mattered, it was just the drugs.

In a matter of months I progressed, if that's the word, from chewing the inside of Benzedrine inhalers to injecting heroin into the vein. And for my education in this department I had Foxy Palmer to thank. Or blame.

I'd first met Foxy at the Bouillabaisse, a Soho drinking club frequented by mainly black US servicemen and newly resident West Indians, of whom Foxy was one. A short, stubby man with a pot belly beneath his extravagantly patterned shirts and a wisp of greying beard, his ears stuck out, fox-like, from the side of his head. A scaled-down Foxy would have made the perfect garden gnome.

'Hey, white boy!' he hailed me from his seat near the piano. 'You here to play?'

'Maybe.'

'Forget your horn?'

For an answer, I straightened my arm and let a pair of hickory drumsticks slide down into the palm of my hand.

A bunch of musicians, mostly refugees from some dance-band gig or other, were jamming their way through 'One O'Clock Jump', but then a couple of younger guys arrived and Foxy pulled my arm towards him with a grin and said, 'Here come the heebie-jeebie boys.'

In the shuffle that followed, Tony Crombie claimed his place behind the drums and after listening to him firing 'I Got Rhythm' at a hundred miles an hour, I slipped my sticks back out of sight.

'So,' Foxy said, planting himself next to me in the gents, 'that Tony, what d'you think?'

'I'm thinking of cutting my arms off just above the wrist.'

Foxy smiled his foxy smile. 'You're interested, I got somethin' less extreme might just do the trick.'

At first I didn't know what he meant.

*

The Bouillabaisse closed down and reopened as the Fullado. Later there was the Modernaires in Old Compton Street, owned by the gangster Jack Spot. Along with half a hundred other out-of-work musicians, I stood around on Archer Street on Monday afternoons, eager to pick up whatever scraps might come my way: depping at the Orchid Ballroom, Purley; a one-night stand with Ambrose at the Samson and Hercules in Norwich. And later, after shooting up, no longer intimidated or afraid, I'd descend the steps into the smoke of Mac's Rehearsal Rooms where Club Eleven had its home and take my turn at sitting in.

For a time I made an effort to hide the track marks on my arms but after that I didn't care.

Junkie – when did I first hear the word?

Applied to me, I mean.

It might have been at the Blue Posts, around the corner from the old Feldman Club, an argument with a US airman that began with a spilt pint of beer and escalated from there.

'Goddamn junkie, why the fuck aren't you in uniform?'

I didn't think he wanted to hear about the trumped-up nervous condition a well-paid GP had attested to, thus ensuring my call-up would be deferred. Instead some pushing and shoving ensued, at the height of which a bottle was broken against the edge of the bar.

Blind luck enabled me to sway clear of the jagged glass as it swung towards my face; luck and sudden rage allowed me to land three punches out of four, the last dropping him to his knees before executing the *coup de grâce*, a swiftly raised knee which caught him underneath the chin and caused him to bite off a sliver of tongue before he slumped, briefly unconscious, to the floor.

As I made my exit, I noticed the thin-faced man sitting close by the door, time enough to think I recognised him from somewhere without being able to put a finger on where that was. Then I was out into the damp November air.

'I hear you takin' up the fight game,' Foxy said with glee, next time I bumped into him. And then, 'I believe you know a friend of mine. Gordon Neville, detective sergeant.'

The thin-faced man leaned forward and held out a hand. 'That little nonsense in the Blue Posts, I liked the way you handled yourself. Impressive.'

I nodded and left it at that.

In the cracked toilet mirror my skin looked like old wax.

'Your pal from CID,' I asked Foxy, 'he okay?'

'Gordon?' Foxy said with a laugh. 'Salt o' the earth, ain't that the truth.'

Probably not, I thought.

He was waiting for me outside, the grey of his raincoat just visible in the soft grey fog that had drifted up from the river. When I turned left he fell into step alongside me, two men taking an evening stroll. Innocent enough.

'A proposition,' Neville said.

I shook my head.

'Hear me out, at least.'

'Sorry, not interested.'

His hand tugged at my sleeve. 'You're carrying, right?'

'Wrong,' I lied.

'You just seen Foxy, you're carrying. No question.'

'So?' The H burning a hole in my inside pocket.

'So you don't want me to search you, haul you in for possession.'

Our voices were muffled by the fog. If Neville knew about Foxy but was allowing him to deal, Foxy had to be paying him off. If what he wanted from me was more backhanders he had another think coming.

'What do you want?' I asked.

A woman emerged from a doorway just ahead of us, took one look at Neville and ducked back in.

'Information,' Neville said.

At the corner he stopped. The fog was thicker here and I could barely see the far side of the street.

'What kind of information?'

'Musicians. In the clubs. The ones you hang around with. Of course, we know who's using. It would just be confirmation.'

'I'm sorry,' I said, 'you've got the wrong guy.'

Smuts were clinging to my face and hair and not for the first time that evening I caught myself wondering where I'd left my hat.

Neville stared at me for a long moment, fixing me with grey-blue eyes; his mouth was drawn straight and thin. 'I don't think so,' he said.

I watched him walk, coat collar up, hat brim pulled down, until the fog had swallowed him up.

'He's a nasty bastard.' The woman had reappeared and stepped up, almost silently, alongside me. Close to, I could see she was little more than a girl. Sixteen, seventeen. Her eyes seemed to belong to someone else's face. 'Don't trust him,' she said and shivered. 'He'll hurt you if he can.'

Ethel, I found out her name was later, and she was, in fact, nineteen. She showed me the birth certificate as proof. Ethel Maude Rastrick, born St Pancras Hospital, seventeeth of March 1937. She kept it with a handful of letters and photographs in an old stationery box hidden away inside the chest of drawers in her room. Not the room where she worked, but the room where she lived. I got to see both in time.

But after that first brief meeting in the fog, I didn't see her for several months. No more than I saw hide nor hair of Detective Sergeant Gordon Neville. I'd like to say I forgot them both, though in Neville's case that wouldn't be entirely true. Somehow I talked myself into a gig with a ten-piece band on a tour of second-rank dance halls – Nuneaton, Llandudno, Wakefield and the like – playing quicksteps and waltzes with the occasional hot number thrown in. The brass players were into booze, but two of the three reeds shared my predilection for something that worked faster on the pulse rate and the brain and, between us, we got by. As long as we turned up on time and played the notes, the leader cast a blind eye.

As a drummer, it was almost the last regular work I had. The same month Bulganin and Khrushchev visited Britain, the spring of '56.

On my second night back in the smoke, I met Ethel again. I'd gone looking for Foxy, of course, looking to score, but to my bewilderment, Foxy hadn't been there. Nobody had seen him in a week or more. Flash Winston was playing piano at the Modernaires and I sat around for a while until I'd managed to acquire some weed and then moved on.

Ethel's was a face at the window, pale despite the small red bulb and lampshade alongside.

I looked up and she looked down.

'*New Young Model*' read the card pinned by the door.

When she waved at me I shook my head and turned away.

Tapping on the window, she gestured for me to wait and moments later I heard her feet upon the stairs. The light over the door was cruel to her face. In the fog I hadn't

noticed what no amount of lipstick could hide, the result
of an operation, partly successful, to remedy the fissure at
the centre of her upper lip.

'Why don't you come up?' she said.

'I haven't got any money.'

'I don't mean business, I mean just, you know, talk.'

Now that I'd noticed, it was difficult not to stare at her
mouth.

She touched my hand. 'Come on,' she said.

An elderly woman in a floral print overall sat like somebody's grandmother at the top of the first flight of stairs
and Ethel introduced her as the maid and told me to give
her ten shillings.

The room was functional and small: bed, sink, bucket,
bedside table. A narrow wardrobe with a mottled mirror
stood against the side wall. Hard against the window was
the straight-backed chair in which she sat, a copy of
yesterday's *Evening News* on the floor nearby.

Now that I was there, she seemed nervous, her hands
rose and fell from her sides.

'Have you got anything?' she said and for an instant I
thought she meant johnnies and wanted business after all,
but then, when I saw the twitch in her eye, I knew.

'Only some reefer,' I said.

'Is that all?'

'It was all I could get.'

She sat on the side of the bed, resigned, and I sat with
her and rolled a cigarette and after the first long drag, she
relaxed and smiled, her hand moving instinctively to cover
the lower half of her face.

'That plain-clothes bloke,' I said. 'Neville. You said not
to trust him.'

'Let's not talk about him,' she said. 'Let's talk about
you.'

225

So I lay back with my head resting where so many other heads had rested, on the wall behind the bed, and told her about my mother who had run off with a salesman in home furnishings and started a new family in the Scottish borders, and my father who worked the halls for years as an illusionist and conjuror until he himself had disappeared. And about the moment when, age eleven, I knew I wanted to be a drummer: going to see my father on stage at Collins Music Hall and watching the comedian Max Bacon, previously a dance-band drummer, topping the bill. He had this huge, to me, drum kit set up at the centre of the stage, all gold and glittering, and at the climax of his act, played a solo, all crash and rolling tom-toms, with the assistance of the band in the pit.

I loved it.

I wanted to be him.

Not the laughter and the jokes or the showy suit, and not fat like he was, certainly not that, but sitting there behind all those shimmering cymbals and drums, the centre of everything.

'Tell us about yourself, Ethel,' I said after a while.

'Oh,' she said, 'there's nothing to tell.' Her fair, mousy hair hung almost to her shoulders and she sat with her head angled forward, chin tucked in.

'Aren't you going to get in trouble,' I said, 'spending all this time with me instead of a client?'

She looked towards the door. 'The maid goes home after twelve and then there's nobody comes round till gone one, sometimes two.'

I presumed she meant her pimp, but I didn't ask.

'Besides,' she said. 'You saw what it's like, it's dead out there.'

She did tell me about her family then. Two sisters and three brothers, all scattered; she and one of her sisters had been fostered out when they were eleven and ten. Her mother worked in a laundry in Dalston, had periods in hospital, times when she couldn't cope. She didn't remember too much about her father, except that he had never held her, never looked at her with anything but distaste. When he was killed towards the end of the war, she'd cried without really knowing what for.

I felt a sort of affinity between us and for one moment I thought I might reach out my hand, lean across and kiss her, but I never did. Not then or later. Not even months down the line when she asked me back to the bedsitter she had near Finsbury Park, a Baby Belling cooker behind a curtain in one corner and the bathroom down the hall. But I did take to stopping by between midnight and one and sharing a little of whatever I had, Ethel's eyes brightening like Christmas if ever it was cocaine.

Foxy was around again, but not as consistently as before; there'd been some falling-out with his suppliers, he implied, whatever arrangements he'd previously enjoyed had been thrown up in the air. And in general the atmosphere had changed: something was clearly going on. Whereas Jack Spot and Albert Dimes had more or less divided the West End between them, Spot lording it over Soho with a certain rough-hewn benevolence, now there were young pretenders coming out of the East End or from abroad, sleek, rapacious, unfeeling, fighting it out amongst themselves.

Rumour had it Gordon Neville had been demoted to a woodentop and forced to walk the beat in uniform; that he'd been shuffled north to patrol the leafy lanes of Totteridge and Whetstone. More likely, that he'd made detective inspector and was lording it in Brighton. Then one evening in the Blue Posts there he was, the same raincoat and trilby hat, same seat by the door. I'd been round the corner at 100 Oxford Street listening to the Lyttelton

Band play 'Creole Serenade' and 'Bad Penny Blues'. Not my kind of thing, really, except he did have Bruce Turner on alto and Turner had studied in the States with Lennie Tristano, which was more my scene.

I should have walked right on past him and out into the street.

'If you can find your way to the bar without getting into a fight,' he said, 'I could use another pint.'

A favourite refrain of my mother's came to mind: *What did your last servant die of?* I kept it to myself.

'Scotch ale,' Neville said, holding out his empty glass.

I bought a half of bitter for myself and shepherded the drinks back through the crowd.

'So,' Neville said, settling back. 'How's business?'

'Which business is that?'

'I thought you were in the bebop business.'

'Once in a while.'

'Lovely tune that.' Pleased with himself, Neville smiled his thin-lipped smile, then supped some ale. 'The Stardust, isn't it?' he said. 'Your little home from home these days.'

The Stardust had sprung up on the site of the old Cuba Club on Gerrard Street and an old pal, Vic Farrell, who played piano there, had talked me into a job as doorman. I kept a snare drum and hi-hat behind the bar and Tommy would let me sit in whenever my hands were steady enough. Which was actually most evenings now. I wasn't clean by a long chalk, but I had it pretty much under control.

'Oscar still running the place, is he?'

Neville had a liking for questions that didn't require an answer.

'What is it with you and coons?' Neville said. 'Taste for the fucking exotic?'

Oscar was a half-caste Trinidadian with a bald head and a gold tooth and a jovial 'Hail fellow, well met' sort of manner. He was fronting the place for a couple of Maltese brothers, his name on the licence, their money. The place ran at a loss, it had to, but they were using it to feel their way in, mark out a little territory, stake a claim.

Neville leaned a shade nearer. 'You could do me a favour there. Comings and goings. Who's paying who. Keep me in the picture.'

I set my glass on the window ledge behind me, half-finished. 'Do your own dirty work,' I said. 'I told you before.'

I got to my feet and as I did so Neville reached out and grabbed me by the balls and twisted hard. Tears sprang to my eyes.

'That ugly little tart of yours. She's come up light more'n a few times lately. Wouldn't want to see anything happen to her, would you?' He twisted again and I thought I might faint. 'Would you?'

'No,' I said, not much above a whisper.

'Say what?'

'No.'

'Good boy.' Releasing me, he wiped his fingers down his trouser front. 'You can give her my love, Ethel, when you see her. Though how you can fuck it without a bag over its head beggars belief.'

So I started slipping him scraps of information, nothing serious, nothing I was close to certain he didn't already know. We'd meet in the Posts or the Two Brewers, sometimes Lyons' tea shop in Piccadilly. It kept him at bay for a while but not for long.

'Stop pullin' my chain,' he said one fine morning, 'and give me something I can fuckin' use.' It was late summer and everything still shining and green.

I thought about it sitting on the steps at the foot of Lower Regent Street, a view clear across the Mall into

St James's Park, Horse Guards Parade. Over the next few weeks I fed him rumours a big shipment of heroin would be passing through the club, smuggled in from the Continent. The Maltese brothers, I assured him, would be there to supervise delivery.

Neville saw it as his chance for the spotlight. The raid was carried out by no fewer than a dozen plain-clothes officers with as many as twenty uniforms in support. One of Neville's cronies, a crime reporter for the *Express*, was on hand to document proceedings.

Of course, the place was clean. I'd seen to that.

When the law burst through the door and down the stairs, Vic Farrell was playing 'Once in a While' in waltz time and the atmosphere resembled nothing so much as a vicarage tea party, orderly and sedate.

'Don't say, you little arsewipe,' Neville spluttered, 'I didn't fuckin' warn you.'

For the next forty-eight hours I watched my back, double-checked the locks on the door to my room, took extra care each time I stepped off the kerb and into the street. And then I understood I wasn't the one at risk.

Wouldn't want to see anything happen to her, would you?

She was lying on her bed, wearing just a slip, a pair of slippers on her feet, and at first I thought she was asleep. And then, from the angle of her torso to her head, I realised someone had twisted her neck until it broke.

He'll hurt you if he can: just about the first words Ethel had said.

I looked at her for a long time and then, daft as it sounds, I touched my fingers to her upper lip, surprised at how smooth and cold it felt.

And then I left.

Discreetly as I could, I asked around.

The maid had taken a couple of days off sick; only the usual slow but steady stream of punters had been seen entering the building. Up and down the street, nobody had noticed anything unusual.

'*Soho Vice Girl Murdered*', the headline read.

I traced Ethel's mother from one of her letters and she promised to come to the funeral but she never did. I stood alone in a little chapel in Kensal Green, fingers drumming a quiet farewell on the back of the pew. Outside, the first leaves were starting to fall. When it was over I took the Tube back to Oxford Circus and met Tom Holland round the corner from the Palladium as arranged.

Holland was young for a detective inspector, no more than thirty-two or -three; something of a high-flyer, he'd recently transferred from the City of London police to run one of the CID squads at West End Central.

The year before, '55, the *Mail* had run a story about police corruption, alleging that many officers in the West End were on the take. The Met issued a bald denial. Everyone from the Commissioner down denied the charge. What evidence existed was discredited or lost. No one was suspended, cautioned, even interviewed. Word was unofficially passed round: be less visible, less greedy.

Holland was the only officer I knew who wasn't snaffling bribes. According to rumour, when a brothel keeper slipped an envelope containing fifty in tens into his pocket, Holland shoved it down his throat and made him eat it.

He was just shy of six foot, I guessed, dark-haired and brown-eyed, and he sat at a table in the rear of the small Italian café, shirtsleeves rolled back, jacket draped across his chair. Early autumn and it was still warm. The coffee came in those glass cups that were all the rage; three sips and it was gone.

I told him about Neville's involvement with pushers and

prostitutes, the percentages he took for protection, for looking the other way. Told him my suspicions concerning Ethel's murder.

Holland listened as if it mattered, his gaze rarely leaving my face.

When I'd finished, he sat a full minute in silence, weighing things over.

'I can't do anything about the girl,' he said. 'Even if Neville did kill her or have her killed, we'd never get any proof. And let's be honest: where she's concerned, nobody gives a toss. But the other stuff, drugs especially. There might be something I could do.'

I thought if I went the right way about it, I could get Foxy to make some kind of statement, off the record, nothing that would come to court, not even close, but it would be a start. Places, times, amounts. And there were others who'd be glad to find a way of doing Neville down, repaying him for all the cash he'd pocketed, the petty cruelties he'd meted out.

'One month,' Holland said. 'Then show me what you've got.'

When I held out my hand to shake his, his eyes fixed on my arm. 'And that habit of yours,' he said. 'Kick it now.'

A favourite trick of Neville's, whenever his men raided a club, was to take the musicians who'd been holding aside – and there were usually one or two – and feign sympathy. Working long hours, playing the way you do, stands to reason you need a little something extra, a little pick-me-up. Nudge, nudge, wink, wink. Men of the world. Just hand it over and we'll say no more about it. Oh, and if you've got a little sweetener for the lads . . . lovely, lovely.

And ever after, if he walked into a club or bumped into them on the street, he would be into them for another fifty plus whatever they were carrying. Let anyone try saying no and they were sorted good.

Inside a matter of weeks I talked with two pianists, a drummer, a guitarist and three sax players – what is it with saxophonists? – who agreed to dish the dirt on Neville if it would get him off their backs. And finally, after a lot of arguing and pleading, I persuaded Foxy to sit down with Holland in an otherwise empty room, neutral territory, and tell him what he knew.

After that, carefully, Holland spoke to a few of Neville's team, officers who were already compromised and eager to protect themselves as best they could. From a distance, he watched Neville himself. Checked, double-checked.

The report he wrote was confidential and he took it to the new Deputy Assistant Commissioner, one of the few high-ranking bosses he thought he could trust.

It was agreed that going public would generate bad publicity for the force and that should be avoided at all costs. Neville was shunted sideways, somewhere safe, and after several months allowed to retire on a full pension for reasons of ill health.

One of his mutually beneficial contacts had been with a businessman from Nicosia, import and export, and that was where Neville hived off to, counting his money, licking his wounds.

I was at the airport to see him off.

Three and a bit years ago now.

I took Tom Holland's advice and cleaned up my act, the occasional drag at some weed aside. Tom, he's a detective chief inspector now and tipped for higher things. I don't play any more, rarely feel the need. There are a couple of bands I manage, groups that's what they call them these days, one from Ilford, one from Palmers Green. And I keep myself fit, swim, work out in the gym. One thing a drummer

has, even a second-rate ex-drummer like me, is strong
wrists, strong hands.

I don't reckon Neville staying in Cyprus for ever, can't
see it somehow; he'll want to come back to the smoke.
And when he does, I'll meet him. Maybe even treat him
to a drink. Ask if he remembers Ethel, the way she lay
back, twisted, on the bed, her broken neck . . .

FAVOUR

Kiley hadn't heard from Adrian Costain in some little time, not since one of Costain's A-list clients had ended up in an all-too-public brawl, the pictures syndicated round the world at the touch of a computer key, and Kiley, who had been hired to prevent exactly that kind of thing happening, had been lucky to get half his fee.

'If we were paying by results,' Costain had said, 'you'd be paying me.'

Kiley had had new cards printed. *'Investigations. Private and Confidential. All kinds of security work undertaken. Ex-Metropolitan Police'*. Telephone and fax numbers underneath. Cheaper by the hundred, the young woman in Easyprint had said, Kiley trying not to stare at the tattoo that snaked up from beneath the belt of her jeans to encircle her navel, the line of tiny silver rings that tinkled like a miniature carillon whenever she moved her head.

Now the cards were pinned, some of them, outside newsagents' shops all up and down the Holloway Road and around; others he'd left discreetly in pubs and cafés in the vicinity; once, hopefully, beside the cash desk at the Holloway Odeon after an afternoon showing of *Insomnia*, Kiley not immune to Maura Tierney's charms.

Most days, the phone didn't ring, the fax failed to ratchet into life.

'Email, that's what you need, Jack,' the Greek in the corner café where he sometimes had breakfast assured him. 'Email, the Net, the World Wide Web.'

What Kiley needed was a new pair of shoes, a way to pay next month's rent, a little luck. Getting laid wouldn't be too bad either: it had been a while.

He was on his way back into the flat, juggling the paper, a pint of milk, a loaf of bread, fidgeting for the keys, when the phone started to ring.

Too late, he pressed recall and held his breath.

'Hello?' The voice at the other end was suave as cheap margarine.

'Adrian?'

'You couldn't meet me in town, I suppose? Later this morning. Coffee.'

Kiley thought that he could.

When he turned the corner of Old Compton Street into Frith Street, Costain was already sitting outside Bar Italia, expensively suited legs lazily crossed, *Times* folded open, cappuccino as yet untouched before him.

Kiley squeezed past a pair of media types earnestly discussing first-draft scripts and European funding, and took a seat at Costain's side.

'Jack,' Costain said. 'It's been too long.' However diligently he practised his urbane, upper-class drawl there was always that telltale tinge of Ilford, like a hair ball at the back of his throat.

Kiley signalled to the waitress and leaned back against

the painted metal framework of the chair. Across the street, Ronnie Scott's was advertising Dianne Adams, foremost amongst its coming attractions.

'I didn't know she was still around,' Kiley said.

'You know her?'

'Not really.'

What Kiley knew were old rumours of walkouts and no-shows, a version of 'Stormy Weather' that had been used a few years back in a television commercial, an album of Gershwin songs he'd once owned but not seen in, oh, a decade or more. Not since Dianne Adams had played London last.

'She's spent a lot of time in Europe since she left the States,' Costain was saying. 'Denmark. Holland. Still plays all the big festivals. Antibes, North Sea.'

Kiley was beginning to think Costain's choice of venue for their meeting was down to more than a love of good coffee. 'You're representing her,' he said.

'In the UK, yes.'

Kiley glanced back across the street. 'How long's she at Ronnie's?'

'Two weeks.'

When Kiley had been a kid and little more, those early cappuccino days, a girl he'd been seeing had questioned the etiquette of eating the chocolate off the top with a spoon. He did it now, two spoonfuls before stirring in the rest, wondering, as he did so, where she might be now, if she still wore her hair in a ponytail, the hazy green in her eyes.

'You could clear a couple of weeks, Jack, I imagine. Nights, of course, afternoons.' Costain smiled and showed some teeth, not his but sparkling just the same. 'You know the life.'

'Not really.'

'Didn't you have a pal? Played trumpet, I believe?'

'Saxophone.'

'Ah, yes.' As if they were interchangeable, a matter of fashion, an easy either-or.

Derek Becker had played Ronnie's once or twice, in his pomp, not headlining, but taking the support slot with his quartet, Derek on tenor and soprano, occasionally baritone, along with the usual piano, bass and drums. That was before the booze really hit him bad.

'Adams,' Costain said, 'it would just be a matter of babysitting, making sure she gets to the club on time, the occasional interview. You know the drill.'

'Hardly seems necessary.'

'She's not been in London in a good while. She'll feel more comfortable with a hand to hold, a shoulder to lean on.' Costain smiled his professional smile. 'That's metaphorically, of course.'

They both knew he needed the money; there was little more, really, to discuss.

'She'll be staying at Le Meridien,' Costain said. 'On Piccadilly. From Friday. You can hook up with her there.'

The meeting was over, Costain was already glancing at his watch, checking for messages on his mobile phone.

'All those years in Europe,' Kiley said, getting to his feet, 'no special reason she's not been back till now?'

Costain shook his head. 'Representation, probably. Timings not quite right.' He flapped a hand vaguely at the air. 'Sometimes it's just the way these things are.'

'A little start-up fund would be good,' Kiley said.

Costain reached into his suit jacket for his wallet and slid out two hundred and fifty in freshly minted twenties and tens. 'Are you still seeing Kate these days?' he asked.

Kiley wasn't sure.

Kate Keenan was a freelance journalist with a free-

238

ranging and often fierce column in the *Independent*. Kiley had met her by chance a little over a year ago and they'd been sparring with one another ever since. She'd been sparring with him. Sometimes, Kiley thought, she took him the way some women took paracetamol.

'Only I was thinking,' Costain said, 'she and Dianne ought to get together. Dianne's a survivor, after all. Beat cancer. Saw off a couple of abusive husbands. Brought up a kid alone. She'd be perfect for one of those pieces Kate does. Profiles. You know the kind of thing.'

'Ask her,' Kiley said.

'I've tried,' Costain said. 'She doesn't seem to be answering my calls.'

There had been an episode, Kiley knew, before he and Kate had met, when she had briefly fallen for Costain's slippery charm. It had been, as she liked to say, like slipping into cow shit on a rainy day.

'Is this part of what you're paying me for?' Kiley asked.

'Merely a favour,' Costain said, smiling. 'A small favour between friends.'

Kiley thought he wouldn't mind an excuse to call Kate himself. 'Okay,' he said, 'I'll do what I can. But I've got a favour to ask you in return.'

*

The night before Dianne Adams opened in Frith Street, Costain organised a reception downstairs at the Pizza on the Park. Jazzers, journalists, publicists and hangers-on, musicians like Guy Barker and Courtney Pine, for fifteen minutes Nicole Farhi and David Hare. Canapés and champagne.

Derek Becker was there with a quartet, playing music for schmoozing. Only it was better than that.

Becker was a hard-faced romantic who loved the fifties recordings of Stan Getz, especially the live sessions from the Shrine with Bob Brookmeyer on valve trombone; he still sent cards, birthday, Christmas and Valentine, to the woman who'd had the good sense not to marry him some twenty years before. And he liked to drink.

A Bass man from way back, he could tolerate most beer, though he preferred it hand-pumped from the wood; in the right mood, he could appreciate a good wine; whisky, he preferred Islay single malts, Lagavulin, say, or Laphroaig. At a pinch, anything would do.

Kiley had come across him once, sprawled along a bench on the southbound platform of the Northern Line at Leicester Square. Vomit still drying on his shirt front, face bruised, a cut splintering the bridge of his nose. Kiley had pulled him straight and used a tissue to wipe what he could from round his mouth and eyes, pushed a tenner down into his top pocket and left him there to sleep it off. Thinking about it still gave him the occasional twinge of guilt.

That had been a good few years back, around the time Kiley had been forced to accept his brief foray into professional soccer was over: the writing on the wall, the stud marks on his shins; the ache in his muscles that never quite went away, one game to the next.

Becker was still playing jazz whenever he could, but instead of Ronnie's, nowadays it was more likely to be the King's Head in Bexley, the Coach and Horses at Isleworth, depping on second tenor at some big-band nostalgia weekend at Pontin's.

And tonight Becker was looking sharp, sharper than Kiley had seen him in years and sounding good. Adams clearly thought so. Calling for silence, she sang a couple of tunes with the band. 'Stormy Weather', of course, and an up-tempo 'Just One of Those Things'. Stepping aside to let Becker solo, she smiled at him broadly. Made a point of praising his playing. After that his eyes followed her everywhere she went.

'She's still got it, hasn't she?' Kate said, appearing at Kiley's shoulder.

Kiley nodded. Kate was wearing an oatmeal-coloured suit that would have made most other people look like something out of storage. Her hair shone.

'You didn't mind me calling you?' Kiley said.

Kate shook her head. 'As long as it was only business.' Accidentally brushing his arm as she moved away.

Later that night – that morning – Kiley, having delivered Dianne Adams safely to her hotel, was sitting with Derek Becker in a club on the edge of Soho. Both men were drinking Scotch, Becker sipping his slowly, plenty of water in between.

Before the reception had wound down, Adams had spoken to Costain, Costain had spoken to the management at Ronnie's and Becker had been added to the trio Adams had brought over from Copenhagen to accompany her.

'I suppose,' Becker said, 'I've got you to thank for that.'

Kiley shook his head. 'Thank whoever straightened you out.'

Becker had another little taste of his Scotch. 'Let me tell you,' he said. 'A year ago, it was as bad as it gets. I was living in Walthamstow, a one-room flat. Hadn't worked in months. The last gig I'd had, a pub over in Chigwell, I hadn't even made the three steps up on to the stage. I was starting the day with a six-pack and by lunch-time it'd be ruby port and cheap wine. Except there wasn't any lunch. I hardly ate anything for weeks at a time and when I did I threw it back up. And I stank. People turned away from me on the street. My clothes stank and my skin stank. The only thing I had left, the only thing I hadn't sold or hocked

241

was my horn and then I hocked that. Bought enough pills, a bottle of cheap Scotch and a packet of old-fashioned razor blades. Enough was more than enough.'

He looked at Kiley and sipped his drink.

'And then I found this.'

Snapping open his saxophone case, Becker flipped up the lid of the small compartment in which he kept his spare reeds. Lifting out something wrapped in dark velvet, he laid it in Kiley's hand.

'Open it.'

Inside the folds was a bracelet, solid gold or merely plated Kiley couldn't be certain, though from the weight of it he guessed the former. Charms swayed and jingled lightly as he raised it up. A pair of dice. A key. What looked to be – an imitation this, surely? – a Fabergé egg.

'I was shitting myself,' Becker said. 'Literally. Shit scared of what I was going to do.' He wiped his hand across his mouth before continuing. 'I'd gone down into the toilets at Waterloo station, locked myself in one of the stalls. I suppose I fell, passed out maybe. Next thing I know I'm on my hands and knees, face down in God knows what and there it was. Waiting for me to find it.'

An old Presley song played for a moment at the back of Kiley's head. 'Your good-luck charm,' he said.

'If you like, yes. The first piece of luck I'd had in months, that's for sure. Years. I mean, I couldn't believe it. I just sat there, staring at it. I don't know, waiting for it to disappear, I suppose.'

'And when it didn't?'

Becker smiled. 'I tipped the pills into the toilet bowl, took a belt at the Scotch and then poured away the rest. The most I've had, that day to this, is a small glass of an evening, maybe two. I know you'll hear people say you can't kick it that way, all or nothing, has to be, but all I can say is it works for me.' He held out his hand, arm extended, no tremor, the fingers perfectly still. 'Well, you've heard me play.'

Kiley nodded. 'And this?' he said.

'The bracelet?'

'Yes.'

Forefinger and thumb, Becker took it from the palm of Kiley's hand.

'Used it to get my horn out of hock, buy a half-decent suit of clothes. When I was sober enough, I started phoning round, chasing work. Bar mitzvahs, weddings, anything, I didn't care. When I had enough I went back and redeemed it.' He rewrapped the bracelet and stowed it carefully away. 'Been with me ever since.' He winked. 'Like you say, my good-luck charm, eh?'

Kiley drained what little remained in his glass. 'Time I wasn't here.'

Standing, Becker shook his hand. 'I owe you one, Jack.'

'Just keep playing like tonight. Okay?'

*

The first few days went down easily enough, the way good days sometimes do. Adam's first set, opening night, was maybe just a little shaky, but after that everything gelled. The reviews were good, better than good, and by mid-week word of mouth had kicked in and the place was packed. Becker, Kiley thought, was playing out of his skull, seizing his chance with both hands. Adams worked up a routine with him on 'Ghost of a Chance', just the two of them, voice and horn, winding around each other tighter and tighter as the song progressed. And, when they were through, Becker gazed at Dianne Adams with a mixture of gratitude and barely disguised desire.

Costain didn't have to call in many favours to have Adams interviewed at length on *Woman's Hour* and more succinctly on *Front Row*; after less than three hours' sleep, she was smiling from behind her make-up on *GMTV*; Claire Martin prerecorded a piece for her Friday jazz show and had Adams and Becker do their thing in the studio. Kate's profile in the *Indy* truthfully presented a woman with a genuine talent, a generous ego and a carapaced heart.

All of this Kiley watched from a close distance, grateful for Costain's money without ever being sure why the agent had thought him necessary. Then, just shy of noon on the Thursday morning, he knew.

Adams paged him and had him come up to her room.

Pacing the floor in a hotel robe, *sans* paint and powder, she looked all of her age and then some. The photographs were spread out across the unmade bed. Dianne Adams on stage at Ronnie Scott's, opening night; walking through a mostly deserted Soho after the show, Kiley at her side; Adams passing through the hotel lobby, walking along the corridor from the lift, unlocking the door to her room. And then several slightly blurred and taken, Kiley guessed, from across the street with a telephoto lens: Adams undressing; sitting on her bed in her underwear talking on the telephone; crossing from the shower, nude save for a towel wrapped round her head.

'When did you get these?' Kiley asked.

'Sometime this morning. An hour ago, maybe. Less. Someone pushed them under the door.'

'No note? No message?'

Adams shook her head.

Kiley looked again at the pictures on the bed. 'This is not just an obsessive fan.'

Adams lit a cigarette and drew the smoke deep into her lungs. 'No.'

He looked at her then. 'You know who these are from.'

Adams sighed and for a moment closed her eyes. 'When I was last in London, '89, I had this . . . this thing.' She shrugged. 'You're on tour, some strange city. It happens.' From the already decimated minibar she took the last miniature of vodka and tipped it into a glass. 'Whatever helps you through the night.'

'He didn't see it that way.'

'He?'

'Whoever this was. The affair. The fling. It meant more to him.'

'To her.'

Kiley caught his breath. 'I see.'

Adams sat on the edge of the bed and lit a cigarette. 'Virginia Pride? I guess you know who she is?'

Kiley nodded. 'I didn't know she was gay.'

'She's not.' Tilting back her head, Adams blew smoke towards the ceiling. 'But then, neither am I. No more than most women, given the right situation.'

'And that's what this was?'

'So it seemed.'

Kiley's mind was working overtime. Virginia Pride had made her name starring in a television soap in the eighties, brittle and sexy and no better than she should be. After that she did a West End play, posed nearly nude for a national daily and had a few well-publicised skirmishes with the law, public order offences, nothing serious. Her wedding to Keith Payne made the front page of both *OK!* and *Hello!* and their subsequent history of breaking up to make up was choreographed lovingly by the tabloid press. If Kiley remembered correctly, Virginia was set to play Maggie in a provincial tour of *Cat on a Hot Tin Roof*.

But he didn't think Virginia was the problem.

'Payne knew about this?' Kiley said.

Adams released smoke towards the ceiling. 'Let's say he found out.'

One image of Keith Payne stuck in Kiley's memory. A newspaper photograph. A tall man, six four or five, Payne was being escorted across the tarmac from a plane, hand-cuffed to one of the two police officers walking alongside. Tanned, hair cut short, he was wearing a dark polo shirt outside dark chinos, what was obviously a Rolex on his wrist. Relaxed, confident, a smile on his handsome face.

Kiley couldn't recall the exact details, save that Payne had been extradited from Portugal to face charges arising from a bullion robbery at Heathrow. The resulting court case had all but collapsed amidst crumbling evidence and accusations of police entrapment, and Payne had finally been sentenced to eight years for conspiracy to commit robbery. He would have been released, Kiley guessed, after serving no more than five. Whereas his former colleague, who had appeared as a witness for the prosecution and was handed down a lenient eighteen months, was the unfortunate victim of a hit-and-run incident less than two weeks after being released from prison. The vehicle was found abandoned half a mile away and the driver never traced.

Payne, Kiley guessed, didn't take kindly to being crossed.

'When he found out,' Kiley said, 'about you and Virginia, what did he do?'

'Bought her flowers, a new dress, took her to the Caprice, knocked out two of her teeth. He came to the hotel where I was staying and trashed the room, smashed the mirror opposite the bed and held a piece of glass to my face. Told me that if he ever as much as saw me near Virginia again he'd carve me up.'

'You believed him.'

'I took the first flight out next morning.'

'And you've not been back since.'

'Till now.'

'Costain knew this?'

'I suppose.'

Yes, Kiley thought, I bet he did.

Adams drained her glass and swivelled towards the telephone. 'I'm calling room service for a drink.'

'Go ahead.'

'You want anything?'

Kiley shook his head. 'So have you seen her?' he asked when she was through.

'No. But she sent me this.' The card had a black-and-white photograph, artfully posed, of lilies in a slim white vase; the message inside read '*Knock 'em dead*' and was signed '*Virginia*' with a large red kiss. 'That and a bottle of champagne on opening night.'

'And that's all?'

'That's all.'

Kiley thought it might be enough.

Adams ran her fingers across the photographs beside her on the bed. 'It's him, isn't it?'

'I imagine so.'

'Why? Why these?'

Some men, Kiley knew, got off on the idea of their wives or girlfriends having affairs with other women, positively encouraged it, but it didn't seem Payne was one of those.

'He's letting you know he knows where you are, knows your every move. If you see Virginia, he'll know.'

Adams' eyes flicked towards the mirror on the hotel wall. 'And if I do, he'll carry out his threat.'

'He'll try.'

'You could stop him.

Kiley wasn't sure. 'Are you going to see her?' he asked.

Adams shook her head. 'What if she tries to see me?'

Kiley smiled; close to a smile, at least. 'We'll try and head her off at the pass.'

That night, after the show, she asked Becker back to her hotel for a drink and, as he sat with his single Scotch and water, invited him to share her bed.

'She's using you,' Kiley said next morning, Becker bleary-eyed over his coffee in Old Compton Street.

Becker found the energy to wink. 'And how,' he said.

Kiley told him about Payne and all Becker did was shrug.

'He's dangerous, Derek.'

'He's just a two-bit gangster, right?'

'You mean like Coltrane was a two-bit sax player?'

'Jack,' Becker said, grasping Kiley by the arm, 'you worry too much, you know that?'

The following afternoon Adams and the band were rehearsing at Ronnie's, Dianne wanting to work up some new numbers for the weekend. Kiley thought it was unlikely Payne would show his hand in such a public place, but rang Costain and asked him to be around in case.

'I thought that was what I was paying you for,' Costain said.

'If he breaks your arm,' Kiley said, 'take it out of my salary.'

Kiley had been checking out the *Stage*. *Cat on a Hot Tin Roof* was already on the road, this week Leicester, next week Richmond. Close enough to make a trip into the centre of London for its star a distinct possibility. He sat in the Haymarket bar and waited for the matinee performance to finish. Thirty minutes after the curtain came down, Virginia Pride was sitting in her robe in her dressing room, most of the make-up removed from her face, a cigarette between her lips. Close up, she didn't look young any more, but she still looked good.

248

'You're from the *Mail*,' she said, crossing her legs.

Kiley leaned back against the door as it closed behind him. 'I lied.'

She studied him then, taking him in. 'Should I call the management? Have you thrown out?' Her voice was still smeared with the southern accent she'd used in the play.

'Probably not.'

'You're not some crazy fan?'

Kiley shook his head.

'No, I suppose you're not.' She took one last drag at her cigarette. 'Just as long as you're here, there's a bottle of wine in that excuse for a fridge. Why don't you grab a couple of those glasses, pour us both a drink? Then you can tell me what you really want.'

The wine was a little sweet for Kiley's taste and not quite cold enough.

'Are you planning to see Dianne Adams while she's in town?' Kiley said.

'Oh, shit!' A little of the wine spilled on Virginia's robe. 'Did Keith send you?'

'I think I'm batting for the other side.'

'You think?'

'He threatened her before.'

'That's just his way.'

'His way sometimes extends to hit and run.'

'That's bullshit!'

'Is it?'

Virginia swung her legs around and faced the mirror; dabbed cream on to some cotton wool and wiped the residue of make-up from around her eyes.

'Keith,' Kiley said. 'You let him know about the card and the champagne.'

'Maybe.'

'Just like you let him know about you and Dianne . . .'

Virginia laughed, low and loud. 'It keeps him on his toes.'

'Then shall we say it's served its purpose this time? You'll keep away? Unless you want her to get hurt, that is?'

She looked at him in the mirror. 'No,' she said. 'I don't want that.'

His phone rang almost as soon as he stepped through the door. Costain.

'Why don't you get yourself a mobile, for fuck's sake? I've been trying to get hold of you the best part of an hour.'

'What happened?'

'Keith Payne came to the club, walked right in off the street in the middle of rehearsals. Couple of his minders with him. One of the staff tried to stop them and got thumped for his trouble. Wanted to talk to Dianne, that's what he said. Talk to her on her own.'

Kiley waited, fearing the worst.

'Your pal, Becker, all of a sudden he's got the balls of a brass monkey. Told Payne to come back that evening, pay his money along with all the other punters. Miss Adams was an artiste and right now she was working.' Costain couldn't quite disguise his admiration. 'I doubt anyone's spoken to Keith Payne like that in twenty years. Not and lived to tell the tale.'

'He didn't do anything?'

'Someone from the club had called the police. Payne obviously didn't think it was worth the hassle. Turned around and left. But you should have seen the expression on his face.'

Kiley thought he could hazard a guess.

Later that evening he phoned Virginia Pride at the theatre. 'Your husband, I need to see him.'

*

250

The house was forty minutes north of London, nestled in the Hertfordshire countryside, the day warm enough for Payne to be on a lounger near the pool. A gofer brought them both a cold beer.

'Hear that,' Payne said. 'Fuckin' birdsong. Amazing.'

Kiley could hear birds sometimes, above the noise of traffic from the Holloway Road. He kept it to himself.

'Ginny says you went to see her.'

'Dianne Adams, I wanted to make sure there wouldn't be any trouble.'

'If that dyke comes sniffin' round . . .'

'She won't.'

'That business with her and Ginny, a soddin' aberration. All it was. Over and done. And then Ginny, all of a sudden she's sending fuckin' champagne and fuck knows what.'

'You want to know what I think?' Kiley said.

A flicker of Payne's pale blue eyes gave permission.

'I think she does it to put a hair up your arse.'

Payne gave it a moment's thought and laughed. 'You could be right.'

'And Becker, he was just sounding off. Trying to look big.'

'People don't talk to me like that. Nobody talks to me like that. Especially a tosser like him.'

'Sticks and stones. Besides, like you say, who is he? Becker? He's nothing.'

Swift to his feet for a big man, Payne held out his hand. 'You're right.'

'You won't hold a grudge?'

Payne's grip was firm. 'You've got my word.'

*

The remainder of Dianne Adams' engagement passed off without incident. Virginia Pride stayed away. By the final weekend it was standing room only and, spurred on by the crowd and the band, Adams' voice seemed to find new dynamics, new depth.

Of course, Becker told her about the bracelet during one of those languorous times when they lay in her hotel bed, feeling the lust slowly ebb away. He even offered it to her as a present, half-hoping she would refuse, which she did. 'It's beautiful,' she said. 'And it's a beautiful thought. But it's your good-luck charm. You don't want to lose it now.'

On the last night at Ronnie's, she thanked him profusely on stage for his playing and presented him with a charm in the shape of a saxophone. 'A little something to remember me by.'

'You know,' she said, outside on the pavement later, 'next month we've got this tour, Italy, Switzerland. You should come with us.'

'I'd like that,' Becker said.

'I'll call you,' she said, and kissed him on the mouth. She never did.

Costain thanked Kiley for a job well done and with part of his fee Kiley acquired an expensive mobile phone and waited for that also to ring.

*

Three weeks later, as Derek Becker was walking through Soho after a gig in Dean Street, gone one a.m., a car pulled up alongside him and three men got out. Quiet and quick. They grabbed Becker and dragged him into an alley and beat him with gloved hands and booted feet. Then they threw him back against the wall and two of them held out his arms at the wrist, fingers spread, while the third drew a pair of pliers from the pocket of his combat pants. One of them stuffed a strip of towelling into his mouth to stifle the screams.

Becker's instrument case had already fallen open to the ground, and as they left, one of the men trod almost nonchalantly on the bell of the saxophone before booting it hard away. A second man picked up the case and hurled it into the darkness at the alley's end, the bracelet, complete with its newly attached charm, sailing unseen into the deepest corner, carrying with it all of Becker's new-found luck.

It was several days before Kiley heard what had happened and went to see Becker in his flat in Walthamstow, bringing a couple of paperbacks and a bottle of single malt.

'Gonna have to turn the pages for me, Jack. Read them as well.'

His hands were still bandaged and his left eye still swollen closed.

'I'm sorry,' Kiley said and opened the Scotch.

'You know what, Jack?' Becker said, after the first sip. 'Next time, don't do me no favours, right?'

ASYLUM

The van had picked them up a little after six, the driver cursing the engine which had stubbornly refused to start; fourteen of them cramped into the back of an ailing Ford as it rattled and lurched along narrow roads, zip-up jackets, boots, jeans, the interior thick with cigarette smoke. Outside, light leaked across the Fens. Jolted against one another, the men sat, mostly silent, heads down, a few staring out absently across the fields. Field after field the same. When anyone did speak it was in heavily accented English, Romanian, Serbo-Croatian, Albanian. There were lights in the isolated farms, the small villages they passed through, children turning in their beds and waking slowly to the half-remembered lines they would sing at Harvest Festival. Thanks for plenty. Hymns of praise. The air was cold.

Some ten miles short of Ely, the van turned off along a rough track and bumped to a halt behind a mud-spattered tractor and several other vans. On trestle tables beneath a makeshift canopy, men and women were already working, sorting and wrapping cauliflowers in cellophane.

254

Towards the far side of the field, indistinct in the havering mist, others moved slowly in the wake of an ancient harvester, straightening and bending, straightening and bending, loading cabbages into the low trailer that rattled behind.

A man in a dark fleece, gloves on his fists, stepped towards the van. 'What sort of fuckin' time d'you call this?'

The driver shrugged and grinned.

'Laugh the other side of your fuckin' face, one o' these fine days.'

The driver laughed nervously and, taking the makings from his pocket, started to roll a cigarette. Most of the men had climbed down from the van and were standing in a rough circle, facing inwards, hands jammed down into their pockets as they stamped their feet. The others, two or three, sat close against the open door, staring out.

'You,' the foreman said, waving his fist. 'You. Yes, you. What d'you think this is? Fuckin' holiday? Get the fuck out of there and get to fuckin' work.'

Across the slow spread of fields to the west, the blunt outline of Ely Cathedral pushed up from the plane of earth and bulked against the sky.

*

A hundred or so miles away, in North London, the purlieu of Highbury Fields, Jack Kiley woke in a bed that was not his own. From the radio at the other side of the room came the sounds of the *Today* programme, John Humphrys at full bite, castigating some hapless politician for something he or she had done or failed to do. Kiley pushed back the quilt and rolled towards the edge of the bed, feet quick to the floor. In the bathroom he relieved himself and washed his hands, splashed cold water in his face. At least now

Kate was allowing him to leave a toothbrush there, a razor too, and he used both before descending.

Kate sat at the breakfast table, head over her laptop, fingers precise and quick across the keys. Kiley knew better than to interrupt. There was coffee in the cafetière and he poured some into Kate's almost empty mug before helping himself. His selflessness was acknowledged by a grunt and a dismissive wave of the hand.

A mound of the day's papers, including the *Independent*, for whom Kate wrote a weekly column, was on a chair near the door, and Kiley carried them across to the padded seat in the window bay. Through the glass he could see the usual dog walkers in the park, joggers skirting the edge, more than one of them pushing those three-wheeler buggies that cost the price of a small second-hand car.

Automatically, he looked at the sports pages first to check the results and saw, with no satisfaction, that one of the teams he used to played for had now gone five matches without scoring a goal. Below the fold on the front page, the second lead was about the wife of a Home Office minister being attacked and robbed not so very far from where he was now.

'*In the early hours of yesterday morning, Helen Forester, wife of . . .*'

What in God's name was she doing, Kiley thought, wandering around the nether end of Stoke Newington at two in the morning? He checked the other papers. Only the disintegrating marriage of a B-celebrity soap star prevented the story from making a full sweep of the tabloids, '*Minister's Wife Mugged*' and similar dominating the rest in one-inch type. A library photograph of Helen Forester accompanying her husband to the last party conference was the most popular, her narrow, rather angular face strained beneath a round, flat-brimmed hat of the kind worn by Spanish bullfighters, her husband mostly cropped out.

'*Mrs Forester was found in a dazed state by passers-by and taken to Homerton hospital, where she was treated for minor injuries and shock.*'

'I know her,' Kate said, looking up from her work. 'Interviewed her for a piece on politicians' wives. After all that fuss about Betsy what's-her-name. I liked her. Intelligent. Mind of her own.'

'Must have been switched off when this happened.'

'Maybe.'

'You think there's more to it than meets the eye?'

'Isn't there always?'

'You're the journalist, you tell me.'

Kate shot him a sour glance and went back to the piece she was writing – '*No More Faking It: the rehabilitation of Meg Ryan in* In the Cut.'

'At least it makes a change,' Kiley said, 'from MPs caught out cottaging on Clapham Common.'

But Kate had already switched him off.

By midday the Minister concerned had issued a brief statement. '*My wife and I are grateful for all of the flowers and messages of support . . .*'

The Shadow Home Secretary materialised long enough to fire the usual tired salvos about the unsafe streets of our cities and the need for more police officers on the beat. Nothing yet about what the unfortunate Mrs Forester had been doing out alone when she might more properly have been tucked up alongside her husband in the safety of their Islington flat or at their constituency home. That, Kiley was sure, would come.

Café tables were spread along the broad pavement north of Belsize Park underground station, and Kiley was sitting in the early autumn sunshine nursing a cappuccino and wondering what to do with the rest of the day.

Almost directly opposite, above the bookshop, his small two-room office held little attraction: the message light on the answerphone was, as far as he knew, not flickering, no urgent faxes lay waiting, any bills he was concerned with paying had been dealt with and his appointment book, had he possessed one, would have been blank. He could walk up the hill on to Hampstead Heath and enjoy the splendours of the turning leaves or stroll across to the Screen on the Hill and sit through the matinee of something exotic and life-affirming.

Then again, he could order another cappuccino, while he considered the possibility of lunch. Irena, the young Romanian waitress who moonlighted two mornings a week as his bookkeeper and secretary, was not on duty, and he caught the eye of a waiter, who by his accent was Spanish and most probably from Latin America. At one of the nearby tables, a May–November couple were holding hands and staring into one another's eyes; at another, a man in a '*Fight Global Capitalism*' T-shirt was listening contentedly to his iPod, and just within his line of vision, a young woman of twenty-two or -three, wearing dark glasses and a seriously abbreviated cerise top, was poring over *The Complete Guide to Yoga*. In small convoys, au pairs propelled their charges along the pavement opposite. The sun continued to shine. What was a seemingly intelligent, middle-aged middle-class woman doing, apparently alone, at the wrong end of Stoke Newington High Street at that hour of the morning? Like a hangnail, it nagged at him and wouldn't let him rest.

*

Dusk prevailed. Lights showed pale under the canopy as the last supermarket loads were packed and readied. The workers, most of them, stood huddled around the vans, the faint glow of their cigarettes pink and red. Mud on their boots and the backs of their legs, along their arms and caked beneath their fingernails. The low line of trees at the far field edge was dark and, beyond it, the cathedral was black against the delicate pink of the sky.

The foreman had counted his men once and now was counting them again.

One short.

He'd had a shouting match with one of them earlier, some barrack-room lawyer from Dubrovnik or some other Godforsaken place, there was always one of them, mouthing off about rest periods and meal breaks.

'You,' he said, poking the nearest with a gloved finger. 'That mate of yours, where is he?'

The man shook his head and looked away. The others stared hard at the ground.

'Where the fuck is he, that fucking Croat cunt?'

Nobody answered, nobody knew.

'Okay,' the foreman said finally, the driver with his engine already idling. 'Get 'em out of here. And tomorrow, be on fuckin' time, right?'

It was later that evening, after a warming dinner of lamb shanks with aubergine and cinnamon and the best part of a bottle of Côtes du Ventoux, the moon plump in the sky, that Audrey Herbert left her husband to load the dishwasher, donned her wellingtons and waterproof jacket and took the Labrador for its final walk. Halfway along the track that ran beside the second field, the dog started barking loudly at something in the drainage ditch and Audrey thought at first he had unearthed a rat. It was only when she shone the torch and saw the body, half-submerged, that she realised it was something more.

*

Kate stood Kiley up that evening to have dinner with Jonathan Sayer. Sayer, until a rather public falling-out and resignation, had been press officer to the Prime Minister and still had close connections with the inner sanctum of government.

'Seems the PM went ape shit,' Sayer confided. They were in an Indian restaurant in Kentish Town, a table well away from the door. 'Tore a strip off the Home Secretary right outside the Cabinet room. Told him if he couldn't keep his underlings and their bloody wives in order, he'd replace him with someone who could.'

'Bit of an overreaction?'

Sayer shrugged. 'You know how he is, scared about weevils coming out of the woodwork. Or wherever it is they come from.'

Kate thought it was flour.

'His ratings, this past six months, last thing he needs now is a juicy bit of scandal.'

'Is that what this is?'

'I shouldn't think so.' Sayer smiled winsomely. 'How's the tarka dhal, by the way?'

'A little too runny, actually.'

'Shame.'

'So. When's it going to hit the fan?'

Sayer looked at her appraisingly. 'First editions tomorrow, most likely.'

'Are you going to make me wait till then?'

'You could always phone your editor.'

'I'm having dinner with you.'

Sayer sighed. 'It seems Helen Forester has not been averse, shall we say, to seeking a little solace on the side. When her husband's work has made him less than attentive.'

'She screws around.'

'Not compulsively.'

'Anyone notable?'

Sayer named a junior MP and a writer whose dissec-
tions of political life under the Tories had come close to
earning him a CBE. 'That's over a period of ten or twelve
years, of course. Restrained by some standards.'

'And Forester knows?'

Sayer nodded. 'There was some talk of divorce, I believe,
but all the usual factors came into play. Children. Careers.
Forgive and forget.'

'So the tabs are going to dish the dirt, encourage their
readers to join the dotted lines. What else was she doing
in the wee small hours if she wasn't on her way home
from some love nest or other?'

'Something like that.'

'Any names being bandied about?'

'Ah . . .' Sayer leaned back in his chair. 'I was rather
hoping you might help me there.'

'Me?'

'You interviewed her recently, got on famously by all
accounts.'

'And you think she might have been a little indiscreet?'

'Two women chatting together, relaxed. It's not impossible she'd have mentioned a name or two, purely in
passing. Besides, it's what you're good at. Getting people
to say things they'd rather keep to themselves.'

Kate smiled and let a piece of well-spiced lady's finger
slide down her throat. 'It's you, actually, Jonathan. Fancies
the balls off you, she really does. Maybe I'll give my editor
a call as you suggest.'

There were times and recently a goodly number of
them, when Kate despaired of her profession. The
following morning, when the press spewed up a mess of
private folly and unsubstantiated rumour, was one of them.
In the cause of public interest, the tabloids took their

usual lead, while the broadsheets, keen to maintain their superiority, merely reported their assertions in words of more than two syllables.

After a decent interval, Kate phoned the number she had for Helen Forester but there was no answer. By the time she tried again later, mid-morning, the line had been disengaged. Jonathan Sayer's mobile was permanently switched off. Kiley, she remembered, had promised to do a little background checking on the client of a solicitor friend. She wondered if a visit to the Olafur Eliasson sun installation at Tate Modern might lift her into a better frame of mind.

*

It was late afternoon before Kiley reported to the offices of Hamblin, Laker and Clarke, a summary of his findings inside a DL manilla envelope, along with a bill for his services. Margaret Hamblin, quietly resplendent in something from Donna Karan, came out into the reception area to thank him.

'I would suggest a glass of wine, Jack. There's a quite nice white from Alsace I'm giving a try. Only there's someone here who wants to see you. Special Branch. You can use my office.'

Someone was plural. One brusque and unsmiling, slight hints of a Scottish accent still lingering, the other, bespectacled, mostly silent and inscrutable.

'Masters,' the first man said, showing identification. 'Detective Superintendent.' He didn't introduce his companion.

'Jack Kiley.'

'You're a private investigator.'

'That's right.'

'And you can make a living doing that?'

'Some days, yes.'

In the parlance of Kiley's recent profession, Masters was a skilful midfielder, not especially tall, wiry, difficult to shake off the ball. He nodded and reached into his pocket. The by-play was over. Inside a small plastic envelope was one of Kiley's business cards, dog-eared and far from pristine.

'Yours?'

'Cheaper by the thousand.'

'There's a phone number, just above your name.' He held it up for Kiley to see. It was Margaret Hamblin's number. 'Is that your writing?'

'Seems to be.'

A Polaroid photograph next, head and shoulders, a deep gash to one side of the temple, lifeless eyes.

'Anyone you know?'

'No.'

'He was found dead in a field last night. Village outside Ely.'

Kiley shook his head.

'Here,' Masters said, handing Kiley the envelope containing the card. 'Turn it round.'

On the back, smudged but still readable was the name '*Adina*'. Just that.

'Ring any bells?'

It rang a few. Adina was a friend of Irena's from Costanza on the Black Sea coast of Romania. Smuggled into the country, she had worked as an exotic dancer, paying off the exorbitant fee for transportation. She had got into a little trouble and Kiley had helped her out. That had been a year ago. Somewhere in that time she had sent Irena a postcard from Bucharest.

'You rode to the rescue,' Masters said. 'Knight in shining armour.'

'Dark armour,' the second man corrected, as if to prove he'd been listening. "A knight in dark armour rescuing a lady".'

'Harry Potter?' asked Kiley guilelessly.

'Philip Marlowe. *The Big Sleep*.'

'You know where she is now, this Adina?' Masters asked.

'Romania?'

'I don't think so. And Alen Markovic . . .'

'Who's that?'

'The man in the photo.'

'The dead man.'

'Exactly. You've no idea how or why he might end up in a drainage ditch with your card on his person? Complete with the name of an illegal immigrant you befriended and the telephone number of a solicitor with a reputation for handling appeals against deportation. And let's discount, shall we, pure chance and coincidence.'

'If I had to guess,' Kiley said, 'I'd say he got it from Adina.'

'You gave it to her, she gave it to him.'

'Something like that.'

'In case of trouble, someone to contact, someone to ring.'

'It's plausible.'

'He didn't call you?'

'No.'

Kiley wondered if they were merely following up stray leads; he wondered if the one blow with a thick-edged implement to Alen Markovic's head had been enough to kill him. On balance, he thought both less than likely.

'We could always try asking this Adina,' Masters said softly, as if the suggestion had just that second occurred to him.

'If we could find her,' Kiley said.

'If she isn't still tied to a tree,' said the second man. He really did know his Chandler backwards.

*

A light rain was beginning to fall. Most of the outside tables had been cleared. Kiley intercepted Irena on her way up from the Tube. Masters stood a little way off, coat collar up. Through the pale strobe of headlights climbing the hill, Kiley could see Masters' colleague in the bookstore opposite, innocently browsing through this and that.

'What is it?' Irena said. 'What's happened?'

Kiley moved her close against one of the plane trees that lined the street. Her features were small and precise and the rain that clung to her short, spiky hair made it shine.

'Adina,' Kiley said. 'Is she back in England?'

'No, of course not.'

Kiley waited, fingers not quite touching the sleeve of her coat. Her eyes avoiding his. 'I shall be late. For work.' Absurdly, he wanted to run his hand across the cap of dark, wet hair.

'Why? Why do you want to know?'

'It's complicated.'

'Is she in trouble?'

'I don't think so.'

'She made me promise not to tell you. She thought, after everything you did, she thought you would be angry. Upset.' There were tears on her face or maybe it was only the rain, which had started to fall more heavily. 'She is working at a club. I think near Leicester Square. I don't know the name.'

'You know where she's living?'

Irena took a set of keys from her pocket and put them in his hand.

'She is living with me.'

Kiley watched her walk away, head down, and then waited for Masters to join him. The dark blue Vauxhall was parked in a side road opposite.

Masters' bibliophile friend was standing by the car, a plastic bag containing several paperbacks clutched against his coat. 'You're lucky,' he said to Kiley. 'More than decent bookshop, that close to where you work.' The glow from the overhead light turned his skin an unhealthy shade of orange.

'You've got a name?' Kiley asked.

'Several.' He took off his glasses, shook them free from rain, blinked, and put them back on again.

'How about one that matches some ID?' Kiley said.

'Jenkins?'

'And you're Special Branch too?'

'Not exactly.'

'Let's get in,' Masters said. 'We're wasting time.'

At the lights by Chalk Farm station, Masters said, 'All we want from your friend is a little information, clarification. We've no interest in her immigration status at this stage.'

Kiley trusted him like he trusted the weather.

Irena lived in two rooms off Inverness Street; actually a single room let into the roof and divided by a rickety partition. A small Velux window gave views towards the market and the canal. Kiley had been there once before, a party for Irena's friends, enough of the Romanian diaspora to cover every available inch of floor and spread back down the stairs.

He had hardly let himself in when Adina came bounding after him, scarf tied round her raven hair, cursing. She was wearing a bustier beneath a flimsy cotton top, skin-tight emerald green trousers and what, after several visits to

266

Cinderella at an early age, would, to Kiley, forever be Dandini boots, folded back high above the knee.

'Oh, my God!' she exclaimed, seeing him. 'Oh, my God, what are you doing here?'

'It's all right,' Kiley said. 'Irena gave me a key.'

'I am just here,' Adina said breathlessly, 'for visit. Holiday.'

'Irena said you were working.'

Adina dumped her things on the floor and threw herself into a chair. 'Work, holiday, what does it matter?'

The headline on the evening paper read *'MINISTER'S WIFE'S MIDNIGHT ASSIGNATION'*. What was an hour or so up against some nice alliteration?

'Adina, there are some people who want to see you.'

'I have visa,' she said. Probably a lie.

'It's not about that.' He paused, the rain persistent on the window. 'You know someone named Alen Markovic?'

Adina jerked forward. 'What's happened to him?'

'You do know him then?'

'Something has happened.'

'Yes.'

'They have killed him.'

'Who?'

She shook her head. Her hair bounced against the tops of her breasts. He thought she might be about to scream or cry, but instead she brought her forearm to her mouth and bit down hard.

'Don't,' he said.

'These people,' Adina said, 'they are police?'

'Yes.'

'Of course they are police.' She stood up and studied the bite mark on her arm. 'You trust them?'

'I don't know.'

'Okay, for Alen's sake I will talk to them. But you must be there with me.'

Kiley nodded. 'The café across the street.'

'Portuguese or Italian?'

'Portuguese.'

'You go. Five minutes, I come.'

'Don't duck out on me.'

'Duck out?'

'Never mind.'

Jenkins sat reading *A Short History of Europeans and the Rest of the World from Antiquity to the Present*. Masters held a small espresso cup in his hand and stared at a lithograph of Lisbon on the wall. Kiley ordered coffee for himself and, believing one of those intense little Portuguese custard tarts was never quite enough, bought two; he didn't offer to share them round.

'When you were helping your friend out of her little difficulty,' Masters said, 'you ran across Sali Mejdani. Aldo Fusco, he sometimes likes to call himself.'

'We had a conversation.'

Jenkins chuckled softly, possibly at something he'd just read.

'He brought her into the country, your Adina?'

'Not directly.'

'Of course. From Romania to Albania and then to Italy, Italy to France, Belgium or Holland. Into Britain from somewhere like Zeebrugge. Fifteen or twenty people a day, seven days a week, three hundred-plus days of the year. Approximately five thousand sterling per head. Even after expenses – drivers, escorts, safe houses, backhanders . . .'

'Plenty of those,' Jenkins said, without looking up.

'. . . it all adds up to a tidy sum. And the punters, what they don't pay in advance, they pay with interest. For women and boys it's the sex trade, for the rest it's hard labour.'

'Mejdani,' Kiley said, 'why can't you arrest him, close him down?'

268

'Ah,' said Jenkins.

'For the last couple of years,' Masters said, 'we've been building a case against him. Ourselves, Immigration, Customs and Excise, the National Crime Squad.' He set down his cup at last. 'You know when you were a kid, building sandcastles on the beach, Broadstairs or some-where, you and your dad. You're putting the finishing touches to this giant, intricate thing, all turrets and towers and windows and doors, and just as you turn over the bucket and tap the last piece into place, one of the bits lower down slides away, and then another, and before you know it you're having to start all over again.'

'Accident?' Kiley said. 'Over-ambition?'

Masters sat back. 'I prefer to think the fault lies in the design.'

'Not the workmanship?'

'Get what you pay for, some might say.'

Jenkins laid aside his book. 'Mejdani certainly would.'

'He's bribing people,' Kiley said, 'to look the other way.'

'I didn't say that.'

Kiley looked across at Masters. Masters shrugged.

''Tis but the way of the world, my masters,' Jenkins said.

'Not Chandler again?'

'A little earlier.'

They all looked round as Adina stepped through the door. She had changed into black jeans and a black roll-neck sweater, an unbuttoned beige topcoat round her shoulders. Some but not all of the make-up had been wiped from her face. She asked at the counter for a Coke with lemon and ice.

Kiley made the introductions while she lit a cigarette.

'Alen,' she said, 'what happened to him?'

Masters showed her the photograph.

For a long moment, she closed her eyes.

'You're not really surprised,' Masters said.

'I don't understand.'

'You thought he might get into difficulties,' Kiley said. 'You gave him my card.'

'Yes, I thought . . . Alen, he was someone important in my country, high up in trade union . . .'

'We used to have those,' Jenkins said, as much to himself as anyone.

'. . . there was disagreement, he had to leave. Rights of workers, something. And here, I don't know, I think it was the same. Already, he told me, the people he work for, they warn him, shut your mouth. Keep your mouth shut. I think he had made threat to go to authorities. The police.'

'You think that's why he was killed.'

'Of course.'

Masters glanced at Jenkins, who gave a barely discernible nod. 'We have a number of names,' he said, 'names and places. We'd like to run them past you and for you to tell us any that you recognise.'

Adina held smoke down in her lungs. What was she, Kiley wondered? All of twenty? Twenty-one? She'd paid to risk her life travelling to England not once, but twice. Paid dearly. And why? Because the strip clubs and massage parlours of London and Wolverhampton were better than the autoroutes in and out of Bucharest? As an official asylum seeker, she could claim thirty quid a week, ten in cash, the rest in vouchers. But she was not official. She did what she could.

She said, 'Okay. If I can.'

'Wait,' Kiley said. 'If she helps you, you have to help her. Make it possible for her to stay, officially.'

'I don't know if we can do that,' Masters said.

'Of course we fucking can,' Jenkins said.

270

Adina lit a fresh cigarette from the butt of the first and asked for another Coke.

Kiley caught the overground to Highbury and Islington. In an Upper Street window a face he recognised stared out from a dozen TVs; the same face was in close-up on the small Sony Kate kept at the foot of the bed.

'Kramer seems to be getting a lot of exposure,' Kiley said.

'The wrong kind.'

Dogmatic, didactic, distinguished by a full beard and sweep of jet black hair, Martin Kramer was an investigative journalist with strong anti-capitalist, anti-American left-wing leanings and a surprisingly high profile. Kiley had always found him too self-righteous by half, even if, much of the time, what he said made some kind of sense.

Kate turned up the volume as the *Newsnight* cameras switched to Jeremy Paxman behind an impressive-looking desk. '. . . if it really is such a small and insignificant point, Mr Kramer, then why not answer my question and move on?'

She flicked the sound back down.

'What was the question?' Kiley asked.

'Was he entertaining Helen Forester in his flat on the night she was attacked?'

'And was he?'

'He won't say.'

'Which means he was.'

'Probably.'

Sitting, propped up against pillows, Kate was wearing the faded Silver Moon T-shirt she sometimes used as nightwear and nothing else. Kiley rested his hand above her knee.

'They were at Cambridge together,' Kate said. 'Maybe they had a thing back then and maybe they didn't.'

'Twenty-five years ago,' Kiley said. 'More.'

Kate turned in a little against his hand. 'Kramer's been making this programme for Channel 4. Illegal workers, gangmasters, people trafficking. Pretty explosive by all accounts.'

'Not the best of times for the wife of a Home Office minister to be sharing his bed.'

'Needs must,' Kate said. 'From time to time.'

*

Helen Forester denied and denied and finally admitted that she had, indeed, had dinner with Martin Kramer on the night in question, had enjoyed possibly a glass of wine too many, and gone for a stroll to clear her head before returning home.

Kramer's programme was moved to a prime-time slot, where it attracted close on seven million viewers, not bad for a polemical documentary on a minority channel. Standing amidst the potato fields of East Anglia, Kramer pontificated about the farming industry's increasing dependence on illegal foreign labour, comparing it to the slave trade of earlier centuries, with gangmasters as the new overseers and Eastern Europeans the new Negroes; from the lobby of a hotel in Bayswater he talked about the dependence of the hotel and catering trades on migrants from Somalia and South-East Asia; and at the port of Dover he made allegations of corruption and bribery running through Customs and Immigration and penetrating right up to the highest levels of the police.

'That's the thing about Kramer,' Masters said, watching a video of the programme in Jenkins' office high above the Thames. 'He always has to go that little bit too far.'

Two days earlier, with the assistance of officers from

the Cambridgeshire force, they had arrested two of Alen Markovic's fellow field workers for his murder. The foreman, they claimed, had given them no choice: get rid of him or get sent back. They had clubbed him to death with a spade and a hoe.

In one of his last actions as a minister before being shuffled on to the back benches, Hugo Forester announced a further toughening of the laws governing entry into the country and the employment of those who have gained access without proper documentation. 'The present system,' he told the House, 'in its efforts to provide refuge and succour to those in genuine need, is unfortunately still too open to exploitation by unscrupulous individuals and criminal gangs. But the House should be assured that the introduction of identity cards to be announced in the Queen's speech will render it virtually impossible for the employment of illegal workers to continue.'

Coordinated raids by the police on safe houses and farms in Kings Lynn and Wisbech resulted in twenty-seven arrests. Two middle-ranking officers in the Immigration Service tendered their resignations and a detective chief inspector stationed at Folkestone retired from duty on medical grounds. A warrant was issued for Sali Mejdani's arrest on twenty-seven separate charges of smuggling illegal immigrants into Britain. Mejdani, travelling under the name of Aldo Fusco, had flown from Heathrow to Amsterdam on the previous morning, and from there to Tirana where he seemed, temporarily, to have disappeared.

Adina was duly given a student visa and enrolled in a course in leisure and travel at the University of North London.

Hugo and Helen Forester announced a trial separation.

Kiley, feeling pleased with himself and for very little reason, volunteered to treat Kate to one hundred and thirty-eight minutes of *Mystic River* with supper afterwards at Café Pasta. Kate thought she could skip the movie.

When she arrived, Kiley was already seated at a side table, Irena bending slightly towards him, the pair in conversation.

'Ordered the wine yet, Jack?' Kate said, slipping off her coat and handing it to Irena. Irena blushed and backed away. 'Oh, and bring us a bottle of the Montepulciano d'Abruzzo, will you? Thanks very much.'

'She was telling me about Adina,' Kiley said.

'How was the film?' Kate asked.

'Good. Pretty good.'

Irena brought the wine and asked Kate if she would like to taste it, which she did.

'She's lovely, isn't she?' Kate said as Irena walked away.

'Who?'

'Irena.'

'Is she?'

JUST FRIENDS

These things I remember about Anna Shepherd: the way a lock of her hair would fall down across her face and she would brush it back with a flick of her hand; the sliver of green, like a shard of glass, high in her left eye; the look of surprise, pleasure and surprise, when she spoke to me that first time – 'And you must be Jimmy, right?'

The way she lied.

It was November, late in the month and the night air bright with cold that numbed your fingers even as it brought a flush of colour to your cheeks. London, the winter of '56, and we were little more than kids then, Patrick, Val and myself, though if anyone had called us that we'd have likely punched him out, Patrick or myself at least, Val in the background, careful, watching.

Friday night it would have been, a toss-up between the Flamingo and Studio 51, and on this occasion Patrick had decreed the Flamingo: this on account of a girl he'd started seeing, on account of Anna. The Flamingo a little more cool, more likely to impress. Hip, I suppose, the word we would have used.

All three of us had first got interested in jazz at school, the trad thing to begin with, British guys doing an earnest imitation of New Orleans; then, for a spell, it was the Alex Welsh band we followed around, a hard-driving crew with echoes of Chicago, brittle and fast, Tuesday nights the Lyttelton place in Oxford Street, Sundays a club out at Wood Green. It was Val who finally got us listening to the more modern stuff, Parker 78s on Savoy, Paul Desmond, the Gerry Mulligan Quartet.

From somewhere, Patrick got himself a trumpet and began practising scales, and I kicked off playing brushes on an old suitcase while saving for the downpayment on a set of drums. Val, we eventually discovered, already had a saxophone – an old Selmer with a dented bell and a third of the keys held on by rubber bands: it had once belonged to his old man. Not only did he have a horn, but he knew how to play. Nothing fancy, not yet, not enough to go steaming through the changes of 'Cherokee' or 'I Got Rhythm' the way he would later, in his pomp, but tunes you could recognise, modulations you could follow.

The first time we heard him, really heard him, the cellar room below a greasy spoon by the Archway, somewhere the owner let us hang out for the price of a few coffees, the occasional pie and chips, we wanted to punch him hard. For holding out on us the way he had. For being so damned good.

Next day, Patrick took the trumpet to the place he'd bought it, Boosey and Hawkes, and sold it back, got the best price he could. 'Sod that for a game of soldiers,' he said, 'too much like hard bloody work. What we need's a bass player, someone half-decent on piano, get Val fronting his own band.' And he pushed a bundle of fivers into my hand. 'Here,' he said, 'go and get those sodding drums.'

276

'What about you?' Val asked, though he probably knew the answer even then. 'What you gonna be doin'?'

'Me?' Patrick said. 'I'm going to be the manager. What else?'

And, for a time, that was how it was.

Private parties, weddings, christenings and bar mitzvahs, support slots at little clubs out in Ealing or Totteridge that couldn't afford anything better. From somewhere Patrick found a pianist who could do a passable Bud Powell, and, together with Val, that kept us afloat. For a while, a year or so at least. By then even Patrick could see Val was too good for the rest of us and we were just holding him back; he spelled it out to me when I was packing my kit away after an all-nighter in Dorking, a brace of tenners eased down into the top pocket of my second-hand Cecil Gee jacket.

'What's this?' I said.

'Severance pay,' said Patrick, and laughed.

Not the first time he paid me off, nor the last.

But I'm getting ahead of myself.

That November evening, we'd been hanging round the Bar Italia on Frith Street pretty much as usual, the best coffee in Soho then and now; Patrick was off to one side, deep in conversation with a dark-skinned guy in a Crombie overcoat, the kind who has to shave twice a day and wore a scar down his cheek like a badge. A conversation I was never meant to hear.

'Jimmy,' Patrick said suddenly, over his shoulder. 'A favour. Anna, I'm supposed to meet her. Leicester Square Tube.' He looked at his watch. 'Any time now. Get down there for me, okay? I'll see you at the club later.'

All I'd seen of Anna up to that point had been a photo-graph, a snapshot barely focused, dark hair worn long, high cheekbones, a slender face. Her eyes – what colour were her eyes?

She came up the steps leading on to Cranbourne Street and I recognised her immediately; tall, taller than I'd imagined, and in that moment – Jesus! – so much more beautiful.

'Anna?' Hands in my pockets, blushing already, trying and failing to look cool. 'Patrick got stuck in some kind of meeting. Business, you know? He asked me to meet you.'

She nodded, looking me over appraisingly. 'And you must be Jimmy, right?' Aside from that slight, quick flicker of green, her eyes were brown, I could see that now, a soft chocolatey brown.

Is it possible to smile ironically? That's what she was doing.

All right, Jimmy,' she said. 'Where are you taking me?'

When we got to the Flamingo, Patrick and Val had still not arrived. The Tony Kinsey Quintet were on the stand, two saxes and rhythm. I pushed my way through to the bar for a couple of drinks and we stood on the edge of the crowd, close but not touching. Anna was wearing a silky kind of dress that clung to her hips, two shades of blue. The band cut the tempo for 'Sweet and Lovely', Don Rendell soloing on tenor.

Anna rested her fingers on my arm. 'Did Patrick tell you to dance with me, too?'

I shook my head.

'Well, let's pretend that he did.'

Six months I suppose they were together, Anna and Patrick, that first time around, and for much of that six months, I rarely saw them one without the other. Towards the end, Patrick took her off for a few days to Paris, a big deal in those days, and managed to secure a gig for Val while he was there, guesting at the *Chat Qui Peche* with René Thomas and Pierre Michelot.

278

After they came back I didn't see either of them for quite a while: Patrick was in one of his mysterious phases, ducking and weaving, doing deals, and Anna – well, I didn't know about Anna. And then, one evening in Soho, hurrying, late for an appointment, I did see her, sitting alone by the window of this trattoria, the Amalfi it would have been, on Old Compton Street, a plate of pasta in front of her, barely touched. I stopped close to the glass, raised my hand and mouthed 'Hi!' before scuttling on, but if she saw me I couldn't be sure. One thing I couldn't miss though, the swelling, shaded purple, around her left eye.

A week after this Patrick rang me and we arranged to meet for a drink at the Bald Faced Stag; when I asked about Anna he looked through me and then carried on as if he'd never heard her name. At this time I was living in two crummy rooms in East Finchley – more a bedsitter with a tiny kitchen attached, the bathroom down the hall – and Patrick gave me a lift home, dropped me at the door. I asked him if he wanted to come in but wasn't surprised when he declined.

Two nights later I was sitting reading some crime novel or other, wearing two sweaters to save putting on the second bar of the electric fire, when there was a short ring on the downstairs bell. For some reason, I thought it might be Patrick, but instead it was Anna. Her hair was pulled back off her face in a way I hadn't seen before, and, a faint finger of yellow aside, all trace of the bruise around her eye had disappeared.

'Well, Jimmy,' she said, 'aren't you going to invite me in?'

She was wearing a cream sweater, a coffee-coloured skirt with a slight flare, high heels which she kicked off the moment she sat on the end of the bed. My drums were out at the other side of the room, not the full kit, just the bass drum, ride cymbal, hi-hat and snare; clothes I'd been intending to iron were folded over the back of a chair.

'I didn't know,' I said, 'you knew where I lived.'

'I didn't. Patrick told me.'

'You're still seeing him then?'

The question hung in the air.

'I don't suppose you've got anything to drink?' Anna said.

There was a half-bottle of Bell's out in the kitchen and I poured what was left into two tumblers and we touched glasses and said, 'Cheers.' Anna sipped hers, made a face, then drank down most of the rest in a single swallow.

'Patrick . . .' I began.

'I don't want to talk about Patrick,' she said.

Her hand touched the buckle of my belt. 'Sit here,' she said.

The mattress shifted with the awkwardness of my weight.

'I didn't know,' she said afterwards, 'it could be so good.'

You see what I mean about the way she lied.

*

Patrick and Anna got married in the French church off Leicester Square and their reception was held in the dance hall conveniently close by; it was one of the last occasions I played drums with any degree of seriousness, one of the last times I played at all. My application to join the Metropolitan Police had already been accepted and within weeks I would be starting off in uniform, a different kind of beat altogether. Val, of course, had put the band together and an all-star affair it was – Art Ellefson, Bill Le Sage, Harry Klein. Val himself was near his mercurial best, just ahead of the flirtations with heroin and free-form jazz that would sideline him in the years ahead.

At the night's end we stood outside, the three of us, ties unfastened, staring up at the sky. Anna was somewhere inside, getting changed.

'Christ!' Patrick said. 'Who'd've fuckin' thought it?'

He took a silver flask from inside his coat and passed it round. We shook hands solemnly and then hugged each other close. When Anna came out, she and Patrick went off in a waiting car to spend the night at a hotel on Park Lane.

'Start off,' Patrick had said with a wink, 'like you mean to continue.'

We drifted apart: met briefly, glimpsed one another across smoky rooms, exchanged phone numbers that were rarely if ever called. Years later I was a detective sergeant working out of West End Central and Patrick had not long since opened his third nightclub in a glitter of flashbulbs and champagne; Joan Collins was there with her sister, Jackie. There were ways of skirting round the edges of the law and, so far, Patrick had found most of them: favours doled out and favours returned; backhanders in brown envelopes; girls who didn't care what you did as long as you didn't kiss them on the mouth. Anna, I heard, had walked out on Patrick; reconciled, Patrick had walked out on her. Now they were back together again, but for how long?

When I came off duty, she was parked across the street, smoking a cigarette, window wound down.

'Give you a lift?'

I'd moved upmarket but not by much, an upper-floor flat in an already ageing mansion block between Chalk Farm and Belsize Park. A photograph of the great drummer, Max Roach, was on the wall; Sillitoe's *Saturday Night and Sunday Morning* next to the Eric Amblers and a few Graham Greenes on the shelf; an Alex Welsh album on the record player, ready to remind me of better times.

'So, how are things?' Anna asked, doing her best to look as if she cared.

'Could be worse,' I said. In the kitchen, I set the kettle to boil and she stood too close while I spooned Nescafé into a pair of china mugs. There was something beneath the scent of her perfume that I remembered too well.

'What does he want?' I asked.

'Who?'

'Patrick, who else?

She paused from stirring sugar into her coffee. 'Is that what it has to be?'

'Probably.'

'What if I just wanted to see you for myself?'

The green in her eye was bright under the unshaded kitchen light. 'I wouldn't let myself believe it,' I said.

She stepped towards me and my arms moved around her as if they had a mind of their own. She kissed me and I kissed her back. She was divorcing him, she said: she didn't know why she hadn't done it before.

'He'll let you go?'

'He'll let me go.'

For a moment, she couldn't hold my gaze. 'There's just one thing,' she said, 'one thing that he wants. This new club of his, someone's trying to have his licence cancelled.'

'Someone?'

'Serving drinks after hours, an allegation, nothing more.'

'He can't make it go away?'

Anna shook her head. 'He's tried.'

I looked at her. 'And that's all?'

'One of the officers, he's accused Patrick of offering him a bribe. It was all a misunderstanding, of course.'

'Of course.'

'Patrick wonders if you'd talk to him, the officer concerned.'

282

'Straighten things out.'

'Yes.'

'Make him see the error of his ways.'

'Look, Jimmy,' she said, touching the back of her hand to my cheek, 'you know I hate doing this, don't you?'

No, I thought. No, I don't.

'Everything has a price,' I said. 'Even friendship. Friendship, especially. And tell Patrick, next time he wants something, to come and ask me himself.'

'He's afraid you'd turn him down.'

'He's right.'

When she lifted her face to mine I turned my head aside. 'Don't let your coffee get cold,' I said.

Five minutes later she was gone. I sorted out Patrick's little problem for him and found a way of letting him know if he stepped out of line again, I'd personally do my best to close him down. Whether either of us believed it, I was never sure. With or without my help, he went from rich to richer; Anna slipped off my radar and when she re-emerged, she was somewhere in Europe, nursing Val after his most recent spell in hospital, encouraging him to get back into playing. Later they got married, Val and Anna, or at least that's what I heard. Some lives took unexpected turns. Not mine.

*

I stayed on in the Met for three years after my thirty and then retired; tried working for a couple of security firms, but somehow it never felt right. With my pension and the little I'd squirrelled away, I found I could manage pretty well without having to look for anything too regular. There was an investigation agency I did a little work for once in a while, nothing too serious, nothing heavy, and that was enough.

Patrick I bumped into occasionally if I went up west, greyer, more distinguished, handsomer than ever; in Soho once, close to the little Italian place where I'd spotted Anna with her bruised eye, he slid a hand into my pocket and when I felt where it had been there were two fifties, crisp and new.

'What's this for?' I asked.

'You look as though you need it,' he said.

I threw the money back in his face and punched him in the mouth. Two of his minders had me spreadeagled on the pavement before he'd wiped the mean line of blood from his chin.

At Val's funeral we barely spoke; acknowledged each other but little more. Anna looked gaunt and beautiful in black, a face like alabaster, tears I liked to think were real. A band played 'Just Friends', with a break of thirty-two bars in the middle where Val's solo would have been. There was a wake at one of Patrick's clubs afterwards, a free bar, and most of the mourners went on there, but I just went home and sat in my chair and thought about the three of us, Val, Patrick and myself, what forty years had brought us to, what we'd wanted then, what we'd done.

I scarcely thought about Anna at all.

Jack Kiley, that's the investigator I was working for, kept throwing bits and pieces my way, nothing strenuous like I say, the occasional tail job, little more. I went into his office one day, a couple of rooms above a bookstore in Belsize Park, and there she sat, Anna, in the easy chair alongside his desk.

'I believe you two know each other,' Jack said.

Once I'd got over the raw surprise of seeing her, what took some adjusting to was how much she'd changed. I suppose I'd never imagined her growing old. But she had.

Under her grey wool suit her body was noticeably thicker;
her face was fuller, puffed and cross-hatched around the
eyes, lined around the mouth. No Botox; no nip and tuck.

'Hello, Jimmy,' she said.

'Anna's got a little problem,' Jack said. 'She thinks you
can make it go away.' He pushed back from his desk. 'I'll
leave you two to talk about it.'

The problem was a shipment of cocaine that should have
made its way seamlessly from the Netherlands to Dublin
via the UK. A street value of a million and a quarter pounds.
Customs and Excise, working on a tip-off, had seized the
drug on arrival, a clean bust marred only by the fact that
the coke had been doctored down to a mockery of its original strength; a double-shot espresso from Caffè Nero
would deliver as much of a charge to the system.

'How in God's name,' I asked, 'did you get involved in
this?'

Anna lit a cigarette and wafted the smoke away from
her face. 'After Val died I went back to Amsterdam, where
we'd been living. There was this guy – he'd been Val's
supplier . . .'

'I thought Val had gone straight,' I said.

'There was this guy,' Anna said again, 'we – well, we
got sort of close. It was a bad time for me. I needed . . .'
She glanced across and shook her head. 'A girl's got to
live, Jimmy. All Val had left behind was debts. This guy,
he offered me a roof over my head. But there was a price.'

'I'll bet.' Even I was surprised how bitter that sounded.

'People he did business with, he wanted me to speak
for him, take meetings. I used to fly to Belfast, then, after
a while, it was Dublin.'

'You were a courier,' I said. 'A mule.'

'No. I never carried the stuff myself. Once the deal was
set up, I'd arrange shipments, make sure things ran smoothly.'

'Patrick would be proud of you,' I said.

'Leave Patrick out of this,' she said. 'This has nothing to do with him.'

I levered myself up out of the seat; it wasn't as easy as it used to be. 'Nor me.' I got as far as the door.

'They think I double-crossed them,' Anna said. 'They think it was me tipped off Customs; they think I cut the coke and kept back the rest so I could sell it myself.'

'And did you?'

She didn't blink. 'These people, Jimmy, they'll kill me. To make an example. I have to convince them it wasn't me; let them have back what they think's their due.'

'A little difficult if you didn't take it in the first place.'

'Will you help me, Jimmy, yes or no?'

'Your pal in Amsterdam, what's wrong with him?'

'He says it's my mess and I have to get myself out of it.'

'Nice guy.'

She leaned towards me, trying for a look that once would have held me transfixed. 'Jimmy, I'm asking. For old time's sake.'

'Which old time is that, Anna?'

She smiled. 'The first time you met me, Jimmy, you remember that? Leicester Square?'

Like yesterday, I thought.

'You ever think about that? You ever think what it would have been like if we'd been together? Really together?'

I shook my head.

'We don't always make the right choices,' she said.

'Get somebody else to help you,' I said.

'I don't want somebody else.'

'Anna, look at me, for fuck's sake. What can I do? I'm an old man.'

'You're not old. What are you? Sixty-odd? These days sixty's not old. Seventy-five. Eighty. That's old.'

'Tell that to my body, Anna. I'm carrying at least a stone more than I ought to; the tendon at the back of my left ankle gives me gyp if ever I run for a bus and my right hip hurts like hell whenever I climb a flight of stairs. Find someone else, anyone.'

'There's nobody else I can trust.'

*

I talked to Jack Kiley about it later; we were sitting in the Starbucks across the street, sunshine doing its wan best to shine through the clouds.

'What do you know about these types?' Jack asked. 'This new bunch of cocaine cowboys from over the old Irish Sea?'

'Sod all,' I said.

'Well, let me give you a bit of background. Ireland has the third-highest cocaine use in Europe and there's fifteen or twenty gangs and upwards beating the bollocks off one another to supply it. Some of them, the more established, have got links with the IRA, or did have, but it's the newer boys that take the pippin. Use the stuff themselves, jack up an Uzi or two and go shooting; a dozen murders in Dublin so far this year and most of the leaves still on the fucking trees.'

'That's Dublin,' I said.

Jack cracked a smile. 'And you think this old flame of yours'll be safe here in Belsize Park or back home in Amsterdam?'

I shrugged. I didn't know what to bloody think.

He leaned closer. 'Just a few months back, a drug smuggler from Cork got into a thing with one of the Dublin gangs – a disagreement about some shipment bought and paid for. He thought he'd lay low till it blew over. Took a false name and passport and holed up in an apartment in the Algarve. They found his body in the freezer. Minus the head. Rumour is whoever carried out the contract on him had it shipped back as proof.'

Something was burning deep in my gut and I didn't think a couple of antacid tablets was going to set it right.

'You want my advice, Jimmy?' he said, and gave it anyway. 'Steer clear. Either that or get in touch with some of your old pals in the Met. Let them handle it.'

Do that, I thought, and there's no way of keeping Anna out of it; somehow I didn't fancy seeing her next when she was locked away on remand.

'I don't suppose you fancy giving a hand?' I said.

Jack was still laughing as he crossed the street back towards his office.

*

At least I didn't have to travel far, just a couple of stops on the Northern Line. Anna had told me where to find them and given me their names. There was some kind of céilidh band playing in the main bar, the sound of the bodhrán tracing my footsteps up the stairs. And, yes, my hip did ache.

The Sweeney brothers were sitting at either end of a leather sofa that had seen better days, and Chris Boyle was standing with his back to a barred window facing down on to the street. Hip-hop was playing from a portable stereo at one side of the room, almost drowning out the traditional music from below. No one could accuse these boys of not keeping up with the times.

There was an almost full bottle of Bushmill's and some glasses on the desk, but I didn't think anyone was about to ask me if I wanted a drink.

One of the Sweeneys giggled when I stepped into the room and I could see the chemical glow in his eyes.

288

'What the fuck you doin' here, old man?' the other one said. 'You should be tucked up in the old folks' home with your fuckin' Ovaltine.'

'Two minutes,' Chris Boyle said. 'Say what you have to fuckin' say then get out.'

'Supposin' we let you,' one of the brothers said and giggled some more. Neither of them looked a whole lot more than nineteen, twenty tops. Boyle was closer to thirty, nearing pensionable age where that crew was concerned. According to Jack, there was a rumour he wore a catheter bag on account of getting shot in the kidneys coming out from the rugby at Lansdowne Road.

'First,' I said, 'Anna knew nothing about either the doctoring of the shipment, nor the fact it was intercepted. You have to believe that.'

Boyle stared back at me, hard-faced.

One of the Sweeneys laughed.

'Second, though she was in no way responsible, as a gesture of good faith, she's willing to hand over a quantity of cocaine, guaranteed at least eighty per cent pure, the amount equal to the original shipment. After that it's all quits, an even playing field, business as before.'

Boyle glanced across at the sofa then nodded agreement.

'We pick the point and time of delivery,' I said. 'Two days' time. I'll need a number on which I can reach you.'

Boyle wrote his mobile number on a scrap of paper and passed it across. 'Now get the fuck out,' he said.

Down below, someone was playing a penny whistle, high-pitched and shrill. I could feel my pulse racing haphazardly and when I managed to get myself across the street, I had to take a grip on a railing and hold fast until my legs had stopped shaking.

*

289

When Jack learned I was going through with it, he offered to lend me a gun, a Smith & Wesson .38, but I declined. There was more chance of shooting myself in the foot than anything else.

I met Anna in the parking area behind Jack's office, barely light enough to make out the colour of her eyes. The cocaine was bubble-wrapped inside a blue canvas bag.

'You always were good to me, Jimmy,' she said, and reaching up, she kissed me on the mouth. 'Will I see you afterwards?'

'No,' I said. 'No, I don't think so.'

The shadows swallowed her as she walked towards the taxi waiting out on the street. I dropped the bag down beside the rear seat of the car, waited several minutes, then slipped the engine into gear.

The place I'd chosen was on Hampstead Heath, a makeshift soccer pitch shielded by lines of trees, a ramshackle wooden building off to one side, open to the weather; sometimes pick-up teams used it to get changed, or kids huddled there to feel one another up, smoke spliffs or sniff glue.

When Patrick, Val and I had been kids ourselves there was a body found close by, someone murdered and left, and the place took on a kind of awe for us, murder in those days being something more rare.

I'd left my car by a mansion block on Heath Road and walked in along a partly overgrown track. The moon was playing fast and loose with the clouds and the stars seemed almost as distant as they were. An earlier shower of rain had made the surface a little slippy and mud clung to the soles of my shoes. There was movement, low in the under-growth to my right-hand side, and, for a moment, my heart stopped as an owl broke with a fell swoop through the trees above my head.

A dog barked and then was still.

I stepped off the path and into the clearing, the weight of the bag real in my left hand. I was perhaps a third of the way across the pitch before I saw them, three or four shapes massed near the hut at the far side and separating as I drew closer, fanning out. Four of them, faces unclear, but Boyle, I thought, at the centre, the Sweeneys to one side of him, another I didn't recognise hanging back. Behind them, behind the hut, the trees were broad and tall and close together, beeches I seemed to remember Val telling me once when I'd claimed them as oaks. 'Beeches, for God's sake,' he'd said, laughing in that soft way of his. 'You, Jimmy, you don't know your arse from your elbow, it's a fact.'

I stopped fifteen feet away and Boyle took a step forward. 'You came alone,' he said.

'That was the deal.'

'He's stupider than I fuckin' thought,' said one or other of the Sweeneys and laughed a girlish little laugh.

'The stuff's all there?' Boyle said, nodding towards the bag.

I walked a few more paces towards him, set the bag on the ground, and stepped back.

Boyle angled his head towards the Sweeneys and one of them went to the bag and pulled it open, slipping a knife from his pocket as he did so; he slit open the package, and, standing straight again, tasted the drug from the blade.

'Well?' Boyle said.

Sweeney finished running his tongue around his teeth. 'It's good,' he said.

'Then we're set,' I said to Boyle.

'Set?'

'We're done here.'

'Oh, yes, we're done.'

The man to Boyle's left, the one I didn't know, moved

forward almost to his shoulder, letting his long coat fall open as he did so, and what light there was glinted dully off the barrels of the shotgun as he brought it to bear. It was almost level when a shot from the trees behind struck him high in the shoulder and spun him round so that the second shot tore through his neck and he fell to the ground as good as dead.

One of the Sweeneys cursed and started to run, while the other dropped to one knee and fumbled for the revolver inside his zip-up jacket.

With all the gunfire and the shouting I couldn't hear the words from Boyle's mouth, but I could lip-read well enough. 'You're dead,' he said, and drew a pistol not much bigger than a child's hand from his side pocket and raised it towards my head. It was either bravery or stupidity or maybe fear that made me charge at him, unarmed, hands outstretched as if in some way to ward off the bullet; it was the muddied turf that made my feet slide away under me and sent me sprawling headlong, two shots sailing over my head before one of the men I'd last seen minding Patrick in Soho stepped up neatly behind Boyle, put the muzzle of a 9mm Beretta hard behind his ear and squeezed the trigger.

Both the Sweeneys had gone down without me noticing; one was already dead and the other had blood gurgling out of his airway and was not long for this world.

Patrick was standing back on the path, scraping flecks of mud from the edges of his soft leather shoes with a piece of stick.

'Look at the state of you,' he said. 'You look a fucking state. If I were you I should burn that lot when you get home, start again.'

I wiped the worst of the mess from the front of my coat and that was when I realised my hands were still shaking. 'Thanks, Pat,' I said.

'What are friends for?' he said.

Behind us his men were tidying up the scene a little, not too much. The later editions of the papers would be full of stories of how the Irish drug wars had come to London, the Celtic Tigers fighting it out on foreign soil.

'You need a lift?' Patrick asked, as we made our way back towards the road.

'No, thanks. I'm fine.'

'Thank Christ for that. Last thing I need, mud all over the inside of the fucking Merc.'

When I got back to the flat I put one of Val's last recordings on the stereo, a session he'd made in Stockholm a few months before he died. Once or twice his fingers didn't match his imagination, and his breathing seemed to be giving him trouble, but his mind was clear. Beeches, I'll always remember that now, that part of the Heath. Beeches, not oaks.

MINOR KEY

It used to be there under '*Birthdays*', some years at least. The daily listing in the paper, the *Guardian*, occasionally the *Times*. September eighteenth. '*Valentine Collins, jazz musician.*' And then his age: twenty-seven, thirty-five, thirty-nine. Not forty. Val never reached forty.

He'd always look, Val, after the first time he was mentioned, made a point of it, checking to see if his name was there. 'Never know,' he'd say, with that soft smile of his. 'Never know if I'm meant to be alive or dead.'

There were times when we all wondered; wondered what it was going to be. Times when he seemed to be chasing death so hard, he had to catch up. Times when he didn't care.

Jimmy rang me this morning, not long after I'd got back from the shops. Bread, milk, eggs – the paper – gives me something to do, a little walk, reason to stretch my legs.

'You all right?' he says.

'Of course I'm all right.'

'You know what day it is?'

294

I hold my breath; there's no point in shouting, losing my temper. 'Yes, Jimmy, I know what day it is.'

There's a silence and I can sense him reaching for the words, the thing to say – You don't fancy meeting up later? A drink, maybe? Nice to have a chat. It's been a while.

'Okay, then, Anna,' he says instead, and then he hangs up.

*

There was a time when we were inseparable, Jimmy, Val, Patrick and myself. Studio 51, the Downbeat Club, all-nighters at the Flamingo, coffee at the Bar Italia, spaghetti at the Amalfi. That place on Wardour Street where Patrick swore the cheese omelettes were the best he'd ever tasted and Val would always punch the same two buttons on the jukebox, B19 and 20, both sides of Ella Fitzgerald's single, 'Manhattan' and 'Every Time We Say Goodbye'.

Val loved that song, especially.

He knew about goodbyes, Val.

Later, anyway.

Back then it was just another sad song, something to still the laughter. Which is what I remember most from those years, the laughter. The four of us marching arm in arm through the middle of Soho, carefree, laughing.

What do they call them? The fifties? The years of austerity? That's not how I remember them, '56, '57, '58. Dancing, music and fun, that's what they were to me. But then, maybe I was too young, too unobservant, too – God! it seems impossible to believe or say – but, yes, too innocent to know what was already there, beneath the surface. Too stupid to read the signs.

Patrick, for instance, turning away from the rest of us to have quick, intense conversations in corners with strangers, men in sharp suits and sharp haircuts, Crombie overcoats. The time Patrick himself suddenly arrived one evening in a spanking new three-piece suit from Cecil Gee, white shirt with a rolled Mr B collar, soft Italian shoes, and when we asked him where the cash came from for all that, only winking and tapping the side of his nose with his index finger – mind yours.

Val, those moments when he'd go quiet and stare off into nowhere and you knew, without anyone saying, that you couldn't speak to him, couldn't touch him, just had to leave him be until he'd turn, almost shyly, and smile with his eyes.

And Jimmy, the way he'd look at me when he thought no one else was noticing; how he couldn't bring himself to say the right words to me, even then.

And if I had seen them, the signs of our future, would it have made any difference, I wonder? Or would it all have turned out the same? Sometimes you only see what you want to until something presses your face so fast up against it there's nothing else you can do.

But in the beginning it was the boys and myself and none of us with a care in the world. Patrick and Jimmy had known one another since they were little kids at primary school, altar boys together at St Pat's; Val had met up with them later, the second year of the grammar school – and me, I'd been lucky enough to live in the same street, catch the same bus in the morning, lucky enough that Jimmy's mother and mine should be friends. The boys were into jazz, jazz and football – though for Patrick it was the Arsenal and Jimmy, Spurs, and the rows they had about that down the years. Val now, in truth I don't think Val ever cared too much about the football, just went along, White Hart Lane or Highbury, he didn't mind.

When it came to jazz, though, it was Val who took the

lead, and where the others would have been happy enough to listen to anything as long as it had rhythm, excitement, as long as it had swing, Val was the one who sat them down and made them listen to Gerry Mulligan with Chet Baker, Desmond with Brubeck, Charlie Parker, Lester Young.

With a few other kids they knew, they made themselves into a band: Patrick on trumpet, Jimmy on drums, Val with an ageing alto saxophone that had belonged to his dad. After the first couple of rehearsals it became clear Val was the only one who could really play. I mean *really* play: the kind of sound that gives you goose bumps on the arms and makes the muscles of your stomach tighten hard.

It wasn't long before Patrick had seen the writing on the wall and turned in his trumpet in favour of becoming agent and manager rolled into one; about the first thing he did was sack Jimmy from the band, Val's was the career to foster and Jimmy was just holding him back.

A couple of years later, Val had moved on from sitting in with Jackie Sharpe and Tubby Hayes at the Manor House and depping with Oscar Rabin's band at the Lyceum, to fronting a quartet that slipped into the lower reaches of the *Melody Maker* small group poll. All this time he was burning the proverbial candle, going on from his regular gig to some club where he'd play till the early hours and taking more Bennies than was prudent to keep himself awake. The result was, more than once, he showed up late for an engagement; occasionally, he didn't show up at all. Patrick gave him warning after warning, Val, in return, made promises he couldn't keep: in the end, Patrick delivered an ultimatum, finally walked away.

Within months the quartet broke up and, needing ready cash, Val took a job with Lou Preager's orchestra at the Lyceum: a musical diet that didn't stretch far beyond playing for dancers, the occasional novelty number and the hits of the day. At least when he'd been with Rabin there'd been a few other jazzers in the band – and Oscar had allowed them one number a night to stretch out and do their thing. But this . . . the boredom, the routine were killing him, and Val, I realised later, had moved swiftly on from chewing the insides of Benzedrine inhalers and smoking cannabis to injecting heroin. When the police raided a club in Old Compton Street in the small hours, there was Val in a back room with a needle in his arm.

Somehow, Patrick knew one of the detectives at West End Central well enough to call in a grudging favour. Grudging, but a favour all the same.

When Val stumbled out on to the pavement, twenty-four hours later and still wearing the clothes he'd puked up on, Patrick pushed him into a cab and took him to the place I was living in Kilburn.

I made tea, poured Patrick the last of a half-bottle of whisky, and ran a bath for Val, who was sitting on the side of my bed in his vest and underpants, shivering.

'You're a stupid bastard. You know that, don't you?' Patrick told him.

Val said nothing.

'He's a musician, I told the copper,' Patrick said. 'A good one. And you know what he said to me? All he is, another black junkie out of his fucking head on smack. Send him back where he fucking came from.'

A shadow of pain passed across Val's face and I looked away, ashamed, not knowing what to say. Val's father was West Indian, his mother Irish, his skin the colour of palest chocolate.

'Can you imagine?' Patrick said, turning to me. 'All those years and I never noticed.' Reaching out, he took hold of Val's jaw and twisted his face upwards towards

298

the light. 'Look at that. Black as the ace of fucking spades. Not one of us at all.'

'Stop it,' I said. 'Stop it, for God's sake. What's the matter with you?'

Patrick loosed his hold and stepped away. 'Trying to shake some sense into him. Make him realise, way he's going, what'll happen if he carries on.'

He moved closer to Val and spoke softly. 'They've got your number now, you know that, don't you? Next time they catch you as much as smelling of reefer they're going to have you inside so fast your feet won't touch the ground. And you won't like it inside, believe me.'

Val closed his eyes.

'What you need is to put a little space between you and them, give them time to forget.' Patrick stepped back. 'Give me a couple of days, I'll sort something. Even if it's the Isle of Man.'

In the event, it was Paris. A two-week engagement at *Le Chat Qui Peche* with an option to extend it by three more.

'You better go with him, Anna. Hold his hand, keep him out of trouble.' And slipping an envelope fat with French francs and two sets of tickets into my hand, he kissed me on the cheek. 'Just his hand, mind.'

The club was on the rue de la Huchette, close to the Seine, a black metal cat perched above a silver-grey fish on the sign outside; downstairs a small, smoky cellar bar with a stage barely big enough for piano, bass and drums, and, for seating, perhaps the most uncomfortable stools I've ever known. Instruments of torture, someone called them and, by the end of the first week, I knew exactly what he meant.

Not surprisingly, the French trio with whom Val was due

to work were suspicious of him at first. His reputation in England may have been on the rise, but across the Channel he was scarcely known. And when you're used to visitors of the calibre of Miles Davis and Bud Powell, Charlie Parker, what gave Val Collins the idea he'd be welcome? Didn't the French have saxophone players of their own?

Both the bassist and the drummer wore white shirts that first evening, I remember, ties loosened, top buttons undone, very cool; the pianist's dark jacket was rucked up at the back, its collar arched awkwardly against his neck, a cigarette smouldering, half-forgotten, at the piano's edge.

The proprietor, Madame Ricard, welcomed us with lavish kisses and led us to a table, where we sat listening, the club not yet half full, Val's foot moving instinctively to the rhythm and his fingers flexing over imaginary keys. At the intermission, she introduced us to the band, who shook hands politely, looked at Val with cursory interest and excused themselves to stretch their legs outside, breathe in a little night air.

'Nice guys,' Val said with a slight edge as they left.

'You'll be fine,' I said and squeezed his arm.

When the trio returned, Val was already on stage, re-angling the mike, adjusting his reed. 'Blues in F,' he said quietly, counting in the tempo, medium-fast. After a single chorus from the piano, he announced himself with a squawk and then a skittering run and they were away. Ten minutes later, when Val stepped back from the microphone, layered in sweat, the drummer gave a little triumphant roll on his snare, the pianist turned and held out his hand and the bass player loosened another button on his shirt and grinned.

'*Et maintenant*,' Val announced, testing his tender vocabulary to the full, '*nous jouons une ballade par Ira Gershwin et Vernon Duke*, "I Can't Get Started." *Merci.*'

And the crowd, accepting him, applauded.

What could go wrong?

At first, nothing it seemed. We both slept late most days
at the hotel on the rue Maitre-Albert where we stayed;
adjacent rooms that held a bed, a small wardrobe and little
else, but with views across towards Notre Dame. After
coffee and croissants – we were in Paris, after all – we
would wander around the city, the streets of Saint-Germain-
des-Prés at first, but then, gradually, we found our way
around Montparnasse and up through Montmartre to Sacre
Coeur. Sometimes we would take in a late-afternoon movie,
and Val would have a nap at the hotel before a leisurely
dinner and on to the club for that evening's session, which
would continue until the early hours.

Six nights a week and on the seventh, rest?

There were other clubs to visit, other musicians to hear.
The Caveau de la Huchette was just across the street, the
Club Saint-Germain-des-Prés and the Trois Mailletz both
a short walk away. Others, like the Tabou and the Blue
Note were a little further afield. I couldn't keep up.

'Go back to the hotel,' Val said, reading the tiredness in
my eyes. 'Get a good night's sleep, a proper rest.' Then,
with the beginnings of a smile, 'You don't have to play
nursemaid all the time, you know.'

'Is that what I'm doing?'

Coming into the club late one evening, I saw him in the
company of an American drummer we'd met a few nights
before and a couple of broad-shouldered French types,
wearing those belted trench coats which made them look
like cops or gangsters or maybe both. As soon as he spotted
me, Val made a quick show of shaking hands and turning
away, but not before I saw a small package pass from hand
to hand and into the inside pocket of his suit.

'Don't look so disapproving,' he said, when I walked
over. 'Just a few pills to keep me awake.'

'And that's all?'

'Of course.' He had a lovely, disarming smile.

'No smack?'

'No smack.'

I could have asked him to show me his arms, but I chose to believe him instead. It would have made little difference if I had; by then I think he was injecting himself in the leg.

The next day Val was up before eleven, dressed and ready, stirring me from sleep.

'What's happening?' I asked. 'What's wrong?'

'Nothing. Just a shame to waste a beautiful day.'

The winter sun reflected from the stonework of the bridge as we walked across to the Isle St Louis arm in arm. Val had taken to affecting a beret, which he wore slanting extravagantly to one side. On the cobbles close to where we sat, drinking coffee, sparrows splashed in the shallow puddles left by last night's rain.

'Why did you do it?' Val asked me.

'Do it?'

'This. All of this. Throwing up your job . . .'

'It wasn't a real job.'

'It was work.'

'It was temping in a lousy office for a lousy boss.'

'And this is better?'

'Of course this is better.'

'I still don't understand why?'

'Why come here with you?'

Val nodded.

'Because he asked me.'

'Patrick.'

'Yes, Patrick.'

'You do everything he asks you?'

I shook my head. 'No. No, I don't.'

'You will,' he said. 'You will.' I couldn't see his eyes; I didn't want to see his eyes.

A foursome of tourists, Scandinavian I think, possibly German, came and sat noisily at a table nearby. When the waiter walked past, Val asked for a cognac, which he poured into what was left of his coffee and downed at a single gulp.

'What I meant,' he said, 'would you have come if it had been anyone else but me?'

'I know what you meant,' I said. 'And, no. No, I don't think I would.'

'Jimmy, perhaps?'

'Yes,' I acknowledged. 'Perhaps Jimmy. Maybe.'

Seeing Val's rueful smile, I reached across and took hold of his hand, but when, a few moments later, he gently squeezed my fingers, I took my hand away.

Patrick was waiting for us at the hotel when we returned.

'Well,' he said, rising from the lobby's solitary chair. 'The lovebirds at last.'

'Bollocks,' Val said, but with a grin.

Patrick kissed the side of my mouth and I could smell Scotch and tobacco and expensive aftershave; he put his arms round Val and gave him a quick hug.

'Been out for lunch?'

'Breakfast,' Val said.

'Fine. Then let's have lunch.'

Over our protests he led us to a small restaurant in the Latin Quarter, where he ordered in a combination of enthusiastic gestures and sixth-form French.

'I went along to the club earlier,' Patrick said, once the waiter had set a basket of bread on the table and poured our wine. 'Sounds as if it's going well. Madame Ricard wants to hold you over for three weeks more. Assuming you're agreeable?'

Val nodded. 'Sure.'

'Anna?'

'I can't stay that long,' I said.

'Why ever not?' Patrick looked surprised, aggrieved.

'I've got a life to live.'

'You've got a bedsit in Kilburn and precious little else.'

Blood rushed to my cheeks. 'All the more reason, then, for not wasting my time here.'

Patrick laughed. 'You hear that, Val? Wasting her time.'

'Let her be,' Val said, forcefully.

Patrick laughed again. 'Found yourself a champion,' he said, looking at me.

Val's knife struck the edge of his plate. 'For fuck's sake! When are you going to stop organising our lives?'

Patrick took his time in answering. 'When I think you can do it for yourselves.'

In his first set that evening, Val was a little below par, nothing most of the audience seemed to notice or be bothered by, but there was less drive than usual to his playing and several of his solos seemed to peter out aimlessly before handing over to the piano. I could sense the tension building in Patrick as he sat beside me, and after the third number he steered me outside; there was a faint rain misting across the headlights of the cars along the Quai Saint-Michel, and from the bridge leading across to the Île de la Cité the river water looked black and unforgiving.

'He's using again,' Patrick said. 'You know that, don't you?'

I shook my head. 'I don't think so.'

'Anna, come on . . .'

'I asked him.'

'You asked him and he said no?'

'Yes.'

'Scout's honour, cross my heart and hope to die. That kind of no?'

I pulled away from him. 'Don't do that.'

'Do what?'

'Treat me as though I'm some child.'

'Then open your eyes.'

'They are open.'

Patrick sighed and I saw the grey of his breath dissembling into the night air.

'I'm not his jailer, Patrick,' I said. 'I'm not his wife, his lover. I can't watch him twenty-four hours of the day.'

'I know.'

He kissed me on the forehead, the sort of kiss you might give to a young girl, his lips cold and quick. A long, low boat passed slowly beneath the bridge.

'I'm opening a club,' he said. 'Soho. Broadwick Street.'

'You?'

'Some friends I know, they're putting up the money. I thought if Val were interested it would be somewhere for him to play.'

'What about the police? Isn't that a risk still?'

Patrick smiled. 'Don't worry about that. It's all squared away.'

How many times would I hear him say that over the years? All squared away. How much cash was shelled out, usually in small denominations, unmarked notes slipped into side pockets or left in grubby holdalls in the left-luggage lockers of suburban railway stations? I never knew the half of it, the paybacks and backhanders and all the false accounting, not even during those years later when we lived together – another story, waiting, one day, to be told.

'Come on,' he said, taking my arm. 'We'll miss the second set.'

When we got back to the club, Val and the American drummer were in animated conversation at the far end of

305

the bar. Seeing us approach, the drummer ducked his head towards Val, spoke quickly and stepped away. 'It's not me you have to worry about, you fucker, remember that.' And then he was pushing his way through the crowd.

'What was all that about?' Patrick asked.

Val shrugged. 'Nothing. Why?'

'He seemed pretty angry.'

'It doesn't mean anything. That's just the way he is.'

'How much do you owe?'

'What?'

'That bastard, how much do you owe?'

'Look . . .'

'No, you look.' Patrick had hold of him by the lapels of his coat. 'I know him. He was busted in London last year, thrown out of Italy before that, jailed in Berlin. He's a user and a dealer, the worst kind of pimp there is.'

'He's okay . . .'

Patrick pushed Val back against the bar. 'He's not fucking okay. You hear me. Keep away from him. Unless you want to end up the same way.'

On the small stage, the pianist was sounding a few chords, trying out a few runs. 'I've got to go,' Val said, and Patrick released his grip.

All of Val's anger came out on stage, channelled first through a blistering 'Cherokee', then a biting up-tempo blues that seemed as if it might never end.

Patrick left Paris the next day, but not before he'd set up a recording date for Val and the trio at the Pathe-Magellan studio. The producer's idea was to cut an album of standards, none of the takes too long and with Val sticking close to the melody, so that, with any luck, some might be issued as singles for the many jukeboxes around. Val always claimed to be less than happy with the results, feeling restricted by the set-up and the selection of tunes.

Easy listening, I suppose it might be called nowadays, dinner jazz, but it's always been one of my favourites, even now.

It was when we were leaving the studio after the last session that the pianist invited us to go along later with him and his girlfriend to hear Lester Young. Val was evasive. Maybe *oui*, maybe *non*. The one night off from *Le Chat*, he might just crash, catch up on some sleep.

'I thought he was one of your favourites,' I said, as we were heading for the *Métro*. 'How come you didn't want to go?'

Val gave a quick shake of the head. 'I hear he's not playing too well.'

Young, I found out later, had already been in Paris for several weeks, playing at the Blue Note on the rue d'Artois and living at the Hotel La Louisiane. A room on the second floor he rarely if ever left except to go to work.

Val had brought a few records with him from England, one of them an LP with a tattered cover and a scratch across one side: Lester Young, some fifteen years earlier, in his prime.

Val sat cross-legged on his bed, listening to the same tracks again and again. I poured what remained of a bottle of wine and took my glass across to a chair opposite the door; traffic noise rose and faded through the partly opened shutters, the occasional voice raised in anger or surprise; the sound of the saxophone lithe and muscular in the room.

When the stylus reached the run-off groove for the umpteenth time, Val reached over and set his glass on the floor. 'Okay,' he said. 'Let's take a chance.'

As we entered the club and walked past the long bar towards the stage, a tune I failed to recognise came to an end and Young, caught in the spotlight, stared out, startled, as the applause riffled out above the continuing conversation.

Up close, he looked gaunt and ill, dark suit hanging ragged from his shrunken frame, pain all too visible behind his eyes.

I took hold of Val's hand and squeezed it hard.

The drummer kicked off the next number at a brisk clip, playing quick patterns on the hi-hat cymbals with his sticks before moving to the snare, a signal for Young, saxophone tilted at an angle away from his body, to begin. Within the first bars, he had dragged the tempo down, slurring his notes across the tune, the same stumbling phrases repeated and then left hanging as he stepped back and caught his breath, the spaces between his playing wider and wider until finally he turned away and stood, head bowed, leaving the guitarist to take over.

'I Can't Get Started' was played at a funereal pace, the sound coarse and almost ugly; 'Tea for Two', one of the tunes Val had been listening to back in the hotel, started promisingly before teetering alarmingly off course; only a measured 'There Will Never Be Another You' rose from its foggy, thick-breathed beginning to become something that had moments of beauty between the self-doubt and misfingerings.

'If I ever get into that state, poor bastard,' Val said, once we were back outside, 'promise you'll take me out and shoot me.'

Yet in the succeeding weeks he went back again, not once but several times, fascinated despite himself, watching one of his idols unravel before his eyes. Then there was the time he went along and Young was no longer there; he'd cancelled his engagement suddenly and returned to the States. Two weeks later he was dead.

The evening he heard the news Val played 'There Will Never Be Another You', just the one chorus, unaccompanied, at the beginning of each set. A day later I walked into his room in the middle of the afternoon, and saw him sitting, half-naked on the bed, needle in hand, searching for a vein.

'Oh, Christ, Val,' I said.

He looked at me with tears in his eyes then slapped the inside of his thigh again.

I slammed the door shut, grabbed my coat and purse and ran out on to the street. For hours I just walked, ending up who knows where. At a corner bar I drank two brandies in quick succession followed by a crème de menthe and was promptly sick. I wanted to go back to the hotel, pack my bag and leave. What the hell was I doing there? What game? What stupid dream? There was vomit on the hem of my dress and on my shoes.

When finally I got to the club it was late and Val was nowhere to be seen, just his saxophone, mouthpiece covered, on its stand. In answer to my unspoken question, the pianist just shrugged and, still playing, gestured with his head towards the street.

I heard Val's shouts, muffled, coming from the alley that ran from close alongside the club down towards the Quai Saint-Michel. Val lay curled in on himself, arms cradling his head, while two men took it in turns to kick him in the back, the chest, the legs, anywhere they could, a third looking on.

'*Espèce d'ordure, je vais te crever la paillasse!*'

I stood, frozen, unable to react, then ran forward, screaming, and, as I threw myself at one of the men, he swung his arm into my face and I went stumbling back against the wall, blood filling my mouth. The sound of police sirens was too indistinct, too far away.

When someone helped me to my feet and I walked, unsteadily, to where Val still lay, unmoving, I thought that they had killed him. I thought he was dead.

For three days I sat by his bed in the hospital and held his hand. At night, I slept in the corridor outside, legs drawn up, on a chair. One of several broken ribs had come close to puncturing a lung. A week later I held his hand again as we walked in the hospital garden, bare earth and the stems of roses that had been cut back against the frost.

'How are you feeling?' I asked him.

'Fine,' he said, wincing as he smiled. 'I feel fine.'

After that there were always dull headaches that prevented him from sleeping and sudden surges of pain, sharp as a needle slipped beneath the skull. Despite the months and years of osteopathy, his back never sat right again, nagging at him each time he played.

*

'*Valentine Collins, jazz musician. Born, September 18th, 1937. Died, April 13th, 1976*'. Thirty years ago. No need any longer to take the ferry to Calais and then the long, slow journey by train, and not caring to fly, I treated myself to Eurostar, first class. A slightly better than aeroplane meal and free champagne. The centre of Paris in less than three hours. Autumn. The bluest of blue skies but cold enough for scarf and gloves. I feel the cold.

The *Métro* from Gare du Nord to Saint-Michel is busy with so many races, so many colours, Val's face would not have stood out at all. Not one of us, Patrick had said, and it was true, though not in the way he meant.

The rue de la Huchette is now a rat-run of kebab houses and crêperies and bars, so crowded, here and there I have to walk along the centre of the narrow street.

Le Chat Qui Peche is now a restaurant and the sign has been taken down. For a while I think I might go inside and have a meal, reminisce a little with the waiter, if he has sufficient English to complement my meagre French. But it is finally enough to stand here at the pavement's edge with people spilling round me, wondering, some of them, perhaps, what this old woman is doing, just standing there, staring at nothing in particular, none of them hearing what I hear, the sound of Val's alto saxophone, a ballad, astringent, keening, 'Every Time We Say Goodbye'.

GHOSTS

It was mid-morning, and Kiley was in his office two floors above a charity shop in Tufnell Park, stranded between his second cup of coffee and his third. *'Investigations'*, read the ad in the local press, *'Private and Confidential. All kinds of security work undertaken. Ex-Metropolitan Police.'* The absence of carpet made it easier to hear footsteps on the stairs. A pause and then a knock.

She was late thirties, dressed ten years younger, and looked all of forty-five, with the eyes of someone who woke up every day expecting to be disappointed and was rarely, if ever, disabused.

'Jack Kiley? Rita Barnes.'

Her hand was all cheap rings and bone.

Kiley knew the name and a moment later he knew why.

'Bradford Barnes, he was my son.'

The flowers had spread across the pavement close to the spot less than a hundred metres away where he'd been killed; tiny candles had burned through the night. Photographs and messages taped to the wall. *'Always remembered*'. '*A tragic waste*'. Bradford had been on the way home from a party, not late, a little after twelve, and had inadvertently brushed the shoulder of a young woman heading the other way. When he'd stopped to apologise, one of the men with her had raised his voice and then his fist. Punches flew and then a knife. When the group sauntered off laughing they left Bradford where he lay. A still-warm statistic, choking on his own blood. The twenty-second young person to have been stabbed to death in the capital that year and still months to go. Gang stuff, drug deals gone sour; the wrong look, the wrong word, the wrong place at the wrong time. Respect.

'I remember,' Kiley said.

The flowers had long since faded and been swept away; the photographs torn down.

'A year ago next week he was killed,' Rita Barnes said, 'three days short of his birthday, an' the police still i'n't got a bloody clue.'

She took an envelope from her bag and counted the notes out on his desk. 'There's two hundred and fifty. I'll get more. Find the bastard as did it, okay?'

What was he supposed to say? It was a waste of his time and her money?

Well, he had the time.

When she'd gone he put in a call to a DI he knew at the local nick. Jackie Ferris met him in the back room of the Assembly House, its dark wood panelling and orna-mented windows harking back to palmier days.

'Not got a clue, that's what she says?' Still on duty, Ferris was drinking lemon and lime.

'She's wrong?'

'We've had more than a clue since day one. Russell Means. It was his girlfriend Barnes bumped into. He's got form and a mouth to go with it, but forensics didn't give us shit and, surprise, surprise, no one's talking. Least, not to us.' Ferris raised her glass. 'You might have more luck.'

Rachel Sams lived on the seventh floor of an eight-floor block close to the closed-down swimming pool on Prince of Wales Road. Three of the flats on her level were boarded up and padlocked fast. The first two occasions Kiley called she refused to open the door and then, when she did, it was only to slam it in his face. It took a fierce squall of rain – Rachel hunched against the wind as she manoeuvred a buggy laden with supermarket carrier bags and containing a wailing two-year-old – for Kiley to open negotiations.

'Here, let me help.'

'Piss off!'

But she stood back while, after freeing the bags and handing them to her, he lifted the buggy and led the way.

Kiley followed her into the flat and, when she didn't complain, closed the door behind him. The interior was dominated by a wide-screen plasma TV, the furniture, most of it, third- or fourth-hand. Toys were scattered, here and there, across the floor. While Rachel changed the child's nappy, Kiley found a jar of instant coffee in the kitchen.

They sat at either end of the sagging settee while the boy piled wooden bricks on top of one another, knocked them down with a loud whoop and started again.

'Gary, for Christ's sake.'

'He's Russell Means' boy?' Kiley said.

'What of it?'

'Russell see him much?'

'When he can be bothered.'

'Bradford Barnes' mother came to see me, a week or so back.'

'So?'

314

'She wants to know what happened to her son.'

'She buried him, didn't she? What else she wanna know?'

'She wants to know who killed him. Wants some kind of – I don't know – justice, I suppose.'

'Yeah, well, she ain't gonna find it here.'

Kiley held her gaze until she looked away.

After that he called round every week or so, sometimes bringing a small present for the boy.

'Listen,' Rachel said, 'if you reckon this is gonna get you into my knickers . . .'

But, stuck up there on the seventh floor, she didn't seem overburdened with friends and now, as soon as he arrived, Gary scrambled up into his lap and happily pulled his hair. Kiley hadn't mentioned Bradford Barnes again.

Ten days short of Christmas, the sky a low, flat, unpromising grey, he got round to the flat to find Rachel hurling bits and pieces over the balcony, tears streaming down her face.

'That bastard! That lousy bastard!'

Kiley tried to calm her down and she lashed out, drawing blood from his lip. When he finally got her back inside, she was still shaking; Gary cowering in the corner, afraid.

'One of my mates rung an' told me, he's only gettin' married, i'n, it? To that skanky whore from down Stockwell. Saw it in Facebook or somethin'.' Picking up a half-empty mug, she hurled it against the wall. 'Well, he's gonna learn he can't treat me like that, i'n he? He's gonna pay.'

Kiley listened while she told him what had happened that night, how Russell Means had stabbed Bradford Barnes three times, once in the neck and twice in the chest, and then walked off laughing. He phoned Jackie Ferris and listened while Rachel told her story again, then promised to look after Gary while the two of them went to the station so that Rachel could make a statement.

Three days later, Russell Means was arrested.

Rita Barnes had tears in her eyes when she came to thank him and ask what more she owed him and Kiley said to forget it, it was fine. He would have given the two-fifty back if it hadn't been for a little matter of paying the rent.

'You're sure?'

'Sure.'

She kissed him on the cheek.

That night, Kiley walked past the spot where Bradford Barnes had been killed. If you looked closely, you could just make out the marks where the photos had been taped, a young man smiling out, his life ahead of him, ghosts on the wall.

TROUBLE IN MIND

Kiley smoothed the page across his desk and read it again: a survey conducted by Littlewoods Pools had concluded that of all ninety-two Premiership and Football League soccer teams, the one most likely to cause its supporters severe stress was Notts County. Notts County! Sitting snug, the last time Kiley had looked, near the midpoint of the League Two table and in immediate danger neither of relegation nor the nail-biting possibilities of promotion via the play-offs. Whereas Charlton Athletic, in whose colours Kiley had turned out towards the end of his short and less than illustrious career, were just one place from the bottom of the Premiership, with only four wins out of a possible twenty-two. Not only that, despite having sacked two successive managers before Christmas, this Saturday just past they had been bundled out of the FA Cup by Nottingham Forest, who had comprehensively stuffed them at the City ground, two–nil.

Stress? Stress didn't even begin to come close.

Kiley looked at the clock.

12:09.

Too late for morning coffee, too early for lunch. From his office window he could see the traffic edging in both directions, a pair of red 134 buses nuzzling up to one another as they prepared to run the gauntlet of Kentish Town Road on their way west towards the city centre, the slow progress of a council recycling lorry holding up those drivers who were heading – God help them – for the Archway roundabout and thence all points north.

His in-tray held a bill from the local processing lab, a begging letter from the Royal National Lifeboat Institution, and a polite reminder from HM Revenue & Customs that the final deadline for filing his tax return was the thirty-first of January – for more details about charges and penalties, see the enclosed leaflet SA352.

His pending file, had he possessed such a thing, would have held details of a course in advanced DNA analysis he'd half-considered after a severe overdose of *CSI*; a letter, handwritten, from a Muswell Hill housewife – a rare, but not extinct breed – wanting to know what Kiley would charge to find out if her husband was slipping around with his office junior – as if – and a second letter, crisply typed on headed notepaper, offering employment in a prestigious security firm run by two former colleagues from the Met. Attractive in its way, but Kiley couldn't see himself happily touching his peaked cap to every four-by-four driver checking out of a private estate in Totteridge and Whetstone on the way to collect Julian and Liberty from private school or indulge in a little gentle shopping at Brent Cross.

Early or not, he thought he'd go to lunch.

The Cook Shop was on the corner of Fortess Road and Raveley Street, a godsend to someone like Kiley who appreciated good, strong coffee or a tasty soup-and-sandwich combo, and which, apart from term-time mornings when it tended to be hysterical with young mums from the local primary school, was pretty well guaranteed to be restful and uncrowded – the owner's abiding penchant for Virgin FM Radio aside.

'The usual?' Andrew said, turning towards the coffee machine as Kiley entered.

'Soup, I think,' Kiley said.

Eyebrow raised, Andrew glanced towards the clock. 'Suit yourself.'

Today it was mushroom and potato, helped along with a few chunks of pale rye bread. Someone had left a newspaper behind and Kiley leafed through it as he ate. Former Labour Education Minister takes her child out of the state system because his needs will be better served elsewhere. Greater transparency urged in NHS. Unseasonably warm weather along the eastern seaboard of the United States. Famous celebrity Kiley had barely heard of walks out of *Big Brother* house in high dudgeon.

An item on the news page caught his eye, down near the bottom of page six. '***Roadside bomb kills British soldier on Basra patrol***. . . . *The death of the soldier, whose name was not immediately released, brought the number of British military fatalities in Iraq since the invasion of 2003, to 130.*'

Iraq, Afghanistan – maybe some day soon, Iran.

Kiley pushed the paper aside, used his last piece of bread to wipe around the inside of the bowl, slipped some coins on to the counter, and walked out into the street. Not sunbathing weather exactly, but mild for the time of year. The few greyish clouds moving slowly across the sky didn't seem to threaten rain. When he got back to his office, Jennie was sitting on the stairs; he didn't recognise her straight off and when he did he couldn't immediately recall her name.

'You don't remember me, do you?'

'Of course I do.'

'Really?' A smile crinkled the skin around her grey-green eyes and he knew her then.

'Jennie,' he said. 'Jennie Calder.'

Her hair, grown back to shoulder length, was the same reddish shade as before.

Jennie's smile broadened. 'You do remember.'

The last time Kiley had seen her she had been standing, newly crop-haired, cigarette in hand, outside a massage parlour on Crouch End Hill, ready to go to work. Two years back, give or take.

'How's your little girl?'

'Alice? Not so little.'

'I suppose not.'

'She's at school. Nursery.'

Kiley nodded. Alice had been clinging to her mother, screaming, wide-eyed, when he had last seen her, watching as Kiley set about the two men who'd been sent by Jennie's former partner to terrorise them, mother and daughter both. Armed with a length of two-by-four and a sense of righteous indignation, he had struck hard first and left the questions for later. Some men, he'd learned, you could best reason with when they were on their knees.

'How did you find me?' he asked.

'*Yellow Pages*,' Jennie grinned. 'Let my fingers do the walking.'

She was what, Kiley wondered, early thirties? No more. Careful make-up, more careful than before; slimmer, too: black trousers with a flare and a grey and white top beneath a long burgundy cardigan, left unfastened.

'You'd best come in.'

The main room of the second-floor flat served as living room and office both: a wooden desk rescued from a skip pushed into service by the window; a swivel chair, second-hand, bought cheap from the office suppliers on Brecknock Road; a metal shelf unit and filing cabinet he'd ferried over from his previous quarters in Belsize Park. For comfort there was an easy chair that had long since shaped itself around him. A few books, directories; computer, fax and answerphone. A Bose Radio/CD player with an eclectic selection of music alongside: Ronnie Lane, Martha Redbone, Mose Allison, Cannonball Adderley, the new Bob Dylan, old Rolling Stones.

One door led into a small kitchen, another into a shower room and lavatory and, beyond that, a bedroom which took, just, a four-foot bed, a chest of drawers and a metal rail from which he hung his clothes.

Home, of a kind.

'You haven't been here long,' Jennie said.

'Observation or have you been asking around?'

Jennie smiled. 'I spoke to the bloke in the charity shop downstairs.'

'A couple of months,' Kiley said. 'The rent in the other place . . .' He shrugged. 'Can I get you something? Tea? Coffee? I think there's some juice.'

She shook her head. 'No, I'm fine.'

'This isn't a social call.'

'Not exactly.'

Kiley sat on one corner of his desk and waved Jennie towards the easy chair. 'Fire away.'

A heavy lorry went past outside, heading for the Great North Road, and the windows shook. The Great North Road, Kiley thought, when had he last heard someone call it that? Seven years in the Met, four in uniform, the remainder in plain clothes; two years of professional soccer and the rest spent scuffling a living as some kind of private investigator. All the while living here or hereabouts.

The Great North Road – maybe it was time he took it himself. He'd been in that part of London for too long.

'This woman,' Jennie said, 'Mary. Mary Anderson. Lives near me. The flats, you know. She used to look after Alice before she started nursery. Just mornings. Alice loved her. Still does. Calls her Gran. She's got this son, Terry. In the Army. Queen's Royal something-or-other, I think it is.'

'Lancers,' Kiley offered.

'That's it. Queen's Royal Lancers. They were out in Iraq. Till – what? – a month ago, something like that. End of last week, he should have gone back.'

'Iraq?'

'I don't know. Yes, I think so. But not, you know, straight off.'

'Report to the barracks first.'

Jennie nodded. 'Yes.'

'And that's what he didn't do?'

She nodded again.

'AWOL.'

Jennie blinked.

'Absent without leave.'

'Yes.'

'Does she know where he is? His mum.'

'All this last week he was staying with her, her flat. Thursday morning, that's when he was due to go back. All his kit there ready in the hall, wearing the uniform she'd ironed for him the night before. He just didn't go. Stood there, not saying anything. Ages, Mary said. Hours. Then he went back into the spare room, where he'd been sleeping and just sat there, staring at the wall. Mary, she had to go out later, mid-morning, not long, just to the shops. When she got back, he'd gone.'

'She's no idea where?'

'No. There was no note, nothing. First, of course, she

322

thought he'd changed his mind. Gone back after all. Then she saw all his stuff, his bag and that, all dumped down beside the bed. ''Cept his uniform. He'd kept his uniform. And his gun.'

Kiley looked at her sharply.

'Mary had seen it, this rifle. Seen him cleaning it. She searched through everything but it wasn't there. He must have took it with him.'

'She's phoned the barracks to make sure . . .'

'They phoned her. When he didn't show. They'd got her number, next of kin. She did her best to put them off, told them he'd been taken ill. Promised to get back in touch.' Jennie shook her head. 'She's worried sick.'

'He's what? Twenty? Twenty-one?'

Jennie shook her head. 'No, that's it. He's not some kid. Thirty-five if he's a day. Sergeant, too. The army, it's a career for him. Mary says it's the only thing he's ever wanted to do.'

'All the more reason to think he'll turn up eventually. Come to his senses.'

Jennie was twisting a silver ring, round and round on her little finger. 'She said, Mary, before this happened, he'd been acting strange.'

'In what way?'

'You'd best ask her.'

'Look, I didn't say—'

'Just talk to her . . .'

'What for?'

'Jack . . .'

'What?'

'Talk to her, come on. What's the harm?'

Kiley sighed and eased his chair back from the desk. The man in the charity shop below was sorting through his collection of vinyl. The strains of some group Kiley vaguely remembered from his childhood filtered up through the board. The Easybeats? The Honeycombs? He could see why people would want to get rid of the stuff, but not why anyone would want to buy it again – not even for charity.

Jennie was still looking at him.

'How did you get here?' Kiley asked. 'Drive?'

'Walked. Suicide Bridge.'

Kiley reached for the phone. 'Let's not tempt face twice. I'll get a cab.'

*

When the council named the roads on the estate after streets in New Orleans they couldn't have known about Hurricane Katrina or its aftermath. Nonetheless, following Jennie through the dog shit and debris and up on to the concrete walkway, Kiley heard inside his head, not the booming hip-hop bass or the occasional metallic shrill of electro-funk that filtered here and there through the open windows, but Dylan's parched voice singing 'The Levee's Gonna Break'.

Mary Anderson's flat was in the same block as Jennie's but two storeys higher, coping missing at irregular intervals from the balcony, the adjacent property boarded up. A rubber mat outside the front door read *'Welcome'*, the area immediately around swept and cleaned that morning, possibly scrubbed. A small vase of plastic flowers was visible through the kitchen window.

Mary Anderson herself was no more than five three or four and slightly built, her neat grey hair and flowered apron making her look older than she probably was.

'This is Jack Kiley,' Jennie said. 'The man I spoke to you about, remember? He's going to help find Terry.'

Kiley shot her a look which she ignored.

'Of course,' Mary said. 'Come in.' She held out her hand. 'Jennie, you know where to go, love. I'll just pop the kettle on.' Despite the cheeriness in her voice, there were tears ready at the corners of her eyes.

They sat in the lavender living room, cups of tea none of them really wanted in their hands, doing their best not to stare at the pictures of Terry Anderson that lined the walls. Terry in the park somewhere, three or four, pointing at the camera with a plastic gun; a school photograph in faded colour, tie askew; Terry and his dad on a shingle beach with bat and ball; a young teenager in cadet uniform, smart on parade. Others, older, head up and shoulders back, a different uniform, recognisable still as the little lad with the plastic gun. Bang, bang, you're dead.

On the mantelpiece, in a silver frame, was a carefully posed shot of Terry on his wedding day – in uniform again and with a tallish brunette in white hanging on his arm, her eyes bright and hopeful, confetti in her hair. Arranged at either side were pictures of two young children, boy and girl, Terry's own children presumably, Mary's grandchildren.

Jennie's cup rattled against its saucer, the small noise loud in the otherwise silent room.

'You've heard nothing from him?' Kiley said.

'Nothing.'

'Not since Thursday?'

'Not a thing.'

'And you've no idea . . . ?'

She was already shaking her head.

'His family . . .' Kiley began, a nod towards the photographs.

'They separated, split up, eighteen months ago. Just after young Keiron's fifth birthday. That's him there. And Billie.

325

I always thought it a funny name for a girl, not quite right, but she insisted . . .'

'Could he have gone there? To see them?'

'Him and Rebecca, they've scarce spoken. Not since it happened.'

'Even so . . .'

'He's not allowed. Not allowed. It makes my blood boil. His own children and the only time he gets to see them it's an hour in some poky little room with Social Services outside the bloody door.' Her voice wobbled and Kiley thought she was going to break down and surrender to tears, but she rallied and her fingers tightened into fists, clenched in her lap.

'You've been in touch all the same?' Kiley said. 'With Rebecca, is it? To be certain.'

'I have not.'

'But—'

'Terry'd not have gone there. Not to her. A clean break, that's what she said. Better for the children. Easier all round.' She sniffed. 'Better for the children. Cutting them off from their own father. It's not natural.'

She looked at him sternly, as if defying him to say she was wrong.

'How about the children?' Kiley asked. 'Do you get to see them at all?'

'Just once since she moved away. This Christmas past. They were staying with her parents, Hertfordshire some-where. Her parents, that's different. That's all right.' Anger made her voice tremble. '"We can't stop long," she said, Rebecca, almost before I could close the door. And then she sat there where you are now, going on and on about how her parents were helping her with the rent on a new house and how they were all making a fresh start and she'd be going back to college now that she'd arranged day care.

And the children sitting on the floor all the time, too scared to speak, poor lambs. Threatened with the Lord know what, I dare say, if they weren't on their best behaviour. Little Billie, she came up to me just as they were going, and whispered, "I love you, Gran," and I hugged her and said, "I love you, too. Both of you." And then she hustled them out the door.'

Kiley reached his cup from the floor. 'Terry, he knows where her parents live? Hertfordshire, you said.'

'I suppose he might.'

'You don't think Rebecca and the children might still be there?'

'I don't think so.'

'All the same, if you had an address . . .'

'I should have it somewhere.'

'Later will do.'

'No trouble, I'll get it now.'

'Let me,' Jennie said.

With a small sigh, Mary pushed herself up from the chair. 'I'm not an invalid yet, you know.'

She came back with a small diary, a number of addresses pencilled into the back in a shaky hand. 'There, that's them. Harpenden.'

Kiley nodded. 'And this,' he said, pointing, 'that's where Rebecca lives now?'

A brief nod. West Bridgford, Nottingham. He doubted if Rebecca had joined the ranks of disheartened County supporters, all the same.

'Thanks,' he said, finishing copying the details into his notebook and passing back the diary.

'A waste of time, though,' Mary said, defiantly. 'That's not where he'll be.'

Kiley nodded. Why was it mothers insisted on knowing their sons better than anyone, evidence to the contrary?

He remembered his own mother – 'Jack, I know you better than you know yourself.' Occasionally, she'd been right; more often than not so wide of the mark it had driven him into a frenzy.

His gaze turned to the pictures on the wall. 'Terry's father . . .'

'Cancer,' Mary said. 'Four years ago this March.' She gave a slow shake of the head. 'At least he didn't live to see this.'

After a moment, Jennie got to her feet. 'I'll make a fresh pot of tea.'

Further along the balcony a door slammed, followed by the sounds of a small dog, excited, yelping, and children's high-pitched voices; from somewhere else the whine of a drill, someone's television, voices raised in anger.

Kiley leaned forward, the movement focusing Mary's attention. 'Jennie said your son had been acting, well, a bit strangely . . .'

He waited. The older woman plaited her fingers slowly in and out, while, out of sight, Jennie busied herself in the kitchen.

'He couldn't sleep,' she said eventually. 'All the time he was here, I don't think he had one decent night's sleep. I'd get up sometimes to go to the lavatory, it didn't matter what time, and he'd be sitting there, in the dark, or standing over by the window, staring down. And then once, the one time he wasn't here, I was, well, surprised. Pleased. That he was sleeping at last. I tiptoed over and eased open the door to his room, just a crack. Wanted to see him, peaceful.' Her fingers stilled, then tightened. 'He was cross-legged on top of the bed, stark naked, staring. Staring right at me. As if, somehow he'd been waiting. And that gun of his, his rifle, he had it right there with him. Pointing. I shut the door as fast as I could. I might have screamed or shouted, I don't know. I just stood there, leaning back, my eyes shut tight. I couldn't move. And my heart, I could feel my heart, here, thumping hard against my chest.'

Slowly, she released her hands and smoothed her apron along her lap. Jennie was standing in the doorway, silent, listening.

'I don't know how long I stayed there. Ages it seemed. Then I went back to my room. I didn't know what else to do. I lay down but, of course, I couldn't sleep, just tossing and turning. And when I asked him, in the morning, what kind of a night he'd had, he just smiled and said, "All right, Mum, you know. Not too bad. Not too bad at all." And drank his tea.'

Jennie stepped forward and rested her hands on the older woman's shoulders.

'You will find him, won't you?' Mary said. 'You'll try. Before he does something. Before something happens.'

What was he supposed to say?

'I can't pay very much, you know. But I will, what I can.' She rummaged round in her bag. 'Here. Here's twenty pounds left over from my pension. I can give you more later, of course.'

Kiley took ten and gave her the other ten back.

'You're sure?'

'Sure.'

'Bless you.'

*

'Terry,' Jenny said. 'What do you think?'

They were walking along the disused railway line that ran east from Crouch Hill towards Finsbury Park, grassed over now to make an urban footpath, the grass itself giving way to mud and gravel, the sides a dumping ground for broken bicycles and bundles of free newspapers no one could be bothered to deliver.

'I think he's taken a lot of stress,' Kiley said. 'Seen things most of us wouldn't even like to consider. But if he stays away there's always the risk of arrest, dishonourable discharge. Even prison. My best guess, he'll get himself to a doctor before it's too late, take whatever time he needs, report back with a medical certificate and a cartload of pills. That way, with any luck he might even hang on to his pension.'

'And if none of that happens?'

A blackbird startled up from the undergrowth to their left and settled again on the branches of a bush a little further along.

'People go missing all the time.'

'People with guns?'

Kiley shortened his stride. 'I'll go out to Harpenden first, make sure they're not still there. Terry could have been in touch, doing the same thing.'

'I met her once,' Jennie said. 'Rebecca.' She made a face. 'Sour as four-day-old milk.'

Kiley grinned. They walked on, saying little, just comfortable enough in each other's company without feeling really at ease, uncertain how far to keep walking, when to stop and turn back.

*

The house was to the north of the town, take a left past the golf club and keep on going; find yourself in Batford, you've gone too far. Of course, he could have done the whole thing on the phone, but in these days of so much cold calling, conversations out of the blue were less than welcome. And Kiley was attuned to sniffing around; accustomed, where possible, to seeing the whites of their eyes. How else could you hope to tell if people were lying?

The house sat back, smug, behind a few straggly poplars and a lawn with too much moss in it for its own good. A mud-splashed four-wheel drive sat off to one side, the space in front of the double garage taken up by a fair-sized boat secured to a trailer. How far in God's name, Kiley wondered, were they from the sea?

The doorbell played something that sounded to Kiley as if it might be by Puccini, but if he were expecting the door itself to be opened by a Filipino maid in a starched uniform or even a grim-faced au pair he was mistaken. The woman appraising him was clearly the lady of the house herself, a fit-looking fiftyish with a fine tan and her hair swept up into what Kiley thought might be called a French roll – or was that twist? She was wearing cream trousers, snug at the hips, and a grey marl sweater with a high collar. There were rings on most of her fingers.

'Mr Kiley?'

Kiley nodded.

'You're very prompt.'

If he were a dog, Kiley thought, she would be offering him a little treat for being good. Instead she held out her hand.

'Christina Hadfield.'

Beneath the smoothness of her skin, her grip was sure and firm.

'Please come in. I'm afraid my husband's not here. Some business or other.'

As he followed her through a square hallway busy with Barbour jackets, green wellingtons and walking boots, the lines from one of his favourite Mose Allison songs came to mind, something about telling a woman's wealth from the way she walks.

The room they went into sported two oversized settees and a small convention of easy chairs and you could have slotted in most of Mary Anderson's flat with space to spare. High windows looked out into the garden, where someone, out of sight, was whistling softly as he – or she – tidied away the leaves. Presumably not Mr H.

Photographs of the two grandchildren, more recent than those on Mary Anderson's wall, stood, silver-framed, on the closed lid of a small piano.

'They're adorable,' she said, following his stare. 'Perfectly sweet. And well behaved. Which is more than you can say for the majority of children nowadays.' She pursed her lips together. 'Discipline in our society, I'm afraid, has become a dirty word.'

'How long did they stay?' Kiley asked.

'A little over a week. Long enough to help undress the tree, take down the decorations.' Christina Hadfield smiled. 'Twelfth Night. Another old tradition gone begging.'

'Terry, their father, he was home on leave while they were here.'

'If you say so.'

'He didn't make any kind of contact?'

'Certainly not.'

'No phone calls, no—'

'He knows better than to do that after what happened.'

'What did happen?'

'When Rebecca first said she was leaving him he refused to believe her. And then when he did, he became violent.'

'He hit her?'

'He threatened to. Threatened her and the children with all manner of things. She called in the police.'

'He was back in England then, when she told him?'

'My daughter is not a coward, Mr Kiley, whatever else. Foolish, I grant you. Slow to acknowledge her mistakes.'

Reaching down towards the low table beside her chair, she offered Kiley a cigarette and when he shook his head, lit one for herself, holding down the smoke before letting it drift up towards the ceiling. 'What possessed her to marry that man I was always at a loss to understand, and unfortunately, circumstances proved my reservations correct. It was a mismatch from the start. And a shame it took the best part of four years in non-commissioned quarters – bad plumbing and condensation streaming down the walls – to bring her to her senses.'

'That's why she left him? For a better class of accommodation?'

Christina Hadfield's mouth tightened. 'She left him because she wanted a better life for her children. As any mother would.'

'His children, too, surely?'

'Is that what you're here for? To be his apologist? To plead his cause?'

'I explained when I called—'

'What you gave me to understand on the telephone was that the unfortunate man was having some kind of a breakdown. To the extent that he might do himself some harm.'

'I think it's possible. I'd like to find him before anything like that happens.'

'In this, you're acting for his mother?'

'Yes.'

'Poor woman.' Smoke drifted from the corners of her mouth. 'After speaking to you, I telephoned Rebecca. As I suspected she's heard nothing from him. Certainly not recently.'

'I see.' Kiley got to his feet. Whoever had been whistling while they worked outside had fallen silent. Christina Hadfield's gaze was unwavering. What must it be like, Kiley thought, to entertain so little doubt? He took a card from his pocket and set it on the table. 'Should Terry get in touch or should your daughter hear from him . . . Unlikely as that might be.'

No call to shake hands again at the door. She stood for a few moments, arms folded, watching him go, making good and sure he left the premises.

Was it the fact that his grandfather – his father's father – had been an engine driver that left Kiley so susceptible to trains? The old man – that was how he had always seemed to Kiley, though he could not have been a good deal older than Kiley himself was now – had worked on the old London and Midland Railway, the LMS, and, later, the LNER. Express trains to Leeds and Newcastle, smuts forever blackening his face and hair. Kiley could see him, home at the end of a lengthy shift, standing by the range in their small kitchen, sipping Camp coffee from the saucer. Rarely speaking.

Now, Kiley, who didn't own a car, and hired one from the local pay-as-you-go schemes when necessary, travelled by train whenever possible. A window seat in the quiet coach, a book to read, his CD Walkman turned low.

His relationship with Kate, a freelance journalist whom he had met when working security at an Iranian Film Festival on the South Bank and who, after some eighteen months, had cast him aside in favour of an earnest video installation artist, had left him, a sore heart and a taste for wine beyond his income aside, with a thing for reading. Some of the stuff that Kate had offloaded on him he couldn't handle – Philip Roth, Zadie Smith, Ian McEwan – while others – Graham Greene, the Chandlers she'd given him as a half-assed joke about his profession, Annie Proulx – he'd taken to easily. Jim Harrison, he'd found on his own. The charity shop below his office, where he'd also discovered Hemingway – a dog-eared Penguin paperback of *To Have and Have Not* with the cover half torn away. Thomas McGuane.

What he was reading now was *The Man Who Liked Slow Tomatoes*, which, when he'd been scanning the shelves in Kentish Town Oxfam, he'd first taken for yet another celebrity cookery book, but which had turned out to be an odd kind of crime novel about Mario Balzic, an ageing cop trying to hold things together in a dying industrial town in Pennsylvania. So far, more than half the book was in dialogue, a lot of which Kiley didn't fully understand, but somehow that didn't seem to matter.

For a few moments, he set the book aside and gazed out of the window. They were just north of Bedford, he guessed, the train gathering speed, and most of the low mist that had earlier been clinging to the hedgerows and rolling out across the sloping fields had disappeared. Off to the east, beyond a bank of threadbare trees, the sun was slowly breaking through. Turning down the Walkman a touch more, Mose Allison's trumpet quietly essaying 'Trouble in Mind', he reopened his book and began chapter thirteen.

Nottingham station, when they arrived, was moderately busy, anonymous and slightly scruffy. The young Asian taxi driver seemed to know where Kiley wanted to go.

Travelling along London Road, he saw the floodlights of the County ground where he had once played. Had it been just the once? He thought it was. Then they were crossing the River Trent with the Forest pitch away to their left – the Brian Clough stand facing towards him – and, almost immediately, passing the high rows of white seats at one end of Trent Bridge, where, in a rare moment of recent glory, the English cricket team had sent the Australians packing.

It was a short street of smallish houses off the Melton Road, the number he was looking for at the far end on the left, a flat-fronted two-storey terraced house with only flaking paintwork to distinguish it from those on either side.

The bell didn't seem to be working and after a couple of tries he knocked instead. A flyer for the local pizza parlour was half-in half-out of the letter-box and, pulling it clear, he bent down and peered through. Nothing moved. When he called, 'Hello!' his voice echoed tinnily back. Crouching there, eyes growing accustomed to the lack of light inside, he could just make out a toy dog, left stranded, splay-legged, in the middle of the narrow hall.

'I think they're away,' a woman's voice said.

She was standing at the open doorway of the house alongside. Sixties, possibly older, spectacles, yellow duster in hand. The floral apron, Kiley thought, must be making a comeback.

'Most often I can hear the kiddies of a morning.' She shook her head. 'Not today. Quiet as the grave.'

'You don't know where they might have gone?'

'No idea, duck. You here for the meter or what?'

Kiley shook his head. 'Friend of a friend. Just called round on the off chance, really.'

The woman nodded.

'She didn't say anything to you?' Kiley asked. 'About going away?'

'Not to me. Keeps herself to herself, mostly. Not unfriendly, but you know . . .'

'You didn't see her leaving? Her and the children?'

'Can't say as I did.'

'And there hasn't been anybody else hanging round? A man?'

'Look, what is this? Are you the police or what?'

Kiley tried for a reassuring smile. 'Nothing like that. Nothing to worry about.'

336

'Well, you could try next door the other side, they might know something. Or the fruit and veg shop back on Melton Road, I've seen her in there a time or two, chatting like.'

Kiley thanked her and rang the next-door bell but there was no one home. Between serving customers, the fruit and veg man was happy enough to pass the time of day, but could provide nothing in the way of useful information.

There was a narrow alley running down behind the houses, mostly taken up with green wheelie bins; a low gate gave access to a small, square yard. The rear curtains were pulled partway across. Through the glass Kiley could see the remains of a sliced loaf, left unwrapped beside the sink; a tub of Flora with no lid; a pot of jam; a wedge of cheese, unwrapped. A child's coat lay bunched on the floor; a chair on its side by the far wall. Signs of unseemly haste.

The back door seemed not to be sitting snug in its frame. When Kiley applied pressure with the flat of his hand it gave a few millimetres, loose on its hinges, rattled, then stuck. No key, Kiley guessed, turned in the lock, but bolted at the top. A swift kick would have it open.

He hesitated, uncertain what to do.

Derek Prentiss' number was in his mobile; Prentiss, whom he'd worked with as a young DC when he'd first made it into plain clothes, and now in line for Commander.

'Derek? Hi! It's Jack. Jack Kiley. . . . No, fine, thanks. Yes, grand. . . . Listen, Derek, you don't happen to know anyone up in Nottingham, do you? Someone you've worked with, maybe? Might be willing to give me the time of day.'

*

Resnick had been up since before five, Lynn heading up some high-power surveillance and needing to be in place to supervise the changeover, a major drugs supplier their target and kudos all round if they could pull it off. Resnick had made them both coffee, toast for himself, a rye loaf he'd picked up on the way home the day before, Lynn crunching her way through Dorset muesli with skimmed milk and a sliced banana.

'Why don't you go back to bed?' she'd said. 'Get another couple of hours.'

She'd kissed him at the door, the morning air cold against her cheek.

'You take care,' he'd said.

'You too.'

One of the cats wandered in from outside, sampled an early breakfast and, despite the presence of a cat flap, miaowed to be let out again.

Instead of taking Lynn's advice, Resnick readied the smaller stovetop pot and made himself fresh coffee. Easing back the curtains in the living room, the outside still dark, he sat thumbing through the previous night's *Evening Post*, listening to Lester Young. Would he rather have been out there where Lynn was, the heart of the action, so-called? Until recently, yes. Now, with possible retirement tapping him on the shoulder, he was less sure.

He was at his desk by eight, nevertheless, breaking the back of the paperwork before it broke him. Derek Prentiss rang a little after eleven and they passed a pleasant enough ten minutes, mostly mulling over old times. There was a lot of that these days, Resnick thought.

At a quarter to twelve, an officer called up from reception to say a Jack Kiley was there to see him. He got to his feet as Kiley entered, extending his hand.

'Jack.'

'Detective Inspector.'

'Charlie.'

338

'Okay, then. Charlie.'

The two men looked at one another. They were of similar height, but with Resnick a good stone and a half heavier, the buttons on his blue shirt straining above his belt. Both still had a fullish head of hair, Resnick's darker and, if anything, a little thicker. Kiley, thinner-faced and a good half a dozen years younger, had a leaner, more athletic build. Resnick, in contrast, had the slightly weary air of a man who has spent too long sitting in the same comfortable chair. Balzic, Kiley thought for a moment, harking back to the book he'd been reading, Mario Balzic.

'Derek Prentiss said you might need a favour,' Resnick said.

'You could call it that.'

Resnick gestured towards a chair. 'Better sit.'

Kiley gave him a succinct version of events, what he knew, what he feared.

'You think they might be inside?'

'I think it's possible.'

Resnick nodded. There had been a case not too long ago, north of the city. A man who'd discovered his wife was having an affair with a colleague and was planning to leave him; he had smothered two of the children with a pillow, smashed their mother's head open with a hammer and left her bleeding on the kitchen floor. The police had found a third child hiding in the airing cupboard, limbs locked in fear.

There were other instances, too.

Almost a commonplace.

'You say the back door's only bolted?'

'So it seems.'

'You didn't go in yourself?'

'I thought about it. Thought it might not be such a great idea.'

Resnick considered, then reached towards the phone.
'I'll organise a car.'

'This could be a wild goose chase,' Kiley said as they
were descending the stairs.

'Let's hope, eh?'

The driver was fresh-faced, carrot-haired, barely out of
training. They're not only getting younger, Kiley thought,
this one can only just see over the top of the steering wheel.

In the back of the car, Resnick was studying Kiley
intently. 'Charlton Athletic, wasn't it?' he said eventually.

Grinning, Kiley nodded.

'Cup game down at Meadow Lane,' Resnick said.

Another nod.

''90/'91.'

'Yes.'

'A good season for us.'

'You had a good team.'

'Tommy Johnson.'

'Mark Draper.'

Resnick smiled, remembering.

'Good Cup year for you, wasn't it?'

'Through to the Sixth Round. Spurs beat us two–one at
White Hart Lane.'

'We should've stopped you sooner.'

'You had your chances.'

Kiley looked out through the window. Off-licence. Estate
agent. Delicatessen. He had spent most of the game on the
bench and only been sent on for the last fifteen minutes.
Before he could adjust to the pace, the ball had come to him
on the edge of the area and, with the centre half closing in
on him, he had let fly and, leaning back too far, his shot had
ballooned over the bar. Then, a goal down and with less than
five minutes to spare, he had nicked the ball away from the
full back, cut inside, and, with only the goalie to beat, had

skewed it wide. At the final whistle he had turned away disgusted as the Notts players ran towards their fans in triumph.

'All a long time ago,' Resnick said. 'Fifteen years.'

'And the rest.'

'Think about it much?'

Kiley shook his head. 'Hardly at all.'

The car swung round into Manvers Road and they were there. Still no one was answering the door. Round at the back, Resnick hesitated only a moment before putting his shoulder to the door, once, twice, before the bolt snapped free. He stepped carefully into the kitchen, Kiley following. Nothing had been moved. The cloth dog, two shades of brown, still sat, neglected, in the hall. The front room was empty and they turned back towards the stairs. A chill spread down the backs of Resnick's legs and along his arms. The stairs creaked a little beneath his weight. A child's blue cardigan lay, discarded, on the landing. The door to the main bedroom was closed.

Drawing a slow breath, Resnick turned the handle. The bed had been hastily made; the wardrobe doors stood open and several garments had slid from their hangers to the floor. There was no one there.

They turned back towards the other room, its door ajar.

The closer of the two, Kiley looked round at Resnick enquiringly then nudged the door wide.

There were bunk beds against the right-hand wall. Posters on the wall, a white melamine set of drawers. Several clear plastic boxes, stacked on top of one another, filled with toys. Stuffed animals and pieces of Lego and picture books strewn across the floor.

Kiley felt the muscles in his stomach relax. 'They're not here.'

'Thank God for that.'

Back downstairs they stood in the kitchen, Resnick taking in the evidence of hasty sandwich making, the fallen chair.

There were a dozen explanations, mostly harmless, some more plausible than the rest. 'You think they've done a runner?' he said.

'I think they might have tried.'

'And if they didn't succeed?'

Kiley released a long, slow breath. 'Then he's taken them, that's what I'd say.'

'Against their will?'

'Odds are.'

Resnick called the station from the car; arranged for the place to be secured and Scene of Crime officers to attend. Jumping to conclusions they might be, but better that than to do nothing and wait for bad news.

*

Terry Anderson had waited, cautious, van parked just around the corner on Exchange Road, back towards the primary school. From there he could see the house, see if Rebecca had any callers, visitors in or out, make sure the coast was clear. Waiting. Watching. Alert. Ready for danger, the least sign. It was nothing to him. What he was trained for. Northern Ireland. Iraq. Afghanistan. Belfast. Basra. Sangin. Someone waiting to take your head off with a rifle or blow you to buggery with an RPG.

Little happened. The occasional couple returning home from visiting friends, an hour in the pub, an evening in town. Men taking their dogs for a last walk around the block, pausing perhaps, to light a cigarette. Television screens flickering brightly between half-closed blinds. House lights going on, going off.

He sat behind the front seats, leaning back, legs stretched in front of him, out of sight to passers-by. Beside him in the van were blankets, sleeping bags, bottles of water. A few basic supplies. First-aid kit. Ammunition. Tools. Tinned food. His uniform, folded neatly. Waterproofs. Rope. Prepared.

As he watched, the downstairs room of Rebecca's house went suddenly dark and he imagined, rather than heard, the sound some moments later as she turned the key in the front door lock. Careful, he liked that. Not careful enough.

Eleven thirty-five.

She'd been watching, he guessed, a rerun of some American soap or a late-night film and had either got bored or found her eyes closing, unbidden. How many times had they sat together like that in the semi-dark, the change in her breathing alerting him to the fact that she had dropped off, unwillingly, to sleep? Her warm breath when he had leaned over to kiss her, her head turning away.

The upstairs light went on and, for a brief moment, he saw her in silhouette, standing there, looking out, looking down; then the curtains were pulled across, leaving a faint yellowish glow.

Automatically, he rechecked his watch.

Imagined the children, already sleeping.

The houses to either side had gone dark long since, but up and down the street there were still signs of life.

He would wait.

*

Rebecca stirred, wondering if she had ever really been asleep and, if so, for how long? The bedside clock read 01:14. It was her bladder that had awoken her and, grudgingly, she slid her legs round from beneath the duvet and touched her feet to the carpeted floor. The house was

smaller than she might have liked, and at times, even for
the three of them, barely large enough – bedlam when one
or more of Keiron's friends came round after school to
play. But the fixtures and fittings were in better nick than
in many of the other places she'd seen and the rent, with
her parents' help, was reasonable enough. If it weren't for
them, she didn't know what she could have done.

Careful not to flush the toilet for fear of waking Billie –
a light sleeper at best – she eased back the door and slipped
into their room. Keiron's thumb was in his mouth and carefully she prised it free, causing him to grunt and turn his
head sharply to one side, but not to wake. Billie, pink pyjama
top gathered at her neck, was clinging to the edge of the
blanket she had slept with since she was three months old.

Straightening, Rebecca shivered as if – what did her
grandmother used to say? – as if someone had just walked
over her grave.

Rubbing her arms beneath the sleeves of the long
T-shirt she was wearing, she turned and went softly back
to bed, this time, hopefully, to sleep through. The morning
would come soon enough.

When she woke again it had just gone two. Levering
herself up on to one elbow, she strained to hear. Had one
of the children woken and cried out? A dream, perhaps? Or
maybe Keiron had got up and gone to the toilet on his own?

No, it was nothing.

The wind, perhaps, rattling the windowpanes.

Her head had barely touched the pillow when she heard
it again, for certain this time, the sound that had awoken
her, a footstep. Next door, it had to be next door. Quite
often, late at night, she heard them moving. Early, too. Her
breath caught in her throat. No. There was somebody in
the house, somebody down below, a footstep on the stairs.

Rebecca froze.

If I close my eyes, will it go away?

It.

He.

Whoever . . .

For the first time she wanted a phone beside the bed, a panic button, something. With a lunge, she threw back the covers and sprang from the bed. Three, four steps and she was at the door and reaching for the light.

Oh, Christ!

The figure of a man, turning at the stop of the stairs.

Christ!

Her hand stifled a scream.

'It's all right,' the voice said. 'It's all right.' A voice she recognised, reassuring, commanding.

'Terry?'

He continued slowly towards her, his face still in shadow.

'Terry?'

'Who else?' Almost smiling. 'Who else?'

With a sob, she sank to her knees, and he reached down and touched her hair, uncertainly at first, easing her head forward until it rested against his body, one of her hands clinging to his leg, the other pressed hard against the floor.

*

They stood in the bedroom, Rebecca with a cotton dressing gown pulled hastily round her. She had stopped shaking, but her breathing was still unsteady. He was wearing a black roll-neck sweater, camouflage trousers, black army boots.

'What are you . . . What are you doing?'

When he smiled, nothing changed in his eyes.

'Terry, what . . .'

'Get the children.'

'What?'

'Get yourself dressed and then get the children.'

'No, you can't . . .'

When he reached towards her, she flinched.

'Just something sensible, jeans. Nothing fancy. Them the same.'

She waited until he turned away.

'Keiron and Billie, they're in back, are they?'

'Yes, but let me go first, you'll frighten them.'

'No, it's okay. You get on.'

'Terry, no . . .'

'Get on.'

'You won't . . .'

He looked at her then. 'Hurt them?'

'Yes.'

He shook his head. 'They're my kids, aren't they?'

Billie was awake when he got to the door and when he moved closer towards her she screamed. Rebecca, half-dressed, came running, brushed past him and took the three-year-old into her arms. 'It's all right, sweetheart, it's only Daddy.'

She sobbed against Rebecca's shoulder.

On the top bunk, Keiron stirred, blinking towards the landing light. 'Dad?'

*

Fingers and thumbs, Rebecca helped them into their clothes, Keiron with a school sweatshirt pulled down over his Forest top, Billie snapped into her blue dungarees.

'Where we going, Mum?' Keiron asked.

'I'm not sure, love.'

'An adventure,' his father said, coming through the door. 'We're going on an adventure.'

'Really?'

'You bet!' He tousled the boy's hair.

'You mean like camping?'

'Yes, a bit like that.'

'Like you in the army.'

'Yes. Like that.'

'Some of the year sixes go camping overnight. Cook their own food and everything. Can we do that?'

'Prob'ly, we'll see.'

'And take a pack-up? Can we take a pack-up?'

'No need, son. I've got all the stuff we need.'

'But they do, carry it with them. Can't we?'

'Yes, all right, then. Why not? Becca, how about it? Like the boy says. Fix us something quick. Sandwich, anything. Go on, I'll finish up here.'

When he got down to the kitchen, a few minutes later, there were bread, a pot of jam and some cheese but no Rebecca; he found her in the front room, texting on her mobile phone.

'The fuck!'

Before he could reach her, she'd pressed delete. Swinging her hard towards him, he snatched the phone from her hand. 'Who was that going to be to? The police? The fucking police?' He hurled the phone against the wall and, pushing her aside, crushed it with the heel of his boot. 'Now get in that kitchen and get finished. Five fucking minutes and we're leaving. Five.'

Keiron was standing, open-mouthed, at the living-room door and behind him somewhere Billie had started to cry.

*

It was early evening and they were sitting in Resnick's office, a light rain blurring the window, the intermittent snarl and hum of traffic from the street.

'Here's what we've got so far,' Resnick said. 'Two sets of adult prints in the house, one we're assuming Terry Anderson's. Looks as if he forced the lock on the back door. Not difficult. Explains why it was only bolted across. There was a mobile phone, Rebecca's, in the front room. Beneath the settee. Broken. Smashed on purpose.'

'Used recently?' Kiley asked.

'One call earlier that evening, to a friend. We've already spoken to her, nothing there.'

'No mention of going away, taking a trip?'

'Nothing.'

'And the husband? She didn't say anything about him? Being worried at all?'

Resnick shook his head. 'We've checked with the school and the nursery where she takes the little girl. Both surprised when the kids didn't turn up this morning. Nursery phoned but got no answer, assumed she'd been taken sick. School, the same.'

Kiley shifted uncomfortably on his chair.

'More luck with the neighbours,' Resnick said. 'Old lady next door, bit of a light sleeper, reckons she heard a child scream. A little after two. Either that or a fox, she couldn't be sure. Person from across the street, sleeps with the window open, thinks he might have heard a vehicle driving away, that would be later, around two thirty. There's not a lot more. A couple of people mentioned seeing a van parked in Exchange Road, just around the corner. Not usually there. Small, white, maybe a black stripe down the side. Could have been a Citroën, according to one. We're following that up, checking CCTV. That time of night, roads shouldn't be too busy. Might spot something.' He leaned back. 'Not a lot else to go on.'

'You've sent out descriptions?' Kiley said.

'As best we can. Local airports. Birmingham.'

'They could have gone with him willingly,' Kiley said. 'Is that what you think?'

'What I'd like to think,' Kiley said. 'Not the same thing.'

*

Keiron helped him put up the tent. The trees in that part of the forest had mostly lost their leaves, but the undergrowth was thick enough to shield them from sight. None of the regular paths came near. Tent up, they foraged for fallen branches and dragged them to the site, arranging them over the bracken. Several times, Keiron cut himself on thorns and briars, but he just sucked at the blood and bit back the tears. Big boy, trying not to be afraid.

'How long?' Rebecca wanted to ask. 'How long are we going to be here?' Reading the look on Anderson's face, she said nothing.

The sandwiches were finished quickly. Amongst the supplies he had provided were tins of corned beef and baked beans, peach slices in syrup. Biscuits. Bottles of water. Tea bags and a jar of instant coffee, though he didn't want the risk of lighting a fire. They had driven the van some way along the main track then gone the rest of the way on foot, making two journeys to carry everything. Still dark. Just the light of a single torch. Taking Keiron with him, Anderson had gone back to move the van.

Before leaving, he had taken Rebecca to one side. 'You'll be here when we get back, you and Billie. Right here. Okay?'

'Yes.' A whisper.

'I'm sorry?'

'I said, yes. Yes, all right.' Not able to look him in the eye.

'It better be.'

By the time they had returned, Keiron was exhausted, out on his feet, and his father had had to carry him the last half-mile. Billie was asleep, stretched across her mother's lap. While he had been away, she had tried walking a little way in each direction, taking Billie with her, careful never to wander too far and lose her way back. She had seen nobody, heard nothing. She felt stupid for not doing anything more, without knowing what, safely, she could have done.

'You look knackered,' Anderson said. 'Tired out. Why don't you get your head down? Get a bit of sleep while you can.'

When she opened her eyes, not so many minutes later, he was sitting cross-legged at the far side of the tent, rifle close beside him, painstakingly cleaning his knife.

*

Not wanting to stand around like a spare part, waiting, Kiley had walked into the city, found a halfway decent place for breakfast and settled down to a bacon cob with brown sauce and a mug of serious tea and tried to concentrate on his book. No such luck. Jennie had rung him earlier on his mobile and he'd hesitated before giving her a truncated version of what little they knew, what they surmised.

'Don't say anything to his mother,' he said. 'Not yet, anyway.'

'What d'you take me for?'

'I'll call you if I know anything more definite.'

'You promise?'

Kiley promised. Breakfast over, he wandered around the city centre. The square in front of the council building was going through some kind of makeover; maybe they were turning it into a car park. The pavements were busy with early shoppers, people hurrying, late, to work, the occasional drinker with his can of cider clutched tight. He walked up the hill towards the Theatre Royal. Duncan Preston in *To Kill a Mockingbird*. All next week, *The Rocky Horror Show*. Big Time American Wrestling at the Royal Concert Hall. He was halfway down King Street, heading back towards the square, when his mobile rang. It was Resnick. They'd found something.

There was an OS map open on the table when Kiley arrived, the blurred image of a van frozen on the computer screen. Night-time. Overhead lights reflected in the road surface. There were several other officers in the room.

'Two sightings of the possible van,' Resnick said.

One of the officers, dark hair, dandruff on his shoulders, set the CCTV footage in motion.

'The first here, junction 27 of the M1, leaving the motorway and heading east towards the A608. And then here – see the time code – not so many minutes later, at the roundabout where it joins the 611. Turning south.'

'Back towards the city?' Kiley said, surprised.

'Could be,' Resnick said, 'but for my money, more likely heading here. Annesley Forest.' He was pointing at a patch of green covering almost two squares of the map.

'Why there?'

'Couple of years back, just north of here, Annesley Woodhouse, this man was found dead outside his home, ex-miner, lacerations to the head and upper body, crossbow found close by.'

'Robin bloody Hood,' someone remarked.

'According to what we heard,' Resnick continued, 'there'd been one heck of a row between the dead man and a neighbour, all harking back to the miners' strike, '84. When we went to talk to the neighbour, of course he'd scarpered, gone to ground right there.' Resnick pointed again. 'Two and a half kilometres of woodland. Then, as if that weren't bad enough, a second man, wanted for turning a shotgun on his own daughter, went missing in the same area. Bloody nightmare. We had extra personnel drafted in from all over, round five hundred all told. Dog teams, helicopters, everything. If that's where Anderson's gone, he could stay holed up for weeks.'

'But we don't know for sure,' Kiley said.

'We know next to bugger all,' one of the officers said.

Resnick silenced him with a look. 'There's forest all around,' he said, 'not just this patch here. A lot of it, though, is criss-crossed with trails, paths going right through. Sherwood Forest especially, up by the Major Oak, even at this time of the year it's pretty busy with visitors. But this is different. Quiet.'

Looking at the map, Kiley nodded. 'How sure are we about the van?' he said.

'Traced the number plate. Citroën Berlingo. Rented from a place in North London – Edgware – two days ago. Name of Terence Alderman. Alderman, Alexander, T.A., close enough. Paid in cash.'

'If he's gone into the woods . . .' Kiley began.

'Then he'll have likely dumped the van. We've got people out looking now. Until that turns up, or we get reports of a sighting, it's still pretty much conjecture. And, as far as we know, nobody's been harmed.'

'I doubt if he's taken them for their own good.'

'Even so. I need a little more before I can order up a major search. Request one, at least.'

By which time, Kiley thought, what they were fearing but not yet saying, could already have happened.

'I thought I might take a ride out that way,' Resnick said. 'Want to come along?'

*

While Rebecca watched, Anderson had talked both children into a game of hide-and-seek, warning them not to stray too far. Billie giggled from the most obvious hiding places, waving her arms, as if the point of the game was to be found. Once, Keiron skinnied down inside a hollow oak and stayed there so silent that his father, fearing maybe he'd run off, had called his name in anger and the boy had only shown himself reluctantly, scared of a telling-off or worse.

They picked at the corned beef, ate biscuits and cold beans, drank the sweet syrupy peach juice straight from the cans.

'We should have done this more often,' Anderson said.

'Done what?' said Rebecca sharply.

'Gone camping,' he said and laughed.

Sitting on the ground outside the tent, he showed his son how to strip down the rifle and reassemble it again.

'Can we go after some rabbits?' Keiron asked.

'Maybe tomorrow.'

'Will we still be here tomorrow?'

He left the question unanswered.

Just out of sight, beyond some trees, Anderson had dug a latrine. Walking back, Rebecca was aware of him watching her, the movement of her body inside her clothes.

'Are you seeing anyone?' he asked.

'Seeing?'

'You know what I mean.'

'No.'

'No man then?'

'No.'
'Why not?'
'I don't know. I'm just not.'
'You should.'
She went on past him and into the tent.

*

The day was sealed in with grey. Low hedgerows and mudded tracks and the occasional ploughed field. Why was it, Kiley asked himself, they didn't seem to plough fields any more, ploughed and left bare? Londoner that he was, he could swear that was what he remembered, travelling north to visit relations in the country. Mile after mile of ploughed fields. That rackety little train that stopped everywhere. What was it? Hemel Hempstead, Kings Langley, Abbots Langley, Berkhamsted, Tring? His uncle, red-faced and – now, he thought, looking back – unreal, waiting outside the station at Leighton Buzzard, to take them home in a Rover that rattled more than the carriages of the train.

Resnick had opted to drive, the two of them up front as they made a careful circuit: Newstead, Papplewick pumping station, Ravenshead, south of Mansfield and back again, the A611 straight as a die from the corner of Cauldwell Wood, across Cox Moor to Robin Hood's Hill and the supposed site of Robin Hood's Cave. Then back down towards the forest, the trees at first bordering both sides of the road and then running thickly to the left.

'Do you ever miss it?' Resnick asked, out of nowhere.

It took Kiley a moment to respond. 'Playing?'

A grunt he took to mean, yes. What answer did he want? 'Sometimes,' Kiley said. 'Once in a while.'

'Like when?'

Kiley smiled. 'Most Saturday afternoons.'

'You don't play at all?'

'Not for years. Helped a friend coach some kids for a while, that was all.'

Resnick eased down on the brake and pulled out to pass an elderly man on a bicycle, raincoat flapping in the wind, cloth cap pulled down, bottoms of his trousers tied up with string.

'Up and down this road, I shouldn't wonder,' Resnick said, 'since 1953 or thereabouts.'

Kiley smiled. 'How about you?' he said. 'County. You still go?'

'For my sins.'

'Perhaps we'll catch a game some time?'

'Perhaps.'

Resnick's phone rang and he answered, slowing to the side of the road. 'We've found the van,' he said, breaking the connection. 'Aldercar Wood. No more than a mile from here. Off the main road to the left.'

It had been driven beyond the end of the track and into some trees, covered over with bracken, the inside stripped clear. The main area of forest was clearly visible across two fields, stretching north and west.

'Looks like your surmise was correct,' Kiley said.

Resnick nodded. 'Looks like.'

*

Anderson had gone silent, drawn back into himself. No more family games. Once, when Keiron had run over to him, excited about something he'd found, his father had just stared at him, blank, and the boy had backed nervously away, before running to his mother and burying his face against her chest.

355

Billie fretted and whined until Rebecca plaited her hair and told her the story of Sleeping Beauty yet again, the little girl's face lighting up at the moment when the princess is kissed awake. She'll learn, Rebecca thought, and hopefully before it's too late.

'How did the prince find her?' Billie asked, not for the first time.

'He cut his way through the undergrowth with his sword.'

'Perhaps someone will find us like that,' Billie said.

Rebecca glanced across at Anderson, but if he had heard he gave no sign.

A light rain had started to fall.

Without preamble, Anderson sprang to his feet and pulled on his cagoule. 'Just a walk,' he said. 'I'll not be long.'

A moment later, he was striding through the trees.

Keiron ran after him, calling; tripped and fell, ran and tripped again; finally turned and came limping towards the tent.

'He isn't coming back,' the boy said, crestfallen.

Rebecca kissed him gently on his head. 'We'll see.'

An hour passed. Two. Once Rebecca thought she heard voices and called out in their direction, but there was no reply and the voices faded away till there were just the sounds of the forest. Distant cars. An aeroplane overhead.

'I told you,' Keiron said accusingly and kicked at the ground.

'Right,' Rebecca said, making up her mind. 'Put on your coats and scarves. We're going.'

'Where? To find Daddy?'

'Yes,' Rebecca lied.

Billie fussed with her buttons and when Rebecca knelt to help her, the child pushed her away. 'I can do it. I can do it myself.'

'Well, get a move on.'

'I am.' Bottom lip stuck petulantly out.

Calm down, Rebecca told herself. Calm down.

Billie pushed the last button into place.

'All right?' Rebecca said. 'Come on, then. Let's go.'

They were a hundred metres away, maybe less, heading in what Rebecca thought was the direction they'd originally come, when they saw him just a short way ahead, walking purposefully towards them.

'Come to meet me? That's nice.'

As the children went into the tent, he pulled her back. 'Try that again and I'll fuckin' kill you, so help me.'

*

There were only a couple of hours of daylight left. By the time they had got a decent-sized search party organised there would be even less. Best to wait until first light.

'I've been talking to the Royal Military Police,' Resnick said. 'Seems as though one sergeant going AWOL isn't too high on their list of priorities. Too many of them, apparently, done the same. Not too keen on hurrying back to fight for someone else's democracy. More interested in tracking down a batch of illicit guns, smuggled into the UK from Iraq via Germany. Bit of a burgeoning trade in exchanging them for drugs and currency. Cocaine, especially. Still, they're sending someone up tomorrow. If we do find Anderson, they'll want to stake their claim.'

'Till then we twiddle our thumbs.'

'Do better than that, I dare say,' Resnick said.

Tony Burns was up from London, sitting in with a local band at the Five Ways. Geoff Pearson on bass, the usual crew. Last time Resnick had heard Burns, a good few years back, he'd been playing mostly baritone, a little alto. Now it was all tenor, a sound not too many miles this side of

Stan Getz. Jake McMahon joined them for the last number, a tear-up through the chords of 'Cherokee'. By now the free cobs were going round, end of the evening, cheese or ham, and Kiley was having a pretty good time.

Resnick had called Lynn and asked her if she wanted to join them, but instead she had opted for an early night. She'd left him a note on the kitchen table, signed with love.

Resnick made coffee and, feeling expansive, cracked open a bottle of Highland Park. They sat listening to Ben Webster and Art Tatum and then Monk fingering his way through 'Between the Devil and the Deep Blue Sea', Kiley not without envy for what seemed, in some respects, a fuller, more comfortable life than his own.

'Well,' said Resnick, finally, levering himself up from his chair. 'Early start.'

'You bet.'

The bed was made up in the spare room, a clean towel laid out and, should he need it, a new toothbrush in its plastic case. He thought he might manage a few more pages of *The Man Who Liked Slow Tomatoes* before dropping off, but when he woke in the morning, the book had fallen to the floor, unread.

*

Wherever he'd gone in those two hours, Anderson had come back with a bottle of Vodka. Stolichnaya. Perhaps he'd had it with him all along. He sat there, close to the entrance to the tent, drinking steadily. Rebecca tried to get the children to eat something but to little avail. She forced herself to try some of the corned beef, though it was something she'd never liked. The children drank water, nibbled biscuits and moped.

The rain outside increased until it began seeping under one corner of the tent.

Billie lay down, sucking her thumb, and, for once, Rebecca made no attempt to stop her. If Keiron, huddled into a blanket near her feet, was asleep or not she wasn't sure.

The bottle was now half-empty.

Anderson stared straight ahead, seeing something she couldn't see.

'Terry?'

At the softness of her voice, he flinched.

'How long is it since you got any sleep?'

Whenever she had awoken in the early hours after they'd arrived, he had been sitting, shoulders hunched, alert and keeping guard.

'How long?'

'I don't know. A long time.'

'What's wrong?'

For an answer he lifted the bottle to his lips.

'Perhaps you should talk to someone? About what's troubling you? Perhaps—'

'Stop it! Just fucking stop it! Shut up!'

'Stop what?'

'Wheedling fucking round me.' He mimicked her voice. 'Perhaps you should talk to someone, Terry? As if you gave a shit.'

'I do.'

'Yeah?' He laughed. 'You don't give a shit about me and I don't give a shit about you. Not any more.'

'Then why are we here?'

'Because of them. Because they have to know.'

'Know what?'

He moved suddenly. 'Wake them. Go on, wake them up.'

'No, look, they're exhausted. Let them sleep.'

But Billie was already stirring and Keiron was awake.

Anderson took another long swallow from the bottle. His skin was sallow and beads of perspiration stood out on his forehead and his temples. When he started talking, his voice seemed distant, even in the confines of the tent.

'We were on patrol, just routine. There'd been a firefight a couple of days before, so we were more on our guard than usual. Against snipers but also for explosives. IEDs. We were passing this house and this woman came out, just her face showing, part of her face, the eyes, and she's waving her arms and wailing and pointing back towards the house as if there's something wrong, and Sean, he jumps down, even though we're telling him not to be stupid, and the next thing we know, he's followed her to the doorway, and the next after that he's been shot. One gets him in the body and knocks him back, but he's wearing his chest plate, thank Christ, so that's all right, but the next one takes him in the neck. By now we're returning fire and the woman's disappeared, nowhere to be fucking seen, Sean's leaking blood into the fucking ground, so we drag him out of there, back into the vehicle and head back to camp.'

Beside Rebecca, Keiron, wide-eyed, listened enthralled. Billie clutched her mother's hand and flinched each time her father swore.

'He died, that's the thing. Sean. The bullet'd torn an artery and the bleeding wouldn't stop. By the time we reached camp, he was dead. He was our mate, a laugh. A real laugh. Always saw the funny side. Just a young bloke. Twenty-one. And stupid. Young and stupid. He'd wanted to help.' Anderson took a quick swallow and wiped his mouth. 'Two days later, we went back. Went back at night, five of us. We'd been drinking beforehand, pretty heavily, talking about what had happened, what they'd done to Sean.'

Rebecca shivered and hugged the children close.

'We went in under cover of darkness. There was no moon, I remember, not then. Sometimes it'd be, you know, huge, filling half the fucking sky, but that night there was nothing. Just a few stars. Everyone inside was sleeping. Women. Men.' He paused. 'Children. Soon as we got inside one of the men reached for his gun, he'd been sleeping with it, under the blankets, and that's when we started firing. Firing at anything that moved. One of the women, she came running at us, screaming, and Steve, he says, "That's her. That's her, the lyin' bitch," and, of course, dressed like she was, like they all were, he had no way of knowing, but that didn't stop him all but emptying his magazine into her.'

'That's enough,' Rebecca said. 'Enough.'

'There was a girl,' Anderson said, ignoring her, 'hiding in one of the other rooms. Twelve, maybe thirteen. I don't know. Could've been younger. Steve grabbed hold of her and threw her down on the floor and then one of the others started to tear off her clothes.'

'Stop,' Rebecca said. 'Please stop. They don't need to hear this.'

'Yes, they do! Yes, they do!'

Keiron was not looking, refusing to look, pressing his face into his mother's side.

'We all knew what was going to happen. Steve's standing over her, pulling off the last of her things, and she calls him a name and spits at him and he leans down and punches her in the face, and then he's on his knees, unzipping himself, and we're all watching, a couple cheering him on, give it to her, give it to her, clapping like it's some game, and that's when I tell him, I tell him twice to stop and he just carries on and I couldn't, I couldn't, I couldn't just stand there and watch – she was just a child! – and I shot him, through the back of the head. Blood and gunk all over the girl's face and she wriggles out from under and grabs her clothes and runs and we're left standing there. All except for Steve. He was my mate, too, they all were, and I'd killed him over some girl who, even before that happened, would've happily seen us blown to smithereens.'

He wiped away some of the sweat that was running into his eyes. Tears were running soundlessly down Rebecca's face.

'We all agreed, the rest of us, to claim he'd got caught in the crossfire. After what had happened, no one was going to want to tell the truth.'

'Except you,' Rebecca said.

'This is different.' He nodded towards the children. 'They needed to know.'

'Why?'

'So they can understand.'

And his hands reached down towards his rifle.

*

Not long after first light, a police helicopter, flying low over the forest, reported a woman and two children standing in a small clearing, waving a makeshift flag.

Armed officers secured the area. Rebecca and the children were escorted to the perimeter, where paramedics were waiting. Anderson was found lying inside the tent, a dark cagoule covering his face, his discharged weapon close at hand. At the hospital later, after she had rested and the medical staff had examined her, Rebecca slowly began to tell Resnick and a female liaison officer her story. The children were in another room with a nurse and their maternal grandmother.

Later still, relishing the chance to stretch his legs, Resnick had walked with Kiley the short distance through the city centre to the railway station. Already, a rush edition of the *Post* was on the streets. It would be national news for a moment, a day, page one beneath the fold, then a short column on page six, a paragraph on page thirteen. Forgotten. One of those things that happen, stress of combat, balance of mind disturbed. Rebecca had told the police her husband's story, as well as she remembered, what he had seen, the attack at night, the confusion, the young Iraqi girl, the fellow soldier caught in the crossfire and killed in front of his eyes. He hadn't been able to sleep, she said, not since that happened. I don't think he could face going back to it again.

'Not what you wanted, Jack,' Resnick said, shaking his hand.

The 15.30 to London St Pancras was on time.

'None of us,' Kiley said.

'We'll catch that game some time.'

'Yes. I'd like that.'

Kiley hurried down the steps on to the platform.

He phoned Jennie Calder from the train. In a little over two hours' time he would be crossing towards the flats where Mary Anderson lived and climbing the stairs, welcome on the mat, but not for him, her face when she opened the door ajar with tears.

FOOTNOTE

Any Notts County supporters reading this will forgive me, I trust, for playing fast and loose with the details of the club's highly successful FA Cup run in 1990/91. Manchester City not Charlton Athletic. Come on, you Pies!

London
January 25 2007

'Sack O' Woe'. First published in *The Blue Religion*, edited by Michael Connelly, Little, Brown, New York, 2008. Reprinted in *Between the Dark and the Daylight*, edited by Ed Gorman and Martin H. Greenberg, Tyrus Books, Madison, 2009.

'Snow, Snow, Snow'. First published in *Greatest Hits*, edited by Robert J. Randisi, Carroll & Graf, New York, 2005.

'Promise'. First published in *Murder Is My Racquet*, edited by Otto Penzler, Mysterious Press, New York, 2005.

'Truth'. First published in *Ellery Queen Mystery Magazine*, September/October 2002.

'Billie's Blues'. First published by Rivages, France, 2002. Reprinted in *Now's the Time*, Heinemann, London, 2002 and *Minor Key*, Five Leaves, Nottingham, 2009.

'The Sun, the Moon and the Stars'. First published in *The Detection Collection,* edited by Simon Brett, Orion, London, 2005. Reprinted in *Minor Key*, Five Leaves, Nottingham, 2009.

'Due North'. First published in *Crime in the City*, edited by Martin Edwards, The Do-Not Press, London, 2002. Reprinted in *The Best British Mysteries*, edited by Maxim Jakubowski, Allison & Busby, London, 2003.

'Smile'. First published in *Birmingham Noir*, edited by Joel Lane & Steve Bishop, Tindal Street Press, Birmingham, 2002.

'Chance'. First published in *Men from Boys*, edited by John Harvey, Heinemann, London, 2003. Reprinted in *The Best British Mysteries 2005*, edited by Maxim Jakubowski, Allison & Busby, London, 2004.

'Well, You Needn't'. First published by Otava, Finland, 2004. Reprinted in *Minor Key*, Five Leaves, Nottingham, 2009.

'Home'. First published in *Sunday Night & Monday Morning*, edited by James Urquhart, Five Leaves, Nottingham, 2005. Reprinted in *Ellery Queen Mystery Magazine*, December 2005, in *The Best British Mysteries IV*, edited by Maxim Jakubowski, Allison & Busby, 2006 and in *Minor Key*, Five Leaves, Nottingham, 2009.

'Drummer Unknown'. First published in *Murder and All That Jazz*, edited by Robert J. Randisi, Signet, New York, 2004. Reprinted in *The Best British Mysteries 2006*, edited by Maxim Jakubowski, Allison & Busby, London, 2005.

'Favour'. First published in *Like a Charm*, edited by Karin Slaughter, Century, London, 2004.

'Asylum'. First published in *Crime on the Move*, edited by Martin Edwards, Do-Not Press, London, 2005.

'Just Friends'. First published in *Damn Near Dead*, edited by Duane Swierczynski, Busted Flush, Houston, 2006. Reprinted in *The Penguin Book of Crime Stories*, edited by Peter Robinson, Penguin, Toronto, 2007 and in *The Mammoth Book of Best British Mysteries*, edited by Maxim Jakubowski, Constable & Robinson, 2008.

'Minor Key'. First published in *Paris Noir*, edited by Maxim Jakubowski, Serpent's Tail, London, 2007. Reprinted in *Minor Key*, Five Leaves, Nottingham, 2009.

'Ghosts'. First published in *Il Giornale*, Italy, August 2008. Reprinted in *Ellery Queen Mystery Magazine*, September/October 2009.

'Trouble in Mind'. First published by Five Leaves, Nottingham, 2007. Reprinted in *Ellery Queen Mystery Magazine*, November 2008.